# EMILY PERCY;

OR,

# THE HEIRESS OF SACKVILLE.

A ROMANCE.

## BY ELLEN T——,

AUTHORESS OF "ROSE SOMMERVILLE," "LOVE AND HONOUR," ETC.

Love, hope, and joy, fair pleasure's smiling train;
Hate, fear, and grief, the family of pain;
These, mix'd with art, and to due bounds confin'd,
Make and maintain the balance of the mind,—
The lights and shades, whose well accorded strife,
Gives all the strength and colour of our life.

POPE.

LONDON:

PUBLISHED BY G. PURKESS, COMPTON-STREET, SOHO; AND W. STRANGE,
PATERNOSTER-ROW.

# PREFACE.

THE imagination, however it may be for a time caught and fascinated by glowing descriptions of stately halls, glistening jewels, rustling silks, harmonious strains, beautiful ladies, and gallant gentlemen, will grow sated in spite of the gorgeousness of the subject; and then, with a placid and calm content, it wends its way into the green fields and quiet villages, to recover from the bustle, and whirl, and tumult of town life.

The authoress of "EMILY PERCY," in penning her romance, has relied upon her knowledge of this fact to produce a work, the plot and style of which, she flatters herself, are alike out of the common and well-trodden track pursued by modern novelists and romancists. She has much cause for self-gratulation in having pursued this course, as, from the success the romance has attained, it has secured a conviction in her mind that the taste of the public (more especially of that portion of it which chooses to recreate its leisure hours, and lose for a short time its recollections of corroding cares and anxieties, among the flower-strewn fields of fiction) is not so vitiated as one half of the canting, hypocritical bigots would have us believe, who are continually preaching against the cheap literature of the day, merely because *it is* cheap, and who, as in a number of well-known instances, only make their rancorous but harmless attacks in consequence of having a direct interest in works of a similar nature, but of a more expensive kind.

The lights and shadows of life in our tale have been varied and striking; but no exaggeration of detail has been used to excite a false sympathy, or create a false interest. Simplicity and truthfulness have been the guiding stars of the writer; and the eagerness with which it has been perused, has spoken forcibly of the amount of interest bestowed by its readers upon the hopes and fears, the joys and sorrows, of the different characters that figure in its pages.

The authoress cannot be blamed for indulging in a little womanly pride at her success; but this pride will stimulate her to further and greater exertion; and she hopes to find that her next essay, improved by experience, may be still more deserving of approbation than the romance now before the public.

# EMILY PERCY;

## OR, THE HEIRESS OF SACKVILLE.

### BY ELLEN T——, AUTHORESS OF "ROSE SOMMERVILLE."

## CHAPTER I.

In the sweet county of Devon, far famed for its beauty and fertility, is situated a pretty, romantic little village, which, for the sake of concealment, we will call Sackville, and which, for the purpose of our history, will serve equally as well as its real name. This village, as we have intimated, is small, and the outskirts are graced by the humble, yet comfortable, and withal pretty cottages of the peasant, each with its little garden in front, trim and neat; here a patch of sweet-scented flowers, and there a sprinkling of vegetables and useful herbs for the winter; while the climbing jasmine and honeysuckle overshaded a rustic porch at the door, where the industrious labourer on an evening at once seeks rest and refreshment after the fatigue of the day, indulging himself with a pipe and mug of ale; while his wife, standing at the little gate, chats with her neighbours, and occasionally with her voice preserving order among the troop of healthy, noisy children who are engaged in mirthful sports by the way-side. Yet, her time too precious to be wasted, she still plies her busy needle, and though the season is one of pleasure, she makes it likewise subservient to utility.

After passing these cottages, which are irregularly built, and form a sort of chain, or connecting link, with the open country around and the main street of the village, you come to the few shops that supply the inhabitants with the necessary articles for consumption and wearing apparel; one technically termed "The Shop," from its vast superiority to the others, and in which may be found almost every article that comprises a separate business in London. Among the others the most prominent is the ale-house, strictly a village one, in front of which are benches tempting the toil-worn wayfarer to rest, and many a one foot-sore and weary, has glanced with a wistful eye towards these very benches, yet, anxious to pursue his journey, has stedfastly resolved not to yield to the almost irresistible impulse he felt to rest awhile, and partake of honest John's famous Devonshire ale. Yet one glance more, and the sight of some fellow traveller, in the act of raising the foaming cup to his lips, and all his wise resolves are forgotten. In the next instant he is himself resting his weary frame and quenching his thirst with a mug of the same refreshing beverage.

Passing these shops, and turning sharp off to the right, you come direct upon the village green, almost facing which is a large, old-fashioned family residence, known to the villagers by the high-sounding title of "The Great House." It is built of bright red bricks, though their colour is now somewhat dimmed with age, and the door and unclosed shutters, as well as the iron railings, are painted of a pretty refreshing green. There is a coach-house and stable adjoining, the doors of which are painted of the same colour. The house altogether bears an appearance of great antiquity; even of the tall trees which stand in front of it (and with their thick foliage shade the rooms from the glare of the noon-day sun), it may be said with truth,—

"Tall trees they were, and old,
And had been old a century."

The inhabitants of this venerable building are but three, exclusive of servants, all of whom, save one, had already grown grey in the service of the master and mistress of the mansion. Mr. Henry Stanhope was a true picture of the old English gentleman, and persevered, with a pertinacity truly astonishing, in adhering to the dress and customs that were in vogue in his youth. Nothing on earth would induce him to regard the numberless changes and innovations of the present day as improvements; of railways in particular he was uncommonly sceptical. Thus, when he first heard of the proposed line, which would carry one actually through his dear native, peaceful village, and within but a short distance of his own residence,—yes, the residence of Henry Stanhope, Esq.,—he was so utterly overwhelmed with astonishment, that he could only hold up his hands, shake his head, and smile at the absurdity of the notion.

"It will never be allowed, sir, I am certain; it never will be allowed," he said, while conversing on this very subject with his friend and neighbour, Squire Elgood, and a benevolent smile played round the corners of his mouth, as though he could afford to pity the absurdity of those who thought it possible that the railway proposition might actually in time be reduced to practice; and yet, although Mr. Stanhope said, "It never will be allowed," with an emphasis that might well be understood to mean, "It never shall," in spite of this, and as it were on purpose to irritate and annoy him, the railroad was began, rapidly carried on, and at length completed, and at certain and regular hours of the day came the noisy engine, with its shrill whistle, and accompanying train of carriages, carrying noise, smoke, and hubbub, into the very heart of the village. This was certainly enough to try the temper of one much more placable than Mr. Henry Stanhope, hitherto reigning almost like a petty sovereign of the village; he was the richest man in it, the greatest landowner, and chief magistrate, and not the slightest alteration had ever before taken place without his full and free consent, asked and obtained; and now this, as he considered it, sad innovation, and replete with demoralizing consequences " to the villagers, inasmuch as it brought them in contact," while the rail was in progress, to use his own words, " with engineers and other low characters from London"—all this was done without him being even so much as consulted. While the surveyors were measuring, planning, and talking, Mr. Stanhope affected to consider it only as a good practical joke; and, with many a shake of the head, and half-waggish smile, was heard to mutter to himself, as he contemplated them at a distance (for he sedulously avoided approaching to their vicinity), "It will never be altered," which, as we have observed, was paramount to saying, " It never shall." But, when the astounding intelligence was brought to him that the first spade of earth was turned, he hurried forth with bewildered looks, forgetful of his usual staid demeanour, to convince himself of the fact beyond the possibility of a doubt. And when he found that, despite all his wise presages, it was really, and in sober earnest, actually commenced, he manifested, as he considered, most Christian forbearance, only shaking his head, and saying to himself, though in a voice loud enough to be heard by all present, " Times are indeed changed," and walking sadly and sorrowfully away.

From that moment no mention of the rail ever passed the lips of Mr. Stanhope; and, by the grave and saddened manner he assumed, whenever it was spoken of in his presence, induced his friends to regard it as a forbidden subject; and, imitating his silence, it was seldom made a topic of discourse by the villagers. But when the rail became so generally used by travellers, that great talk was made about taking off the road the " Tallyho" coach, that with its four horses, coachman, and guard had regularly dashed through the little village twice a day, to the infinite delight of all the idle urchins, as long, aye, and longer, than Mr. Henry Stanhope could remember—this was too much; it was trying to his temper, beyond what he (as all allowed), a most peaceful, quiet, country gentleman, could bear; and he indulged in invectives loud and long against railroads, surveyors, engineers, shareholders, and, though last, not least, that terrible innovation on the custom of his forefathers,—steam. And just about the time, a most sad and disastrous accident, involving both loss of life and limb, afforded him ample scope on which to discourse of the direful consequences likely to accrue from the employment of a power that, in his opinion, never was intended, and never ought to be used for the purpose of locomotion. And yet, notwithstanding all he urged on the subject (and much he did urge), travellers were still mad enough to abandon the safe old coach, that had never been known, even in the roughest weather and heaviest state of the roads, to incur an accident more perilous to the passengers than a few bruises; but people, as Mr. Henry Stanhope very sagely observed, in these altered times, " seemed to prefer celerity to safety." And as they wilfully and wickedly chose to run the risk, when such dreadful odds were against them, it was certainly no business of his, though for himself he deemed it right to set his face so strongly against this fearful peril, that he would not even transmit a parcel, otherwise than through the ordinary conveyance, ere steam and its concomitant evils had monopolised the carrier's business, who would have been knocked off the road long before, had not Mr. Stanhope kept him constantly running at his own expense; at least, so it was pretty generally asserted in the village, though neither the carrier (a bluff, weather-beaten old fellow), or Mr. Stanhope, himself, ever spoke to the truth of the assertion.

And now, when talk was made of putting a stop to the running of the old coach, they both shook their heads very wisely. And the carrier (who was as fondly attached to old customs, and as bitter against railroads as even Mr. Henry Stanhope himself) was fre-

quently heard to re-echo his master's favourite observation, " It never will be allowed !"
And, indeed, it has been whispered, by those who were most intimate with him, that in
this case he spoke in the positive degree, and was boldly heard to declare, " It never
shall !" and, for this once, he was right.

The Tallyho, with its four horses, coachman, and guard, continued to fulfil their
wonted occupation ; and on the very day that it was confidently asserted the coach would
be put down, it came dashing into the village at a most furious and alarming pace, the
horses' heads decked with scarlet ribbons, "like streamers, long and gay ;" and the
train belonging to the railway chancing to be just on the point of starting, the guard
seized his horn, and blew a blast long, shrill, and loud, as it were in the very madness of
victory, and in utter defiance of all the railroads in the known world.

With all his eccentricities and irritability of temperament, Mr. Henry Stanhope was a
kind and benevolent man ; and though obliging his steward, who occupied a pretty cottage close to the mansion of his master, to strictly enforce payments from his tenantry,
and never, on any account, to allow them to fall into arrears, yet has he been frequently
known clandestinely to visit the cottages of those whom he had reason to believe, from
sickness, or other calamities, would not be able to meet the forthcoming quarter-day,
and supply them with the money to pay the steward, enjoining, at the same time, strict
secrecy on their part.   This was literally doing good by stealth, and not allowing his left
hand to know what his right hand did.   And thus were his benevolent actions ever
performed.

In person Mr. Henry Stanhope was tall, moderately stout, and of commanding exterior.
Time had dealt very leniently with him, for he was now fast approaching to his seventieth
birthday ; yet he was hale, strong, and hearty. His features bore the appearance of having
been remarkably handsome in his younger days ; his complexion delicately fair, and his
hair of silvery whiteness—that is, what remained of it, for he was very bald, especially
round the forehead and temples—his cheeks were of a florid hue, that showed, though
Mr. Stanhope was not addicted to intemperance, he was yet fond of a bottle of generous
wine, and still fonder of sharing it with a friend.

He was the last surviving member, in the male line, of one of the most ancient and
respectable families in England, and now inherited the mansion of his forefathers and its
contiguous estate, with the sorrowful reflection that with him the name of his family would
become extinct.   This had for many years embittered his cup of happiness ; he was so
proud of his ancestry, so fond of boasting of their numberless virtues, which had in itself
ennobled them, that to think so bright and untarnished a name as they had bequeathed to
him must, in the course of a few years, sink into oblivion, filled his heart with sadness, and
not unfrequently his eyes with tears.

In politics Mr. Stanhope was a stanch Tory, according to his own statement ; but his
friends fancied they could, of late years, perceive a gradual veering round towards the
liberal interest ; at least many of his actions implied as much, though, had he been taxed
with it, there is no doubt but he would have repudiated it with anger and disdain.   A
more regular or zealous attendant at the village church was not to be found in the entire
parish, as the good curate, Mr. George Ellis, could well testify.   Indeed, it had been remarked by many of the villagers, that, in the course of his duty, his eye wandered more
frequently towards Mr. Stanhope's pew than was absolutely necessary.   This may be accounted for by the fact, that there existed the warmest friendship between them, or, if that
will not satisfy our readers, as the curate was a young man—say scarcely five-and-twenty
—his gaze may have been attracted to the pew by the bright eyes and glossy curls of Mr.
Stanhope's niece, Emily, who never failed to accompany her uncle and aunt to their devotions.   Be this as it may, his eye would most certainly wander in the direction of that
particular pew more often than in any other.

The father of Mr. Henry Stanhope had been just such another good-hearted, warm,
independent country gentleman as himself; he was an only child, and much anxiety was
manifested by his parents to see him suitably married.   Unfortunately, he had, when
very young, placed his affections on a lady, his friends thought beneath the dignity of
being allowed to share what they considered his brilliant destiny, and, with much pain
and trouble, they at length succeeded in setting aside the intended match.   Thus separated from his first and early love, the father of Mr. Henry Stanhope became indifferent
as to whom he formed an alliance with, and was consequently guided entirely by his parents ; and, at the age of eight-and-twenty, was united, with much form and ceremony,

to the Honourable Eliza Villiers, a match his friends looked upon as possessing every requirement to ensure happiness; but, alas! it turned out the very reverse.

The Honourable Eliza Villiers was the sixth daughter of Lord Gordon Villiers, a man who had dissipated his estate and impoverished his family by a long continued attendance at the gaming-table, and having a large family, was only too glad to accept the proposal of the wealthy commoner, never, for a moment, so much as dreaming of consulting his daughter on the subject; and when ordered by her unfeeling and haughty father to prepare for the union, it was in vain that she wept, and prayed of him to allow her to refuse it. He insisted on her compliance, and the unfortunate girl, who had no mother to whom to impart the sorrows of her breast, prepared, with an almost broken heart, to do the stern bidding of her unrelenting parent, and her hand was given to Charles Stanhope at the altar.

There was, however, no exchange of hearts on that occasion, neither had any to bestow: Eliza's had long been given to a young and gallant sailor, who, though high in command of his ship, standing second alone to the captain, yet had no wealth to lavish on his bride. No, he was dependent almost entirely on the value of his services, and this was the reason that had prevented Eliza allowing him, as he earnestly wished, to seek her father's consent to the marriage. They had secretly plighted their troth to each other, and arranged that on his return from this one voyage, Eliza should give him her hand as a reward for his enduring affection. He did return, full of hope and love, and loaded with bridal presents, to present to his beloved, from whom his heart had never once wavered since their last parting. How deep and heartfelt his anguish, then, to find her the wife of another.

In the extremity of his anguish he sought her residence, to learn from her own lips the truth of what he had heard. She was already the mother of one child, a fine boy, who was called Henry, and pregnant with a second.

When they met, Ernest Percival was too heart-broken to upbraid the object of his tenderest love, especially when he heard she had but obeyed the commands of a father, whom she had ever feared, and trembled at his violence; and he was far away, or it had never been. That one sad meeting led to others, and before many months had passed, Eliza left her husband's roof, and fled with her former lover. Such precaution had they taken, that for awhile they baffled all attempts to track them out.

Mr. Charles Stanhope had never loved the woman he had made his wife; consequently the shock to his feelings on discovering her flight was but trifling. She had left him one son, the undoubted heir to his large estates, and was pregnant with a second child, likewise his own; which being the case, he was anxious to discover her retreat, that, after her accouchement, he might remove the child to his own roof. With great difficulty he at length succeeded in discovering her, when she gave him her assurance that the child she was pregnant with when she left his house was still-born. Satisfied with this statement, he immediately set about procuring a divorce, and ultimately married the very lady his parents had been at so much pains to separate from him.

This lady, though of humble birth, was truly amiable and deserving; and being, moreover, fondly attached to him, they lived together for many years in happiness and peace. In the course of time she became the mother of a little girl, who shared equally with the youthful Henry in the tender love and care of their father.

As they both approached to maturity, Mr. Charles Stanhope deemed it right to acquaint his son that the mother of his sister (who bore the name of Emily) stood not in that tender relationship towards himself, else he had never known it, so truly and lovingly had she extended towards him her maternal care. The brother and sister had ever been most devotedly attached to each other, which continued warm and unabated after they were respectively married.

Henry Stanhope had early placed his affections on the only daughter of a neighbouring landowner, which meeting with the approbation of their parents, they were married, and had now lived together for upwards of forty years, in as much, or more felicity than commonly falls to the lot of mortals. There was, indeed, but one drawback to their happiness; but Mr. Henry Stanhope would have sacrificed many of the comforts and enjoyments by which he was surrounded could he have removed that one bar to his felicity. They were childless: for many years he had encouraged the hope that his wife might ultimately bring him an heir to his estate, but in vain; time rolled on, and he was at length forced to abandon the hope he had so long nourished. He had seen his revered parent gathered to his fathers, and might now, at the commencement of our narrative, be well considered to be looking out in constant expectation for his own summons to depart, and then the race of the Stanhopes would be at an end. His sister Emily, who was eight years his junior, had, by her extreme beauty, attracted the regard of the only son of a rich baronet, who, dying, bequeathed his entire property to him, and Henry had the pleasure, six years after his own marriage, of witnessing the union of his sister with Sir Beaumont Percy. For many years this marriage was likewise barren, which was a source of sorrow to all concerned; when, after they had given up all hope of children, Emily became pregnant, and was safely and happily delivered of a daughter.

This unexpected event was a source of great joy; and though all would have preferred a son, yet the little stranger was warmly received, and gifts showered upon her in abundance, ere she could know or appreciate their value. She was wrapped in the richest velvet, and her infant face shaded with the finest lace and cambric that could be procured; and the spark of life, which at first seemed very flickering, fanned and nursed so carefully, that it at length burst into a strong and stedfast flame. The old proverb avers that "it is better to be born lucky than rich;" but we incline to think that, all things considered, it is by no means a bad thing to be born rich. It is pleasanter for an infant to be rocked to sleep on downy cushions, and defended by warm mantles from the piercing cold, and its every murmur hushed and lulled to rest, far pleasanter, than to possess parents whose arduous duties leave them but little time to attend to the wants of an infant, and are forced when it cries, frequently from cold and hunger, to allow it to cry itself to sleep.

The infant daughter of Sir Beaumont and Lady Percy was baptised in an elegantly chased silver font, the gift of her uncle, Henry Stanhope, who stood god-father on the occasion, and gave his niece her mother's maiden name, Emily Stanhope. She had scarcely attained her third year, when her father, who was in the constant habit of taking daily equestrian exercise, was killed by a fall from his horse, and brought back to his home, that he had left but a few short hours before in the full health and strength of manhood, a corpse; the dreadful shock so affected the nerves of his afflicted widow, that in less than three months she followed him to the grave, leaving her orphan daughter to the tender care of a brother, whom she well knew worthy of the trust reposed in him.

"I need not, my dear Henry," she said, as he hung in anguish over her dying couch, "recommend my child to your love and protection, as I well know, that for my sake, if not her own, she will be fondly cherished, both by you and your inestimable partner. I would rather, on the contrary, guard you against extreme indulgence; receive her from my hands as your own child, and warn and admonish her as such. She will be rich; teach her how to use her wealth, that it may become a blessing in her hands, and through her to many. She already betrays sensibility beyond her years; warn her against giving way to it, as it may become prejudicial, if too much indulged in. My voice fails me, or I would say more; but let it suffice, that I pray you to be to her a father; raise her, my dear brother, that I may press my last dying kiss upon her lips, and with it bequeath the best legacy—a mother's blessing." A short time after this, and Lady Percy had breathed her last.

The little Emily was instantly removed to her uncle's home, and every tender attention lavished on her by her kind and, in every respect, excellent aunt, Mrs. Elizabeth Stanhope; and in introducing this lady, it may be as well to say, that she was as pertinaciously fond of old customs and observances as her husband, Mr. Henry Stanhope; was the very pink of propriety, and though nearly as old as her husband, a very fine-looking woman, and so tenderly attached to him, that his will was held by her as law, even on the most trivial subjects.

When the youthful Emily was received by this worthy couple, they had been married turned of twenty-six years, and had long given up the hope of having children of their own; consequently their little charge stood in great danger of being spoiled by indulgence. Mr. Stanhope, it is true, remembered his sister's dying caution, and strove hard to admonish and reprove her when she did wrong; but Emily had such pretty winning ways, and laughed so gaily when her uncle looked grave, and then he could never find it in his heart to be really cross, or even seemingly unkind to her, that despite his wish to curb and control her somewhat stubborn will and fiery spirit, Emily was allowed to do almost as she pleased, till her uncle, seeing there was no hope of educating her under his own roof, placed her, when of a suitable age, at a fashionable boarding-school in the adjoining town; and notwithstanding many tears and entreaties, insisted on her remaining there for five years, at the close of which period he himself fetched and brought her back, as it were in triumph, in the very identical Tallyho coach, that it was so strongly suspected he kept running at his own expense. And the moment that his niece, leaning affectionately on his arm, ascended the broad stone steps of his family mansion, while her pleased and playful glance wandered over the scenes dear to her, as connected with childhood's joys, that moment was one of the proudest of Mr. Stanhope's life. Nor was it less so to his revered partner, who received them in the hall, in a rustling dress of rich brocade, and small mob cap of the finest lace, while her own grey hair was brushed from her forehead, and confined to the back of her head; and warmly and affectionately she embraced her niece, and bade her welcome to the home of her forefathers; and yet even this glad return, when Mr. Stanhope looked upon his niece with the proud consciousness that he had performed his duty towards her, even at the sacrifice of his own feelings, which would have prompted him to have given way to the tearful entreaties of his niece, and have allowed her to complete her education at home; but even this proud moment of his life was embittered with the painful reflection that it was a niece, and not a nephew, that he was thus introducing to his ancestral seat. Had Emily been a boy, the occasion would indeed have been one of unmixed gladness; the name of Stanhope would not then, as, alas! it was now doomed, sink into oblivion, for even if Emily married, and gave birth to a son, who by assuming the name and arms of the family, might prevent them from becoming extinct, yet the family would not be continued in the regular unbroken line of male descent, as it had hitherto been; but Mr. Stanhope was a wise man, and therefore consoled himself with the reflection, that it was wrong to impugn the ordinations of a wise and merciful God, and that instead of murmuring at his just decree, he should be thankful that there was yet left one fair flower to blossom on their ancestral tree, which but a few short years before he had trembled to think was in imminent danger of being left without a single bud.

Thus reasoning with himself, Mr. Stanhope, with the air of a courtier, formally led his niece up the grand staircase, and into the carved oak dining-room. The uncle and niece afforded a strange and striking contrast to each other: he, in the now old-fashioned costume of his youth, and full of years, and, like the rich, ripe, yellow corn, ready for the sickle, which the grim, stern mower, Death, would undoubtedly ere long put in and gather to his fathers; she, in the light heyday of youth and beauty, just bursting into womanhood, with all the world and its enjoyments spread before her, and her ready hand eager to gather the flowers that were strewn in profusion over her path, yet leaning on the arm of age for succour and support, as though conscious of her own weakness, and anxious to keep her feet from slipping; and he gazing on her with half-tearful eyes, as the thought crossed his mind that in that fair girl he beheld the last of his race, while, like the ivy that clings to the mouldering wall, they each at once gave and received support.

---

## CHAPTER II.

AT the opening of our narrative, Emily, or Miss Stanhope, as she was usually called, had just entered her nineteenth year, and resided at the mansion we have already described with her uncle and aunt, by whom she was most fondly loved and cherished. Naturally warm, open-hearted, and generous, and possessing that best blessing, an excellent temper, united to a cheerful disposition, she was greatly loved and respected by the few friends and acquaintances that visited the mansion, and regarded as a most pleasant and amiable young lady by the servants, and, indeed, all the villagers. If any one had a favour to ask of Mr. Stanhope, it was always done through the medium of his niece; and when once she promised her interposition, they were sure of success. Thus, thought well of by all, Emily had by no means a mean or contemptible opinion of herself. Was she not Miss Stanhope Percy, the daughter of a baronet, and heiress to no inconsiderable amount of landed and funded property? Was not every one eager to bow to her decision, and pleased to have an opportunity of obliging her; and her dear uncle and aunt, who all allowed to be wisdom's oracle, in the constant habit of praising everything she said and did? Therefore, under all circumstances, it would be positively wrong in her not to entertain an excellent opinion of her own deserts. So thought Emily Stanhope; and this thought infused an air of pride into her manners and bearing, which, upon a first acquaintance, caused her to be rather disliked than otherwise; but those who knew her rightly, attributed it to the result of the well-meant though ill-judged praise bestowed upon her by her tender relatives.

Sir Beaumont Percy, the father of Emily, had, indeed, most amply provided for his daughter, and by his will left Mr. Stanhope as her only guardian and sole controller of her property and vast estate, not a farthing of which she could make use of, without his consent, till she arrived at the age of twenty-one; but from this she experienced no inconvenience, as Mr. Stanhope kept her most liberally supplied with money, and which, it is but right to say, though exceedingly fond of dress, and expensive ornaments, she yet, upon the whole, made a good use of. Her ear was never deaf to the appeals of charity; let the object be worthy or unworthy, it was all the same to Emily; her hand was immediately stretched out to aid the supplicant. It is true, that give what she might (and it was never a niggard boon that she bestowed), her own purse suffered no diminution, for whenever she found it growing light, one word to her uncle, and it was refilled, as it were, by magic; yet it was something to be of a generous disposition, and her readiness to give showed a feeling heart. We have now noticed the best traits of her character, for all was not excellence that pertained to Emily, though she herself thought so; for she had an uncommonly proud spirit, and a most determined will, added to which (though possessed naturally of an excellent understanding), she had been foolishly indulged, immediately after her return from school, in being allowed to read all the old novels of the neighbouring circulating library, which had been the means of vitiating her taste for good reading, and filling her mind with absurd notions utterly unfit for every day life. She had read of heroines in distress, and preserving their virtue chaste and uncorrupted in the midst of the most direful temptations and heart-rending sorrows; and of noble, gallant heroes in disguise, performing the most wonderful exploits, and wresting their lady loves from ruthless captors, till, in the end, they were made happy for life.

She had read and studied all this till the greatest ambition of her life was to become a heroine. She absolutely sighed for adventure, and would have resigned every farthing of her expected fortune to have been exalted into a heroine; to have had some mysterious personage flitting across her path, and ever and anon conveying to her some strange warning as regarded her future destiny. And, as to marriage, the idea of going in a coach to church, and accompanied by her friends, walking up the aisle and repeating the marriage ceremony, she regarded as a most dull, flat, insipid affair.

An escape with a rope-ladder from her bed-room window, a hurried flight to Gretna-green, pursued by merciless and unrelenting friends, was, to her mind, the most delightful thing in the world. There were even times in which she regretted being blessed with such kind, indulgent friends. A cruel and unfeeling guardian would have been one step, she deemed, towards becoming what she so much wished—a heroine. But no; fortune, in this darling wish of her heart, appeared to have frowned upon her most terribly, for she had now nearly completed her nineteenth year without having met with even the shadow of an adventure.

In person, too, she was not what heroines generally are; that is to say, by no means divinely beautiful, or of faultless proportions. Her figure was certainly good, and her deportment graceful and pleasing; rather above the middle height, and of tolerable proportions as regards symmetry. Her face was somewhat of a pensive cast, and its usual expression mild and gentle; her nose was aquiline, and her eyes of a soft hazel in colour; her hair, of a light chestnut, was simply plaited behind, and hung pendant in loose curls on either side of her face; her forehead was high, polished, and commanding. In conversation she could be at once dignified and playful, as the subject, or her own inclination dictated; and though at times whimsical and capricious, she was an affectionate and attentive niece, thinking of her relatives' comfort and happiness in preference to her own. Frequently has she refused to join a gay party that she might remain at home with her uncle when he has been attacked with a fit of the gout, and no one could attend to his comfort so well or so tenderly as Emily; and her light and cheerful converse would often cause him to forget his pain, and bless God for having given to him so kind and dutiful a niece.

Among the most frequent visitors at the mansion, or great house, as it was called in the village, was the curate of the little church, Mr. George Ellis, a young man of most blameless and unspotted integrity; as ready and willing to perform his sacred office to the poor as to the rich. He had now been curate of the village of Sackville for three years,

THE INTRODUCTION OF THE HEIRESS TO HER FUTURE HOME.

[The moment that his niece, leaning affectionately on his arm, ascended the broad stone steps of his family mansion, while her pleased and playful glance wandered over the scenes dear to her, as connected with childhood's joys and pleasures, that moment was one of the proudest of Mr. Stanhope's life.]

having accepted the curacy about the time that Emily first returned from school. He was a tall, well-made young man, and particularly gentlemanly both in his person and manners. He was a character that no one would ever dare to take a liberty with, or approach to a freedom beyond what he allowed. His hair was rather light, but of glossy smoothness, and his mild, grey eyes were capable of being lit up with an expressive softness unknown to more brilliant orbs.

Mr. Ellis was ever a most welcome guest at the residence of Mr. Stanhope, who entertained a sincere respect for him; and thinking his poor pittance of fifty pounds a year (which was all he received as equivalent for his services) an insufficient sum for one of his holy calling, would have augmented his income out of his own private purse; but Mr. Ellis was proud, and shrank with an innate feeling of delicacy from receiving money, as it were, in charity; and not only contrived to subsist upon his paltry income, but, though it was not generally known, he was in the habit of sending a part of it to his widowed mother and orphan sister.

The father of Mr. Ellis had for years confidently relied upon coming into the possession of a princely estate, he being the next of kin to an old bachelor, who had ever treated him as his son and heir, and as such allowed him a handsome income; but, alas! after having for a number of years given way to all his whims and fancies, he unfortunately offended his relative, who, in a fit of spleen, married; and, what was still worse, shortly after became the father of a son, thus entirely cutting off the hopes he had so long, but fruitlessly, encouraged in Mr. Ellis. Unfortunately, immediately after the old gentleman's marriage, Mr. Ellis, instead of endeavouring to conciliate him, in a fit of passion reproached him for his apparent duplicity; when, exasperated by his conduct, his relative intimated that, unless he was more guarded for the future, he should withhold the allowance he had hitherto supplied him with. Mr. Ellis was at this time turned of forty, married, and the father of two children—a son and daughter. His son had been educated for the church, in consequence of his relative having several valuable livings at his disposal; but, alas! after he became himself the father of a boy, he gradually got entirely weaned from the Ellis family, and ultimately departed this life, without making the slightest provision for any of them. This so preyed upon the spirits of the elder Mr. Ellis, that it brought on a low nervous fever, which terminated fatally in six weeks. His widow, never accustomed to exertion of any kind, was totally incapacitated from procuring a livelihood either for herself or daughter—a beautiful, but delicate, girl of sixteen. Her son George, who was several years older, deemed himself fortunate in procuring the curacy of Sackville, and willingly denied himself everything beyond bare necessaries, that he might be enabled to send a moiety of his income to his beloved parent; and bitter anxiety often swelled the breast of the curate, as he thought upon the temptations and trials to which his sister was daily exposed, and of which her extreme loveliness and unprotected state but rendered her the more likely to become the victim. And yet he felt he could rely upon the virtue and upright conduct of his sister; she was not the girl to be overcome by any light or trivial temptation. The unmeaning flattery and hollow sophistry of the worldling fell but lightly on her ear, and made no impression whatever on her mind. She perfectly understood and appreciated true excellence of character, and loved it far more than a showy exterior or handsome face. Though thoroughly convinced of this, still Mr. Ellis would have been happier could he have kept his sister near him; but that was impossible. She had ever been exceedingly clever with her needle; consequently, she found no difficulty in procuring a permanent situation at a fashionable milliner's at the west end of London; but this placed many miles between the brother and sister, who had never before been separated. But the poor have no choice; and, though tenderly and delicately nurtured, they each, with praiseworthy zeal, pursued their different avocations without a murmur. Happy, indeed, Mr. Ellis would have deemed himself could his own exertions have supported both, even had it involved a double amount of labour; but it could not be, and Mr. Ellis departed for Sackville alone.

The first visit he paid, after his arrival, was to the house of Mr. Stanhope, where he was greatly charmed with the eccentric, yet worthy, old couple. Their niece, too, strongly interested him. There was something about her that reminded him of his sister, though, in most respects, the two were essentially different; and, both as regards beauty of person and stability of character, few would have hesitated to give Miss Ellis the decided preference; but then she was the poor, hard-working, and badly-paid milliner, not the proud, high-born, and wealthy heiress, whom all were anxious to please. And here it is but justice to Mr. Ellis to state that, in the deep interest he felt awakening in his mind towards Miss Stanhope, he was actuated by no mercenary motive. No ; he simply looked upon her as an amiable young lady, whose cheerful converse and agreeable manners rendered her a pleasant and desirable companion ; and, thinking of her and treating her as though she were, in truth, his sister, he not unfrequently mingled with his converse a word or two of brotherly advice and tender counsel. He considered himself, likewise, as her pastoral teacher, and, as such, deemed it his absolute duty to reprove and admonish her when in error. And it was wonderful how well Emily bore with his censure—her, so utterly unaccustomed to reproof ; but she respected Mr. Ellis, and, knowing him to be poor, would not on any account hurt his feelings, by allowing him, even for a moment, to suppose she regarded him as an inferior. And then, too, the reader must remember that her greatest desire was to be a heroine, and heroines always bore all things patiently. Likewise, it was a perfect novelty to her to be chided, and novelty always carries with it a charm for the young.

Among the other persons who resided in the village, was a good-looking, dashing young widow, who had lately come to reside there, and occupied a pretty, tasty-looking cottage, within ten minutes' walk of the mansion, and which she in all humility was in the constant habit of calling her " little box."

There was a something bold and even disagreeable to the curate in the manners of this lady, and consequently he felt much grieved and vexed to observe the close and constant intimacy that took place between her and his young friend, Emily. From curtseying when they met at church, or in their walks, they soon got as far as wishing each other good-day, and from that to converse about the weather or any other common-place topic ; till at length they became so intimate that they were seldom or never apart.

Mrs. Harley was certainly a most unfit and dangerous companion for such a girl as Emily ; for, though endeavouring to throw around all her actions an air of openness and candour, the curate had seen enough of the world to enable him to discover that she was evidently an adept at intrigue, and that while she frequently laughed at Emily's desire for adventure, she yet secretly encouraged her in the absurd and ridiculous notions she entertained regarding love and marriage. Yet all Mr. Ellis could do was to take every opportunity of warning Emily against the fascinations of this lady, and which he certainly was not backward in doing ; but though Emily took all he said in good part, and thanked him for his friendly interest, yet she parried all he could urge against her new acquaintance with such zealous ardour as completely startled him ; and when he spoke of her external attractions and lively manners, as making her a dangerous companion, she absolutely laughed outright, and holding up her finger with the most provoking air of caution, while her eyes shone with moisture, brought there by the merriment he had unintentionally excited, she exclaimed, making an effort to look serious,—

" Oh ! Mr. Ellis, if that is indeed your true opinion of Mrs. Harley, let me entreat you to abandon all care for me, and rally all your forces to guard the avenue to your own heart, for I absolutely fear that it is in danger of a siege."

" I am sorry," replied Mr. Ellis, seriously, " to see my well-meant remarks turned into ridicule. True, I have no right to censure your conduct, and, therefore, may be considered as having drawn it upon myself ; still you have ever borne my reproofs so mildly that I confess I am more pained than I should have imagined possible. I have always spoken to you, Miss Stanhope, and must consequently trust to your goodness to excuse me now, and, that I may not offend further, will wish you good morning at once ;" and taking his hat, Mr. Ellis turned to leave the room, but was arrested in his intention by Emily, who, grieved indeed to have hurt the feelings of the curate, hastened to obtain his pardon.

" Stop, Mr. Ellis, I beseech of you," she exclaimed, " or you will be the means of making me really unhappy. I had no thought, I assure you, that any foolish remark of mine would have possessed the power to affect you thus, neither had I the slightest intention of turning aught that you said into ridicule : on the contrary."

" Say no more about it," replied Mr. Ellis ; " doubtless I am most to blame ; but I have felt so honoured by your friendship, and the kind and sisterly manner in which you ever listened to me, that I fear," he continued, smiling, " it has had the effect of causing me to regard it almost as a right, instead of receiving it as a favour."

" You have a right," returned Emily, with unaffected earnestness, " to expect that I should listen seriously to advice intended wholly and solely for my good. Still, I am at a loss to conceive what should prejudice your mind so much against Mrs. Harley ; you, that generally entertain so charitable an opinion of every one."

"And I trust," rejoined Mr. Ellis, "that I am not uncharitable in my opinion of her ; I merely wish to warn you, as I do not consider her a character that is likely to do you any good."

"And yet you allow her to possess personal attractions and agreeable manners?"

"Most certainly ; but that has nothing whatever to do with her character."

"Tell me, Mr. Ellis," replied Emily, with an air of frankness that it much pleased the curate to observe, "tell me of any one bad trait in it, and I will instantly resign her acquaintance. I cherish your friendship more than I can well tell you, for I consider it a friendship worth having ; and did you find less fault with me, I should probably like you less."

"Then you will not feel offended with me for saying that you are too apt to run into extremes. I had no desire to see you resign the acquaintance of Mrs. Harley altogether ; I rather wished to prevent you making so intimate a friend of her ; treat her as an acquaintance only, and I shall be satisfied."

"I cannot," replied Emily, smiling ; "Mrs. Harley is a woman that must be, to such a one as I am, all, or nothing."

"And therefore does she become a dangerous character, and one that will do you more harm than good."

"I cannot see it ; you have not even attempted to point out a single failing that she possesses, or a solitary instance in which her example is likely to become injurious to me, and I think I may charitably suppose that it is because you cannot ; consequently, as I find her company pleasant and agreeable, and her friendship in many respects desirable, I do not consider myself called upon to relinquish it merely because you entertain a contrary opinion of her merits, or I should, perhaps, rather say, demerits."

"I cannot argue with you, Miss Stanhope ; I was ever bad at controversy, and you have unquestionably the advantage of me in this, as in most things. Still, though I cannot argue the point, I am convinced that I see farther into the real character of Mrs. Harley than you do. I have had more experience in the world, have seen its dull, as well as its sunny side ; have experienced sad and bitter reverses, felt not so much on my account as for those who are bound to me by the dearest and tenderest ties ;—but I forget ; this, Miss Stanhope, cannot, of course, be interesting to you."

"You mistake, Mr. Ellis, it does interest me : I had no idea, till now, that you had any near connexion ; especially, as you intimate, in trouble. It would be a pleasure to me to be the means of assisting, to the utmost of my ability, any friend or relative."

"Pardon me, Miss Stanhope," hastily interrupted the curate, while a blush forced its way to his cheek ; "I have a mother and sister residing in London, which circumstance I never before imparted to you. Yet it arose from no desire to conceal what I am but too proud to own, but I had not the vanity to suppose that anything relative to my private affairs would prove interesting to you ; and I am thankful to say that, though in humble circumstances, they are yet above receiving charity, especially from Miss Stanhope."

"Good God ! Mr. Ellis, how terribly you misunderstand me," exclaimed Emily, shocked at having wounded the sensitive pride of the curate.

"Let us change the subject," he replied, "or rather return to our original discussion ; forgetting, if possible, this idle digression, which is entirely to be attributed to myself."

"Well, then," said Emily, "we were speaking of Mrs. Harley, and I again ask it as a favour, that if you know anything to her prejudice, you will at once declare it to me. And then, as I before said, you will find me open to conviction, and willing to resign her friendship."

"It is painful to speak ill of another ; neither do I know aught positively wrong in her character ; it is the freedom and boldness of her general manners that has caused me to dislike her."

"Dislike, is a very strong way of expressing your feelings towards her."

"It is nevertheless the true one."

"I can hardly conceive, Mr. Ellis," said Emily, with unusual warmth, "that you can have any just cause to dislike a person who entertains the strongest respect for you both as a public and private character ; indeed, she ever speaks of you in the warmest terms."

Emily was at a loss to imagine what there was in her remark to call the blood so tumultuously to the cheeks and temples of the curate as he answered, with an evident attempt to be composed,—

" I am, indeed, much obliged to her for her good opinion of me."

And after he was gone, she thought it well over, and endeavoured, but in vain, to make something of it. Could it be that Mr. Ellis was in love with her, and sought to conceal it, by a pretended dislike. She had read of such things in some of her favourite novels, and, had he been a different sort of man, she would thus have interpreted his conduct ; but even Emily, with all her desire to think otherwise, could not do the curate the injustice of supposing him capable of saying one thing and meaning another, and she felt, though she knew not why, much more pleased and happy, when she arrived at the conclusion, that his professed dislike of Mrs. Harley proceeded direct from his heart, and that, under it, there lurked, in truth, no tender feeling. This was strange, considering the warm friendship she herself entertained towards that lady, and her readiness to battle with the prejudice of Mr. Ellis, and, if possible, make him think better of her ; but Emily was made up of strange contrarieties, and, though a girl of warm feelings and affectionate disposition, yet, as we have said, there was so much contradistinction in her character, that even Mr. Ellis, who studied her more than most persons, was sometimes puzzled to make her out.

It may not here be amiss, perhaps, to say a word or two concerning Mrs. Harley, of whom the two principal characters in our history entertained so different an opinion. Mrs. Harley, then, was the widow of an elderly gentleman, of an exceedingly mean and avaricious disposition, and whom she had married when very young, in obedience to the wish of her parents ; and no sooner was the ceremony over, than she heartily wished him in the grave, in order that he might make room for a more favoured suitor ; but her wishes were for a long time vain. He lived, as it were, on purpose to be a continual torment to her, and, indeed, to all whom he was connected with. Having amassed considerable wealth (by, it was whispered, no very honest or praiseworthy means), his great ambition was to have a son, to whom to transmit it ; and the disappointment of this cherished wish had the effect of souring his temper, never at any time very amiable. Still his wife bore patiently with all his whims and caprices, keeping ever before her mind the great end for which she had married him, namely, the hope of soon getting effectually rid of him by death ; and then, being left a rich widow, with no one's happiness or pleasure to consult but her own ; then she deemed she would be well repaid for the misery and privation of her present position. How deep then her mortification and disappointment, when, after ten years of almost continual worry, and self-denial, death at length closed the career of Mr. Harley, and she deemed herself to have reached the goal she had so long sighed after, on opening his will, to find that he had bequeathed the bulk of his property to his nephew, Frank Harley, a careless, open-hearted, yet dissolute young fellow, whom in his lifetime he had ever affected to despise, and for whom, to please her husband, Mrs. Harley had professed to entertain feelings little short of hatred ; but scandal accused her of being by no means indifferent to him. Be that as it may, it was never suspected by the deceased husband, and, to the uter astonishment of Frank, who never expected to be left a farthing, he found himself by his uncle's death in possession of a handsome competence, while Mrs. Harley, who had so depended on being left a large and independent fortune, was bequeathed only a small annuity, and even that to be forfeited unless she lived entirely in the country.

Great as Mrs. Harley's mortification was on this humiliating discovery, she yet possessed sufficient tact to conceal it from her nephew, whom she warmly congratulated on his accession to wealth, protested that what was left to herself was amply sufficient to supply her moderate wants, and that a country life was what she had long sighed after ; and that, amid sylvan scenes, her spirits, she doubted not, would again revive, and that the fresh pure air of the country would re-establish her health, which her long and exhausting attendance on the sick bed of her husband had much injured.

Mr. Harley had left the choice of a residence entirely to the discretion of his widow, only stipulating that it should be at least upwards of twenty miles from the great metropolis, and had likewise kindly allowed her six months to seek for a suitable spot on which to take up her future abode. Mrs. Harley determined to avail herself of this kind consideration to visit every place of amusement or interest with which London abounds ; and thither she was constantly attended by the gay and gallant Frank, and so pleasant and agreeable did he make his company to the young widow, that, as the six months drew to a close, her spirits sank to the lowest ebb at the thought of parting with so delightful a nephew; and there is little doubt that had Frank chosen to avail himself of her condescension, he would have found no difficulty in persuading her to resign her legacy, and, abandoning all thoughts of the country, and the nominal relationship that existed between them, do him the honour of becoming his wife. But, alas! so dull and apathetic was Frank, that he never appeared conscious of his own power over the widow; and, though he bemoaned with her that her stay in London was forced to be so short, and regretted that they were obliged to relinquish many pleasant jaunts they had planned; yet it never seemed to occur to him that he was capable (if he chose to do so), of fixing her there for life; and notwithstanding numberless hints thrown out at various times by Mrs. Harley, yet so stupidly senseless was he, that they produced no more effect on him than they would have done on a block of wood.

The widow was out of all patience, and had it not been that she strongly suspected his stupidity on that particular subject was assumed, because he did not wish to understand, she would have told him in plain language, that she was willing to become his bride. As it was, she had nothing for it but to prepare for her departure, though where to fix her residence she knew not; yet some place must be chosen, for time was creeping on, and the six months fast drawing to a close. When, on descending to the breakfast-room one morning (after a long debate with her nephew the previous evening, concerning her future residence), to her surprise, she found him already there, waiting her arrival.

"My dear aunt," he began, as he rose to meet her (she hated to be called so), "I have been thinking of you all night" (she smiled, but affected to look incredulous). "I have, upon my soul," he continued, leading her to a seat; "and this morning rose two hours before my usual time, and have walked down here positively without breaking my fast, in hopes of gaining your consent to ——" and he hesitated; she smiled yet more sweetly as she answered in an encouraging tone,—

"Do not be afraid to go on, dear Frank, or to ask any favour of me that it is in my power to grant. I have told you before, that I feel so deep an interest in your welfare, that I would not hesitate to consult your happiness in preference to my own."

"Yes, aunt, I well remember your having frequently said as much; still, though what I wish to gain your consent to, I shall ask as a favour to myself; yet your comfort and happiness will be most promoted by what I desire; at least, I hope so."

"Very likely, dear Frank; a woman's comfort and happiness centres more in home than a man's; consequently, you are right in supposing mine to be more at stake than your own."

"You have hit it exactly, aunt"—("I wish," thought Mrs. Harley, "he would drop that odious title")—"and that is the reason why I so much desire to see you settled for life in a pleasant and comfortable abode."

The widow smiled still sweeter than before; she could positively have hugged the dear creature who had thus so opportunely come to his senses (it wanted but a fortnight to the completion of the six months).

"And now, dear aunt," he resumed, after a momentary silence, "as we understand each other, do give me some breakfast, for I am devilishly hungry, and we can discuss our plans as well, or better, on a full stomach, as an empty one."

"Aunt again" thought she; "what can he be thinking of? Under our present position, it is absolutely nonsense;" and in obedience to his wish, she moved towards the breakfast-table. She had but little appetite herself; but Frank made ample amends for that circumstance, by eating enough for both; and, as if determined to verify the truth of his assertion, "that he was devilishly hungry," caused eggs, bacon, rolls, and toast, to disappear, as it were, by magic.

Never did any breakfast—no, not even in her deceased's husband's life time, when they were usually seasoned by a pretty good sprinkling of ill humour, and a tolerable share of fault finding, to render, as it were, the viands more piquant, and the appetite to enjoy them more keen—yet never before did any breakfast appear half so long or tedious as this. "But all things must have an end," had ever been a favourite proverb with Mrs. Harley, and with this she now consoled herself; and at length her nephew announced his hunger appeased.

This was received, indeed, as glad tidings; but, still Mrs. Harley's impatience had to be tried a little longer. The servant was summoned to remove the breakfast equipage, and he seemed on this occasion more dilatory than usual. At last he departed, and closing the door, left his mistress and Mr. Francis, as he was usually called, alone. When, instantly turning to her companion, with a smile of pleasure, the widow thus began,—

"My dear Frank, I am now at liberty to converse with you without restraint, and must confess that I am a little impatient to learn what brought you so early a visitant to my house this morning."

"Why, I thought," replied Frank, taking a cigar, "that you had pretty well guessed the object of my visit."

"So far as it refers to my own settlement, you have already told me that my surmises are correct."

"Yes, that is it exactly," he returned, deliberately lighting his cigar (he was a most inveterate smoker). "You see," he continued, removing it from his mouth, after taking a few preliminary puffs, "that in another fortnight you will be compelled to quit your present residence."

"Undoubtedly," replied the widow; "such are the arbitrary terms of my late husband's will; though, as far as I am individually concerned, it will grieve me to be so entirely separated from you, Frank, for whom (at the risk of being thought premature and forward) I do not hesitate to declare I entertain a sincere regard, though, perhaps, I ought to blush for saying so much."

"I see no reason," he replied, in the interval of puffing, "why you should blush to declare an affection for me, who, I think, have always given you reason to believe sincere in my attachment to yourself. Say, aunty, have I not ever been a kind and dutiful nephew?"

"Why, Frank," replied the widow, forcing a laugh, "how exceedingly humourous you are; but, do try and be serious, for once in your life; remember, we are conversing on no light or trivial matter."

"I assure you, aunt, I am perfectly serious," he replied, removing the cigar from his mouth, and staring at her with unfeigned astonishment; "and, to prove to you that I am in earnest, I will tell you at once what I have done, and which I came here purposely to acquaint you with this morning."

"Well, Frank," she returned, impatiently, seeing he hesitated, and made a motion of carrying the cigar again to his mouth, "do pray go on."

"Well, then," he continued, "knowing that in another fortnight you must positively leave London, I have purchased" (the widow made sure he was going to say a license) "a very pretty cottage, standing, the advertisement says, in its own grounds, and most delightfully situated, being within five minutes' walk of the railway—in short, it possesses every requisite for ensuring the happiness and comfort of persons fond of retirement, and lovers of nature."

"Well, Frank," said Mrs. Harley, but with a perceptible change in her tone, from gay to sad, "what then?"

"Why, aunt, I wish to beg your acceptance of it; as, from all I can learn, it is the very thing for you; and, being in a sporting country, and the purchasing of the cottage giving the owner a right to shoot over a certain quantity of land, I thought, if agreeable, I could occasionally come down and spend a few weeks with you; and, at the same time, enjoy my favourite sport. What do you think of my plan, aunt?"

"I think it a very excellent one, and shall unhesitatingly accept of your generous gift," she replied, delighted with the prospect of having him so much with her, and never doubting but that ultimately he would regard her with a warmer feeling than at present he appeared to entertain ; at least, she determined to leave no stone unturned in her efforts to do so.

And, within the prescribed fortnight, behold the widow settled in the humble, but pretty village of Sackville, whither she was attended by her affectionate nephew, who, having stayed with her for a few weeks, took his leave, promising shortly to renew his visit, and during his absence enliven her solitude with a letter once a week.

And now, having given the reader an insight into the character of Mrs. Harley, whom in person we have already said was good-looking, and carried with her an air of *ton*, and in age under thirty, we will proceed to introduce one or two other characters with whom it is necessary for the reader to become acquainted.

## CHAPTER III.

Mr. Elgood, or Squire Elgood, as he was generally called, occupied a large, rambling, old-fashioned house, approaching to the outskirts of the village. He was a warm, hos-- pitable, good-hearted man, but of rough, unpolished exterior. He was much beloved in the village—more, indeed, it was believed, than by his own family, who were constantly endeavouring to modernise him, and make him leave off what they termed his vulgar ways. He had been for many years a persevering, honest merchant of the famous city of London, and, by dint of industry and economy, had saved a sufficient sum to enable him to retire with a handsome fortune, some ten years before the opening of this narrative. His family consisted of his lady, a stiff, starched, proud, yet matronly dame, of about eight-and-forty, exceedingly fond of chess, and of somewhat showy exterior, inasmuch as she possessed a tolerable figure for her years, and never failed to show it off to the best advantage, in the most becoming dress and ornaments ; indeed, her personal appearance, and that of her daughters, occupied her constant care and attention, to the exclusion of more important matters. She was uncommonly anxious to be thought a lady of fashion and experience in the *mode ;* and her sister having married a baronet, was a constant source of exultation to Mrs. Elgood ; and though, unfortunately, he used her so ill that she died of a broken heart within sixteen months after marriage, yet Mrs. Elgood confined this circumstance entirely to her own bosom, and never failed to extol Sir John Thornton, the morose, ill-tempered old widower of her much--injured sister, as a very paragon of perfection. Truly this was making rank and wealth (instead of charity) cover a multitude of sins, and sins of not very light complexion either. Mrs. Elgood was the mother of four children ; three daughters and a son.

The three Misses Elgood were tall, fine-looking girls, of dark complexion, hair, and eyes, and much resembled their mother in taste and disposition. Indeed, they had been so thoroughly tutored from their earliest infancy into her ideas and feelings, that it would have been strange had they grown up otherwise. Caroline and Jane, the two eldest, certainly more largely partook of their mother's character than Louisa, who was several years younger, and more lively and amiable than the others, and certainly the greatest favourite with the squire. It was no uncommon thing to see them walking, arm in arm, of a summer's morning, chatting with that easy, pleasant familiarity which should ever mark the intercourse of that tender relationship, father and daughter. But it was very rare to see him with either of his other daughters as a companion ; they more naturally chose their mother, her ideas and feelings coinciding with their own. All of them professed the strongest friendship towards Emily Stanhope, though Mrs. Elgood and her two eldest daughters frequently, in her absence, laughed at her absurd ideas of romance. Louisa and the squire never joined them on these occasions in their mirth, and, indeed, Louisa would sometimes venture to expostulate with her sisters on their duplicity.

John, the only son of Mr. and Mrs. Elgood, was their third child, Louisa being the youngest of the family. He had been given the name he bore in compliment to their relative, Sir John Thornton, who, having no children of his own, they confidently hoped would adopt his nephew as his heir.

John Thornton Elgood was about eighteen years of age ; very tall, very fair, and moderately stout. He was an awkward, ungainly sort of youth, though not bad looking. His complexion was a mixture of red and white, that betokened good health ; and his smiling and somewhat dignified mouth, spoke to his likewise possessing good temper ; yet, with these advantages, he was so uncommonly bashful, especially in the presence of ladies, that it gave him an appearance of sheepishness that did not properly belong to his character. He was, like his father, an excellent sportsman, and prodigiously fond of the field. There he was in his element, and shone forth quite a different character to what he did in his mother's drawing-room in the evening, especially if she entertained company. He seemed, on those occasions, to be so thoroughly conscious that he was out of place, that his position was really painful to witness by any sensitive beholder.

To this youth Mrs. Elgood had spoken in such strong praise of Emily, had dwelt upon her personal beauty, her delightful conversational powers, her elegance, her graceful figure ; and last, though by no means least, in her estimation, of her wealth, and her uncle's princely estate ; which she doubted not, at Mr. Stanhope's decease, would revert

THE INTERVIEW BETWEEN MR. ELLIS AND THE YOUNG STRANGER.

["This is a most painful subject," returned the young man; "let us drop it for ever." . . . . . "But one word more," interrupted the curate. "Isabel ——"—"Name her not—name her not!" he replied, as he pressed his hands upon his ears, as if to shut out the name.]

No. 3.

to Emily. This had been so strongly impressed upon the mind of John, was so constantly dinned into his ears, and hints thrown out that Miss Stanhope was by no means indifferent to his numberless good qualities, and which Emily had herself unconsciously strengthened by (out of pity for the young man's bashfulness and evident embarassment in her company), taking more notice of him than any other young lady had ever condescended to do, till at last John Elgood honestly thought himself desperately in love with the heiress, and took great credit to himself that her money by no means enhanced her value in his eyes. No, it was Emily and Emily alone, he deemed he loved, and had declared on several occasions to his mother and sisters, that had she been the honest village girl in Sackville, she would have been equally dear to his heart. Nay, he even went further, and had been heard to regret, with the most touching pathos of manner, that she was so rich in this world's goods; had she been poor he would have experienced no difficulty in wooing and winning her for his bride ; but now, alas, he could only mourn in secret over what he had been heard to term his ill-fated passion. Whether or not it proved to be so, we must leave the development of our history to determine. But we should here acquaint our readers that for many reasons John was somewhat of a favourite with the curate, who, conceiving that he wanted encouraging and bringing forward, always devoted the greater part of his ministerial calls at the squire's to conversing with his son on any topic that appeared most to please or interest him. And not unfrequently would he request his company to join him in a walk, always (such was the kindness of his disposition) asking it as a favour to himself; thus inferring that he conceived him a pleasant and desirable companion. This unwonted kindness was not lost upon the youth, who, in return, regarded the curate with a warmer friendship than he entertained for any other person in Sackville. And it was remarkable that he so identified himself with his friend, that he never spoke of himself alone. In relating any circumstance, he would say, "Mr. Ellis and myself" saw such a thing, or "we" called at such a place, or some one told "us" so and so; in fact, he always spoke in the plural, never in the singular number. If asked if he was going to the fair, the races, or anything else, at the next town, he would answer, "We have not yet quite made up our minds, but it is most probable we shall." And what is even still more curious, he used to say, when speaking on the subject of his love for Emily, "We are absolutely dying for Miss Stanhope ; but though very kind and condescending, we dare not hope that she returns our affection." This used to annoy and vex his mother and elder sisters greatly ; and, arguing with her brother on the subject one day, Caroline exclaimed,—

"La, John, what nonsense you do talk; who do you mean is in love with Miss Stanhope?"

"Who," he replied with astonishment, "why, myself, to be sure ; and ——" but recollecting himself in time, he stopped.

"And Mr. Ellis," said Louisa, laughing immoderately.

"I am sure I did not say so," replied her brother.

"No, John, I know you did not, in so many words, but you said, 'we are in love with Miss Stanhope,' and we know that with you, we stands for yourself and Mr. Ellis," said Louisa, still laughing.

"I forgot myself at the moment," he returned ; "for I am certain Mr. Ellis has never given me reason to suppose that he likes Miss Stanhope better than you, or either of my other sisters."

"Very likely not, John; and yet I think there are many more improbable things than Mr. Ellis being in love with the handsome and wealthy heiress."

"That is just like you, Louisa," said Jane, joining in the conversation ; "you think every one must of necessity be in love with Miss Stanhope, as if there was no good looking girl in the village but her ;" and she cast an approving glance in the opposite mirror, adjusting, at the same time, her glossy ringlets.

Jane was the best looking of the family, consequently Louisa took no notice of this, as she deemed it a pardonable piece of vanity. Yet the reader must not suppose that Jane had any desire to captivate the curate; on the contrary, she regarded him as far too humble to be worth even a smile from her, and often expressed her surprise that Miss Stanhope should admit him to so much familiarity.

"But then," she would say, "Emily is such a strange, unaccountable girl, that one need not be surprised at any absurdity she may commit."

"Still, my love," would argue her mother, " Mr. Ellis, though only a poor curate, is certainly a perfect gentleman. I am sure he was well born, and has most likely, through some unfortunate occurrence, become reduced in life. I am certain I am correct in my surmises; for it is so easy to tell when persons have been well born—they carry an air with them that is perfectly unmistakeable. For instance, there is your uncle, the baronet, Sir John Thornton; now see him where you would, or under the most peculiar circumstances, it would be impossible to take him for a common person."

"But surely, mamma," said Caroline, raising her eyes from her embroidery frame, "you do not mean to insinuate that it is probable that Mr. Ellis is the son of a baronet?"

"No, my love," replied the lady mother, "I do not mean you to draw such an inference from my remarks. What I wished you to understand was, that Mr. Ellis comes, I feel certain, of a respectable family."

"That may be the case," replied Jane; "but, for myself, I cannot say that I much like his manners; he is so very stiff, and, whenever he calls, appears to think that he is conferring a favour on us by so doing; and scarcely ever addresses even so much as a remark to any one but John or papa."

"I cannot tell how you can expect him to converse with you, when you never give him the slightest encouragement to do so," said John, who thought it necessary to defend his friend against the ill-natured remarks of his sister. "Now, Miss Stanhope ——"

"Is all perfection, of course," said Caroline, not allowing her brother to finish the sentence.

"As near it as it is possible for any one to be," replied John, with more spirit than he usually showed.

"My dear brother," said Louisa, smiling good-naturedly, and anxious to put a stop to the conversation, "we all know that you are in love, and, therefore, not a competent judge; for lovers always suppose their mistresses perfect, though an unprejudiced person may perceive in them a thousand faults."

"Well, Louisa," replied Mrs. Elgood, "instead of a thousand, I think Miss Stanhope cannot rightfully be accused of having more than one fault, and which is more to be attributed to the absurd notions inculcated by that old-fashioned, eccentric old couple, her uncle and aunt. Had she been brought up and properly instructed by a person who understood the observances of fashionable life, and who had been accustomed to move in the highest circles, I make no doubt but Miss Stanhope would have been a very different creature. As it is, she must at present be humoured in her romantic ideas; for to attempt to pluck them out, would only have the effect of causing her to dislike us."

"That would indeed be the completion of my wretchedness," said John, with a deep sigh.

"Do not talk of wretchedness, John," replied his mother, with a meaning smile. "It would afford us all pleasure to welcome her as your bride; but remember, that though she at present favours you, 'that faint heart never won fair lady.' You must talk, or at least, write to her of love. She is very fond of anything that can be called romantic; you should, therefore, mingle a little of it in your conversations with her."

"La! mamma," said Jane, laughing; "John never enters into conversation with Miss Stanhope. She certainly talks to him; but he never answers more than 'Yes,' or 'No.'"

"He must determine to begin, then," replied Mrs. Elgood, glancing encouragingly on her son; "and he will gain confidence as he proceeds."

"And first," said Louisa, laughing good-naturedly, "he must turn poet, if only to prove the truth of his affection, for love, you know, makes all men poets."

"By no means a bad thought," replied Mrs. Elgood; "a few verses would have a wonderful effect upon such a romantic girl as Emily."

"Especially if sent anonymously, and announcing the writer desperately in love with her," said Louisa, laughing still more.

"Good again," replied her mother, "and worthy of being acted upon. I protest, child, you have quite a genius."

"Wait, dear mother, till I can give you a better proof of it, before you praise me for what I own I cannot at present lay any claim to. I was only amusing myself a little at the expense of Miss Stanhope's fondness for romance; not of course for an instant being serious in my suggestion."

"It matters not, child," replied Mrs. Elgood; "a word sometimes spoken in jest has been the means of producing events long desired but little hoped for. I mean, of course, well acted upon by a person who was capable of reducing even the lightest hint to practice when occasion required.  Now I remember many years ago that your uncle, the baronet ——"

John at these words managed to slip unobserved from the room; he knew it was the signal for some thrice-told tale, and was glad to escape for this once, at least, the hearing.

We have now made the reader acquainted with the most aristocratic persons residing in Sackville; the select few who look upon themselves as the heads of the village, and down upon all the other residents as of beings of an inferior grade, if we except Doctor Harding, who was a general favourite, and gladly welcomed to every house and cottage in the village, from the noble mansion of Mr. Stanhope down to the humblest abode of the peasant.  He was a short, stout, middle-aged man, with a ruddy, good-humoured face, and possessed an inexhaustible fund of merriment; so that it has frequently occurred that some individuals have fancied themselves almost at the point of death, when, after a short visit, Doctor Harding has left them so far recovered that they have smiled at their own mournful anticipations, and have quickly regained their wonted health and spirits.  No wonder that " the doctor," as he was called, was considered in the light of a friend, as well as a medical adviser, by the entire inhabitants of the village.

His house, which was of modern build, was situated half-way betwen the main street and the little green that faced the lordly mansion of Mr. Stanhope.  His name and profession were made known by a large, bright brass-plate, the admiration and pride of the village.   The windows of his parlour, or surgery as he best liked it called, were polished to an unwonted brightness, and shaded from the gaze of passengers by dwarf Venetian blinds of a light drab colour; and at the moment we describe it, they bore likewise a very neatly-written paper, announcing the important intelligence, "Apartments to let furnished." The windows above were festooned with snow-white drapery, and, in short, everything about the house bore, like himself, an air at once of extreme cleanliness and comfort. There was something even in the very knocker of the door that spoke to the same; it was none of your long, angular, awkward-looking things, but a round, portly, comfortable-looking knocker, such as you could not for a moment suppose to belong to any one but a jolly, good-humoured, good-hearted, and contented man; and such was Doctor Harding.

He was a bachelor, and consequently did not require the whole of his house for his own use, and was in the habit of letting a part, which during the summer months he found no difficulty in doing.   The picturesque beauty of Sackville, its salubrious air, and the advantages it offered in point of retirement and quiet, drew many individuals to pay it a visit; and, during their stay, Doctor Harding's professional skill was taxed to the utmost in order to restore them to health.   And it was his proud boast that he had sent many away perfectly recovered, and among them some who had been suffering under their complaints for many months, and had tried in vain relief from the prescriptions of the most eminent of the London physicians, and which could be attested, if need be, by reference to the patients themselves.   And all the village were ready to declaim upon the alteration that took place in a few weeks for the better, without even a solitary exception, in invalids who had become inmates of his house.   But while conversing on the subject, the doctor never failed to give the climate of Sackville its modicum of praise.

" What absurdity," he would remark, " it is to send persons to seek for health in a foreign clime when there are such sweet, sunny, healthy spots in Old England as this ; if the balmy air of Devon cannot eradicate disease, no air on earth can.   I bless God I have never had so much as an hour's illness since my residence here ; and, when I lived in London, there was not a more sickly, miserable-looking person on earth ; and, if that is not something in proof of the beauty of the climate, I should like to know what is."

" Why, doctor," said Mrs. Elgood, to whom these remarks happened to be addressed, " your love for Sackville makes you quite poetical."

" I have spoken the truth, madam, the plain, unsophisticated truth, and nothing more."

" Well, I confess," she returned, " I fully believe your ideas on the subject are perfectly correct ; and it is this belief that induces me to reside so constantly here ; however, my brother-in-law, the baronet ——"

" I am delighted, madam, to see you display such good sense," interrupted the doctor, " and, from what I know of the constitution of yourself and family, I feel certain that if you were to reside in London for one year—mark, madam, I say for only one year—it would cause your death."

" Yes, doctor, that is exactly what I tell my brother-in-law, Sir John Thornton, when he urges me to quit my solitude, and mix once more in the festivities of London."

" When once a person has been accustomed for a number of years to breathe a pure and salubrious air, to transplant them to a smoky, foggy atmosphere, such as London, is sure to cause their deaths," replied the doctor, "and that, too, in a very short time."

" We entirely agree in our opinions, doctor; consequently I am resolved, even at the risk of offending my brother-in-law, the ——"

" So, mamma," interrupted Jane, who was seated at the window which commanded a view of the road, " here is Mr. Ellis coming up the avenue; I shall go and call John, for he is his visitor, not mine—good morning doctor."  And she hastened from the room.

Almost immediately afterwards Mr. Ellis entered; and the doctor, pleading press of business as an excuse for his short stay, took his leave.  We have said Doctor Harding was a bachelor, and middle aged; that is, he had passed the grand climacteric.  Notwithstanding his bachelor state, his little household was arranged with that air of comfort that so peculiarly belonged to the doctor; and, knowing that a table richly spread was nothing without a lady at its head, he had engaged a stout, rosy, comely dame, of about forty years of age, in the capacity of companion and housekeeper, to the great indignation of all the middle-aged spinsters in Sackville, who expressed themselves rather strongly on the subject.

" If Doctor Harding required a female companion, which of course all men did, or should do, why not have selected a virtuous female of his own age, or thereabout, and have given himself a legal right and title to her services by marrying her, instead of bringing such a creature as Mrs. Blake among them (the housekeeper had been selected from the neighbouring town).

" For my part," said Miss Tabitha Fraser, a sour vinegar-faced old maid, " I shall never, on any account, give the slightest countenance to that creature he has brought from town.  I am sure she ought to be ashamed of herself thus to digrace her sex by living with a single man, without even so much as having the delicacy to call herself his wife; that would have been bad enough, but it would have proved that she was not quite lost to all sense of delicacy; but, as it is, she perfectly outrages all ideas of propriety and decorum."

Yet, gentle reader, you will, perhaps, scarcely believe that Miss Tabitha confined all her bitterness entirely to the housekeeping, and never let fly at the doctor even a spark of her virtuous indignation   But whenever she was the slightest indisposed, Dr. Harding was sent for instantly, and received with the greatest kindness and condescension; indeed it was reported in the village, that she had, on more than one occasion, feigned indisposition, in order to procure a visit from the doctor; but this was probably only scandal, for Miss Tabitha, to use her own words, " enjoyed very bad health," though what enjoyment she found in it, if we except the visits of Dr. Harding, we think Miss Tabitha herself would have been puzzled to say, unless it was the occasional pastoral calls of Mr. Ellis, who was an immense favourite with this lady; and though we cannot with truth declare that the feeling was reciprocal, still, as she was one of the most devoted and constant attendants at his little church, never having been known to be absent when it was open for public worship, let the weather be ever so rough or the roads ever so dark or miry, let who might be absent, notwithstanding her delicate health, Miss Tabitha's seat would most certainly be occupied.  Consequently the curate, in a measure, felt bound to comply with that lady's request to favour her with a call, and nowhere was he more cordially received; and yet, strange to say, Mr. Ellis's visits to her were always performed as a duty, never indulged in as a pleasant relaxation from his ministerial labours; and then they were always made as short as possible, frequently to the great discomfiture of Miss Tabitha.  Yet Mr. Ellis was forced occasionally to do, what he considered, penance—that is, drink tea, and spend the evening with Miss Fraser and a small coterie of her female friends, and great indeed were the preparations to do him honour. On these occasions there was a regular process of washing, scrubbing, sweeping, and polishing for at least a week beforehand.  And then what an alarming, an unusual demand, was made upon the miller for the best—yes, the best, wheaten flour for the production of dainties, such as tea-cakes, seed-cakes, plum-cakes, and—but it would be useless to attempt to recount the varieties of delicacies that were prepared especially to tempt the appetite of the curate.  And then the dragging forth, from strange nooks and corners, of glass and china, never desecrated to the useful purposes for which they were expressly made, except on such great occasions as the present—great indeed, to Miss Tabitha, who was desirous to show Mr. Ellis that with her he could be as hospitably, ay, and as grandly entertained, as at the wealthy Mr. Stanhope's, for whose splendid mansion and noble estate she ever professed the greatest contempt. And for his niece, Emily, she could scarcely conceal her dislike even from the curate, though knowing it was bad policy to speak ill of one for whom all the village accused him of entertaining a lively regard. And not even Mr. Ellis's mild and amiable disposition could preserve him from scandal; for it was universally believed that it was the wealth of the heiress, and not any excellent qualities, either in her person or disposition, that rendered her desirable in his eyes.

"A bold, forward minx," Miss Tabitha would say, when speaking of Miss Stanhope; "it is well for her that she is accounted so wealthy, or I am certain she would never obtain the slightest notice. It is a very true proverb, 'that birds of a feather flock together;' and I have frequently seen her laughing and talking with that Mrs. Blake, just as though she were her equal; whereas she can scarcely condescend to nod to a decent, respectable person like myself. But I can see very well how it is; she knows that I am not deceived by her assumed airs of decorum, which she puts on to entrap Mr. Ellis, though he, poor man, is quite taken in by it."

"I cannot tell," urged a friend of Miss Fraser's, rather more charitably disposed than herself, "why Miss Stanhope should desire to entrap Mr. Ellis; he is poor, certainly not handsome, and by no means the man likely to please such a girl as her; there is every inducement for him to desire her notice, and nothing for her to seek for his."

"Oh, you do not understand her," replied Miss Tabitha; "she desires the notice of every man she comes in contact with, no matter whether they are poor or rich, handsome or ugly; not that she, for a moment, intends to bestow upon either one of them the broad lands which constitute her dower. No, depend upon it, if she ever does marry, it will not be any one residing in Sackville; her uncle will take good care to prevent that, even if she were so disposed. And I am sure I quite pity poor Mr. Ellis for being so imposed upon by her specious behaviour to him."

It is somewhat strange that Miss Tabitha Fraser and Emily Stanhope had unconsciously adopted the same expression when speaking of the curate; for when either of them spoke of him in his absence, they would say, "Poor Mr. Ellis." We have seen the reason Miss Tabitha entertained for supposing him an object of pity and commiseration, and for which, we think, we may safely say, the curate would not have thanked her. And Emily had prefixed the epithet "poor," before his name, on account of the humble opinion he ever held of himself, and the exceeding mildness of his general manners, which, joined to the amiability of his disposition, had the effect of inducing her to regard him with the warmest friendship, such as she extended but to few; and now, having premised this much, which is necessary for the proper development of our narrative, we will not longer try the patience of our readers, but proceed at once to another chapter.

---

## CHAPTER IV.

IT is autumn, but such an autumn as our variable climate is seldom blest with—bright, warm, and beautiful. Everything is softened and mellowed with the rich tints of the declining summer, which (as though it were unwilling to give place to stern, barren winter) held its fair and undisputed sway to the latest moment of its existence; and though its days were perceptibly shortened, and its career fast drawing to a close, yet its warmth and beauty remained almost undiminished. True, the evenings were cool, and family parties were glad to gather round the social hearth, and enjoy together the cheering influence of the blazing fire, a sweet foretaste of winter's joys, without its dreary and sometimes dispiriting effects. And then the days (but for the falling leaves, the season might well have been mistaken for spring), so soft and balmy, so delightfully cheering to the exhausted mind; this would tempt the veriest book-worm, that has been chained to the seclusion of his study the entire summer, to cast aside his books, and sally forth with invigorated spirits, anxious to enjoy the benign influence of the season, which could not, in the natural course of things, be expected to last long. And a walk in the fields and forests of old England, on a beautiful day in the fall of the year, may be productive of much reflection, which, if we would but lay it to heart, might be the means of making us wiser and better for the remainder our lives.   As we gaze upon the noble trees but lately rich in foliage, which crowned them with glory and with pride, now stripped of their bright plumage, which lies thickly scattered over the path; and the fresh green of summer, changed into the sad sombre hue of autumn; all things gradually sinking to decay—the flowers, that had so much delighted us, and which we have fondly cherished, now droop their graceful heads,.as if in sorrow for their own fleeting charms ; while the plaintive whistle of the robin sounds like the wail of the departing summer.   This surely must strongly remind us of our own fragility, how few comparatively are allowed to descend to the autumn of life, when the hoary head must bow before the hand of the reaper ; but this season also, to the reflective mind, teems with thoughts of days and hours mispent, and which we never can recall;   therefore, no wonder that it tinges our minds with sadness, and that our hopes for the future partake of the hue of the autumn leaf. But we forbear ; all have at times doubtless felt what we have attempted to describe, and, begging the reader pardon for this digression, which was unintentional on our part, we return to the spot from whence we started.

We were saying that it was autumn, but still warm and beautiful, especially at Sackville.   Nature had not yet wholly laid aside her summer garment, though preparing to change it for the darker mantle of winter.   Outdoor pleasures were zealously sought for by all; the fields presented a gayer appearance (being thronged with pedestrians), than they had done in the summer's prime.   Every one seemed determined to take advantage of the fine weather, and enjoy it while they could.   It was towards the close of a most lovely day, and the evening threatened to set in colder than usual, that a young man entered the little village of Sackville, and walked rather slowly up the main street, glancing for a moment at every shop as he passed it.   On arriving at the ale-house, he paused, and seemed debating in his own mind whether or not to enter ; but after hesitating a few moments, and throwing a somewhat searching look within, and observing it crowded with idlers, who were just returning from their day's toil, he quickened his pace, and pursued his walk.   He was evidently a traveller, and a stranger to the village.   He was dressed in a loose great coat, which completely enveloped his form; but his bearing was firm and erect, and he trod with the step of one who was accustomed to walking, and carried in his hand a small leather portmanteau.   He continued his pace till he reached the house of Doctor Harding, when, casting a glance towards it, the bill we have mentioned in the window caught his attention ; and, after a moment's hesitation, he knocked modestly at the door.   It was instantly opened by Mrs. Blake, the housekeeper, to whom he mentioned his desire to look at the apartments ; having seen which, he expressed his perfect satisfaction, and intimated his desire to take possession at once ; at the same time drawing forth his purse, he tendered half a sovereign as a deposit, stating that being a perfect stranger in the village, he was not of course prepared to offer any reference as to his respectability.

"I have been induced to seek this spot both on account of the salubrity of its air, and the advantages it offers, in point of retirement and quiet, of which I stand greatly in need.   I, therefore, trust that I may depend on being left perfectly undisturbed by idle and obtrusive curiosity," said the stranger, to Mrs. Blake, as she was about leaving the room.

" There is no one here," replied the lady, with an air of offended pride, " whose curiosity," and she laid great emphasis on the word, " would induce them to obtrude upon your privacy, or wish to pry into your motives for desiring to remain in retirement, I am sure."

" Very well, my good woman, that will do," interrupted the stranger; " yet," he added, as she was in the act of closing the door behind her, " you had better send some one to kindle a fire, for this room seems uncommonly cold."

" The evenings must be expected to get cold now," returned the housekeeper, as she prepared to do his bidding ; " it is getting late in the autumn, though, to be sure, the weather is so fine and beautiful, that one can scarcely believe it wants but ten weeks to Christmas, as I was saying this afternoon to Miss Stanhope."

At the mention of this name, the stranger raised his eyes from the carpet upon which they had previously been fixed, and apparently endeavouring to recollect himself, said,—

" Stanhope! I think I have heard that name somewhere before—at any rate, it seems familiar to my ears, though it is scarcely possible I have met with a person of whom you speak, unless, indeed, she may be in the habit of visiting London."

" I can undertake to assure you," replied the housekeeper, glad of an opportunity of indulging her loquacity, " that she has never been nearer to it than the next town; but a good, amiable, and most generous young lady she is—God bless her, and not the least bit of pride does she ever show in her conversation, even to the humblest peasant, though she is so rich that she is known as 'the Heiress of Sackville.' Now, Squire Elgood's daughters ——"

" Upon my word," replied the stranger, smiling, " your village seems to contain a perfect aristocracy—a wealthy heiress and a squire. After this I shall not be surprised to hear of an earl, or at least a baronet."

" You have heard of the daughter of a baronet already," replied the housekeeper, somewhat offended at the others manners.

" Indeed! then I am to suppose that the father of this Miss Stanhope, of whom you speak in such warm terms, is ——"

" Was, for he has long since departed this life, having been killed by a fall from his horse, and his lady unfortunately survived him but six short months."

" Consequently," returned the stranger, " Miss Stanhope is an orphan, and, I suppose, holds undisputed possession of the family estate, and that may account for her generosity."

There was an evident bitterness in the tone of the young man as he spoke these words, which did not escape the observation of Mrs. Blake, who hastened to undeceive him by saying,—

" You are entirely mistaken, sir; Miss Stanhope is not yet of age, and resides with her uncle and aunt, to whose control she willingly submits. Indeed, Mr. and Mrs. Stanhope are as much beloved in the village as their niece."

" And have they no children of their own?" inquired the stranger, apparently interested in the subject of conversation.

The housekeeper answered in the negative, and having concluded her task, she left the room, and the stranger drew his chair towards the fire, which now gave forth so cheerful a blaze, that it was no wonder the young man appeared to regard it as a companion. A bright blazing hearth will often supply the place of an absent friend, and sweet it is to recall to memory (as we watch the sparks flying upwards, and listen to the crackling of the wood, which at once affords us warmth, light, and company), past converse, which in happy hours have lightened our bosoms of its care, and we have imparted " to the few we liked, the one we loved," every thought and feeling of our hearts, and they in return have done the like by us. Seated alone by a bright, cheerful fire, " how will our thoughts, to long past moments turning," recall feelings and hopes long buried in oblivion. Yet soft as the shadowy light by which we are surrounded, and as wrapt in meditation we watch the fantastic shapes of the burning fuel, to our fanciful imagination they image forth scenes and circumstances belonging to past times, but which, like Banquo's ghost, seem standing boldly before us, though invisible to all other eyes. We live again in days gone by. Many who have long since descended to the tomb are once more smiling upon us; we hear the very tone of the loved one's voice, erst so sweet to hear, and revel over the brightest hours of our existence. Thus sunk in deep and apparently at times painful meditation, the young man remained for a considerable time, his earnest gaze bent upon the fire; one leg was mechanically crossed over the other, and his arms folded moodily over his breast. He was very tall, and exceedingly well proportioned; his complexion dark, and his eyes and hair of jet black; his forehead was unusually high and beautifully polished, without even the vestige of a wrinkle. There was an unwonted fire in his eye, and a curl of the upper lip, that betokened there was a mingling of contempt for some person or things connected with his reflections.

He was roused from his reverie by the entrance of Mrs. Blake, bearing a candlestick in her hand, which having placed on the table, she was about to withdraw, when the stranger stopped her, by inquiring if she knew where Mr. Ellis, the curate of the village, lived.

" Oh, dear, yes, sir," replied the lady; " he resides in a little cottage almost facing the church, with the widow of the former curate, Mrs. Fairlawn, and if you would wish to see him, I am sure he would gladly come. A dear good young man he is, and never backward at offering spiritual consolation to those who stand in need of it; so, if you please, I will send to him at once."

" My case is not so pressing but that it may safely wait over to-morrow," returned the stranger, smiling at the simplicity of the housekeeper. " I am indisposed both in

## THE BOUDOIR OF THE HEIRESS.

[Touching the handle of the bell rather sharply, soon brought into the apartment a smartly dressed damsel, who officiated as her waiting-maid, of whom she made inquiries concerning the strange gentleman she had just seen.]

body and mind, and shall be glad to retire early. To-morrow I may, probably, avail myself of the kindness of Mr. Ellis, and seek an interview with him."

"As you please, sir," replied Mrs. Blake, curtseying a good night to her lodger, about whom there was a something she did not exactly like, though it is probable she would have been puzzled to say what it was.

The following morning, the doctor, having been previously made acquainted that his house contained a new inmate, hastened to offer his services to his lodger, and apologise for his apparent neglect of the previous night, by assuring him that he was in close attendance upon a sick patient, till an hour too late to permit him to pay his respects, and which he was thus most unwillingly obliged to postpone to the present moment.

"Make no apology, I beg of you," returned the stranger. "The more I am left in undisturbed quiet, the better I shall be pleased, as I had the honour of informing your good lady last night."

"Mrs. Blake is my housekeeper, not my wife," replied the doctor, with his usual suavity.

"Indeed! I beg your pardon," said the stranger; "but I dare say it is of small consequence. And, as I really have no occasion for your services, you will excuse me for saying plainly that I prefer to be alone."

"My housekeeper informed me," replied the doctor, "that you stated to her that you were indisposed, and that was partly your reason for your seeking the retirement of this sweet, salubrious spot. And though, perhaps, you may think light of my professional skill, yet I can assure you that ——"

"Stop!" said the stranger, with an air of irritation in his manner, quite at variance with the smooth, persuasive tones of the doctor. "Can you minister to a mind diseased?"

"It is not so utterly impossible as you imagine; and if you will allow me to introduce you to cheerful society, and, at the same time, to prescribe ——"

"Once for all," interrupted the stranger, "let me inform you that I am determined to live in perfect seclusion, troubling myself with the affairs of none, and all I require is, that no one shall meddle with mine. I wish to be asked no question, or be interfered with on any one point. Knowing this, if it suits you for me to remain in your house, well and good; if not, I will seek for a residence elsewhere."

The doctor was sorry to have given offence, and was quite certain that nothing was farther from his thoughts than intruding upon the privacy of any one; and, trusting that he should be pardoned this once, promised not to offend in like manner again, and withdrew, and shortly after joined his housekeeper at the breakfast-table.

The merits and demerits of their new lodger formed the subject of conversation during the meal, and both agreed that though, in many respects, a most eccentric character, and altogether not a very agreeable one, still he might make a good inmate for the winter months, when lodgers were not so plentiful, that they could afford to be particular.

In the midst of their cogitations they were disturbed by the ringing of the lodger's bell, and Mrs. Blake hastened to receive his orders; when he handed her a note addressed to Mr. Ellis, saying, at the same time,—

"You have assured me that your curate is ever willing to offer his services to any who may wish to avail themselves of his kindness; consequently, upon the faith of that assurance, I have ventured to ask of him, as a personal favour, to call here this morning as early as convenient. I trust that he will not think that, being a perfect stranger, I am taking too great a liberty."

"Make yourself perfectly easy on that score," replied the housekeeper; "for I can ——"

"Then," interrupted the stranger, "I will trouble you to send some one with that note immediately; and when Mr. Ellis calls, show him in here."

A boy was quickly dispatched with the note, and quickly returned with the curate, who was instantly ushered into the presence of the stranger. The door was closed upon the two, and Mrs. Blake, though very curious to learn the subject of their converse, was obliged to retire with her curiosity unappeased. They had merely bowed as perfect strangers while she was in the room; but no sooner was she gone, and the last echo of her step heard upon the stairs, than the curate, addressing the other as an intimate friend, spoke thus:—

"And is it possible, Mordaunt, that we again meet? I had long given over the hope—

I had almost said the wish—that we should do so; and even now I know not whether this meeting may be most productive of pleasure or of pain."

"We are both changed," he returned; "six years has had its wasting effect on each, though fortune has frowned on the one and smiled on the other."

"Six short years," replied the curate, "has, indeed, made a wonderful difference between us, in point of worldly fortune; but, in me, you now behold the same pure hopes cherished as fondly as of yore, the same kindly feelings towards my fellows are nourished in my bosom, and though it is impossible to love all, I yet trust that I despise none; but you, I have discovered, with deep regret, have been led to entertain feelings of distrust and hatred towards the whole human race."

"And, oh! have I not had bitter cause to make me do so?"

"No, James, I will not allow it; the injustice and oppression of one individual, can never be pleaded in excuse for your hatred of all."

"This is a most painful subject," returned the other; "let us drop it for ever; I never intended it as a topic of discussion between us."

"But one word more," interrupted the curate—"Isabel."

"Name her not—name her not," he replied, as he pressed his hands upon his ears, as if to shut out the name.

There was a pause of a few moments, when the curate again resumed,—

"I know that by pressing my inquiry, I am probing a deep and painful wound; yet I feel it no less my duty to do so, Mordaunt," he continued, raising his voice. "You are rich."

"Aye," he returned, stopping abruptly, in his hurried walk, while a contemptuous sneer curled his lip; "and you do well to remind me of it in connection with her you have named; it stems the current of my blood, and causes me to think of her as I most wish to do."

"Such thoughts are wholly unworthy of you; cast them, I beseech you, from your mind, and, in their place, encourage thoughts more befitting both her and yourself; remember, that with all her faults she is still ——"

"Faults!" he vehemently interrupted; "say, rather, crimes, and those of the deepest dye; but cease such thoughts, they bring with them misery too acute even for me to bear. I once thought that there was a solitary oasis in life's desert, even for me, oppressed and trampled on as I have been; and on that green and sunny spot, I had garnered every hope and feeling of my bosom, had lavished all the love and affection it was ever my lot to possess; but storms have broken over it and nearly buried me under their whelming influence. Oh! Ellis," he continued, "pardon these tears, they shame my manhood, but when I think of the past I am not myself; yet," he continued, stifling the rising emotion, "I desired your presence here this morning, not to speak of myself, or aught concerning me it was for your sake alone I wished this interview, and to inform you of a circumstance that I know will pain you much. I arrived at this place last evening, direct from London, on purpose to acquaint you with the sudden and alarming indisposition of your mother."

"Alas!" exclaimed Mr. Ellis, clasping his hands, and turning deadly pale; "and why did you delay your information so long? The difficulty, you must know, that I should encounter in procuring a suitable person to fulfil my duty to-morrow, for, most unfortunately, this is Saturday, ought to have induced you instantly, on your arrival, to have imparted to me your distressing intelligence; I might then, perchance, have found a substitute, but now, alas! I can scarcely hope to do so."

"Do not distress yourself," returned his friend; "I but waited to inform you of your parent's illness, till I could say, at the same moment, hasten instantly to her; I am now able to do so, having just received a satisfactory an answer from the young man I applied to, to fulfil your duties as long as your absence may render it necessary. You have truly said, that I am rich; you will not, therefore, feel any delicacy in my remunerating him for his services, or in accepting this trifle for your own expenses;" saying which, he extended a paper towards him.

"Mordaunt," replied Mr. Ellis, averting his face from the other's gaze, "you have proved to me that you are still capable of performing a generous, a noble action, and the knowledge of this affords me the sincerest pleasure; for the future, you may cavil at your fellow man, and affect an enmity towards your race, without exciting the painful feelings in my breast that you have hitherto done, for I shall feel assured that your words belie yourself; and, that in truth, you are the same kind, noble being, that I ever deemed you; that you still love to do good; and though happiness and yourself are for the present separated from each other, yet you strive to make others acquainted with it. And now, Mordaunt," he continued, "I feel no hesitation in availing myself of your kindness, and shall hasten to my poor mother instantly. God grant that I may not be too late to receive her blessing."

"Farewell, Ellis," returned Mordaunt; (but seeing he avoided his proffered gift) "you will not refuse to accept this trifle, which I purposely made so small, that I never for an instant even dreamed it would hurt your pride to receive it."

"My dear friend," replied the curate, "did I require any sum, I would not, as you say, hesitate to receive it from you; but I assure you I am amply provided for my journey—nay, more, I have also sufficient for my mother's wants."

"You were ever proud, Ellis," returned his friend; "and, knowing this, I cannot take offence at your refusal. Give me one promise, and I will press you on this subject no further."

"Name it," replied Mr. Ellis.

"It is simply this, that if, after your arrival in London, you find your parent's illness make greater demands on your purse than it is able to meet, you will ——"

"Most unhesitatingly apply to you," interrupted the curate; "and now I must hasten my departure; we shall probably hereafter meet again."

"I must detain you one moment longer," replied his friend. "Listen to me an instant. When you return to Sackville, be your absence long or short, you will, unless any unforeseen circumstance should arise, find me still here; but I wish you, for reasons which I stated in my note, to regard me, if ever we chance to meet in public, as an entire stranger. I have represented myself as known to none in this neighbourhood, and, if I except you, I have spoken the truth."

"I shall not forget," returned the curate; "nor the generosity you have manifested towards me this day, as kind as it was unexpected;" and extending his hand, which was cordially grasped by the other, without either exchanging another word, he left the room.

As soon as he found himself in the street, Mr. Ellis almost mechanically bent his steps towards the residence of Mr. Stanhope. He was received by the kind old gentleman and his partner with the warm, affectionate greeting they ever bestowed upon him, and who failed not instantly to note a shadow on his brow not usually seen there; nor did the curate delay to acquaint them with the cause, and ready sympathy offered all the consolation in its power.

"You had better, my dear sir, prepare for your departure immediately. The coach will be passing in half an hour at the farthest," said Mr. Stanhope. "No, my dear sir; I beg pardon," added the precise old gentleman, consulting his watch, "it will be about five-and-thirty minutes, as near as possible. You will have just time to prepare for your journey, so I will not detain you a moment longer."

"Will you pardon me, sir," replied Mr. Ellis, with a respect for Mr. Stanhope's prejudice exceedingly praiseworthy under the existing circumstances, "if, for this once, I determine to avail myself of the speed of the railway conveyance."

The old gentleman's countenance changed as he answered,—

"Surely, Mr. Ellis, my dear sir, you will not allow the slight difference of an hour or so, to induce you to risk your life—a life so justly dear to your parishioners? Be advised," he continued, earnestly, "by an old man, yet one who has your welfare truly at heart, and go by a slower yet safe and pleasant vehicle."

"My mother," replied the curate, endeavouring to conceal his emotion, "is now on a bed of sickness, from which it is only too probable she may never rise again. Think, then, Mr. Stanhope, what must be the feelings of her only son; and, oh! do not deem me wanting in respect or kindness towards yourself, when I say that I have no choice, but must hurry to her by the readiest and quickest conveyance, even were it at the risk of my own life, which, however, I do not think will be endangered."

"As you please, sir," returned the old gentleman; "though I trust, under other circumstances ——"

"I should most unquestionably go by the coach," interrupted Mr. Ellis.

"I believe you," returned Mr. Stanhope, something mollified by this assurance; "and though nothing on earth should induce myself, or any one over whom I exercised control to make use of any other conveyance than was formerly found to answer every purpose of locomotion, still young people will, I find, depart from the customs of their forefathers; and, considering the pressing nature of the case, I cannot, my dear sir, find it in my heart to be angry with you."

This was much from Mr. Stanhope, and the curate felt it to be so; and yet, though most anxious to be at the bedside of his parent, he still lingered even after the old gentleman had most courteously bade him adieu, and extracted from him a promise of writing immediately on his arrival in London; providing, of course, that he escaped the numberless dangers to which he would be exposed on his journey, and arrived there safe; still the curate, as we have said, lingered, and seemed unwilling to be gone, to the great surprise of Mr. Stanhope; but his good lady appeared to comprehend him better; and at length said,—

"Emily will be greatly disappointed at not having the opportunity of bidding you adieu."

"Miss Stanhope is from home, then?" replied Mr. Ellis, rather hastily.

"She has just left to call upon her friend, Mrs. Harley," returned her aunt, "and will, as I said before, be much grieved when she hears of your unexpected departure, and more especially when made acquainted with the cause."

"You do me too much honour, madam," said the curate, who now appeared as anxious to depart, as he had previously been tardy; and after polite greetings had been once more exchanged, he hastened towards his own humble abode; arriving at which, he selected a few trifling articles from his but scantily stocked wardrobe, and with a sorrowing heart, prepared to leave the village. He was walking at no very rapid pace, it must be confessed, towards the railway terminus, carrying his little parcel under his arm, when, raising his eyes from the ground on which they had been bent, they encountered three persons coming towards him. His heart beat quick as he recognised them to be Mrs. Harley, her nephew, and Emily Stanhope; they were walking very cheerfully, and praising the brightness of the weather, and so entirely engaged with themselves, that he was totally unobserved; and for an instant, the curate felt disposed to cross the road, and thus avoid a recognition; but then the thought arose, that if Emily should discover him in the act of doing so, she would deem it disrespectful, and she had treated him so kindly, that he should be sorry for her to suppose, even for an instant, that he would purposely avoid her. Thus communing with himself, he pursued his walk.

"What! is that you, Mr. Ellis?" said Emily, as they approached, and who was the first to observe him. "It is rather unusual to see you abroad so early of a Saturday."

"I have just been to take leave of your aunt and uncle," he returned, rather coldly, as he remarked that she leaned familiarly on the arm of her male companion, "and am now going by the train to town."

"Surely," observed the widow, with one of her blandest smiles, "it can be no common occurrence that can so suddenly deprive us of the pleasure of your society;" and she, more versed in the knowledge of a man's heart, had released her arm from that of her nephew's, immediately she recognised Mr. Ellis.

"It is as you observe, madam," he replied, "no common occurrence that thus so suddenly takes me from Sackville; not that I could for a moment have the vanity to suppose that my absence would be felt as a loss by any who have condescended to receive me as a friend;" and he cast a reproachful glance towards Emily, who remarking it, observed, in a tone something akin to his own,—

"I know not what Mr. Ellis's friends can have done to induce him to entertain so mean an opinion of them in the hour of parting. I think it would be more generous of him to regard them more favourably."

"It was of myself alone I spoke," he returned, with increased coldness; "but I desire not to detain you from your walk, and will therefore wish you a good morning."

"Will it be attributed to curiosity if I presume to inquire into the nature of the business that takes you so suddenly to London?" said Mrs. Harley, in the same soft tones she had first spoken.

"By no means," returned the curate; "I have just received intelligence of the severe illness of my dear mother, and as I have fortunately procured a young man to perform my duties here, it cannot be deemed surprising that I should be desirous of hastening to her."

"Surprising! oh, dear, no, Mr. Ellis; it would be wonderful, indeed, if you were not.

God grant that you may find your mother better than you have been led to expect," replied the widow, affecting the greatest commiseration for the unhappy event; and stretching out her small white hand, she cordially bade him adieu.

The curate received it politely, but without any emotion of pleasure, and thanking her for the interest she manifested in his welfare, returned her farewell greeting.

This was the first time Emily had ever been treated with coolness by one of the opposite sex, and not perceiving any cause for it in herself, felt not a little mortified by it, and consequently returned the curate's farewell bow with an hauteur quite unusual to her.

Mr. Ellis and Frank Harley had not exchanged a single word during the interview, for the curate had imbibed, he knew not why, a strong dislike to the young man, which was by no means lessened by his observing the familiarity that appeared to exist between him and Emily; he had therefore only bestowed a formal bow upon him.

"What a strange, unaccountable man, Mr. Ellis is," said Emily, as soon as they had parted company; "I feel quite vexed with myself for being annoyed at his rude treatment of me, and which I am perfectly at a loss to account for."

"Then trouble yourself no more about it, *ma chere amie*," replied the gallant Frank, pressing the hand that rested on his arm; "it is easy enough to perceive that the curate is confoundedly jealous."

"Mr. Ellis jealous!" replied Emily; "absurd!" and a blush crept to her cheek, she knew not why.

"Absurd, indeed!" said Mrs. Harley. "For the future, Frank, do not attempt to interpret the feelings of others, for you do it very badly, I assure you. Jealous!" and the widow laughed at the bare idea.

But, though Emily had pronounced it absurd—and she generally deemed herself infallible—she was not altogether satisfied or pleased with Mrs. Harley for taking the same view of it as herself. This was strange, for Emily usually liked her friend to confirm her in her opinion; but now she felt uneasy, and wished that the parting between herself and the curate had been a more friendly one; but it was of no use to grieve about it now, and so, inwardly resolving to greet him with redoubled kindness on his return, she endeavoured to banish him for the present from her thoughts.

---

## CHAPTER V.

As Mr. Ellis pursued his walk, he endeavoured to tranquillise his ruffled feelings. "What right had I to expect her to interest herself with aught that concerned me?" was his inward exclamation; and yet, spite of himself, and his wish to think the contrary, he felt that he had expected it, and till this, to him, unfortunate morning, she had ever treated him with the kindest consideration; and, as he thought it over, he began rightly to attribute the blame to himself; "but, however," he continued, musing on what had passed, it is quite clear that she cares nothing at all for me. I did wish her to regard me as a friend, and were this Mr. Harley a suitable person to match with such a one as her, it would please me to forward it all in my power; but no, for her own sake, I trust her affections will never be placed on such a reckless, heedless young man. When I return here, I must take an opportunity of advising with her on the subject."

Thus busily engaged with his own thoughts, Mr. Ellis did not perceive young Elgood, who had been for the last two or three minutes walking by his side; but who, perceiving that he was sunk in meditation, had not ventured to interrupt him, till, raising his head, the curate became aware of his presence, and speaking with his usual kindness, asked him whither he was going.

"If agreeable," replied the youth, timidly, "I thought of accompanying you to the railway."

"How happens it, John," replied Mr. Ellis, smiling, "that you were aware of my intention of proceeding there? It is not a usual walk of mine."

"I but this moment met Miss Stanhope, who informed me that you were going by the rail to London instantly; when, quickening my steps, I have been fortunate enough to overtake you."

"It is very kind of you, John," said the curate, pressing the hand of the youth; "and I am much pleased to have an opportunity of bidding you good bye; and be assured

that I shall often think of you while away;" and then, after a pause, he continued,—
" What do you suppose, John, I was thinking of at the moment you joined me?"

" I am sure I cannot tell," replied the youth, with great *naivete;* "unless it was of Miss Stanhope. She told me she had just met you, and ——"

" Consequently," interrupted the curate, " you deemed it by no means improbable that I was thinking of her, and for this once you are not far out in your calculation ; but I was likewise thinking that if I were about to leave Sackville for ever, instead of, as I fully hope, a few short days, or, at most, weeks, I should not leave one person behind who would grieve for my departure. Now, John, you have convinced me I was in error; for I can plainly see traces of sorrow in your countenance at the idea of parting with me for only a short time."

" Indeed, sir, it does grieve me to be obliged to bid you farewell, and I shall be dull and sadly out of place till you return."

" I believe you, John," replied the curate ; " but let us hasten our steps, or we shall be too late for the train."

They had just reached the terminus, when, to the surprise of both, they encountered Mr. Stanhope, who, with anxious looks, was waiting their arrival.

" My dear sir," began the old gentleman, addressing Mr. Ellis, " I have come to see you safe off, and God grant that your perilous journey may conclude without accident. I wish indeed that you had taken my advice and gone by the coach. It is not even now too late to alter your determination."

These words being overheard by the bystanders occasioned a smile, and one stylishly-dressed young man, forgetful of the laws of politeness, laughed outright, and inquired what there was in a journey of a few hours so perilous ?

" It is not the journey," replied Mr. Stanhope, with his usual courtly air, " but the manner of performing it, that, I conceive, I rightly deemed perilous."

" But you surely would not advise your friend," replied the young man, " to be daudling along the road in a heavy lumbering old coach for nearly a whole day, when he might perform the journey in a few hours?"

" And is safety to be put down as nothing?" rejoined Mr. Stanhope.

" Safety, sir," replied the other; " if you lay so much stress on that, I can tell you that I have travelled many thousand miles by the rail, and have never once met with even the slightest accident."

" You have been fortunate, sir," returned Mr. Stanhope ; " and I can only hope that you will continue to prove so."

" This is exceedingly kind of you, sir," said Mr. Ellis, drawing him aside ; " do not, I beg of you, make yourself at all uneasy concerning me, and on my return, as speed will be but of little importance, rest assured I shall make use of the coach. And now, dear sir, farewell, and you, my dear John," turning to his more youthful companion, " for the present, adieu. As soon as I arrive in London, I will acquaint you with my welfare." Saying which, and cordially shaking the hand of each, Mr. Ellis stepped into the carriages.

And now the loud, shrill whistle is given, and the heavy strokes of the engine, and the loud puffing of the steam as it escapes, sounds like the laboured breathing of some living gigantic frame ; and now the ponderous machine is in motion, drawing after it the long train of carriages, clattering along the line, till Mr. Stanhope actually turned pale, and his brain grew dizzy, for this was the first time he had ever viewed the wonderful power of steam, as applied to the purpose of locomotion ; and taking the arm of young Elgood, he quietly wended his way from the spot, for awhile completely absorbed in deep meditation on what he had seen, till at length he broke the silence by asking the opinion of his youthful companion of what they had witnessed.

" I think, sir, that it is a wonderful power; and, if rightly managed, and proper caution be taken to guard against accident, that it will prove of great service to man," replied John Elgood, and who was indebted for these remarks to his friend, Mr. Ellis.

" My dear young man," replied Mr. Stanhope, " you are partly right in your ideas, and partly wrong. In the first place, it truly is a wonderful power ; yet it never was intended to be used for the purpose to which man has most wantonly applied it; and, in my opinion, I hold that it is impossible for man to govern and manage it in such a manner as to secure himself from accident. And when accident does occur, it is almost invariably attended with the most frightful consequences, from the very nature of the power man has so presumptuously arrogated to his use. I have seen many changes," continued the old gentleman, mournfully, " many sad innovations on the customs of my forefathers ; but this has caused more pain than all the others put together; for I am almost daily hearing of the death of my countrymen, with the sad conviction forced upon me, that it is entirely owing to their own folly."

John Elgood was ready and open to conviction, and before they reached Mr. Stanhope's residence, he had succeeded in fixing on his mind a strong and abiding dislike of railways, and a most mournful presentiment as to the safety of his friend.

In the meanwhile, Mr. Ellis was speeding away towards London ; the novelty of his journey (for it was the first time he had travelled by the rail) afforded him some amusement, and the loquacity of his fellow traveller, who expatiated in glowing terms on the superiority of steam over every other known power, helped to relieve the tedium of the way, and the anxiety he endured on account of his parent; and himself apprehending no danger, he half forgot the uneasiness Mr. Stanhope entertained on his account ; but could he have known that Emily participated in her uncle's hopes and fears regarding him, there is every reason to believe that it would have been uppermost in the mind of the curate ; but yet, though he knew it not, Emily was as anxious to hear of his safe arrival as Mr. Stanhope himself. She had, it is true, continued her walk with Mrs. Harley and her nephew, and never had she seemed more gay or in better spirits ; for Emily was a proud girl, and could not bear the idea of others discovering the exact state of her feelings ; and, deeming Mr. Ellis had treated her with marked discourtesy, she was anxious to conceal from her friends how much she was affected by it; and, indeed, Emily was surprised and vexed at herself for taking it so seriously to heart.  But, then, Emily did not take into account the kindness and respect with which she had ever been considered by every individual with whom she had been brought in contact.  And this is one of the greatest evils of being accounted rich ; it causes persons to be so flattered and caressed— their wishes and opinions to be held as law, that to young people, especially, it has frequently proved ruin.  They do not place all this at its proper estimate, and regard it as nothing more than an offering at the shrine of their wealth; but, unfortunately, look upon themselves as far superior to most others, never for a moment doubting that every one regards them in the same light.  This is an error which of course grows upon them, and has rendered many a young person, who would otherwise have been amiable and agreeable, not only the contrary, but sometimes even ridiculous in the eyes of those who are wiser than to worship that idol at whose shrine so many prostrate their talents— that god who rules the greater part of the world, and always with a ruthless sway, hardening the hearts of his votaries, drowning every soft and gentle feeling in one unconquerable thirst for gold.

When Emily parted with her friends, and returned to her uncle's mansion, she observed he wore an air of great anxiety, and, on inquiring the cause, learnt that it was occasioned by the obstinacy of the curate, who had positively refused to take Mr. Stanhope's advice of prosecuting his journey in the old-fashioned style.

" Well," replied Emily, who had naturally imbibed some of her uncle's prejudice, " I think it really unkind of Mr. Ellis to cause you this uneasiness on his account; the difference of a few hours could not be of such very great importance."

" Still, my love," said her aunt, " before you pronounce your decision against him, which may have the effect of inducing others to think he has, without sufficient cause, awakened the fears of your uncle on his behalf, you must remember, Emily, that he is hastening probably to the death-bed of his mother, and the delay of a few hours might be the means of preventing him ever seeing her alive again."

" Yes—yes," replied Mr. Stanhope; " he would not, I am sure, were the case less pressing, have trusted his life to that uncertain and, in my opinion, perilous mode of performing his journey, that he has, under the existing circumstances, deemed it right to adopt ; and yet, though I am willing and anxious to hope that he may arrive at his destination in safety, I feel a strange, and no less painful foreboding, that he will sustain some serious and alarming accident, perhaps even lose his life."

" Stop—stop! dear uncle," replied Emily, and for a moment the rich bloom vacated its usual place upon her cheek; " you must not allow your fears thus, I fully believe, unnecessarily to alarm you, though I cannot help thinking Mr. Ellis is to blame in exposing you to anxiety on his account, and I am likewise surprised that he should hold his life of so little value as to peril it in the manner he is doing.  I met him this morning on

THE CHURCH OF THE VILLAGE OF SACKVILLE.

[The responses were followed by the entire congregation, with the exception of the stranger, who remained throughout the service a mute spectator of the scene—his arms folded across his breast.]

his road to the terminus, and had he not behaved almost rudely to me, I should have stongly urged him not to go by the rail."

" Behaved rudely to you, my dear Emily!" replied the uncle, with evident surprise; " I could scarcely have thought it possible Mr. Ellis would have behaved rude to any person, much less to one who has ever been so kind to him; and I really feel quite hurt that he should have done so. Were you alone when you met him?"

" No, I was in company with Mrs Harley."

" Depend upon it then, my love," returned Mr. Stanhope, " that you mistake him; he was doubtless vexed at seeing you together. You know that he has imbibed a prejudice against Mrs. Harley."

" I am sure I am infinitely obliged to him," returned Emily, with an air of satire, " for taking so great an interest in my affairs, that he must needs choose my companions for me; at the same time, I think I am capable of performing that office for myself, and consequently shall continue my friendship towards Mrs. Harley, even at the risk of incurring his displeasure."

" You certainly have a right, my dear child," replied her uncle, " to extend your friendship towards whom you please, and I never knew a young person exercise more judgment in the choice of friends; and you must not, my Emily, feel hurt that our good curate should occasionally remonstrate with you a little; but bear in mind, that he considers it a part of his duty."

Mrs. Stanhope had remained a listener to the foregoing conversation between her husband and her niece, smiling occasionally at the remarks of each; but though she had not joined in the conversation, being a lady of few words, yet she was an acute observer, and saw, under the affected indignation with which Emily spoke of the curate, a larger amount of affection for him than she deemed Mr. Stanhope would be pleased to know existed in the inmost recesses of her heart. Yet the old lady knew well that opposition was a certain strengthener of love, and, to Emily especially, would have the effect of fanning the spark of love, which was but just kindled in her bosom, into so strong a fire that nothing would be able to smother it; whereas, if left to itself, in all probability, the spark would gradually become extinguished Consequently, though she deemed she had discovered an affection which even Emily was as yet unconscious existed, she determined to keep the secret strictly confined to her own heart, at the same time losing no opportunity of watching the progress or extinction of the flame.

In the meantime, Mr. Ellis's departure became generally known to the villagers, and truly and deeply were his sorrows sympathised with by all who knew him; so much so, that could the curate have known how sincerely regretted he was in the village, he would have become fully convinced how hastily and erroneously he had judged, when he acknowledged to John Elgood, that the thought had occurred to him, if he was leaving Sackville for ever, not one would grieve for his departure. And much speculation was abroad in the village concerning the new inmate of Doctor Harding's house, described to her gossips by Mrs. Blake as a strange, mysterious sort of a man, though undoubtedly a perfect gentleman, inasmuch as he wore suspended round his neck a superb gold chain, attached to which was a magnificent watch, and seemed to entertain no more regard for money, or money's worth, than a prince.

Dinner was over at the great house, and Emily had sought the retirement of her boudoir, an elegant, and even spacious apartment, furnished with regard to luxurious comfort; and modern refinement smiled upon the old-fashioned carved oak-panelling of the room, and the light, tasty furniture of the present day, seemed sadly out of place in the lofty apartment. The handsome muslin curtains were certainly never intended to shade the gothic windows which admitted the light into a room whose appointments gave evidence of its being of considerable antiquity; but Emily had willed it to be so, and her will in that apartment at least was held as law. Ranged round the room were some mahogany bookshelves, containing a goodly array of books, radiant with rich gilding; and in the middle was a library table, and near it was a large and particularly comfortable-looking chair, into which Emily, at the time we describe the apartment, had just thrown herself. In the recess facing where she sat was a modern upright pianoforte, and on her left a very splendid harp.

Emily had reached one of her favourite volumes of romance, and was endeavouring to give herself up to the enjoyment of its contents; but for this once it failed in affordin her the amusement she sought, and throwing it down, after several ineffectual attemp continue her perusal, she rose from her seat, touched a few notes of her pianoforte and then of her harp; but music interested her still less than reading, and sauntering towards the window, she stood for some minutes looking out into the street, heartily wishing herself one of the heroines whose distresses so frequently awakened her interest. But, no; she began to despair of ever meeting with what she so earnestly sought after, namely, adventure; and she was on the point of turning away, when her attention was caught by a tall, gentlemanly-looking person, who was advancing towards the house.

He was evidently a stranger; and Emily remained lost in thought, as to whom he could be, when, having arrived in front of Mr. Stanhope's residence, he halted for an instant in his walk, and gazed earnestly upon the ancient structure. There was nothing very remarkable in this, as a stranger might very naturally be supposed to regard the noble mansion with interest; but there was something in the air and bearing of the stranger that awakened Emily's sympathy instantly on his behalf. There was something about him that reminded her strongly of her favourite poet, Lord Byron. Whether it was that he had a high and noble forehead, and wore his shirt collar turned down, that caused Emily to fancy she detected a likeness to that great author, or that there was something of the cynic in his countenance, we cannot exactly determine; but in her own mind she instantly characterised him as a very Byronian-looking man, and felt an earnest desire to become acquainted with him; and when for an instant their eyes met, as the stranger raised his to take a further survey of the building, the blood rushed to her cheek; yet, when the other, perceiving he was observed, as Emily thought, gracefully raised his hat, though not a passing smile illumined his pale face, she was perfectly enraptured; and, after watching his retreating steps till he was no longer visible, she turned from the window, and touching the handle of a bell rather sharply, soon brought into the apartment a neatly-dressed damsel, who officiated as her waiting-maid, of whom she made inquiries concerning the strange gentleman she had just seen. The maid was delighted to have an opportunity of showing her knowledge, and in answer to Emily's query as to whether she knew anything of him, replied,—

"Oh, la! yes, miss. I was going to tell you all about it this morning, only somehow you were in a hurry to get out, and that, I suppose, caused it to slip my memory."

"Well, never mind," returned Emily, impatiently. "You can tell me now."

"Well, then, miss, his name is Mordaunt, and he arrived at the village last evening, and took apartments at Doctor Harding's."

"Oh, then," said Emily, "I suppose he is an invalid?"

"Oh, dear, no, miss! for Mrs. Blake told me this morning—for hearing a report in the village that a strange sort of person had come to reside at the doctor's, I made an excuse to call, that I might learn all the particulars from Mrs. Blake ——"

"And what did she tell you?" said Emily, with apparent eagerness.

"Why, she said, miss, that when the doctor paid his respects to him, and made him any offer of his services—for you must know, miss, he came when the doctor was out ——"

"Never mind that," interrupted Emily; "tell me what he said to Doctor Harding."

"Well, then, miss, Mrs. Blake assured me that he behaved quite rudely to him, and said something about his mind being diseased, which was certainly a very strange thing, because, you know, miss, mad people generally think themselves perfectly reasonable."

"You do not suppose, Jane, surely," said Emily, "that he meant that he was mad?"

"What else could he mean, miss?" replied the waiting maid, rather annoyed at being thought in the wrong.

"Why, Jane, he only meant to infer that he was unhappy."

"It is strange what he can have to make him unhappy; he is evidently very rich—indeed, Mrs. Blake heard him tell Mr. Ellis so."

"Mr. Ellis!" replied Emily, with astonishment.

"I forgot to tell you," replied the girl, "that he seemed very strange and dull last night, and inquired of Mrs. Blake where the curate lived, and this morning sent him a note desiring to see him; and Mr. Ellis came almost directly afterwards, and stayed a long time; and Mrs. Blake having occasion to pass the door of the room they were in, during his stay, she heard the strange gentleman telling Mr. Ellis that he was very rich."

"Indeed," said Emily; "and what answer did Mr. Ellis make?"

"They spoke so low, that she heard no more; and it is very unfortunate that Mr. Ellis has gone so suddenly to town, as, I dare say, he would have told you all that passed between them."

"I am by no means so sure of that as you appear to be," replied Emily; "but, taking the sudden departure of Mr. Ellis in connection with his apparent acquaintance with the stranger, I think we may reasonably infer that it was from him he gained the intelligence of his mother's illness."

"I hardly think so," returned the waiting maid; "as this Mr. Mordaunt told Mrs. Blake that he knew not a single person in the village."

"Then, what could he possibly want with Mr. Ellis, so soon, too, after his arrival?"

"He seems so melancholy and reserved," replied the other, "that Mrs. Blake feels certain that he has something on his mind, and most likely wished to unburden himself to a clergyman; indeed, he almost said as much."

"He is, undoubtedly, a gentleman," said Emily; "indeed, there is an air of superiority about him that is quite unmistakeable."

"Oh, yes, miss; he spends money, Mrs. Blake says, like a prince, and talks quite grand; but, for all that, she is sorry he ever came to the house; for, when she asks him even a necessary question, he will sometimes answer her quite snappishly; and when he rings the bell she is absolutely obliged to leave whatever she may be about, and fly to attend upon him instantly; and then his meals must be ready to a minute."

"Which shows that he is accustomed to command," replied Emily; "and, really, I feel greatly interested in him. His name alone speaks good birth; who ever heard of a common person being named Mordaunt?"

"Well, to be sure, miss, there is no accounting for taste; but he is not at all the sort of person I should fancy. Mrs. Blake says he is so mopish and stern-like, that she feels quite uncomfortable in his presence; and then, too, he can't bear company, but says that he intends to live perfectly alone; and, when the doctor offered to introduce him to a few of his friends, said that he was determined to remain in the most perfect exclusion."

"Seclusion, I suppose you mean," interrupted Emily, smiling.

"Well, miss, it is all the same; but I was going to say that this strange gentleman ——"

"Call him Mr. Mordaunt," said Emily.

"Mr. Mordaunt, then, said that, if the doctor ever intruded his company upon him again, he should be forced to seek for lodgings elsewhere."

"All this convinces me," said Emily, with an air of importance, "that he has some bitter sorrow that he wishes to nourish in secret, and that has induced him to visit this retired and peaceful village. I can well understand the feelings that would induce him to conceal his sorrows from an unfeeling world."

"I am sure, miss," replied the waiting-maid, "there is no one unfeeling about here, unless it is that old maid, Miss Fraser, and one or two more of that sort; but then the doctor would never, I am sure, have introduced him to her."

"You do not understand exactly what I mean," said Emily; "but a refined mind shrinks from the pity of strangers."

"I don't know that he has much to be pitied for, miss," returned the other; "I only know, that if I was as rich as he appears to be, I should care for no one's pity."

"But, suppose," said Emily, trying to express herself so as to be understood by the other, "he had placed his affections on some person who did not, or could not, return them; he would then, notwithstanding his riches, have good reason to be miserable?"

"A gentleman that has got lots of money, as it seems, from his own account that he has, must be a fool to make himself miserable about anything of the sort; just as though there was no other woman in the world but one. Now, if I lose a lover, you know, miss, I always comfort myself with the thought that if one goes, another is sure to come; and, if I was but rich, which, worse luck for me, I am not, I should not care a pin how often they went; and, of course, a fine-looking gentleman like him, had never need be at a loss for some one to keep company with. I make no doubt but there are many pretty women who would be glad enough to have him for a lover."

"All, unfortunately, cannot adopt your wise resolve, Jane," replied her mistress, "or there would be much less unhappiness in the world; for myself I can truly say, that I have never yet loved; but when I do, it will be for ever. I should like to win one true, noble, affectionate heart, who would be entirely devoted to myself, and then I should scarcely even look at another."

"La, miss, what fun on earth would there be in that?"

"Fun!" replied Emily, with an air of angry surprise. "I am quite convinced, Jane, that you know nothing whatever about love, or you would not deprecte the name by coupling it with such a word as that; but you may go now, and if you should learn any-more concerning Mr. Mordaunt, you can tell me in the evening."

"Very well, miss," said the smiling Abigail; "I am going to the shop this evening, to buy a new ribbon for my bonnet; and it is very probable that I may chance to fall in with Mrs. Blake, and then, depend upon it, I will get everything out of her I can."

"Yes; but do not mention my name."

"Oh, la, no, miss; I know better, of course, than to let it appear you are interested about this strange gentleman; I mean interested about Mr. Mordaunt;" and the self-satis-fied waiting-maid left the room; and Emily, throwing herself into the easy-chair, gave herself up to pleasing meditation.

"This looks well," thought Emily, "and, certainly, savours strongly of mystery. Here is a tall, strange, melancholy-looking man, about whom there evidently hangs some painful adventure, some mournful secret which he wishes to conceal; and, consequently, seeks retirement in a secluded village; and even then refuses to mix with any of the in-habitants but the curate, to whom it is supposed he wishes to unburden his mind, and receive of him spiritual consolation."

These, Emily thought, were sufficient materials for her imagination to work upon; till she was quick enough to imagine that there must have been some previous intimacy be-tween Mr. Ellis and the stranger; indeed, she shrewdly suspected, that from him the curate must have received the intelligence of his mother's illness. Consequently, resolv-ing on his return to watch them both narrowly, whenever opportunity should offer, she doubted not but in time she should become acquainted with the secret, for she had deter-mined there was one that now, to use her own words, seemed involved in mystery. While Emily was busied with these thoughts, her uncle, in a fit of restless anxiety con-cerning his young friend, the curate, had betaken himself to the railway terminus, in hopes of learning from the train, which was now momentarily expected in, whether the up one had arrived in safety. Mrs. Stanhope had deemed it an unnecessary fatigue (for the old gentleman rarely stayed out after dinner), and proposed sending the powdered foot-man; but Mr. Stanhope seemed bent upon going himself, and accordingly sallied forth. What befel him there, the reader will learn in the next chapter.

---

## CHAPTER VI.

ON reaching the terminus, Mr. Stanhope found that the expected down-train had ap-parently just arrived, and so many persons were assembled that he found some difficulty in forcing his way through them; and this circumstance caused the old gentleman many wise reflections on the disadvantages and annoyance attributable to the departure from what he termed the good old customs of our forefathers. Wrapt in these thoughts, Mr. Stanhope did not take particular heed as to where he was wending his way, his only desire being to reach the platform, where he would have an opportunity of speaking with some person who could afford him the information he wished to obtain, when he was sud-denly stopped by a coarse, surly-looking fellow, in the dress of a guard, who called out,

"Hilloa! old gentleman, where are you going? We don't allow any one loitering about here, so you had better be off at once."

It was impossible for Mr. Stanhope (and which, in our humble opinion, shows a true gentleman, and belongs, we are sorry to be obliged to say, more to the old school than the new),—it was impossible, we were saying, for Mr. Stanhope, let him be addressed ever so rudely, to forget the politeness that was so pleasing a feature in his character; and he, therefore, mildly explained the nature of his errand, and begged his coarse interrogator to direct him to some person who would be able to satisfy his anxiety; "for," continued the old gentleman, in conclusion, "I have had a presentiment all day that some accident would occur on this line."

"And what the deuce did you have a presentiment for? We should have enough to do, did we pay attention to every old fool who chooses to trouble himself about things he don't understand; so you had better walk off at once."

"But," politely urged Mr. Stanhope, "I have a friend who went to town by the up-train this morning, and, surely, you will not be so uncivil as to refuse to inform me whe-ther it arrived in safety."

"And a nice treat it would be, were we to answer the inquiries of every one who had friends going to town. We have bother enough without answering the questions of every one who chooses to come here making inquiries."

And the fellow turned upon his heel, leaving Mr. Stanhope perfectly astonished at his want of civility, and which he attributed as one of the bad signs that men and things were sadly different to what they were in his youthful days. And this is no overdrawn sketch of the treatment persons receive from guards and others connected railways; on the contrary, their incivility and want of even common politeness is so notorious, that unless it fortunately meets with a salutary check, it will ere long become quite proverbial. This is surely enough to call a blush upon our cheeks, at an age when we are priding ourselves upon the march of science, of intellect, of improvements (as we are fond of terming them) of every kind. It may be, perhaps, that man is so engrossed, so entirely taken up with his superior acquirements, that he has neither the time nor inclination to bestow upon that civility which is surely due from man to man. We are not now speaking of politeness and good breeding, which once formed a most essential part of education, but merely of obtaining a civil answer to a question civilly put, which it is rare indeed to meet with at any of the railways; we particularise none, but, taking them as an entire body, we cannot help thinking that the rude, uncouth behaviour of the men employed on them, and with whom travellers are necessarily brought in contact, forms a marked contrast to the civil and sometimes even polite behaviour of the now almost obsolete coachman and guard, who were wont to while away the tedium of the journey, and amuse the outside travellers by tales of the road, and strange anecdotes, and still stranger mischances that had befallen them, but of which they had ever come off victorious, quite as a matter of course, and taking no praise whatever to themselves for so doing; in fact, rather making it appear that it would have been impossible for them to have done otherwise, even had they been so inclined.

But we forget that we are leaving Mr. Stanhope standing all this while, a piece of rudeness of which he would not have been guilty to even the meanest of his peasantry. By no means discouraged by the rude treatment he had met with, Mr. Stanhope determined to pursue his inquiry, and hoping to meet with more civility elsewhere, continued his walk, when suddenly he encountered the sorrowful face of John Elgood, who, surrounded by a small knot of persons, was evidently listening to some painful intelligence.

"John," said Mr. Stanhope, while an undefinable feeling of fear took possession of his mind.

The young man started at the sound of his name, and turning to see from whence it came, to his astonishment beheld Mr. Stanhope. He instantly disengaged himself from the group, and was at the old gentleman's side, and drawing his arm through his own, kindly led him away, though without speaking a word.

"John," began Mr. Stanhope, after a silence of a few moments, " I am convinced that you came here on the same errand as myself, namely, to make inquiry concerning the safe arrival of the train by which Mr. Ellis left here this morning, and that you have heard of some sad accident, realising my worst fears on his account. Speak, my dear John," continued the old gentleman, seeing the youth hesitate; " I am fully prepared to hear all."

"Then, sir," replied John, " your forebodings have not proved incorrect; there has been, from all accounts, a most disastrous accident on the line. Yet, though two persons have been killed, and several severely injured, yet many of the passengers have escaped without any injury; consequently I trust that Mr. Ellis is fortunately unhurt, more especially as you must remember, sir, there was but one person beside him in the first-class carriage; that smartly dressed gentleman who laughed at your fears?"

"I remember, John," replied Mr. Stanhope; " but pray go on."

"Well, sir, as I was saying, there were but those two in the first-class carriage, and one of the guards just now informed me, that but one first-class passenger was injured, the other having escaped with a few bruises."

"But," said Mr. Stanhope, with evident anxiety, " may it not be Mr. Ellis that has sustained such serious injury?"

"I think not, sir," replied the youth, respectfully; " as, from what I have been enabled to learn, the description of the injured party does not at all resemble our friend; on the contrary, it answers in almost every respect to the person who spoke to you so rudely this morning."

"God grant that it may prove so," replied Mr. Stanley, emphatically; " and now, my dear John, I fear we can do nothing, but must wait patiently till we hear from Mr.

Ellis. If, most fortunately, he has escaped even with slight injury, he will immediately write, 1 am certain, and acquaint us with the joyful intelligence."

" Indeed, sir, I am quite sure he will be most anxious to inform us of his safety."

" He will—he will. You are perfectly right, my dear John ; but, alas ! I had, as you say, a sad, a very sad foreboding, that his journey would be attended with fearful consequences. And that unfortunate young man, I fear, has found, to his sorrow, that 1 rightly termed the journey perilous."

" I thought, at the moment he was treating your fears so light, that ere long he would entertain a different opinion," replied the youth.

." Did you, indeed, John ?" said Mr. Stanhope ; "well, I must confess that the same thought occurred to me ; and yet, in spite of this fearful accident, and many others, there will still be found people mad enough to venture their lives, aye, and lose them, too, in this new and most dangerous mode of travelling."

" It is frightful to think, John," continued the old gentleman to his willing listener, " how many valuable lives have been lost through this sad innovation upon the customs of our forefathers. Steam, taken as a power, might prove a useful auxiliary to man, when applied to the exclusive purposes of machinery ; but it never was intended as an agent in locomotion, and I can scarcely attribute it to anything but a species of mania that has induced the legislature to allow it to be thus applied ; but the numberless accidents that are almost daily occurring, should induce every one who has any regard for his fellow man, to do his utmost to put a stop to these frightful occurrences ; but, alas ! an apathy the most strange, and at the same time most painful, pervades apparently all classes, and the evil is allowed to continue with scarcely so much as one dissentient voice. Alas ! my dear John, things and men likewise are sadly altered, since I was a young man like you."

They had by this time reached the noble mansion of Mr. Stanhope, who began to feel greatly interested in his youthful companion, and he unceremoniously invited him to enter. John Elgood and Mr. Stanhope had never been thrown so much together before, for John, as the reader is aware, was naturally of a retiring disposition, added to which, he was unfortunately very diffident, and consequently had associated with scarcely any one in the village but Mr. Ellis, to whom he was sincerely attached ; but this day, circumstances, singular and unforeseen, had brought the two in closer contact, and wrought a greater intimacy between them than years of every-day occurrence had been able to perform ; and Mr. Stanhope began to reproach himself for having overlooked so pleasant and amiable a youth, and to determine for the future to make him ample amends, by cultivating his friendship, and bestowing on him much of his company ; and here, it must be confessed, that John being a most excellent listener, and having little or no opinion of his own, had gone far in securing the favour of the somewhat prejudiced, yet worthy old gentleman, who now cordially invited him to enter the house, and John, nothing loth, followed him into the drawing-room, where Mrs. Stanhope and Emily were seated.

The elegant service of Dresden china that had been in vogue when Mr. Stanhope's father was young, was arranged on the richly carved table, that vied with it in age. Everything in the room was quaint and old-fashioned, from the straight, high-backed chairs, down to the chimney ornaments, but they were all in keeping with Mr. Stanhope and his lady ; their dress and appearance were characteristic of, as they termed it, " the good old times," when the suits of rooms through which they moved were in all their pristine glory ; they seemed, indeed, part and parcel of the mansion, which would have appeared incomplete without them, and themselves would have been sadly out of place elsewhere—in fact, they helped each other out ; and, when seated on either side of the broad, open fire-place, they bore an exact resemblance to one of those old-fashioned pictures that are occasionally to be met with. But Emily, all life and gaiety, a creature of momentary impulse, and filled with ideas of romance, which bordered closely on the absurd, and in every respect, both as regards dress and manners, a perfectly modern belle, seemed to have no business there ; and yet how fondly she was cherished by the good old couple! Even her very faults were looked upon by them as virtues ; in her their youthful days were again revived, and they loved to boast of her excellent qualities. and the exceeding amiability of her disposition, and, in short, her great superiority to the generality of young people of the present day.

Emily was bending over the tea-table when her uncle and John Elgood entered. Her rich chesnut curls swept the table and she bowed her head over a small volume, which lay open before her, displaying a highly finished engraving of the portrait of Lord Byron, on which Emily gazed with an interest as deep as though it for the first time met her eyes.   The candles were not yet lighted, but the dancing reflection of the fire played upon her polished brow, and her features, naturally of a pensive cast, now wore a melancholy tinge, far from unpleasing ; and, seen by that subdued and mellow light, which displayed the outlines of her figure and her whole contour to the best advantage, John Elgood might well be pardoned for deeming her one of the loveliest of her sex.

Mrs. Stanhope, who, notwithstanding her age, was of unbending uprightness, sat erect in her chair, perusing a large book, with brazen hasp and hinge, and type so large as scarcely to require the gold eye-glass which she held before it.

"Emily, my love," said Mr. Stanhope, addressing his niece.

She turned instantly, and closing the volume, rose to meet him.

"My dear, dear uncle," she said, kissing his cheek, as she urged him towards the chair which was already drawn close to the fire, ready to receive him on his return, "you are, I am sure, greatly fatigued.   You look quite pale and harassed !   I am sorry, indeed, that you should have gone out this afternoon, and can scarcely forgive Mr. Ellis for causing you so much anxiety and fatigue on his account." .

"What Emily says is perfectly correct," said Mrs. Stanhope, gazing anxiously at her partner.   "You do, indeed, my dear Henry, look very unwell."

"Not caused by fatigue, for I have encountered none : but by the sad realisation of my gloomy forebodings."

"What is it you say, uncle ?" replied Emily, hastily.   "I trust no accident has ———"

Mrs. Stanhope spoke not, but continued looking earnestly upon her husband.

"A sad and fearful accident has occurred, my Emily," replied Mr. Stanhope, "involving the loss of life to more than one individual."

At this moment, the aged servant, who, on Mr. Stanhope's entrance, had commenced lighting the four tall wax candles, concluded his task, and John Elgood perceived that Emily's face was of ashy whiteness, and that she trembled in every limb; and these mute, but certain signs of deep interest in the fate of his friend, made her appear in his eyes still more lovely than before.   Oh ! how he longed to beseech her to calm her apprehensions, for he entertained no fear that the curate was among the injured persons.   But John was too diffident to speak unless spoken to, and so he continued silent, but his eyes riveted on Emily, who falteringly begged her uncle to relate the particulars he had gleaned concerning the accident.

"We have reason, God be praised !" replied Mr. Stanhope, "to hope that our friend the curate has escaped, at least, with but slight injury."

"Oh, God, indeed, be praised !" said Emily, earnestly.   "But tell me, uncle, how you were able to ascertain that fact."

"Of myself, I have been able to ascertain nothing ; but here is John Elgood," he replied, turning to the youth.

Emily turned likewise, and to her astonishment now, for the first time, became aware of his presence.   He blushed deeply as she extended her hand, and smilingly inquired after his health.

"Then I am to suppose," said Emily, addressing her uncle, "that John has been your informant ?"

"He has told me all," replied Mr. Stanhope, "that I as yet know concerning the sad calamity that has occurred, and to him I must refer you for anything further you wish to ascertain."

Emily invited the young man to a seat by her side, and for this one night, at least, John felt himself exalted into a hero.   Emily had so many questions to ask regarding the terrible accident, and wanted him so frequently to confirm her hopes that Mr. Ellis had sustained no injury, that the youth conversed with more freedom than he had ever done before, and began almost to believe the truth of his mother's so frequent assertion, that he was by no means indifferent to the object of his heart's adoration : and when he rose to depart, and Mr. Stanhope thanked him for the kind attention he had shown him when they met at the railway terminus in the afternoon, and praised him for the deep interest he had shown for his friend ; and Mrs. Stanhope assured him that his modest, unobtrusive manners reminded her of what young men used to be in the good old times that were past and gone, and was far more becoming than the bold, forward manner of young men of the present day ; and Emily begged him, if he received a letter from Mr.

THE RESULT OF THE JOURNEY BY RAIL TO LONDON.

[Mr. Ellis engaged the earliest care of the surgeon on the young man's behalf, who pronounced his life, to the worthy curate's great joy, to be in no immediate danger.]

Ellis, to let her know immediately—at all events, to call there again early on Monday, as no doubt her uncle would hear from him by that time. "And, as I cannot bear suspense myself, John," she added, in conclusion, "I should be wrong to impose it upon you one moment longer than is absolutely necessary. And now, for the present, farewell."

Emily never said "good-bye,"—it was a common, every-day term; she therefore adopted the word "farewell," as being far more suited to her romantic mind. But, to return to John Elgood. His head was completely bewildered, and during his walk home he painted the most bright and fairy-like visions for his future life. "This has been in many respects a most fortunate day for us"—for he was accustomed to think as well as speak in the plural number—was John's inward exclamation. "It is a great thing to have gained favour with the aunt and uncle; and now I feel certain they will offer no objection; on the contrary, they are more likely to persuade Emily to accept me."

Thus soliloquising with himself, John wended his way towards his father's house. In the gaiety of his heart he had commenced humming a tune, when he was intercepted by the approach of a tall figure enveloped in a cloak. The moon was shining resplendently in the heavens, making it almost as light as noonday; and John perceived, as they drew near, that the person who approached him was an entire stranger; he therefore would have passed without any salutation, had not the other stopped short, and begging pardon for the intrusion, inquired if there were any truth in a report he had heard was spread about the village, of an accident that had occurred on that line of rail.

"I am sorry to say that it is perfectly true," he replied; "the more so, that Mr. Ellis went to town by the very train to which the accident occurred; though I have every reason to hope he escaped without serious injury."

"Mr. Ellis, I presume, is a friend of yours?" returned the other.

"He is, indeed, a true and sincere friend; but I forget you are a stranger, and possibly may not be aware that he is the curate of this village."

"I am, indeed, an entire stranger; but you say you have reason to believe that your curate has escaped without accident?"

"I have; and which is a source of joy not only to myself, but to every person in the village."

"I may conclude, then, that he is a general favourite?" replied the stranger; and John thought there was something satirical in his tone, and replied with a deserved eulogium on his friend, and concluded by saying,—

"He is truly beloved by young and old."

"Then he is truly fortunate," returned the stranger, laying great emphasis on the adverb; "but I am unnecessarily keeping you standing, sir, and will therefore do myself the honour of wishing you a very good night;" saying which, he turned and pursued his way, leaving John absolutely astonished at his strange manners.

"Well, I am sure," said John, apostrophising the stranger, "you are a rum sort of fellow; as uncouth and queer an animal as ever I met with. But I can tell you, my boy, this sort of thing won't do here; people are not accustomed, in this part, to be spoken to in a manner that makes them think, all the while they are civilly answering your questions, that they are being laughed at for their pains. It may be the fashion where you came from, but I would advise you not to try it on here, unless you want to get thoroughly hated; in that case, why, you may do it as much as you please, only you won't find many persons who will answer your questions when you feel disposed to make inquiries, that's all." And having thus eased his mind, and watched the object of his indignation out of sight, John, who was upon the whole a good-tempered fellow, resumed at once his tune and his walk, and by the time he reached home had entirely forgotten the circumstance.

---

## CHAPTER VII.

THE village church of Sackville formed a pretty and picturesque feature in the surrounding landscape. It was of the gothic style of architecture, and its long slender spire towered gracefully towards the skies; and on the morning following the events recorded in our last chapter, the sun shone so brightly upon it that its fair outlines appeared traced on the background of deep blue, where not a single fleecy cloud was seen; and the gilt cross that decked the top of the spire reflected the sun's pure rays so vividly, that it looked as if it was composed of molten gold. It stood upon a quiet, sequestered spot, though but a very short distance removed from the main street of the village, and was skirted on either side by fields that were still fresh and green: and snow-white sheep cropped the verdant grass; and horses, released from plough and harness, stretched themselves in the sunniest spots; and sleeping cows lay down beside the limpid stream that flowed gently through the meadow, and in a sort of half dreamy enjoyment watched the gnats as they sported on the surface; the birds twittered on the leafless branches of the trees, and seemed, so balmy was the air, to forget the near approach of winter. All things were in harmony with the still, soft beauty of the scene, and seemed to usher in the Sabbath as a welcome day of rest—refreshing rest—and enjoyment both to man and beast; everything looked fresh and gay, and appeared to wear a smile of joy and thankfulness that God, in his mercy, had appointed one day out of the seven as a season of cessation from the labour and turmoil of the other six.

And all the inhabitants of Sackville (for it contained no bigots) regarded the Sabbath as a holiday—a day of pleasure, which was devoted to innocent mirth and enjoyment; and by so using it, the peasant returned to his week's toil with invigorated spirit; his mind and body alike refreshed, he was enabled to pursue his customary occupation with renewed and increased vigour. Mr. Stanhope, as we have intimated, belonged to the old school, and his ideas of the Sabbath were commensurate with that time when no one dreamed of there being any harm in encouraging the tenantry to regard it not only as a day of relaxation from toil, but also as one of recreation and joy; consequently, he loved to see the villagers in the full enjoyment of the Sabbath, and took care that every one possessed the means of procuring some little extra indulgence; and, as a matter of course, all loved the Sabbath, and hailed its approach with joy and gladness. Service was held in the church twice in the day—morning and afternoon; and all the inhabitants of Sackville made it a point to attend, clean and neat; none were absent, except in cases of sickness; and each with the well-thumbed prayer-book repeated the responses in an audible voice, led by Mr. Stanhope. And when the curate, in simple but well-chosen language, exhorted them to the well performance of their duties, both to God and man, he received the undivided attention of his flock; no stray glances wandered round the church—every eye was fixed upon the preacher; and when the benediction was given, all departed quietly to their homes. And a pretty sight it was to see the happy contented faces of the peasants, leading their healthy, rosy children from the house of God, all in good, comfortable clothing. No squalid poverty was ever seen or heard of in Sackville; poor was there—as it ever should be,—only a comparative phrase; it was never understood to mean the wanting any of the necessaries, or, indeed, many of the comforts, of life; it was merely used in contradistinction to being the possessor of wealth.

Thus was passed the earlier part of the Sabbath, and the evening was devoted entirely to amusement. In summer, out-door pleasure was sought by all; and in the winter, social parties were formed, and the laugh and joke went round, and the mug of ale was quaffed, and each did their best to contribute to the amusement of the whole. And surely this is a reasonable and proper way of spending the Sabbath; none should seek to curtail the enjoyments of the labouring classes, or make the only day that is vouchsafed them from toil, one of weariness and irksome restraint. Let the rich man, who has every day at his command, and can spend them as he will—let him, we say, reflect seriously before he ventures to interfere with, or break up the small space of time that is allotted for the amusement and enjoyment of the poor. It is but common justice that those who labour unremittingly for six days, should be allowed to devote the seventh to pleasure and relaxation. It is not enough that the poor have a day of rest, if it be not also one of happiness and joy.

But now the bell of the church sent forth its summons to the house of prayer, and all were ready and eager to obey its call. Mr. Stanhope, with that courtly grace which so distinguished him, led his lady and his niece down the broad stone steps of his mansion, and supporting one on either arm, set the excellent example of being early in his attendance at church. The pew which had been occupied by the Stanhopes, and descended from father to son, from time immemorial, was entered from the outside of the church, and exactly faced the pulpit. The floor was covered with rich carpeting, and the back and sides hung with crimson cloth. The front communicated with the church, and was only divided from it by a gothic arch, which supported curtains of the same rich colour, capable of being closed or drawn aside at pleasure; chairs remarkable for their antiquity were ranged round the pew. Two with arms, and otherwise commodious, had ever been appropriated to the heads of the family, and were now occupied by Mr. Stanhope and his lady; one of the others, and placed between her uncle and aunt's, was made use of by Emily; the rest were of course empty, and Mr. Stanhope had frequently been observed to glance towards them with a sorrowful countenance, as though grieving that his family was reduced to so small a number. The back of the pew was graced by a large escutcheon containing the family arms, and immediately under the pew was the vault in which his so much boasted ancestry lay crumbling and mouldering to dust, and whither Mr. Stanhope, in the course of a few years, would inevitably join them; and to this the good old man looked forward with the greatest complacency, and would take his place on the Sabbath in that arm-chair, that had regularly been filled in succession by father and son, in one unbroken descent, for so many generations. Alas! it could be so no longer; he most unfortunately was the last male of his race, and this was the drop of bitterness in his cup that so frequently turned his happiness into gall and wormwood. He would willingly have laid down his life without a sigh could he have left behind him a worthy successor; and, though loving his niece dearly, yet it was a constant source of regret to Mr. Stanhope that she was not a boy. As a sister's son, though belonging to the female branch of the family, he could have regarded her as having a legal right and title to the inheritance upon taking the name and arms of Stanhope for herself and heirs for ever. And though as it was, the male line ceasing, Emily would be entitled to the estate, and had promised her uncle that, marry whom she might, the hereditary honours of her husband should be merged in that of his, yet Mr. Stanhope felt a deep, though he knew it was an unavailing sorrow, at thus witnessing what he regarded an almost extinction of his race.

On this particular Sabbath morning, as the trio took their respective places in the old family pew, they each wore an unusual sadness on their countenances, for as yet their fears concerning the curate were not entirely removed.

The pew appertaining to Squire Elgood was opposite the chancel, and to the left of Mr. Stanhope's; and here Mrs. Elgood and her three daughters, redolent with perfume, and radiant in finery, arranged themselves "in order due," the squire and his son bringing up the rear; and John, ere he seated himself, contrived to gain a smile of recognition from Emily.

Presently the widow, leaning on the arm of her nephew, walked up the aisle with a mincing air, and placed herself in the seat assigned her; and Frank Harley manifested as much anxiety to win a glance from Emily as John Elgood had done before him, but her eyes were wandering in a different direction. She had detected, in the tall, erect figure of a young man who had just seated himself near the door, and removed from the vulgar gaze, the strange mysterious lodger of Doctor Harding, who had so politely greeted her the previous evening; and so intently were her thoughts engaged with that personage, that Doctor Harding had himself, with his usual urbanity, thrice bowed without attracting her notice. And Miss Tabitha Fraser had taken the compliment to herself, and smilingly returned it, to the infinite amusement of Frank, who was forced to bow his head to conceal the risibility it excited, which was rendered more grotesque from the doctor in his turn being perfectly innocent of the condescension of the lady.

At length all the congregation was assembled, and the young man, who for that day performed Mr. Ellis's duty, commenced reading the prayers. The responses were made by Mr. Stanhope, in a loud, sonorous voice, followed by the entire congregation, with the exception of the stranger, who remained throughout the service a mute spectator of the scene; his arms folded across his breast, and his head bent down.

Of this Emily was perhaps more perfectly aware than any other person in the church, if we except the preacher. The interest she had avowed awakening in her bosom on his behalf, was now fast increasing; there was something in his form noble and commanding, and his countenance gave evidence that "melancholy had marked him for her own." This was sufficient to interest, deeply interest, her in his behalf.

The service over, before she turned to leave the church, Emily bent her gaze once more on the stranger, and, to her great surprise, discovered his eyes fixed on her with an earnest melancholy expression; but, observing himself discovered, he instantly removed them, while a satirical smile, approaching, Emily thought, almost to a sneer, for an instant curled the corners of his mouth. She blushed deeply, and, averting her eyes, affected to be busily engaged in putting away the bibles and prayer books that had been used during the service. This done, she once more placed her arm in that of her uncle's, and, in the same order as they had entered the church, they took their departure.

The afternoon witnessed the assembling of the same persons who had been gathered together in the morning, the same solemnity was observed, each occupied the exact spot they had done when they last met; in short, it was a complete repetition of the morning scene. But Emily, though endeavouring to give her attention to the service, found her thoughts wandering to things of a less spiritual nature. She had, as soon as she entered the church, glanced, though in a manner not to be remarked by others, towards the seat occupied by the stranger in the morning; but it was vacant, and though her eyes frequently strayed in that direction, yet the service began, proceeded, and at length concluded, without the stranger making his appearance. Emily felt greatly disappointed, and yet vexed with herself for being so; and on her return home she sought her own room, and summoning her maid, inquired whether she had been able to learn anything further concerning Mr. Mordaunt.

"La, no, miss! I saw Mrs. Blake last evening, as I told you I should, but she knows no more about him than what I told you yesterday; but, to be sure, miss, how he did stare at you all church time, and looked so melancholy and wretched-like, that I cannot help thinking that he is in love."

"I think that it is very probable," replied Emily, musingly, "that he has met with some very painful disappointment; he does, as you say, Jane, look very melancholy, and it can scarcely be attributed to the death of one to whom he might have been tenderly attached, for he does not, you know, wear mourning."

"La, miss, I have quite forgotten to tell you the strangest thing of all. In the course of conversation with him, Mrs. Blake happened to mention your name, when he asked her if you had ever been to London, as he had a recollection of meeting with some person of that name before."

"There is nothing so very wonderful in that, Jane," replied Emily; "in such a place as London, there are, probably, many who bear the name of Stanhope."

"Not so very many, miss; for I have a brother, you know, who has been living in London this last twelvemonth, and though he sends me an account of all the grand folks who visit his master and mistress, yet he has never once mentioned any one of that name."

"Well, I do not think, Jane, that it is very common; still, if Mr. Mordaunt has met with a person of the name of Stanhope, you know it could not possibly be me, or my aunt, for the very best reason, that we have never been to London; consequently it follows, as a matter of course, that it must have been some one else," said Emily, smiling.

"It is certainly a great pity, miss, that Mr. Ellis has gone there just now, because I am certain he would have told you all that took place between him and Mr. Mordaunt, the morning he went away."

"I do not think Mr. Ellis would have felt inclined to betray the confidence placed in him, even if I could have so far forgotten myself as to ask it of him, which, under any circumstances, I trust I never should."

"Well, miss, you know best about asking him; but I am positive that, had you done so, he would instantly have told you all. Everybody knows how delighted he is to have an opportunity of obliging you; and what is the good, miss, of having a lover, if you don't make use of him?"

"Mr. Ellis is no lover of mine, Jane," said Emily, in a tone of mild reproof.

"When I said lover," replied the maid, "I merely meant that he was in love with you. I did not, of course, suppose for a moment, miss, that you ever intended to give him any encouragement. I should think, indeed, that you knew your value better than to give a thought even to a poor curate like him."

"I cannot allow you to speak in that way, Jane; I am afraid I have given you too much liberty of tongue, or you would not dare to speak in such disrespectful terms of an intimate friend and favoured guest of my uncle, which alone should have prohibited you from mentioning his name otherwise than respectfully; but Mr. Ellis is likewise a gentleman, both by birth and education, and though I desire to dispossess your mind of the erroneous idea you appear to entertain—I mean that Mr. Ellis regards me with any other feeling than that of friendship—still I must at the same time insist, that whenever you mention his name, either to myself or any other person, you forbear to connect with it any disparaging terms."

These words were spoken with an earnestness that convinced her hearer, that Emily was disposed to be seriously angry; she therefore hastened to make the " amend honour-able," though inwardly exclaiming,—

" Well, to be sure, I had no idea that Miss Stanhope was in love with Mr. Ellis, a proud, disdainful sort of man, that thinks every girl but her beneath his notice; but he shall never have her, though, if I can help it; on the contrary, he may depend on my doing all that lays in my power to prevent it."

But the girl had too much cunning to allow her mistress to discover her real senti-ments, and therefore answered, with every appearance of regret for what she had care-lessly given utterance to,—

" I am sure, miss, I am very sorry to have given you offence, and assure you I had no intention of doing so, and for the future will be careful not to repeat it. And as to his being in love with you, I think there is nothing very strange in that, and I am sure every one in the village declares it to be the truth; but, howsomever, miss, you of course must know best, and if you say he only regards you as a friend, I dare say he does not."

" I fully believe that to be the case," returned Emily, in a more softened tone; " and you should never forget, Jane, that a clergyman is entitled to respect; and, though he may not possess affluence, he is yet received into the highest circles, and admitted as an equal; in short, he stands inferior to none."

The waiting-maid listened to this with affected humility, and with an air of being per-fectly convinced, and heartily sorry for having, in a thoughtless moment, spoken lightly of one her mistress held in such high esteem; and, being satisfied with this, Emily dis-missed her, and shortly afterwards joined her uncle and aunt in the drawing-room. The evening passed slowly away. Emily had refused a most pressing invitation from her friend, Mrs. Harley, to spend the evening with her and Frank; that lady had, indeed, declared that she positively could take no denial, but Emily had made it a rule never to spend any part of the Sunday away from her aged relatives, and she was not a girl to be easily persuaded to neglect the performance of what she deemed a duty, and, therefore, stedfastly declined the invitation. And Sunday evenings usually passed very quickly and pleasantly at the mansion, for Mr. Ellis invariably made one of the family, to the great vexation of many in the village, who would have liked occasionally the good curate to join their social parties; yet he always refused to do so, alleging, in excuse, that he ever considered himself on that day engaged to Mr. Stanhope; and this, at length, became so much the custom, that none endeavoured to intrude upon it.

He was, certainly, a most pleasant, lively companion, and had been heard to ex-press to Mr. Stanhope the pleasure he found in these Sunday evening visits, which was perfectly reciprocated by the warm-hearted old gentleman and his lady; and the bright smiles and happy countenance of his niece showed that she likewise considered the company of the curate a pleasant addition to their little circle; and on this first evening of his absence, since his residence at Sackville, he was missed and regretted by all of them. Emily strove to exert herself to amuse her uncle and aunt, but all her efforts failed. Mr. Stanhope's thoughts were bent upon the absent one.

" Had he gone to visit his relatives as a pleasant relaxation, and we might now fully hope that he was happy in their company, I would not be so selfish as to mourn his de-parture," said Mr. Stanhope; " but, alas! if he has even, fortunately, escaped the peril of his journey, he is now engaged in attending on the death-bed of his mother."

" Surely, uncle," said Emily, striving to banish her own sadness, " we may not only hope that he has arrived in London safely, but also that his mother may be progressing towards recovery. Sudden and alarming illness sometimes, you know, my dear uncle the soonest abates."

" A favourable change may have taken place," said Mrs. Stanhope; " but, should it prove otherwise, let us hope that Mr. Ellis may have fortitude to sustain his loss."

" He will strive, my love, doubtless, to bear it as a man; but then, as the immortal bard says, he ' must also feel it as a man," replied Mr. Stanhope, in a voice and intonation that did perfect justice to the beautiful poetic sentiment he had quoted.

The evening, as we have said, wore drearily away. Emily felt an unusual depression of spirits, and though, at her uncle's request, she played and sang some of his favourite hymns, in which both he and Mrs. Stanhope joined, yet she missed the fine tenor voice that usually lent them its aid on these occasions, and the thought that it was possible that voice might be now mute in death, banished the blood from her cheek, and caused her such a chilliness of heart as she had never before felt.

At length they separated for the night, and never did any night seem so sad and tedious to Emily. The consciousness that the morrow would confirm their hopes of the curate's safety, or realise their dreadful fears on his behalf, forbade her even to close her eyes; and when at length sleep did "weigh her eyelids down," the same thoughts pursued her in the shape of

> "Dreams of troubled sleep,
> From which 'twas joy to wake and weep."

It was singular that all her fears concerning Mr. Ellis were redoubled now that the time drew near when they might with certainty expect to hear from the object of their solicitude. Till now she had hoped far more than she had feared; but hope itself had began to sicken, and mournful forebodings filled its place; and the consciousness that their parting had not been marked with that friendly feeling which previously existed between them, caused her a severe pang.

And here it may not be entirely out of place to remark, that we might frequently spare ourselves much bitter sorrow and self-accusation, did we, at the sacrifice even of a little of our natural pride and self-importance, make allowance for the weakness of others, and passing over what we may deem provocation, never give them cause to deem themselves treated with unkindness and neglect, much less behave to them with intentional severity; for we know not that we may ever have an opportunity of renewing our kindness, or acknowledging our error. If we conceive ourselves wrongly judged, or our actions misinterpreted, let us rather, by kind and conciliatory words, endeavour to rectify the mistake, and place our conduct in its proper light, explaining our motives for having, perhaps unintentionally, given offence; for surely the severest pang a rightly constituted mind can feel, is caused by the bitter reflection that we have acted unkindly towards one to whom some unforeseen circumstance has deprived us of the power ever to express our contrition; and as we cannot possibly foresee how soon the object of our resentment may be called away, let us be wary—very wary—how we lay up for ourselves sorrow and remorse. There is sufficient grief and bitterness scattered along the brightest path, and mingling with even the fairest and freshest flowers; consequently, none need wilfully add to their own anxieties, or give themselves unnecessary cause for self-reproach.

We write chiefly for the guidance of the young, and this must be our excuse for offering the foregoing remarks. We deem no tale, however much it may charm the imagination, or how great soever the ability it may display, of any real benefit, unless it convey some moral truth, or good example, either in the shape of incentive to virtue, or an abhorrence of vice, more especially if designed for the perusal of the young; it then becomes imperative that reproof and counsel should be conveyed through the medium of fiction.

---

## CHAPTER VIII.

WE last left Mr. Ellis pursuing his journey to London, little dreaming of the alarming accident that was so soon to befal the train by which he was travelling, and which, of course, had it been possible he could have foreseen, he would doubtless have taken Mr. Stanhope's advice, and have chosen the slower, but, as it proved, safer conveyance. We have intimated that he had but one companion in the carriage with him, and who was no other than the stylishly dressed young man who laughed so rudely at the old gentleman's prejudice against steam. One half their journey was performed in perfect safety, and Mr. Ellis had began to congratulate himself on having resisted Mr. Stanhope's entreaties in favour of the famed Tally-ho coach, and his fellow-traveller had just laughingly inquired whether or not he had found his journey attended with that peril his friend had so sadly and woefully predicted.

Mr. Ellis was unable to answer, for scarcely had the young man given utterance to the words, when they became conscious of a tremendous shock, and the next instant they were rolled, engine, carriages and all, over a steep embankment, accompanied with the most direful screams of frightened women and children that Mr. Ellis had ever heard. For a few minutes he was completely stunned with the violence of his fall; but, quickly

recovering his senses, his first impulse was to return brief, but heartfelt thanks for hi
wonderful preservation to that Being to whom alone he was indebted for his life.   The
next, as he lay uppermost, was to endeavour to raise his companion, who was bleeding
profusely, and, to all appearance, lifeless.   The carriage had fallen on its right side, and
the glass, being of course completely shattered, had severely wounded the unfortunate
young man about the head and face, and Mr. Ellis found it almost impossible to extricate
him; so, opening the uppermost door of the carriage, he managed to get out, in order to
seek for further assistance for his less fortunate companion.   But the sight that met his
eyes, though in a measure prepared for it, completely unmanned him.   In a confused
mass lay human beings, some dead, and others apparently dying; those that had escaped
with slight injury, were weeping and mourning over their wounded friends and relatives,
and the carriages were broken, and strewn in fragments around.   The precise cause of
the accident could not at present be ascertained, but that it was occasioned by something
being left on the rails, though the usual signal had been given them that they might proceed with safety, was the full belief of those who best understood such things.   And
as Mr. Ellis gazed around at the fearful consequence that had resulted apparently from
want of care and attention, which, if properly exercised, would most undoubtedly have
prevented this fatal catastrophe, he thought, and perhaps not altogether without truth,
that Mr. Stanhope's dislike of railways resulted from something more than mere prejudice, and that his so frequent assurance that life was not thus perilled in the good old
times, had with it much of truth.   And most certainly life at the present day seems held
at an uncommon low estimate; how else can we account for the number of railway accidents caused most frequently by the wilful negligence of persons, who thus prove themselves totally unfit to be entrusted with the public safety; and, indeed, they have sometimes been found entirely ignorant of the power they have been employed to govern.
Even when that is not the case, the most culpable carelessness has prevailed, such as
making wrong signals, miscalculating the time, so as to run down other trains who have
started earlier, or being themselves run down by trains that start afterwards, or things
being left on the line by persons whose business it is to see that they are clear; thus causing loss of life and property to an extent almost incalculable; and such accidents as these
are so notorious, that it would be a perfectly needless task to attempt to convince the
reader of the truth of our statement, feeling assured that it will not for an instant be
doubted by any.   Let us rather, then, charitably hope that the proprietors of railways
will ere long select such persons to fill the various offices connected with them, so as to
ensure the public safety, so far as ignorance and negligence now endanger it, and at the
same time teach them to exercise civility towards travellers, who are, in a measure,
obliged to adopt that mode of travelling, coaches being now almost exploded.

Mr. Ellis had time for such reflections as these, while he assisted to the utmost the
injured parties.   One guard, and a third-class passenger, were beyond all human help;
but many others remembered the kind sympathy and affectionate attention shown to
them by the curate, who, forgetful of his own bruises, sought to lessen the sufferings of
his fellow travellers.   First of all his more immediate companion engaged his care;
with the assistance of another passenger, who like himself had fortunately escaped unhurt, he succeeded in removing him from the carriage; he was certainly seriously
injured, but, to Mr. Ellis's infinite joy, he discovered that he still breathed; but further
help was so distant, that he almost despaired of his surviving till such time as it could
be procured.   A full hour elapsed before the messenger who had been despatched to the
nearest farm-house returned; but when he at length appeared, it was with a light waggon
to take the persons who were most seriously injured.   In the meantime, a fresh train had
arrived, and conveyed all who were disposed to, and capable of pursuing their journey
on to London; but Mr. Ellis, though most desirous of arriving in town with as little
delay as possible, yet could not determine to leave his fellow-traveller, in whom he felt
an unusual degree of interest, till he had seen him placed under proper medical treatment; he having, therefore, carefully and tenderly placed him in the waggon, along with
several others more or less injured, walked himself by the side of it.   When they reached
the farm-house, they found warm beds prepared by the hospitable inmates, and a surgeon
already in attendance.

With the affectionate solicitude of a brother, Mr. Ellis assisted in conveying the in-
animate form of his unfortunate companion to the room appointed for his reception, and
engaged the earliest care of the surgeon on his behalf, who pronounced his life, to Mr.

THE LOST ONE AND THE MINISTER OF MERCY.

[" God is my witness," she exclaimed, stretching forth her hand impressively, " that I have—that I do most bitterly repent of that one dark sin which has sullied my previous spotless name."]

Ellis's great joy, to be in no immediate danger; still he could not bear the thought of leaving him in a state of insensibility, and nothing but the alarming illness of his parent would have induced him for an instant to have so determined; but having done all for him that the nature of the case would admit, he sent a labourer from the farm to the nearest town, to procure a post-chaise, in order that he might conclude his journey as expeditiously as possible. The interval that elapsed previous to the arrival of the vehicle, he spent by the bedside of the patient, watching his countenance, which wore the hue of death, and wondering if he had any near relative, who might suffer anxiety and sorrow on his account. While thus mournfully musing, the sick man manifested an appearance of returning sensibility, which was joyfully hailed by the curate, who, bending over him, inquired how he felt. The stranger opened his eyes, and regarded him with a confused expression of countenance, as though endeavouring to recall his scattered senses, and at length, in a low voice, asked what had happened.

" The train in which we were fellow-travellers, has met with a disastrous accident," replied Mr. Ellis.

" And I ?" returned the other.

" Have sustained severe, yet, I trust not, dangerous injury," replied the curate.

" And you have ———"

" Escaped," interrupted Mr. Ellis, " with only a few bruises. I trust," he continued, after a short pause, " you will endeavour to keep your mind perfectly at ease. I regret that I shall shortly be obliged to leave you; but if you remember, during our journey, I informed you that I was hastening to the sick bed of my only parent; otherwise nothing should induce me to quit this place till you were more perfectly recovered. As it is, I am assured that you will want for neither kindness or attention."

" Thank you," returned the other; " I am perfectly sensible of your kindness, though at present unable to express my feelings."

" Say no more on that subject. I have only acted as I am certain you would have done had our situations been reversed," replied Mr. Ellis; " but tell me if you have any relative whom you would desire to see?"

At this question, the curate remarked there was a slight convulsive movement of the upper lip of the injured man; but he spoke in a calm voice, as he said, in a tone of inquiry,—

" You are going to London ?"

" Most certainly," returned the curate, " and shall be happy to execute any commission with which you may entrust me."

" Will you have the kindness then to seek for my pocket-book, in which you will find a card ?"

" Your pocket-book is here," replied Mr. Ellis, " together with your watch and guard," moving towards a small dressing-table.

" Be kind enough, then, to look for the card."

" I presume this is it," answered the curate, drawing a small embossed card from the pocket-book, and holding it before the eyes of the other.

" Yes, that is correct," he replied; " and I wish you to add to the obligation I am already under to you, by calling at that address, and acquainting my "———and he hesitated for a moment, and then, with a tremor in his voice, said, " wife with the accident that has befallen me. She is expecting me in town this evening, and will suffer extreme uneasiness at my non-arrival."

" You may depend," said the curate, kindly, " that I will break it to her as gently as possible."

" And do not lead her to suppose that my life is in any danger; but assure her she may expect to see me in a very short time, as I hope ere long to be sufficiently recovered to bear the fatigue of removal."

" I am afraid," said Mr. Ellis, mildly, " that it will be some time before you are capable of leaving your bed; had I not rather desire your lady to come to you?"

" Oh, no," replied the other, eagerly; " the sight of me as I am now, would be the death of her. No, no, she must not come. Do not tell her where I am, or her love may induce her to come here, in spite of my desire to the contrary. Promise me this," he added, with anxiety, " or I shall be in constant fear of her coming."

" Certainly, I will do exactly as you wish," said the curate. " I only thought your own desire was to have her in attendance upon you."

"That desire must be sacrificed," interrupted the other. "I tell you it would be the death of her."

"Do not agitate yourself," returned Mr. Ellis. "I promise to inform her of nothing more than you wish her to know; give me a message, and I promise to deliver it verbatim."

"Convey to her, then," replied the other, in a calmer tone, "my tenderest regard, and acquaint her that I have met with a slight accident, which will prevent me, at present, pursuing my journey; but, immediately on my recovery, I will hasten to her. In the meantime, beg of her not to entertain any apprehensions on my behalf."

"You may depend upon my seeing her to-night, and delivering to her your message; but she will, doubtless, wish to know where you are; indeed, I can scarcely tell how to keep it from her knowledge."

"You must do so, nevertheless," replied the other; "and yet," he continued, musingly, "I do not think it probable she would come if you told her I did not wish it; on the contrary, I feel assured she would not; therefore, if she is very pressing on that subject, you may tell her where I am, but, at the same time, state that I expressly desire her not to come; at least," he added, after a moment's pause, "not at present."

Mr. Ellis reiterated his assurance that he would strictly comply with his wishes, and, the post-chaise being announced, prepared to take his leave.

"It is, my dear sir," he said, as he bent over him, "with extreme reluctance that I feel myself compelled to quit you; but I earnestly hope that you will soon be so far recovered as to permit of your removal. Though, as I said before, you will not want for anything in this abode that the good-hearted inmates can procure, still ——"

"Make yourself perfectly happy regarding me," replied the stranger, "and receive my warm thanks for your disinterested kindness. And now, my dear sir," he added, stretching out his hand, "I will not detain you longer; so, farewell."

"Farewell!" returned Mr. Ellis, warmly pressing the proffered hand; and, without a word more, he hurried from the room. He was a particularly feeling, tender-hearted man and the unusual events of the day had greatly affected him, and he threw himself back in the chaise, and endeavoured so far to forget them as to rally the strength of mind he so greatly stood in need of, to support him through the sorrowful meeting that was speedily to take place between him and his beloved parent. The startling events we have recorded were utterly at variance with the calm, even tenor in which his time usually glided so smoothly and pleasantly on, at once removed from the bustle and strife of the busy world, and its concomitant amount of anxiety, and the sad dreariness which most commonly attends a total exclusion from it; no wonder, then, that the good curate felt depressed in no light degree, and his gloomy imagination pictured his beloved parent as having already passed from earth away.

"Alas!" he exclaimed, "this sad accident may have delayed me so long, that my arrival may be too late for me to receive her last blessing."

And as the thought forced itself upon his mind, the tears coursed each other unheeded down his cheeks. At length, recovering in a measure his usual composure, he drew from his pocket the card from his new acquaintance; it bore the name of "Mr. Thornton," and he perceived the address was to one of the fashionable squares at the west-end; and as he must necessarily pass close to it on his way to his mother's abode, he determined to call there first; so, giving orders to the postilion where to stop, he began to consider in what manner he had better break the distressing intelligence to the lady. She, doubtless, he considered, would feel much hurt at being prohibited from hastening to the sick bed of her husband, and her alarmed feelings, on hearing of the accident, would probably induce her to think him even more seriously injured than he really was; he might too have a difficulty in persuading her that he still lived. Altogether, he deemed he had to execute a delicate and painful mission; and though no one was more calculated to perform it than Mr. Ellis, yet he shrank from the self-imposed task the more as he approached the spot. He was a perfect stranger to the lady, and scarcely knew how to introduce the subject with which he had undertaken to make her acquainted. Still, it must be done; so, endeavouring to rally his spirits, and shake off the sadness that hung over them, he turned his thoughts back to Sackville, and the kind friends he had left behind him, wondering if they had heard of the accident, and picturing their fears on his account, and resolving to remove them by writing, as soon as he arrived at his mother's residence; for there was but a very small quantity of selfishness in Mr. Ellis's composition ; and if even he was plunged into the depths of sorrow by finding his parent no more, it most certainly would not have the effect of causing him to forget the anxiety of his friends.   But for the present we will leave the curate to his reflections, and take a peep into the house to which he is hastening to communicate such painful tidings.

---

## CHAPTER IX.

THE house indicated in the card given to Mr. Ellis by his new acquaintance, was, we have said, situated in one of the most fashionable squares, and thither we now wish to introduce the reader.   The house is large and elegantly furnished, profusion scatters its lavish gifts around, and everything speaks of the wealth and good taste of the inmates. Splendid suits of rooms vie with each other in costly expenditure and appointments ; superb paintings from the first masters decorate the walls ; the floors are covered with such thick, yet soft carpets, that the foot sinks into them like down.

In one particular apartment of this truly princely abode, fitted up in a style of elegance superior even to the rest, a large fire is burning brightly, and a magnificent ormolu lamp sheds a brilliant light round the room, reflected on all sides by splendid mirrors, giving the place an appearance of enchantment.   A table, richly inlaid with pearl, stands in the middle of the room, on which are thrown, with an appearance of carelessness, a number of embossed books, containing, as was apparent from some that were open, engravings in the best style of the art.   A settee, covered with crimson velvet, ornaments one side of the room, on which, half reclining, is seated a young and beautiful woman—we say beautiful, but there was something almost angelic in the face and figure of that fair being.   She was slight-made, but of most exquisite proportion, which was displayed to advantage in a dress of pale dove-coloured satin, which was confined at the waist, and then descended in thick folds to her feet.   The sleeves fitted tight to her arm, but reached no further than the elbow, a broad ruffle of Brussels lace forming an elegant and graceful finish.   Rich gold bracelets were clasped round the lower part of her arm, in which the diamonds glittered perceptibly.   Her dress was rather low on the neck and shoulders ; but ample amends were made for that circumstance by the thick cluster of fair tresses which hung like a curtain around her.   At the moment we describe her, she raised her head, and, with an impatient movement, flung back the curls from her face, and, by so doing, displayed small but beautifully-formed features, wearing an expression of such sweet and touching innocence as to seem almost child-like in their beauty.   Her eyes were of a soft blue, and

> " So pure, that at their ray
> Dark vice would turn, abash'd, away."

Her complexion was white as Parian marble, with the exception of the cheeks, on which a warm glow was perceptible.   An open book lay by her side, but she seemed to have abandoned herself to thought.

Suddenly a knock was heard at the door, and, starting from her recumbent position, she threw an anxious glance at the opposite mirror, and never had it reflected a more lovely countenance, at the same time hastily adjusting her truant curls, and causing each to fall in its proper place, while a pleased smile played round her dimpled mouth.

At this instant the room door opened, and a footman in gorgeous livery presented himself.

" There is a gentleman, madam, particularly desires to speak with you.   He comes, he says, on very painful business."

" His name, John ?" interrupted the lady, hastily.

" He declines to give it, madam, being, he says, an entire stranger to you, and but just arrived in London from Devonshire."

" He brings me news, doubtless, from—from your master.   By all means show him in here."

" Yes, madam ;" and the man departed to do her bidding.

During his absence, she seemed endeavouring to suppress some painful emotion, that blanched her cheek and shook her frame ; but she appeared to have a remarkable power (for one so young) over her feelings.   And when the footman returned, ushering in the stranger, the soft colour had resumed its wonted place upon her cheek ; and she rose with graceful dignity, and an appearance of thorough self-possession, to receive her visitor, whom our readers will have already guessed was no other than Mr. Ellis. Emerging as he did from the comparatively dark streets of London into the full glare of that elegant and brilliantly illuminated apartment, it was some minutes before he became sufficiently accustomed to the light to be thoroughly conscious of surrounding objects. His first thought was the unfitness of his own travel-soiled dress for the splendour and beauty of the place ; therefore, hastening to apologise and fulfil his mission, that he might depart to scenes far more humble, but ten times more dear, he thus began,—

"You must excuse me, madam, intruding upon you in my present dishabille, but I am come on an errand painful in the extreme. Your husband, whom you are expecting in town this evening, has, I am sorry to say, met with a severe, though I trust not danger- ous, accident on his journey from Devonshire. I was a fellow-traveller in the same car- riage as himself, and having urgent business in London, which forced me to continue my journey as soon as circumstances would permit, he deputed to me the painful task of making known to you this distressing intelligence."

She had allowed the curate to proceed without the slightest interruption ; not even a sigh had escaped her ; her hands were firmly clasped upon her breast, and her head bowed down. She seemed the victim of speechless agony, her long hair hanging in weeping folds over her bosom. The curate, feeling for the mute sorrow of one so young and lovely, advanced a few paces nearer to her side, and endeavoured by gentle words to soothe her anguish, when she raised her head, and fixed her large blue eyes, now flashing with almost unearthly excitement, on the face of her visitor. Seeing he started back, while sorrow and amazement were plainly depicted on his countenance, she exclaimed,—

"You know me now. Alas! Mr. Ellis, you know me now ; yet can no longer offer me consolation, though I stand in need of it—God knows how greatly I stand in need of it." And her slight frame shook with a convulsive movement.

The curate remained gazing on her, with mournful, but mute surprise.

"Speak," she exclaimed, and there was a wildness in her tone, "reproach me. I de- serve it, and can bear it all—anything but that disdainful silence."

"I am silent," replied the curate, "not from disdain, but pity. Yes," he continued, glancing round at the costliness and splendour of the apartment, "in spite of all this, I consider you an object of my pity, and, I had almost said, abhorrence."

"Say on," she continued ; "you cannot think worse of me than I think of myself. Yet, think not that I was tempted to guilt, to ruin, by these glittering yet worthless toys," and she threw a glance of contempt on the beautiful objects which surrounded her. "No, no ; it was grief, it was madness did it all ;" and burying her face in her hands,

> "She hung her head, and wept for shame,
> Sighing as if a heart-string broke
> With every deep-heaved sob that came."

It was impossible for the curate to view such terrible grief as this unmoved, and, regard- ing it as a proof of penitence, he stretched forth his hand, and laying it gently on her arm, he thus spoke,—

"You repent,—I think bitterly and truly repent of the guilt which has not only ruined your own happiness, but planted a thorn in the bosom of one who by nature was formed for noble and generous deeds,—who for your sake bowed his pride, and was content to bear any humiliation or suffering for you, but felt it not."

The curate paused an instant, but she spoke not ; the blue veins in her forehead stood out like cords, so violent was her emotion ; but she remained motionless. Mr. Ellis again began,—

"I feel assured that you sincerely repent of your guilt ; then far be it from me further to reproach you with it. Let us leave this place at once, and for ever. I can promise you an asylum with my sister—humble it is true, yet removed from want."

"Mr. Ellis," she said, raising her head, "I can never consent to be a burden either to yourself or sister ; and I am utterly incapable of providing for my own wants, or of her who is a thousand times dearer to me than myself. Had it been otherwise, I never should have fallen so low as this."

"You would not be a burden to us ; there is one whom I am sure would not allow it. Were he assured that you had voluntarily returned to a life of virtue, he would himself supply your wants."

" And do you think," she replied, while the blood mounted to her face, suffusing not only that, but her neck likewise, with the deepest crimson—" do you think that I would ever receive aught from him? Oh! no, no—surely it is impossible!"

" If you feel all that pride," returned the curate, "you cannot have repented of your sins as I wished, and, indeed, hoped you had."

" God is my witness," she exclaimed, stretching forth her hand impressively, " that I have—that I do most bitterly repent of that one dark sin which has sullied my previously spotless name."

" And," resumed the curate, " for the most 'unworthy motives. You were not led astray through an undue attachment to an unworthy object, who basely took advantage of your love to beguile you into sin. That being the case, I could have pitied and forgiven you—nay, I should have placed your guilt to the account of another; but as it is ——"

" You despise me," she returned; " I know it; but not more—oh! not more than I despise myself. And yet, just God! I was driven mad by the accumulation of sufferings that were heaped upon the head of my innocent and unconscious offspring. I saw her pining day by day for food, and I none to bestow. I had given her the last crust, and knew not how to procure more. I had parted with almost every article of clothing; starvation stared me in the face on one hand; riches, luxury, splendour, courted our acceptance on the other. What wonder, then, if my reason, weakened by privation, gave way, and I yielded myself to the insidious temptation."

" But the price," returned the curate. " Did it never occur to you how dearly you must purchase the life of your child, if that thought, as you say, urged you to sacrifice your every hope of heaven?"

" I knew it all; but I was beside myself. The only thought upon which I could rest with anything approaching to satisfaction, was that of saving my child at the sacrifice of all else on earth."

" And now," returned the curate, " that you are aware of the enormity of your guilt, your sin will be doubled—trebled, if you do not instantly recant your error, and return to the path from which you have so sadly strayed. There is hope for you yet," he continued, with increased animation. " Oh! bless God that you are not without the pale of mercy! Need I urge more? Oh! surely—surely it is needless. You will no longer hesitate to go with me. Everything favours your flight. He who alone might endeavour to prevent it, is incapacitated from so doing. He is lying upon a bed of suffering, from which it is impossible he can rise for many weeks. Lose not, then, the golden opportunity—an opportunity that may never again occur. How fortunate that I should have been delegated to convey to you the account of his accident. Oh! it was purposely ordained that I should come here and snatch you from utter destruction."

While the curate thus spoke, she had hidden her face once more in her clasped hands, and now, as he paused for her to reply, she startlingly motioned him away. He heeded it not, but continued looking stedfastly at her. At length, having succeeded in subduing her emotion, she once more raised her face, bathed in tears; but brushing them hastily away, she spoke in a low but firm voice,—

" Mr. Ellis, I thank you for the friendly interest you manifest towards me; but the same motives that drove me into guilt, still prevail to keep me in it; I am utterly helpless and without resource for myself and child; for to live upon the generosity of one too deeply injured, I never can consent; besides," she continued, " do not persuade me to add ingratitude to the list of my sins."

" Speak not of ingratitude," returned the curate, " to one who has succeeded in placing you in the degrading position you now occupy; far from having any claim upon your gratitude, he should be regarded with detestation. Do not, I entreat of you, deceive yourself; say, has he acted generously, or even fairly, by you?"

" I cannot," she replied, " palliate my own sin, by thinking ill of another, who has provided a home and every comfort for myself and child."

" He lavishes upon you," said Mr. Ellis, " what it has cost him no effort to obtain; he has suffered nothing for you, either in the shape of self-denial, or adversity; he deprives himself of no luxury, pleasure, or happiness, to bestow it upon you; he merely provides for you out of his abundant superfluity, and which you have already dearly paid for, purchasing it at the inestimable price of all that made you lovely. Every minute I spend here is precious to me, for my mother is expecting me at her sick couch; and yet, oh, yet, I cannot withdraw myself from your presence till I have exhausted every endeavour to induce you to accompany me."

" Leave me, I pray you," she replied; "every effort will prove unavailing; I cannot quit this place at present."

" Say, rather, that you will not."

" Well, then, be it so; under existing circumstances I will not. I have chosen my own path, and even at the price of suffering for it hereafter, I must persevere in it now."

" Oh, speak not thus lightly of another state," returned the curate, with a solemnity in his tone; " nor so wilfully and readily pronounce your own doom. Once more I entreat of you, be persuaded, ere it is too late, and come with me; I promise you a sister's love, and a welcome to all that she can give."

" I can only reiterate my thanks, but at the same time my refusal to accept of your generous offer; not that I hold it lightly, or of trivial value; but I would not cast myself a burden upon any one, more especially upon those whom I know have scarcely sufficient to maintain themselves, and what little they have is obtained ——"

" By honest industry," interrupted the curate; " and sweeter, far sweeter is the morsel thus earned, than the most luxurious fare purchased by sin."

" I believe you," she returned; " for often, indeed, have I eaten of the bread of bitterness."

" Then why eat of it any longer?"

"Cease," she replied, " I may not listen to you; do not linger here, in the hope of inducing me to comply with your wishes, kind and generous as they are. I can only unhesitatingly decline them. You cannot justly appreciate my motives for so doing; yet, to me, they are strong and urgent. To do as you desire, I should, in my own eyes, be adding the blackest ingratitude to my other sins, of no light magnitude already. It is probable—most probable, we may never meet again; yet, believe me, I shall often think of you, and always with a grateful feeling; and if the prayers of one so fallen can avail aught, your path through life will be bright and pleasant."

" The day, I feel assured, will come," returned Mr. Ellis, " when sorrow and bitterness will be your portion; if my counsel or kindness can alleviate it in the remotest degree, you will not find me less willing to extend it to you then, than now."

" No—no," she hastily interrupted; " I refuse your offer of shelter, not only now that I do not require it, but for ever; we meet no more on earth; our paths are, indeed, distinct and separate. When you entered this room, I recognised you immediately, and thought that when you became aware whom you were addressing, you would treat me with scorn and contempt, and I would have borne it unrepiningly; for, oh! I know how richly I deserved it. But when, instead of that, you spoke to me words of kindness and consideration, it melted my whole soul; and the memory of this meeting will ever be fondly cherished in my heart. Farewell! and take with you ——"

" Stop," interrupted the curate; " you have said we shall meet no more on earth;" and there was an increased solemnity in his manner. " What hope have we that we shall ever meet in Heaven? You persist in living a life of guilt, knowing well that it is so; you are not blinded to your real position, but see it as clearly as I, who am an unwilling witness of your sin; therefore, you are inexcusable. You voluntarily proclaim yourself an outcast from that blest inheritance, which might otherwise be your portion; and when you are stretched on the bed of death, you will repent, bitterly repent having turned a deaf ear to my solicitation;" and without giving her time to offer any further remark, he turned from the room. After he had descended a few stairs, he stopped for a minute, and listened attentively, in the vain hope that she might alter her determination and call him back, to acquaint him with it. But no; all was profoundly still, and with a sorrowful heart, the curate regained the street.

---

## CHAPTER X.

IN the same fashionable quarter of the town, and not far removed from the splendid house we have described in our last chapter, was a long and exceedingly narrow street, containing houses on either side, which had evidently seen better days; they were large, but most incommodiously built, some of them having stables adjoining, but which were now only used as a sort of out-houses. It was one of those dark, dull streets, which even in the brightest summer's day, could boast no more than a slight patch of sunshine scarcely perceptible, only as it made surrounding objects a shade more gloomy by its rays. The smoke and dust of years remained in undisturbed repose upon the windows, which were ornamented with dirty, yellow-looking curtains. It was a street that a pedestrian would gladly go a mile out of his way to avoid, had it been necessary; but it was not, inasmuch as it contained no thoroughfare. It was greatly favoured by laundresses, almost every other house exhibiting a board or card to that effect. There was also a dyer's, with a large pole thrust out from the upper windows, on which were displayed great coats, trowsers, and other wearing apparel, waving to and fro in the breeze, in a most melancholy and woe-begone manner.

The houses were very old and shaky, and seemed to lean upon each other for support; and, for want of necessary repairs, had been allowed to fall into a very dilapidated state; yet they were crowded with inhabitants from the garret to the kitchen. Not a room was unoccupied, except when, occasionally, a bill would announce an apartment to let, and this was not often the case; but, when it so occurred that there was a room vacant, it very shortly found a fresh occupant. Children, too, there were in plenty, from babies at the breast to the rough-clad urchin of ten or twelve, who would frequently disturb the inhabitants, especially at the time of year of which we write, by letting off squibs and other fireworks in the street, to the very great indignation of an old gentleman, who lived at the corner of the most aristocratic end—that is, the end which had an outlet—and which house he was allowed to occupy free, on condition of his looking sharp after the other tenants, and preventing them running away without paying their rent, should any be so minded.

About ten houses down this street, the second floor window on the right hand side of the way displayed two pots of geraniums, one of myrtle, another of fuschia, and two of pinks. The curtains, moreover, were of an unusual whiteness for the neighbourhood; and, hanging near the window, in a wire cage, was a young, merry little goldfinch, who hopped from perch to perch, and chirruped with such lively notes, in a manner that was truly astonishing, considering the dull, close neighbourhood in which he was doomed to pass his existence. But he was a contented little bird; and though, at times, he must, undoubtedly, have had yearnings for the green fields and deep blue skies, where the purest breezes played o'er Nature's fairest landscape, and from which he had been transplanted to the thick, smoky atmosphere he now breathed, yet he seemed resolved to make the best of the change; and, consequently, whistled as lively as in days of yore. Just beneath his cage was a small work-table, which, by day, was in constant use—ay, and frequently by night also. A pretty, delicate female, whose pallid brow betokened much care and anxiety, while her long taper fingers almost mechanically performed their task, was seated at the table, her eye glancing occasionally down the street, as if in expectation of the approach of some person; and as, time after time, they turned from the window in disappointment, the anxiety depicted on her countenance visibly increased. At length all out-door objects were wrapped in gloom; when, laying down her work, she drew the curtain before the window, and, rising from her seat, walked to the further end of the room, and approached a small bed, covered with a snow white quilt, on which lay her sick mother. Stooping down, she bent noiselessly over her; then, turning away, she commenced preparing tea and toast for the invalid. Having finished this occupation, she drew a table to the bedside, and, once more bending down, said, in a soft, musical voice,—

"Mother, dear mother!" The invalid opened her eyes, and gazed upon her affectionately. "You have slept long, dear mother; and, I trust, feel refreshed. I have prepared you a little tea, and after partaking of it, I hope you will be better, much better."

"Is he come?" replied her mother, in a faint voice, and looking anxiously at her.

"Not yet, dear mother, but he will be here shortly, I am convinced he will. Let me raise you in bed, and do try and eat a little bit of this toast."

"Thank you, my child," she returned, in the same weak voice she had first spoken. "I will endeavour to do as you wish. Yet, Mary, love, do not deceive yourself with the belief that I can ever recover; I feel that my time here is short, so short, that unless George soon arrives I shall not live to see him. I feel a greater difficulty in breathing, even than I did yesterday; each hour I grow weaker, and there is an unusual coldness at my heart which tells me that death is nigh; indeed, I now feel his icy hand grasping me, and ere long, my child, we must part. Do not weep," she continued, as the unhappy girl threw herself on her knees by the bedside, and buried her face in the clothes. "God

THE MEETING BETWEEN MR. ELLIS AND HIS SISTER.

[Footsteps were heard ascending the stairs. Mary Ellis hastily dropped her work, and, opening the door, sunk almost fainting into her brother's arms.]

will reward and protect you for all the dutiful and affectionate love you have shown towards me, your widowed mother. It grieves me that you are forced to work so hard for your daily bread; yet, my child, persevere, nor let aught seduce you into the broad, and apparently flowery paths of vice."

The weeping girl here raised her dark and tearful eyes to her mother's face.

"I do not, my love, doubt you," she continued; "but when I am gone, you will be left without a protector, your brother being too far removed to perform towards you that office he would otherwise delight in; and, oh! my child, London abounds with temptations for unsuspecting females. Yes," she added, in a firmer tone; "I know I can trust you. Kiss me, my love; talking has exhausted me, and I will endeavour to take some tea, it may refresh me."

The young girl rose from her knees, and hastened to attend to her mother's request. After a short time, the invalid once more sunk into a quiet sleep, and the younger female renewed her work; for the poor are forced to labour, let their hearts be ever so sad and weary. Yet the work she was employed upon, was sadly at variance with her own humble attire, and certainly out of place in that sick chamber; she was engaged in making a bridal robe of delicate satin, and which out, of consideration for her mother's illness, the rich milliner had allowed her to do at home; for Mary Ellis was most proficient in the art of dressmaking. While plying her needle the tears flowed in such torrents from her eyes, that they frequently completely obscured her vision, and she was obliged to drop her work, while she hastily wiped them away; indeed, she had much ado to prevent them staining the rich satin, that was to deck the graceful form of a youthful bride, who, at that precise moment, was glancing with pleased satisfaction over her superb and costly trousseau, which was complete with the exception of this one dress, that was destined for the bridal day; her face radiant with joy and pride; a tear occasionally, for a passing moment, dimmed the lustre of her vision; but, oh, it was a tear consecrated at the shrine of bliss, not such as fell from the eyes of Mary Ellis.

And here we cannot refrain from remarking, that we never look upon an elegant and costly toilet, without wandering in thought to the close work-room where so many slaves of the needle are engaged "from morn to night, and oft to morn again;" condemned to an occupation which, if not laborious, is, in many respects, far worse, as moderate labour may be considered as conducive to health, whereas, there is no employment at once more unhealthy and irksome than that of constant and unceasing occupation at needlework, and which is likewise most wretchedly paid. The milliner reaps the golden harvest, for dressmaking, in the first instance, is an excellent and profitable business; but the number of young females they employ are engaged at a small weekly salary, and into that portion of time the greatest possible amount of labour is condensed. Who, then, that has ever been into one of those crowded work-rooms, and marked with what astonishing rapidity the needle is made to perform its office, and know that a stipulated task is frequently assigned to each, and which the uninitiated would consider it an impossibility to perform in the given time—we say, after this, who can wonder at the sunken cheek and pallid brow of the dressmaker? And yet how many—how very many young and interesting females are condemned to this species of slavery! Well would it be for them, and creditable to ourselves, if, while we are boasting of having put an end to slavery abroad, and are collecting money to be reckoned by thousands of pounds yearly, to teach the gospel to the heathen, we looked a little more at home, and directed our energies to our suffering countrywomen. The gospel that we are so anxious to promulgate abroad teaches us—nay, commands us to love and help one another—and yet, forgetful of the sorrowing slaves in our own free and Christian land, we pass them by, and seek for objects on which to expend our wealth and pity in a foreign clime.

We confess we look with a jealous eye on charitable contributions that, laid out in our own country, under proper management, might be the means of making many an aching, sorrowing heart to ring for joy, but which, alas! are destined for the conversion of the heathen to Christianity. And far be it from us to decry such an expenditure of money, were there not so much real suffering and distress in our own country; but while we are daily hearing of deaths caused by utter destitution, and the actual want of the means of supporting life, we cannot do otherwise than regret—deeply and bitterly regret, that it is not applied to snatching them from destruction.

Poor Mary Ellis had continued engaged upon her employment for nearly an hour, when steps were heard ascending the stairs. She hastily dropped her work, and, opening the door, sunk almost fainting into her brother's arms.

"Dear Mary, I am not too late—thank God, I am not too late," said Mr. Ellis, as he glanced towards the bed upon which, in a calm and tranquil sleep, lay his dying parent.

Recovering from the mingled emotions of joy and sorrow that her brother's sudden appearance had caused nearly to overcome her, she led him to the further end of the room, dreading, that should her mother awaken and behold him she so longed to see by her side, it might be the means of extinguishing the spark of life, that burnt with such a flickering, unsteady flame, that the slightest emotion might prove fatal to its continuance.

"Oh, why, dear George, did you delay so long?" said his sister; "we expected you hours ago, and our mother has been getting weaker and weaker the entire day, and I much feared she would have expired without seeing you."

"Do not blame me, dear Mary," returned Mr. Ellis. "I should, indeed, have been here, as you anticipated, hours ago; but the train by which I journeyed met with a most disastrous accident, and it is, indeed, a most providential circumstance that I have escaped unhurt."

"Oh, thank God!" replied Mary, with evident emotion, "that he has, in his mercy, spared me this further calamity; and, my dear brother, do not think I meant unkindly; on the contrary, I was certain that some untoward event must have detained you against your will."

"And you did me no more than justice," replied Mr. Ellis. "With what bitter anguish have I counted the time by moments that kept me from this spot, on which every thought has been fixed since I received the painful intelligence, which was but this morning."

"You heard it, of course," returned his sister, "from Mr. Mordaunt?"

"Yes; he arrived at Sackville last night, but I was not aware of his having done so till the morning."

"It was a very singular circumstance," she replied, "that he arrived in town, and called here at the very moment I had determined on writing to acquaint you with our mother's illness, and urge you, if possible, to come immediately; when he instantly set out for Sackville, at the same time writing to a person whom he thought would be willing to fill your place while you were absent."

"It was kindly done," returned Mr. Ellis; "and to that alone you may attribute my presence here so soon. I know not how else I could have procured a substitute; but tell me, Mary, how long has our mother been so ill, and why you did not acquaint me with it earlier?"

Mary Ellis informed her brother that their sole surviving parent had been ailing for a considerable time; but, neither of them entertaining any apprehensions for the result, they had, out of kindness, concealed it from his knowledge.

"But," said Mary, in conclusion, "I now fear that her constitution has been weakened by the want of wine, and other expensive nutriment she had previously been accustomed to, but which, of late years, our altered circumstances would not allow us to procure."

And, as she gave utterance to the painful thought, the tears once more gushed in torrents from her eyes.

"And yet," she continued, when her emotion was a little subsided, "though she must have felt the privations which were nothing to me, who had youth and health to support me through it; but, at her time of life, and always of a weak and delicate frame, the privations must have, consequently, been very severe. Yet she never complained, or appeared to feel the change our circumstances had undergone; on the contrary, she was ever so cheerful and contented, that I had no idea she was sinking slowly, but surely, to the tomb, till this last week, when she became so much worse that she could no longer conceal it from me. Still I had no thought she was so near her end; and, when the surgeon whom I sent for, at my earnest request to know if he thought there was any danger, informed me that it was impossible she could survive many days, I could scarcely realise the distressing intelligence, and, for a while, encouraged the hope that he must be mistaken; but, alas! that hope was soon torn from me, though I clung to it Heaven only knows how tenaciously!"

"Comfort yourself, dear Mary," replied the curate, as his sister once more abandoned herself to the full bitterness of grief, though the tears that glistened in his eyes gave evidence of his own anguish.

Mary Ellis possessed a firm mind, and, consequently, brushing away the tears, she once more resumed her work.

With a sorrowful expression Mr. Ellis fixed his eyes on the delicate satin, and watched his sister, as with dextrous hand, she plaited it in graceful folds, and wondered if the wearer were half so amiable, as meek, enduring, as her, who, in the midst of anguish and sorrow of heart, yet performed with a willing hand the irksome toil which procured her daily bread; and then, as, in mournful silence, he gazed round the scantily-furnished apartment, his thoughts winged themselves back to the elegant and costly abode he had lately visited under such peculiar circumstances, and there, with the lovely image of the fair mistress of that mansion full before his mind's eye, he looked upon the high and polished brow of his sister, and the black hair, which, arranged in the Madonna style, afforded a marked and chilling contrast to the whiteness of her cheek, which grief and toil had robbed of the bloom that once sat upon it, and he marked the sweet air of modesty that pervaded every feature, and was plainly perceptible in every movement. He deemed her a thousand times more lovely, though care had set his seal upon her young brow, than her whom every charm adorned, save that sweet ornament, without which all other grace and beauty is nothing. This is so well known, so entirely beyond all doubt, that those who have lost all modesty, when they most desire to please, endeavour to throw around them the charm of its presence. This alone speaks more in praise of virtue than volumes of written arguments in its favour; for who would be at the pains of counterfeiting aught that was not valuable?

Thus, busily engaged in thought, the hours passed slowly on; neither Mr. Ellis or his sister were inclined for converse; their hearts were too full of the absorbing sorrow that weighed them down; though, had they met under different circumstances, how much they would have had to communicate to each other.

At length the invalid gave signs of once more awakening from her sleep. Mary was instantly at her side.

"Are you any better, dear mother?" she inquired, tenderly stooping to kiss her pallid cheek.

"Has your brother come, my child?" she replied, turning her lustreless eyes upon her daughter.

"Yes, dear mother, he has been here some time. Do you feel strong enough to see him?"

"Oh, yes, my child," she returned, making a feeble attempt to rise in bed; "let him come at once."

Mr. Ellis approached the bed, and, raising the cold hand of his parent to his lips, essayed to speak, but his heart was too full to allow him to give utterance to what he wished to say.

"My son, my dear, dear son," said Mrs. Ellis, while an expression of joy illumined her countenance, "God has granted my desire to see you once more before I die, and now I am ready and willing to depart. My children," she continued, glancing affectionately from one to the other, "you have both been good and dutiful, and though I shall not live to see it, God will assuredly bless and reward you. Mary, dearest, never forget your mother's dying command, to persevere in the path of virtue, even though it may involve the sacrifice of all else on earth. Though, I trust, indeed, you may never be put to so severe a trial. As yet, your affections are disengaged——"

At these words the face of Mary Ellis became like crimson, and, to hide her confusion, she pretended to be engaged in smoothing the pillows of the invalid, whose notice it escaped, and she continued as before,—

"And, oh, Mary, let them not be lightly won; scan well the merits of the man who seeks to gain them, and give heed that they are not bestowed on an unworthy object. You will, my child, give me this assurance?"

"I promise, dear mother," replied Mary Ellis, as she sank upon her knees by the bedside.

"And you, my son, will guide and protect her as far as it is possible for you to do so. For yourself I have no apprehension; neither, indeed, for your sister, beyond what her sex and unprotected situation demands."

Having spoken these words, which had caused her great exertion, Mrs. Ellis sunk back in the bed exhausted. Mary Ellis rose from her knees, and commenced packing up the work she had executed.

"I am thankful it is finished," she remarked to her brother, as she enclosed it in a wicker basket.

"So am I too, dear Mary," he replied. "I wonder, indeed, how you have been enabled to do it."

Taking the basket in her hand, she left the room, and descended the stairs to seek for some person to whom she could entrust it to deliver at the milliner's.

"Is that you, Miss Ellis, dear?" said a swarthy and rather over-dressed young woman, opening the door of the room she was passing, and looking out.

"Yes, it is me, Mrs. Herbert," replied Mary. "I wish to find some person who will take this (exhibiting her basket) to Madame Florenzi for me."

"Oh, come in for one instant," returned the first speaker; "I have something of importance to tell you."

"I have neither time or inclination to attend to you now," replied Miss Ellis; "my dear mother, I feel, is sinking fast, and I must hasten back to her." And as she gave utterance to the words, her tears again gushed forth.

"Oh, pray, Miss Ellis, dear, do not take on so. But I will not detain you an instant; I only wanted to tell you that Fred has been here, and begged so hard for me to call you down for five minutes, that I hardly knew how to refuse; but I remembered the promise you exacted from me, and consequently would not do as he wished."

"You were quite right, Mrs. Herbert; and I thank you for your attention to my request. Did," and the colour mounted to her cheek, "did Frederick leave any message for me?"

"Oh, yes; he told me to give his kindest love, and hoped that if your mother still continued so ill that you could not see him, that you would endeavour to write him a few lines. At the same time he thought it rather unkind that you would not consent to grant him an interview at least of a few minutes; and, indeed, Miss Ellis, I cannot think that you entertain much regard for him, or, when he had troubled himself to come all this distance on purpose to see you, you would not have refused to speak even one word to him."

"Alas! Mrs. Herbert," replied Mary, sinking into a chair, "you know not my heart, or how truly his image is enshrined there, to the utter exclusion of all others. I have loved only too well and fondly, though it has been nourished in secret, which has caused me many a severe pang. I had no right, I feel it now, to conceal this affection from my mother. Oh, it was a proof that it was an unworthy attachment, and yet he has ever treated me with the greatest respect and consideration."

"Why, you know, Miss Ellis, dear," returned the other, in an encouraging tone, "you could not have told your mother of this attachment, unless you were prepared instantly to renounce it. She never would have believed that he meant honourable towards you."

"And, alas!" returned Miss Ellis, "how do I know what his intentions towards me are? It is scarcely probable that he will marry the poor needlewoman; he may be even now laughing at my absurd hopes. Oh! Mrs. Herbert, would that we had never, never seen them."

"I am sure I cannot tell what cause you have to regret it—it has been the means of procuring us many happy hours."

"Scarcely so, at least, to me," replied Miss Ellis; "the thought that I was acting with deception towards one of the kindest and best of parents, poisoned my happiness—turned it, indeed, into sorrow and remorse; and now that she is stretched upon her deathbed, and I can no more hope for an opportunity of repairing my sin, I feel it a thousand times more acutely. I do not blame you, Mrs. Herbert," she continued, seeing the other seemed hurt at her remarks, "it is myself alone I blame."

"I was going to tell you," she replied, "that hearing from me how ill your mother was, and how hard you were obliged to work to provide for her and yourself, Fred wished to leave a present of money to be expended on your mother; but knowing how particular you are, I refused to take it."

The face of Mary Ellis was suffused with the deepest crimson at these words, and she exclaimed indignantly,—

"I am astonished that Mr. Maitland could for an instant suppose that I would receive any pecuniary present from him, and you, Mrs. Herbert, have done very wrong to a quaint him with my limited means; but rather than receive anything from him, I would work without ceasing, day and night, and feel thankful that I had it to do."

" Well, do not be angry, Miss Ellis; I refused his offer, and that should satisfy you; though, had I been in your place, I should have been very pleased to accept it. As it is, you know I have had several presents from William, and always think it very kind of him to give them me."

" That is nothing to me," replied Miss Ellis; " our ideas on that, as on many other subjects, are totally different; but I am wasting my time here; if you will be kind enough to send some person you can depend upon with this basket, I shall feel much obliged."

" Oh! certainly, Miss Ellis, dear; do not make yourself at all uneasy about that, I will see it safe off."

" I thank you," she replied, rising, and moving towards the door, " and will now wish you good evening, and return to my poor mother."

------

## CHAPTER XI.

EMILY STANHOPE, as we have said, passed a restless and anxious night, and arose in the morning with a sense of trouble hanging over her, she had seldom if ever felt. A few hours now would assuredly remove, or confirm her fears, regarding the curate; and when she joined her uncle and aunt in the breakfast-room, after the first salutations were exchanged, the conversation naturally reverted to the object of their anxiety.

" Oh! how much I wish it was the post-hour!" said Emily, with an air of feverish impatience.

" It will shortly be here, my love," replied her aunt, smiling, " and I am sure your uncle and myself desire it equally as much as you."

" We do, indeed, my dear Emily," rejoined Mr. Stanhope, " but age has taught us a little more patience. I remember, ah! when I was young and impatient of delay as yourself—but that is long ago, and times are sadly changed since then. I sometimes think," he added, glancing affectionately at his aged partner, " when I see the sad innovations on the customs of our forefathers, that we have lived almost too long."

" Oh! dear—dear uncle, say not so," exclaimed Emily, rising, and throwing her arms round his neck; " without you, what would become of your orphan niece?—remember, you stand in the double character of father and guardian—that you, and my dear aunt, are not merely the only protectors, but likewise the only relatives I possess in the wide world."

" True—true, my child," replied the old gentleman, straining her kindly to his bosom; " in thee, my Emily, I behold the last of my race; would, indeed, it were not so; but it is useless to repine—nay, rather let me bless God for having given me so kind and dutiful a niece. Emily, love," he continued, after a moment's pause, " listen to me a few minutes."

" Yes, uncle," she replied, raising her head from his shoulder, and gazing affectionately on his face.

" When I am gone, my love, these broad lands will become your property."

Emily again bowed her head to hide the tears that gathered to her eyes, at the thought of parting with so dear and kind a relative.

" God grant, dear uncle, that that day may be far, very far distant," she said, in a voice that betrayed her emotion.

" It cannot be very far, my love. I have already reached an age which but few are permitted to attain, and I am thankful that I have lived, my Emily, to see you grow to womanhood; and, when this mansion and the contiguous estate, which has been the property of the Stanhopes for—yes," he added, with a show of pardonable pride, " for centuries—when you become its mistress, there will be a master; yes, my Emily, to you will be delegated the task of founding the family afresh, and I hope, in the course of years, it will flourish once more, as it hath done in days gone by. It has been my painful lot to see it gradually dwindling, till I have become the last of the name; for you, my Emily, more properly belong to the Percy family, of which you may be justly proud. Yet never, my girl, forget that on your mother's side, you are descended from the Stanhopes; and, as you will become possessor of their large estate, it will be your duty to uphold the family name."

" I know it, uncle, and have promised you that I will do so."

" Yes, Emily, and I am certain you will not recant it; but there is one subject on which we have never spoken, and I wish to do so now—it is, my love, the important one of marriage. As I said in the commencement of our conversation, I cannot reasonably look forward to many more years, and it would be a considerable gratification to me could I see you united to a man worthy to share this estate with you, and who, upon taking our name, I would gladly regard as a son."

" Yes, uncle," said Emily, seeing he paused for her to reply; "and I could have no objection to give my hand to such a one; but"—and a playful smile passed over her countenance—" the difficulty is, where to find him."

" I have thought of that, Emily," returned her uncle; "and it is, as you say, the difficulty."

" And a very formidable one," replied his niece ; " so much so, that I fear I must, for the present, be content to remain single. Yet I promise you, uncle, that, should any gallant knight stray to this spot, and be induced to burden himself for life with so troublesome a charge as your Emily, he shall find her nothing loth."

" I was in earnest, Emily," said Mr. Stanhope; "nor do I consider this subject a fit matter for jest."

" Forgive me, uncle, if I have vexed you," said Emily; "but, seriously, you know there is no one at Sackville with whom you would wish me to wed, so there remains nothing but to wait till we meet with a suitable person. But," she exclaimed eagerly, glancing at the window, "I see the man with the letter-bag approaching. God grant we may hear from Mr. Ellis!"

Mrs. Stanhope regarded her stedfastly as she spoke, though without appearing to do so; and the secret conclusion she drew was, that, as far as Emily was concerned, it would not be difficult to find a husband for her, even in the neighbourhood of Sackville. Whether the old lady was correct in her surmise, the sequel must determine. At present she was prevented pursuing her thoughts further by the entrance of the venerable servant whose office it was to wait upon the master and mistress of the house.

" A letter for my uncle, John ?" said Emily, glancing at one he held in his hand.

" Yes, miss;" and, privileged by his long and faithful service, he added, bowing his powdered head, "it contains news, I hope, of our good curate."

" It is, indeed, his hand-writing," replied Emily; "God be praised !" and the sudden confirmation of hopes she had till this moment scarcely dared to entertain, blanched her cheek to the whiteness of fear.

Indeed, joy has often been known to prove as fatal as grief; and, in the suddenness of its first effects, it would be impossible to distinguish between the two. But, oh! when, as in Emily's case, it is but momentary, how sweet is the consciousness of the realisation of our hopes—how delightful the certainty that all our fears are dissipated—how speedily we are enabled to realise the fullness of our bliss. Everything appears to wear a brighter aspect than it did but a few minutes previously. We congratulate ourselves on the certainty of our happiness, and smile at our former fears. We drop, so to speak, the burden that oppressed us, and our hearts feel light and free.

Mr. Stanhope drew forth his gold spectacles, and deliberately placed them on his nose; at the same time, with his usual affability, addressing the servant, who was preparing to leave the room, said,—

" I am certain, John, you feel equally interested in Mr. Ellis as ourselves; consequently, you are free to remain while I read the letter, that, as you have partaken of our anxiety, you may also share in the joyful tidings that I trust it contains."

The man bowed in acknowledgment of the kindness of his master, and placed himself in an attentive position near the door. Having adjusted his spectacles, Emily thought, with unusual precision, he drew forth a small pen-knife, and commenced carefully cutting round the seal which secured the envelope, a custom he invariably adopted, and which, indeed, his father had done before him. This concluded, he gently unfolded the letter, smoothed out the creases with the greatest deliberation, and, at length, when poor Emily's patience was almost exhausted, began, in a clear voice, to read aloud the contents.

The letter was not very long ; it gave them a slight account of the accident, his own fortunate escape, the injury of his fellow-traveller, and concluded with his own safe arrival in town, and the hopeless condition in which he found his parent.

An expression of joy burst from the lips of his hearers as Mr. Stanhope read the passage which contained the intelligence of Mr. Ellis's safety, in which the good old gentleman stopped for a moment to join ; and after he had concluded with the affectionate remembrance of the curate to Mrs. Stanhope, Emily, and John Elgood, by name, and the rest of his parishioners generally, he indulged in a long invective against the baneful effects of steam, to the infinite delight of the old servant, who held his master's opinion law upon every subject, and only wished that some part of the railway company was there to hear him, feeling assured, as he afterwards declared in the kitchen, that they would have gone away convinced of the dreadful wickedness of encouraging the use of a power that so constantly resulted in the death of their fellow-creatures.

Mr. Stanhope, indeed, had attentive auditors, and he proceeded for a long time denouncing what he termed the terrible innovation, steam, as applied to locomotion, and bemoaning the sad departure from the customs of his forefathers, and sighing over the good old times when he was young. This was his great failing ; but we think we may with truth apply to him the words of the poet, and say,—

"That e'en his failings leaned to virtue's side ;"

at all events, they were such as injured none, and could be easily pardoned by all.

We were saying that Mr. Stanhope proceeded for a long time discoursing on his favourite subject, and it is most probable he would have continued much longer, had he not been interrupted by the entrance of John Elgood, whom he warmly greeted, and placed the curate's open letter in his hand. We need not say that John was equally pleased and delighted to hear of Mr. Ellis's fortunate escape as Mr. Stanhope and his family, and, after some minutes spent in mutual congratulation, Emily arose, and announced her intention of calling on Mrs. Harley, to acquaint her with the joyful intelligence, when John suddenly recollected that he had promised his mother and his sisters to return and inform them directly he gained any news of the curate.

"That being the case, my dear John," said the polite old gentleman, extending his hand, "I will not detain you another instant ; had it been different, I could not have parted with you so soon : as it is, I hope speedily to have the pleasure of seeing you again."

After this, John had nothing to do but to make his exit ; but whether he contemplated quite a speedy departure, is, at least, we think, uncertain. Probably, his road home laying the same way as Emily must necessarily take to pay her proposed visit to Mrs. Harley, he had thought, if possible, he might have the pleasure of walking with her.

Emily, herself, seemed thus to interpret his wishes, for she smiled at his apparently disconcerted air when her uncle thus politely bowed him from the apartment, which, quitting herself at the same time, she hastened up stairs to attire herself for her walk. The morning was fine and beautiful, and Emily proceeded towards the residence of Mrs. Harley with a light heart and cheerful countenance, stopping occasionally in her walk to communicate the glad tidings of the curate's welfare to the villagers whom she met, and all of whom rejoiced, and blessed God for his preservation. She had passed down the main street, and was turning off towards the more open country, when her eye detected a tall figure, enveloped in a cloak, which was folded across his chest, approaching, and whom she instantly recognised as the stranger, about whom she felt so strongly interested. As they drew near to each other, he likewise appeared to recognise her, and raising his hat, he spoke in the following words :—

"I believe I have the honour of addressing Miss Stanhope."

"That is my name, sir," she returned.

"Will you, then, permit me to inquire whether you have received any intelligence from Mrs. Ellis?"

"My uncle received a letter from him this morning, in which he informs us of his safe arrival in London."

"Without having sustained any injury?" replied the stranger, hastily.

"Without having sustained the slightest injury," returned Emily ; "but you seem interested in the curate, sir ; consequently, I may presume that you are acquainted with him."

"He is an old and esteemed friend of mine, Miss Stanhope, though I do not wish it

THE YOUNG OFFICER DECLINES TO FOLLOW HIS BROTHER'S ADVICE.

["You don't drink, Fred. The wine is particularly fine—a present, you know, from the colonel, and such as cannot be obtained every day"—and he held his glass before the candle, and criticised it with the air of a connoisseur.]

generally known. I have urgent reasons for wishing to remain here in the strictest seclusion; the anxiety I felt concerning him, alone induced me to intrude upon your company, and that must be my apology."

"No apology is necessary, sir," replied Emily; "neither do I consider your having inquired of me concerning Mr. Ellis, any intrusion; on the contrary, I am happy to have been the means of relieving your anxiety."

"I am much obliged to you, Miss Stanhope; but do not allow me to detain you from your walk: the morning is so fine, that I have myself been some distance, and the country around here is as beautiful as any I have ever witnessed."

"It is indeed, sir, considered very fine; though, for myself, I cannot boast of being a judge, inasmuch as I have never wandered from this spot."

"You will be fortunate," replied the other, "if you never do."

"Indeed, sir! I cannot agree with you," returned Emily; "for I have a great desire to witness other scenes; for though they may prove inferior in beauty to these, they will, to me, possess at least the charm of novelty."

"And is novelty so very charming then?" said the stranger, while a smile of peculiar bitterness passed over his countenance; "but," he added, "I need not ask; it is, I know, irresistible to your sex."

The reader must not suppose the two were standing still during this conversation; for, when the stranger had intimated his desire not to detain her, Emily had resumed her walk. Still he kept by her side.

At his last remark, Emily was conscious of looking confused. She had gone on saying just what she at the moment thought, and had thus unconsciously given the stranger a bad opinion of herself, and which she felt she did not deserve, and yet knew not what to say in mitigation of her thoughtless speech, and consequently remained silent. After a short pause, the stranger resumed,—

"The short time I have been in this village, I have heard much in praise of your amiability and kindness of heart. That being the case, Miss Stanhope, has emboldened me to make a request, which I hope you will have the goodness to grant."

"Name it, sir," replied Emily, "and you may depend on finding me willing to oblige you."

"I had the honour of informing you just now that Mr. Ellis was an old and esteemed friend of mine; yet he possesses such sensitive delicacy regarding pecuniary matters, that though I am certain he stands in need of assistance, he will not receive it from me. I offered him a sum so trifling, that I thought he would not hesitate to accept it, the morning he left here; but, to my surprise and disappointment, he persisted in refusing. I had previously endeavoured to force it upon his sister, but with the same ill success."

He hesitated for a moment, but Emily only bowed, and he again went on,—

"Illness is at all times expensive, Miss Stanhope, and Mrs. Ellis has nothing to depend on for the common necessaries of life but what her daughter can procure by constant toil. Yes, though her mother is stretched upon her dying bed, and she is her only attendant, yet Mary Ellis is forced to work, too frequently by night as well as day, to procure for her the comforts she so greatly stands in need of."

"Good God!" exclaimed Emily, "is it possible that there are persons in such distress?"

The stranger smiled at her observation.

"Indeed, Miss Stanhope, you have seen but little of the world, if you imagine I am overdrawing the picture. I could tell you of distress, to which that would, in comparison, be riches. You may well bear the character of being virtuous, amiable, and good; for poverty and sorrow seem wholly unknown to you. Others have appeared all, if not more than you now are, but they have fallen before that terrible monster poverty, which stalks through the land, laying the heart open to temptations it would otherwise have never even dreamed of."

And as he spoke these words his brow contracted, and his breath came short and thick, and some painful reminiscence seemed to harrow his frame. Emily gazed on him with astonishment; she knew not what to think. "Surely," she inwardly exclaimed, "he can never himself have known the distress he thus so vividly depicts; or is it possible that he has felt the stings of poverty, and been driven by it to commit some dreadful deed, by which he has acquired riches, but lost the power of enjoying it."

She shuddered as the thought forced itself upon her with the sense of certainty, and she continued silent, brooding over the strange manners of her companion, who, after a while recovering his composure, again addressed her, though without any apology for his previous abruptness.

"I was saying, Miss Stanhope, that I am convinced Mr. Ellis, or rather his mother and sister, stand in need of pecuniary assistance; yet, as I before intimated, they will not receive it from me. Now, as a great personal favour, I wish you to find some means of sending them occasionally a trifling sum. I leave it entirely to your own judgment how to do so, only let it be in such a manner as cannot hurt their pride, and will enable me to declare that I had nothing to do with the sending of it."

"Certainly," replied Emily, "I thoroughly understand you, and will gladly undertake the mission."

"Thank you," returned the stranger; "I knew no one else to whom I could apply, or I would not have troubled you;" saying which, he drew forth his purse, and tendered a bank note to Emily; but she shrank from receiving it.

"This is perfectly unnecessary, sir, at least," she added, "at present."

"How, Miss Stanhope," he replied; "do you think I will allow you to perform this mission for me, unless you receive the money? I did not apply to you to rid myself of an unpleasant duty. Could I, by any means, have performed it without your aid, rest assured I would not have troubled you with the matter; but, perhaps, I misunderstand you. From what I have said regarding poverty, you may, perhaps, have inferred that I am suffering from its stings; if that is the case, let me assure you, Miss Stanhope, that I am rich, as far as money can make a man so;" and a sarcastic smile curled the corners of his mouth.

Emily hastened to reply,—

"Oh, no, it was not as you suppose; that is, I mean I am willing to take the money and do with it as you wish;" saying which, she extended her hand, and received the proffered note.

"You will add to the obligation you are conferring on me, Miss Stanhope," said the stranger, "if you will allow this transaction to remain strictly secret from all but our two selves."

Emily bowed, and assured him of her readiness to oblige him.

"We will now part," he returned; "when you again hear news of the curate, you will, perhaps, meet me at the spot where we accidentally encountered each other this morning."

"I shall be pleased to do so," replied Emily; "but how can I make sure of seeing you?"

"Every morning at this hour I shall walk in this direction; consequently, when you may have aught to impart, you will find me here."

Emily again bowed, and, after exchanging polite greetings, the two separated; Emily to pursue her walk, filled with a vague apprehension that the money she had received from Mr. Mordaunt had not been acquired by honest or honourable means. Yet Emily's self-importance was considerably raised by the interview she had held with the mysterious stranger; for mysterious in every respect she most certainly considered him. And her fertile imagination had now good ground to work upon, and she began really to regard herself as an heroine; for not even among her most favoured romances had she ever read of a more strange, dark, mysterious character than Mr. Mordaunt, between whom and herself there existed a secret, involving private assignations, and about whom there hung some crime, which it would doubtless be her lot ultimately to discover; yet she was assured there were palliating circumstances connected with it, that would, in a great measure, exculpate him. Filled with these thoughts, there is no knowing where her imagination would have carried her, had she not fortunately at this juncture arrived at her destination.

Mrs. Harley and her nephew were seated in the drawing-room—Frank puffing away at his eternal pipe—when Emily was announced, and immediately ushered into their presence.

"Oh, my dearest Emily," said Mrs. Harley, affectionately embracing her, "this is indeed kind of you, and an unexpected pleasure; is it not, Frank?" turning towards her nephew.

"Why, yes," replied the gentleman, knocking the ashes out of his pipe, and preparing to refill it by cutting up a square piece of tobacco into small chips—"why, yes, Miss

Stanhope, your presence is as welcome, and equally as cheering, as the sunshine after a week of rain and gloom."

Emily smiled in acknowledgment of the compliment, and immediately proceeded to acquaint Mrs. Harley with the good news she had purposely come to inform her of.

That lady was, of course, in raptures on learning of the curate's welfare ; and, in very touching language, described the dreadful anxiety she had suffered on his account.

"I would not, my dear Emily, allow you to know how really distressed I felt, and the numberless fears I entertained concerning him, because I saw how much anxiety you were yourself enduring ; and you, my dear Emily, are so unaccustomed to trouble, that it is infinitely worse for you to endure distress, or anxiety of any kind, than for myself, who have gone through so much severe affliction, that I have in a manner become inured to it ; therefore I concealed from you the anxiety I endured on account of Mr. Ellis, in hopes of mitigating yours."

"It was very kind of you," returned Emily, in answer to this soft speech. "I thought at the time you were more uneasy about him than you wished me to suppose."

"Did you, indeed," replied the widow, smiling ; "well, I must confess that I am very bad at deception. I always find it the most difficult thing in the world to disguise my feelings, especially from persons for whom I entertain a sincere regard."

While this conversation was passing between Emily and Mrs. Harley, Frank had re-lighted his pipe, and was once more puffing away without having had the politeness to inquire whether it was agreeable ; and he now, for a moment, removed it from his mouth to enable him to address Emily as follows,—

"I was very sorry, Miss Stanhope, that you were not with us last evening, for we were confoundedly dull without you."

Whether or not the widow considered this speech at all complimentary to herself, we cannot exactly say, but she answered with her usual persuasive softness,—

"We should, indeed, my dear Emily, have been delighted with your company ; but, for myself, I so truly appreciated your motive for declining our invitation, that I could not, under the circumstances, desire your company."

And now, if the reader pleases, we will leave the trio to pursue their conversation (which, though doubtless interesting and agreeable to themselves, is scarcely so to others), while we take a glance at another part of this history, and introduce to the reader two entirely different characters.

---

## CHAPTER XII.

In an elegant and spacious apartment, in the vicinity of St. James's, two young men were seated on either side of a cheerful fire ; rich curtains, of crimson damask, were lowered before the windows, and candles in massive silver candlesticks were burning brightly on the table, on which, likewise, were placed fruit and wine.

With all these "appliances and means to boot," the young men did not appear to be altogether in a humour for enjoying conversation. They had both preserved an impenetrable silence for some time ; the elder found constant employment in filling and emptying his glass ; the younger sat with his eyes bent upon the fire, in, as it appeared, somewhat sullen silence.

The two were evidently brothers, from the strong resemblance that existed between them, and were both dressed in military uniform, from which it was likewise evident they belonged to the same regiment. The younger of the two was exceedingly handsome, though of a kind that could not altogether be considered as masculine beauty. His face was soft and smooth, almost as a woman's ; delicately fair, and with a bashful carmine glow upon his cheeks, which was at once the envy and admiration of the fair sex ; his eyes were of a dark and dazzling blue, added to which, he possessed a small and beautifully formed mouth, with teeth that rivalled ivory in their whiteness ; a handsome Grecian nose, and an ample forehead, over which his dark brown hair waved in thick clustering curls.

His brother, who was at least a good ten or twelve years his senior, possessed features which, taken separately, were equally as good, and had doubtless, when of the same age, been as attractive in personal appearance as his young brother now was ; but the soul-beaming intellect, without which the most beautiful features are insipid and entirely fail to charm, in him was obscured by an air of dissipation, that was only too perceptible in his countenance. There was something, too, about the mouth, in expression anything but pleasing, and which prejudiced the beholder greatly in his disfavour.

Had it not been for these disadvantages, the elder brother might well have been considered the handsomest man, inasmuch as he was the tallest and best proportioned of the two. Moreover, his upper lip was graced with a fine moustache; but here the comparison ceases, for, as we have said, his face was wanting in the greatest attribute of beauty, intellectual expression, and which was so strongly impressed on the younger brother's countenance. His eyes, too, were dull, and void of fire, and his whole appearance spoke to his being addicted to excess of every kind, but more especially in his devotion to the bottle.

The brothers had remained silent for some time, when the elder, again replenishing his glass, pushed the decanter towards his brother, and broke the silence by saying,—

"You don't drink, Fred. If you are out of humour with me, don't be so with the wine, which cannot possibly have offended you. And this is particularly fine; a present, you know, from the colonel, and such as cannot be obtained every day"—and he held his glass before the candle, and criticised its colour with the air of a connoisseur. "Come, fill your glass, my boy," he added, after a short pause. "You won't!" he exclaimed, as the other made a gesture of denial. "I am sorry for you, then; it is showing a bad spirit, Fred—a very bad spirit. The wine, as I before said, cannot have offended you, and yet you persist in maintaining an ill-humour towards it—a most deuced ill-humour. Not that it matters to me—certainly not—only I don't like to see you evince such a bad spirit—curse me if I do!"

"If it don't matter to you," replied the younger brother, "I wish you would hold your tongue, and not keep on worrying me in this fool's manner. You can keep quiet a few minutes, I suppose? I told you, just now, I was in no humour for talking this evening, and wish you would be satisfied with drinking the wine yourself, and not bother me any more about it."

"Certainly, Fred, I can do that," returned the other; "and, by Jove! it is no hardship to drink this wine; on the contrary, I consider it a very pleasant and agreeable occupation; at the same time, Fred, I should be glad to see you behave with a little more respect towards ——"

"Pshaw," interrupted his brother; "do leave off this cursed nonsense."

"Very well—very well, Fred. I believe this is not exactly the recognised mode of addressing an elder brother, and likewise a superior officer; but I am not offended—not at all offended, Fred; for your own sake, I am sorry to see you so wanting in respect to your superior."

"Why do you not act in a manner to command respect, if you wish it shown to you?" replied the younger man, whose voice was soft and musical, with an almost imperceptible provincial accent.

"If to bear patiently an inferior officer's deuced ill-humour would entitle a fellow to respect, I think, Fred, I have this right."

"Stop a minute," interrupted his brother. "Let us first consider the provocation that has put me into an ill-humour; remember, you have been advising, I had almost said, ordering me, to play the villain."

"Really, Fred, I wish you would be a little more particular in your choice of words; villain has a very awkward sound; and I beg you to bear in mind, that I have recommended you to do no such thing. Also remember, my dear fellow, that I have promised our mother to keep a strict watch upon your conduct; and on no account to allow you to commit any mad act. You surely cannot forget, Fred, that it was only on this condition, I induced her to purchase an ensigncy in my regiment; and being under age, I am liberty, should you manifest any symptoms of disgracing the family, to send you back immediately to Worcestershire; nay, the old lady has absolutely commanded me to do so."

"Disgracing the family! I should like to know which would be the greatest disgrace, to ruin an innocent and unprotected female, or to marry a lovely and virtuous woman, whose only drawback is, that she is forced to earn her livelihood by working with her needle—a terrible disgrace to be sure!" and his flexible voice assumed a tone of bitter sarcasm.

"Well, Fred, that is, certainly, entirely a matter of opinion. I well know which our mother would consider the greater disgrace; but I am not inclined to discuss the merits of it now; let us rather look at the whole affair in a proper light. First, then, Fred, soon after your arrival in town, we accidentally encountered two pretty women in the park, one fine evening; and being a couple of handsome fellows, we found them by no means disinclined to enter into conversation with us."

"Say one of them," interrupted his brother.

"Certainly; as you please, Fred; we'll say one of them; and we induced that one to allow us to see them home, and also gained permission to call on a future day. Well, Fred, when we came to talk the adventure over between ourselves, we found that we both gave the preference to the youngest, and, as we considered, the prettiest of the two. I believe I am perfectly correct, Fred," he added, pausing for an instant.

"Yes," returned the other; "but all this is nothing to the point."

"I beg your pardon, Fred, but must differ from you. I will, however, proceed. I was saying we both gave the preference to the same young lady; and, instead, as many would have done, endeavouring to ingratiate myself into her favour—when, knowing the sex so much better than you, I could scarcely have failed of success—yet, wishing to do what was honourable, and afford you an equal chance with myself, I proposed that we should write the names of both females on a piece of paper, and fold them exactly alike; after which, shake them up in a box, and each draw one, exchanging our words, that whichever female we chanced to draw, we would confine our attentions wholly to that one. You consented to my proposition and drew the prize; consequently, acting with strict honour, and as I should have expected you to have done, had I been victor, I have given you every opportunity of wooing and winning the lady, while I have brought my numberless attractive qualities to bear upon her companion, and I am proud to say, not without success, for, though certainly not so pretty as the younger female, I certainly consider her a fine woman, and by no means a contemptible conquest; while you, Fred, have not as yet advanced a single step."

"I have gained her affections," replied his brother, somewhat sullenly.

"But, Fred, what is the use of talking that nonsense—gained her affections!—and what will they profit you, if you do not gain the lady? I have had to encounter a thousand more difficulties than you, yet have surmounted them all. I don't generally like to have anything to do with married ladies. Husbands are troublesome things, especially when they have good reason to be jealous. Yet, for this once I set aside my scruples, and induced the lady to do the same with hers."

"I told you," returned his brother, in the same dogged tone he had before spoken, "you wished me to play the villain, but I cannot find it in my heart to do so. I have gained, as I before said, the young lady's affections, and I think, if I offered her marriage, she would accept it."

"Ha, ha, ha! Think she would! why, Fred, of course she would; that is undoubtedly what she is aiming at. She sees you are a raw country chap, and, therefore, makes a great show of virtue, in order to draw you in. But, to be serious, Fred, it is my duty to see you do nothing of the sort."

"I have been serious all along; it is you that seem to regard this subject as a matter for jest."

"Well, Fred," said his brother, filling his glass, and tossing off the contents, "I must confess, that when I hear a young fellow like you, scarcely nineteen years of age, coolly and deliberately talking of marriage, because you cannot win the woman you wish to gain without it——"

"I did not say that I could not gain her without marriage, but that I thought it cruel and selfish in the extreme to do so."

"'Pon my word, Fred, you ought to have been a parson with those old-fashioned ideas of your's about cruelty and selfishness; how excellently you could discourse upon the wickedness of such devil-me-care-fellows as I, and lots of others who love wine and women, and woo them both with open arms, and are troubled with none of that squeamishness which robs them both of half their charms, and makes the recollection of our devotions, instead of a matter to boast of, a constant source of worry and annoyance. In good truth, Fred, I would seriously advise you to doff the red coat, bid adieu to London, and retire for life to our ancestral hall in Worcestershire—be guided in your choice of a wife by our lady mother, and settle yourself down into a respectable married man."

"And could I marry whom I chose, I would willingly take your advice; but I am in love, and cannot separate myself from the object of my attachment."

"In love, Fred! Pshaw! you are in no such thing. I know you better, my good fellow, than you know yourself, and can safely affirm that you are no more in love than I am. You like the girl, and would be pleased to win her, only you are troubled with the most absurd scruples."

"In one word, I love her, and would gladly marry her, only ———"

"Only I cannot allow it. I should be sorry, Fred, to be obliged to insist upon you returning to the country; but I am your elder brother, and constituted likewise your guardian; and consequently I consider it my duty to prevent you running your head blindly into the noose of matrimony, and which, when you came to your senses, you would bitterly repent doing. This is an unpleasant subject, Fred—a very unpleasant subject. I'll just trouble you to push the other decanter towards me. The wine, as I before said, is truly excellent, and I am sorry that you decline to drink. I was saying, I believe, that this was an unpleasant subject, and I wish to give you one word of advice, and then dismiss it."

"It is equally unpleasant to me; and if the advice you are about to give me is the same that you have already done, I had rather be excused a repetition of it."

"As you please, Fred; only be careful how you talk about my having advised you to be a villain; as, so far from having done so, I should be very sorry indeed to see you thus commit yourself."

"Have you not told me to do my best to ruin an innocent and confiding girl, whom I am assured loves me? and if that is not being a villain, I know not what is."

"My dear Fred, I only pointed out to you the course any other man would pursue under the circumstances; at the same time, let me assure you I have not the least desire to see you adopt that course—not in the least, Fred."

"What am I to do, then?" replied the other petulantly; "you won't consent to my marrying her."

"Marriage, my dear boy, is entirely out of the question. Either gain the girl without, or (perhaps which would suit you best, though, by Jove, it wouldn't me) forget her altogether."

"Forget her! It is utterly impossible. Besides, she loves me, and, having won her affections, it would be dishonourable to forsake her now."

"Well, Fred, I have placed two courses of action before you; you are at liberty to follow the one you like best; whichever that may be, is to myself a matter of equal indifference. Only remember, Fred, that I shall keep a strict watch upon your conduct. It is exceedingly painful for me to be obliged to do so; but I deem it a matter of imperative necessity, otherwise I would not trouble myself about it. You know, Fred, that I have never interfered with your private affairs, but have left you entirely to your own guidance. You will not attempt to gainsay that."

"Oh, dear, no; you would, without interruption, have allowed me to run headlong into all sorts of vice, had I been so disposed; indeed, have you not introduced me to scenes, I should, of myself, never have visited."

"You say perfectly right, Fred; I have endeavoured to show you a little of life, and familiarize you with the means of making it pass agreeably and merrily."

"More properly speaking, with the means of shortening it."

"Well, we will not dispute about terms. 'Let us live while we live,' is, you know, our family motto, and I have endeavoured to reduce it to practice in my own person, and so far have succeeded to admiration; have experienced all the joys, and none of the cares of life. 'What have we with care to do?

Sons of toil, 'twas made for you."

And once more filling his glass, he emptied it at a draught; and then, drawing forth his gold repeater, exclaimed,

"Dear me, Fred, I had no idea that it was so late; I have an engagement for the evening at the Marchioness of Lansdown's; if you have no better way of passing your time, perhaps you will accompany me."

"I shall not go out to-night," returned the other.

"I am afraid, Fred, you will find it uncommonly dull sitting here by yourself; the wine is certainly a good companion, only you don't seem to appreciate its good qualities."

"I want no companion," replied his brother, testily; "I prefer being alone."

" That being the case, Fred, I will leave you; at the same time I can't help thinking you will find it more dull than you imagine, and would fain persuade you to join me. The marchioness has two very charming daughters, and such a handsome fellow as you, will be sure to find favour in their eyes. Come, Fred, don't be so devilishly obstinate; I half promised them I would bring you."

" I have told you that I prefer being alone, therefore don't bother me any more about the marchioness or her daughters. I care not for any of them."

" I certainly had no idea, Fred, that you could show such a cursed bad spirit; for myself, I consider it a mark of excessive low breeding, to be out of humour; therefore, wishing you all the benefit that can possible result from such a deuced ill-temper as you have this night manifested, I will at once take my leave, and seek for more agreeable companions in the saloon of the marchioness."

Saying which, he walked to the door, having reached which, he turned round for an instant, politely waved his hand, exclaiming at the same time, " *au revoir*," and then made his exit. His brother took not the slightest notice of this parting salute, but resumed the same attitude he had assumed previous to the commencement of this conversation.

---

## CHAPTER XIII.

THE two young officers whose conversation we listened to in the foregoing chapter, were the only children of the Lady Elizabeth Maitland, a high-born, haughty dame. When young, she had strongly resembled her sons, and even now that her charms were somewhat matured, there yet remained traces of great beauty on her countenance; but her proud, commanding manners, and the unfeeling nature she assumed towards any whom she regarded as inferiors, greatly neutralized the effect of her personal attractions. She was herself an only child, the daughter of an earl, and consequently a lady in her own right; but beauty and high birth were almost the only attractions she possessed. Her mind was narrow and uncultivated, for being naturally of a violent and ungovernable temper, her preceptors had no influence over her, and she was allowed to learn or not, as she thought proper; and having had the misfortune to lose her mother in her infancy, and her father being a weak, indulgent man, over whom she speedily contrived to possess almost unlimited control, she grew to womanhood, unloved, nay, even disliked by every one, but her foolishly indulgent parent.

The Earl of Vilroy, though ranking high among his fellow men, and his peerage being one of the oldest in England, yet was by no means a rich man. When, on the death of his father, he came into possession of the family estates, he found them much impoverished, and which his own expensive style of living by no means tended to decrease; and knowing that at his decease they would necessarily revert to a very distant member of the family, whom he neither liked or respected, his greatest desire was to benefit as much as he could by them during his own life; and, consequently, acting up to this selfish wish, he scattered with a lavish hand the choicest pleasures and luxuries around his path. For his daughter, he deemed her beauty sufficient to procure her a rich husband, and farther he never dreamed of inquiring.

Accustomed from her earliest infancy to regard wealth and rank as the *ne plus ultra* of existence, the Lady Elizabeth would have been equally as willing as her father to accept the proposals of the first wealthy man that offered; but, unfortunately for her, her proud and haughty bearing destroyed the effect her great beauty would otherwise have made upon the hearts of the rich aristocracy with whom she mingled, and the proud beauty, as she was constantly termed, was left entirely unsought; while the winning smiles and soft, gentle tones of other females, less favoured in personal charms, but far more attractive in the amiable disposition and sweeter beauties of the mind, which surpasseth a thousand times the most lovely form or face, won the hearts of their companions; and the Lady Elizabeth, notwithstanding her boasted beauty, was left to spend her days in " single blessedness," which neither met the views of her father or herself.

The earl's redeeming quality was his affection for his daughter; and having so firmly depended upon seeing her settled in life previous to his own demise, he had neglected making the slightest provision for her. And when she had reached her thirtieth year,

THE MARRIAGE OF MAITLAND AND LADY ELIZABETH.

[As seen as the preliminaries were arranged, he led her a willing bride to the altar of St. George's, Hanover-square, and a goodly number of his former friends assembled to witness the ceremony.]

and well nigh earned the appellation of the old maid, he found it a little too late in life to set about what he should have begun years ago—namely, denying himself some of those luxuries he so selfishly indulged in, in order to provide in a suitable manner for his only child. He had certainly deemed that beauty, such as she possessed, must be of itself a passport to every heart; and that far from having no offer of marriage to decline or accept, that she would be absolutely overwhelmed with suitors, and the only difficulty she would have to encounter would be which to choose; therefore his mortification and disappointment at this untoward state of things was very severe. He had accustomed his daughter to the gratification of the most expensive taste and pursuit—never once taught her to practise self-denial; but constantly surrounded her with at least the semblance of wealth. And now (for he was an old man, having married late in life) in a few short years she must necessarily be left totally unprovided for.

Deeply affected at this unpromising state of affairs, the Earl of Vilroy was yet as equally perplexed how to avoid them. At this critical juncture, a young man named Maitland held the humble situation of clerk to the earl's attorney, and had thus opportunities afforded him of occasionally seeing the Lady Elizabeth, with whom he had speedily become passionately enamoured, though without the most distant hope of ever obtaining her hand; they had never, indeed, exchanged a word; but, upon one occasion, when she had called with her father at the attorney's office, young Maitland had been allowed the honour of assisting her ladyship to alight, for which service he had not received even a bow in return. His fellow clerks had, indeed, often laughed at his mad passion, as they called it, and jeered at the impossibility of his ever gaining so much as a smile from his lady-love. Yet the young man bore it all very patiently, and as year after year passed on, and she still remained single, began to hope almost against hope that he might, at some distant period, succeed in winning the object of his secret adoration. This, as it appeared, absurd hope of young Maitland's, was a never failing source of merriment and jest to the clerks who were daily engaged in the same office as himself, and they would frequently ask him when the wedding was coming off, and if he intended to be married at St. George's, or anticipated a flight to Gretna Green; to which he would invariably reply, that he fully intended to proceed to Hanover-square in all pomp and state; which speech was immediately received with loud shouts of laughter.

Nothing daunted by the mirth of his companions, young Maitland steadily pursued his career, and had actually deposited in the bank a by no means paltry sum, when the unexpected death of a relative in the prime of life, and just on the point of marriage, placed Mr. Maitland in the possession, as rightful heir, of an ample estate in Worcestershire.

This was a most unlooked-for occurrence, as his cousin, as we have said, was in the prime of life, and in the enjoyment of health that gave promise of old age; and had he but lived a few years longer, would, in all probability, have left a family, and thus excluded Maitland from the estates, which, indeed, he never entertained an expectation of enjoying; yet, now, this, to him fortunate occurrence, was hailed with the greatest pleasure, and he resolved to lose no time in suing for the hand of the fair Elizabeth.

His old companions, who crowded round him to wish him joy and happiness on this sudden accession to wealth, still smiled at the hope he had so long fondly cherished, and now nourished with the certainty of its speedy realization; yet Maitland bid them prepare to witness the solemnization of his nuptials in St. George's church; and when they shook their heads, and bade him prepare for disappointment, as they were assured the proud old earl would never consent to his marriage with his only daughter, he laughed outright, and told them he now felt certain of the speedy accomplishment of his long cherished, but at one time almost preposterous hopes.

And yet, though Maitland had determined on success, it was with a very fluttering heart that he proceeded to the town residence of his lordship; and having knocked at the door, sent in a card, desiring an audience with the great man, which was granted, and he managed, though in somewhat faltering accents, to acquaint him with his bold, but ardent, wishes regarding his daughter, laying before his lordship, at the same time, a plain statement of his circumstances, and his munificent desires regarding settlements, and so forth.

Prepared as young Maitland was to receive the earl's consent to the union, yet he was absolutely astonished to find his proposals so cordially and graciously received, on condition that they met with his daughter's consent, of which he gave him every reason to hope he would find no difficulty in gaining.

In less than a week from this interview, Maitland was received by the earl as his future son, and he who, a short time previously, was considered beneath the proud beauty's slightest acknowledgment, had now lavished on him her most bewitching smiles, and which he had no rival competitor to share with him.

And, as soon as the preliminaries were arranged, he led her, a willing bride, to the altar of St. George's, Hanover-square, and a goodly number of his former friends assembled to witness the ceremony.

Not long after he became a husband, young Maitland discovered that his choice was an unfortunate one; his high-born haughty lady, whom he had for so many years regarded with a species of adoration, proved herself utterly unworthy of the disinterested affection he had so lavishly bestowed upon her. The marriage was in every respect, for him, an unhappy one. Accustomed to rule, and taking advantage of his love, which at first induced him to implicitly obey her slightest wish, she at length contrived to exercise over him, as she had previously done over her father, the most absolute control, so much so that he became an object of pity even to his own servants; and there is little doubt that her unkind treatment, preying upon a mind peculiarly sensitive and alive to the unfeeling conduct of one to whom he was so tenderly attached, was the primary cause of his premature decease. He lived but twelve years after his unpropitious nuptials, leaving behind him two sons; the eldest, a fine promising boy of eleven years, and the youngest, an infant in arms.

To the Lady Elizabeth Maitland devolved the education of these tender charges, and it would have been scarcely possible to have found a more unfit person. She had early instilled into her eldest son her own proud and haughty spirit, and taught him to value wealth and rank above all things else. He naturally partook of her ideas on almost every subject, though, in temper and manners, mild and pleasing as his father; indeed, had he been properly educated, he would undoubtedly have proved an amiable and deserving character. As it was, he early made pleasure his entire study—in that much resembling the earl, his grandfather, who had long since departed this world. There was also about him a capability of deceit in no common degree; he could seem, in fact, the very reverse of what he was, if it answered any purpose to do so. With all this, he was selfish to a degree; and when he came of age, and took possession of his estates, he regarded the claims of his younger brother, which his mother repeatedly urged upon his notice, with a very jealous eye, and was by no means inclined to make any settlement on him; for, though his income was liberal, his own pleasures and enjoyments engaged it all.

The younger son, on the contrary, was without any provision, for Lady Elizabeth, equally as selfish as her eldest son, considered that her jointure, though ample, was by no means more than sufficed to maintain her in a manner suitable to her rank; and, as the youth grew to manhood, it was exceedingly galling to his proud spirit (for that he inherited from his mother) to find himself regarded as a sort of supernumerary, and to be allowed only a trifle of pocket-money, while his brother was living and spending money like a prince. Frequently, indeed, had he entreated of his mother to place him in some situation (and he cared not what, so as it was not absolutely menial) that he might at least have the satisfaction of feeling independent. But no; he was her son, and could not, therefore, be allowed to disgrace the family by engaging in any useful and honourable employment; he was, therefore, kept at home with his mother, who resided constantly at Annesley Hall, on her son's estate, in Worcestershire, who had long been a captain in the —— th Hussars. Not caring to purchase a higher commission, and being a soldier in nothing but name, the fascination of the dress gratifying his pride, his being in the army afforded him ample excuse for spending the greater part of his time in London, where, among the officers of his regiment, he met, to use his own words, with many choice spirits, who helped to make old time jog on at a pleasant and rapid trot. Frederick, the younger son, was thus made bitterly to rue the comparatively slight circumstance, though, to him, fraught with sad consequences, of coming into the world some few years later than his more favoured brother. In person, we have noticed him as being remarkably handsome, and in disposition naturally amiable and agreeable; but, through constantly brooding over his conceived wrongs, he had become of a sullen temper, which (though in every other respect a far more worthy character than his brother) caused him to be much less liked or admired by casual acquaintances. His mother, too, was far more proud of, and thought much higher of her eldest son, and frequently held him up as a pattern of excellence to Frederick, that he would do well to copy.

Shortly before we introduced them to the reader, Captain William Maitland had paid a transitory visit to Worcestershire, and, during his stay, his mother again strongly urged the claim his brother had to his consideration, inasmuch as she greatly feared that if he were not provided for in some way, he would disgrace the rank of his parent by seeking employment in a capacity wholly beneath the respectability of his family.

After a great deal of discussion, and still greater hesitation as to what had better be done with him, or for him, the captain proposed to his mother to purchase an ensign's commission for him in the regiment to which he was himself attached, and promising, on that consideration, to allow him a yearly income, sufficient to maintain him in the army with credit to themselves.

Seeing no better course of action, the lady mother resolved to adopt the proposition of her son, thankful to get Frederick off her hands, and knowing that in London he would be constantly under the eye of his brother, whom she earnestly besought to take the greatest heed that he committed no act that would in any manner compromise the dignity of the family. This arrangement was made and completed without the person who might naturally be supposed the most interested party, being even once consulted on the matter, and not till the commission was presented to him, did Frederick become aware what course of life he was required to follow. Heartily sick of the dependent life he had so long led, and glad to avail himself of anything that promised a change, with a willing mind Frederick accompanied his brother to town, where all things pleased, for life itself was new. Yet, having lived in such seclusion, he was not altogether delighted with the gay scenes to which his brother introduced him, and so far from desiring to follow the vicious course his brother pursued, it acted, on the contrary, as a beacon to warn him where shoals and quicksands lay concealed beneath a smooth and apparently safe surface.

Drink, especially, he shunned, from having seen his brother frequently in a state of helpless intoxication; not that Frederick Maitland lacked the good taste to enjoy occasionally the social cheer, where the generous sparkling wine added to the hilarity of the evening's enjoyments; on the contrary, he loved much to join with the officers of his regiment in so rational a way of spending the evening; and possessing a rich, mellow voice, and a great love for sweet sounds—himself, and one or two others of the same cast, would frequently beguile the time with song and harmony. So far all went well; his brother had certainly determined on breaking down the barrier Frederick had reared up to protect himself from falling into the follies and sins of one who, as his senior in years and experience, should have shielded him from the temptations he wantonly led him into; but at present he had not succeeded.

His brother was cast in a different mould to himself, and well for him that he was; there are not many young men by nature so viciously inclined as William Maitland. Frederick was happy in his new situation, and much beloved by his companions; and could he have steeled his heart against the tender passion, he would have continued happy, and thankful for the change that had taken place in his fortune, and which he undoubtedly regarded as a lucky occurrence; but, alas! he unfortunately—most unfortunately became deeply in love with (we are sure the reader has guessed whom) Miss Ellis, and which resulted in the conversation between him and his brother, we have already transcribed, and from which it will be gathered, he regarded her with an honourable attachment—an attachment that shrunk from the cruel and unfeeling suggestions of his brother to gain her if possible without marriage, or forget her altogether.

After the captain had gaily taken his leave, Frederick sat for hours in deep musing over the fire; he loved, and it was the first time he had ever regarded one woman more favourably than another. He had ever been an admirer of the sex, but now he really loved, and knew not what to do; he saw not the slightest hope of ever being in a situation to enable him to marry the choice his heart had made; he was entirely dependent on his brother's bounty, and felt assured that if he so far committed himself as to marry the poor milliner, though rich in everything but this world's goods, he would be utterly cast off by his brother, and thus left without the means of supporting either himself or her he so fondly loved. Under these circumstances, his conscience whispered that he would be only acting honourable and kind towards Miss Ellis, if he immediately made her acquainted with his inability ever to make her his wife, and then resolve to forget her—at all events, never see her more. This he knew was the only course he could with honour pursue, but he could not resolve so to act. Once or twice the thought crossed his mind that his brother's disipated life might become the means of his premature death, and then—but no, he would not voluntarily pursue such a train of thoughts, though the ideas conjured up were fraught with bliss; but he resolutely bade them depart, and blushed even at the want of feeling they betrayed.

"And yet," he murmured half aloud, "had I only the means of gratifying my ardent love, by marrying a girl I feel in every respect worthy of myself, I would covet no man's wealth; he"—apparently alluding to his brother, "might revel on, and I never so much as give a thought that the inheritance might be one day mine. But to be allowed no will or desire of my own, to act only as he thinks proper; and, with all his sophistry, he would make me, if possible, contemptible even in my own eyes."

Yet, though Frederick Maitland reasoned so well and accurately, he could not, or rather would not, give up the love of Mary Ellis. No, he would still visit her the same, and hope for some fortunate event to turn up in his favour. False, delusive hope! alas, into what a labyrinth does it lead its votaries, and whither indeed may it not carry Frederick Maitland! Better, a thousand times better had he have renounced a passion that could not be honourably entertained; for while he continued by his attentions to excite the hopes of her he loved, that they might ultimately end in marriage, he was acting towards her with cruelty and deception. No matter what his motive might be, nothing could justify his conduct in this respect; in fact, it arose chiefly from selfishness; he could not bear to deny himself the gratification he felt in enjoying her society, or to crush the desire that he might at some future time be able to seek her for his bride. Yes, it aróse from selfishness; and when is man not selfish in his affection and regard to woman? Seldom, if ever. No; to woman alone exclusively belongs that self-denying, enduring affection, which prefers the welfare of him she loves, to her own; who is content to suffer any anguish or sorrow, if it will tend to the accomplishment of her most ardent wishes, the happiness of him her soul worships; and, though forsaken and forgotten, yet

> " The heart if she truly loves never forgets,
>   But as truly loves on to the close;
> As the sun-flower turns on his god when he sets,
>   The same look which he turned when he rose."

---

## CHAPTER XIV.

MR. ELLIS has been in London nearly a week, and himself and sister are still engaged in affectionate attendance on their beloved parent, whose end was now fast approaching; indeed, it was wonderful that exhausted nature had held on for so long a time.

Poor Mary, to her brother's deep sorrow, was still obliged, almost unremittingly, to ply her needle, in order to procure for her mother the few comforts her situation so imperatively demanded. Thus, body and mind fully employed, she had no time to comply with her lover's earnest request to write to him, had she even the inclination to do so, which is, at least, doubtful. Her heart was filled with bitter regret at having acted with deception towards her now dying mother, who, constantly praising her for her love and duty, affected her to tears of self-reproach. Oh! what would she not have given to live over again the last few months; for, alas!—

> " Her fatal flame was nursed in sorrow, silence, shame ;
>   A passion without hope or pleasure, in her soul's darkness buried deep."

And yet how fondly and truthfully had she clung to it; but now she felt the dream was o'er, and, oh! how sad the awakening—how desolate and dreary seemed the world deprived of that one bright vision. Oh! if men did but know the depths of a woman's love—the devotedness with which she sacrifices all things else upon the altar she has reared in her breast, as sacred to his image; and the utter desolation of her heart, when conscious that love must be no longer cherished—we say, did but men know this, surely, surely, they would hesitate ere, to gratify a passing passion, they exposed the young and helpless to this utter abandonment of sorrow. Many, very many, have sunk to an early tomb, and been duly registered as victims to that fell disease, consumption ; when, if we could trace their disorder to its real source, we should most undoubtedly have found that it arose from some ill-fated passion, nourished, perchance, too long to be eradicated, even by the unworthiness of the object ; and, like a fading flower, they have drooped slowly and sadly, day by day, its sweet-scented leaves falling one by one, till all on earth is over, and death, frequently gladly welcomed by the sufferer, closes the farewell scene, and the curtain is dropped for ever. Oh! that the knowledge of this might act as a warning to others ; it is no exaggerated or overwrought statement, but a plain, simple fact.

We were saying Mary Ellis felt that her bright dream of love was over, though she hoped better things of Frederick. Yet his brother's conduct towards her friend, Mrs. Herbert, and to which she had been long, perhaps, wilfully blind, occasioned her many doubts regarding his own intentions towards herself. True, he had never breathed a word that could call a blush upon her cheek, had ever treated her with marked respect, and his vows of love had ever been paid with courteous admiration ; but—and, oh! what agony of mind it cost her—she had now finally resolved never to see him more ; she would not even write to him. No ; better, she deemed, had he regard her as capricious (that, indeed, might be the means of healing the wound his bosom might, perchance, receive), than, by affording him the means of seeing or writing to her, expose herself to the temptation of his renewed addresses. She knew her own weakness—for, oh! how fondly she loved—and, consequently, determined to shield it from temptation. Wise resolve!—brave determination! Yes! Frederick, that young girl has shown herself to be more firm in purpose—more determined to act with integrity—than yourself!

In the midst of thoughts and resolves such as we have noticed, Mary Ellis had occasion to leave the room on some errand for her dying parent. On the stairs she encountered Mrs. Herbert, who placed a letter in her hands, saying,—

"My dear Miss Ellis, this letter has been here some time ; but I did not like to bring it up to you, thinking it might be from ——"

"It is doubtless from Frederick," replied Mary, as she received it from her, with a quivering lip and trembling hand ; and tearing open the envelope, she allowed a bank note to drop unheeded at her feet, while she perused the following lines :—

"A friend whom you have never seen, but who has frequently heard you extolled as possessing almost every virtue that can adorn and elevate your sex, requests your acceptance of the enclosed note, which will shortly be renewed ; therefore fear not to apply it in liquidation of expenses illness must necessarily have incurred, and, at least, while your mother requires your attendance, refrain from the fatiguing employment in which your days are usually spent."

The handwriting was evidently a feigned one, and Mary Ellis doubted not for an instant that it came from her lover ; and picking up the note, with a sorrowful expression of countenance, she said,—

"It is kind of him thus to think of me ; but, oh, Frederick! I may not receive your gift. I could not feel comfortable to do so, even if I intended still to encourage your addresses. As it is, of course, it would be dishonourable so to do ;" and, as the thought flashed across her mind of his brother's munificent gifts to Mrs. Herbert, her usually pale cheek matched the rose in its colour.

"Surely," said Mrs. Herbert, regarding her stedfastly, "you do not mean to abandon Fred, who is, I am convinced, tenderly attached to you. Indeed, William tells me ——"

"Do not mention his brother's name to me," replied Mary ; "he has my utmost abhorrence ; and if I am to judge of Frederick's desire regarding me by the manner his brother has behaved to you, then I may, indeed, be truly thankful for the determination I have come to, never to see him more."

"Oh, surely, Miss Ellis, you will not act so unkindly towards poor Fred, who has never given you any just cause of offence ; and if you persist in doing as you say, it will, I am certain, break his heart."

Mary smiled faintly as she answered,—

"Men's hearts, Mrs. Herbert, are not so easily broken ; they are, indeed, made of sterner stuff than you appear to imagine ; at the same time I will do Frederick the justice of allowing that I think it will at first somewhat affect him. But the knowledge of this does not for an instant cause me to waver in my purpose ; for it will not, cannot make him even one half as wretched as it has done, and still will do me ; and this gift," she continued, gazing upon the note she held in her hand, "though I am willing to believe meant in all kindness, yet must be returned to him. I shall not, indeed, feel comfortable till I have done so. I will, therefore, enclose it in an envelope, and send it to him at once."

"It will, without doubt, greatly hurt his feelings," replied Mrs. Herbert; "but what does he say in the note?"

Mary instantly offered it for her perusal; she received it, and commenced reading; but had scarcely read the first line, when surprise strongly manifested itself on her countenance, and hastily finishing the perusal, she exclaimed,—

"Why, my dear Miss Ellis, whatever could have induced you to suppose that this letter came from Fred, when it expressly intimates that the writer has never seen you?"

"That is very easily explained," replied Mary. "Frederick has employed some person to write for him."

"It may, indeed, be as you say," returned the other, with apparent reluctance.

"It may be!" replied Mary; "without doubt, it most certainly is. I am very sorry that Frederick should thus endeavour to force the money upon me, which I cannot, nay, more, will not, receive."

"He will, no doubt," replied the other, in a half musing tone, "attribute your refusal to pride."

"And he will do right," returned Mary, with dignity; "it does arouse my pride; but it is the pride which belongs to a woman, and which she cannot wave without detracting from the purity and excellence of her character."

There was something in the words, and the tone in which they were uttered, that touched a chord in the heart of the hearer, and which instantly responded to the touch, for Mrs. Herbert turned aside her head to hide a tear that had forced itself to her eyes; but she replied not, and Mary, unheeded, left the room.

It may not here be entirely out of place to say a few words concerning Mrs. Herbert, who, with all her faults, was kind and affectionate to Mary Ellis, who had so few friends that she readily awarded her a place in her affections.

Mrs. Herbert, then, was young, and pretty withal, but of a most unfortunately weak and vacillating character, which the want of education had left to manifest itself in all its deformity. An extravagant love of dress was perhaps her greatest foible. She had early been married to an industrious and deserving young man, whose employment taking him constantly from home, she was left entirely mistress of her own actions. Being of a pleasant and agreeable disposition, it is by no means surprising that when Mary Ellis was forced, by her altered circumstances, to become an inmate of the same house, that an intimacy should have sprung up between them, nor that Mrs. Ellis should have encouraged an acquaintance that afforded her daughter a little cheerful society, when the welcome sabbath dawned a day of rest from the fatiguing labours of the other six.

And it was during a walk in one of the parks on a warm summer's evening that they encountered the two officers, who were afterwards doomed to play so prominent a part in the history of their lives.

From the conversation that took place between the brothers, we have seen, that though both gave the preference to the modest, unobtrusive beauty of Mary Ellis, yet they each agreed to confine their attentions to one; and Frederick, with a declaration of an honourable attachment, succeeded, though not without great difficulty, in winning the love of Mary.

His brother unfortunately found but an easy victim in her friend, whose weak mind could not resist the fascinations of the handsome officer, who, skilled in a woman's heart, had vowed that, were she unmarried, he would have sought her for his bride, and necessity alone compelled him to seek her on other terms.

After the conversation we have just related between Miss Ellis and Mrs. Herbert, Mary returned to her mother's room, who, in a weak voice, exclaimed,—

"Mary, my love, how long you have been absent!"

"Forgive me, dear mother," she replied, hastening to her; "how do you feel now?"

"Well, my love, quite well, with the exception of this weakness. I am entirely free from pain, and yet I feel a coldness creeping over me, which I think, Mary, dear, must be the chill of death; but where is your brother? I have been for a long while alone."

"I am here, dear mother," replied Mr. Ellis, "and have been all the morning; and Mary has only left the room for a few minutes. Your memory, I fear, fails you."

"I fear it does, my son," returned his parent; "but both of you remain by my side, and I think I can sleep."

Mary and her brother instantly placed themselves on either side of the bed.

"I think she sleeps," said Mary, after a silence of some minutes, bending over her.

She did sleep; but it was that sleep which knows no waking.

When convinced that all was over, and her mother torn from her for ever, poor Mary gave way to the most heart-rending anguish. Mr. Ellis, though almost equally affected, yet strove with Christian fortitude to subdue his own sorrow, and, if possible, administer consolation to his almost heart-broken sister.

Mary, we have before said, possessed a firm mind, and was not insensible to her brother's affectionate words of comfort, who tenderly pointed out the wickedness of indulging in such inordinate sorrow for one whom it would be selfish indeed to wish back again to earth.

"Let us, my dear sister," said Mr. Ellis, "rather rejoice that she is for ever removed far beyond the reach of sin and grief; we, dear Mary, have still to wrestle with the cares and temptations of this busy world, and we know not what of anguish or trial there may yet be in store for us; perchance, there is much for us to encounter, both of mental and bodily suffering; but, oh!"—and his voice increased in animation—"our dear mother is at rest for ever. And, if the bright above can look down on those they loved below, depend upon it, she will often look upon us both; and it would be a pleasurable satisfaction to her to know that we resigned her without a murmur."

Thus did the good curate seek to abate the distress and tears of his sister, nor did he so strive in vain. Mary called all her fortitude to assist her to sustain the loss of her parent, at least, unrepiningly; and the varied duties which the poor are obliged to perform themselves, lacking the means wherewith to delegate them to an hireling, forbade her sitting down to indulge in her grief, but called all her energies into action, and this certainly removed much of the bitterness of her sorrow.

We have frequently heard the poor designated as unfeeling, because they so speedily, after the death of a near relative, resume the active business of their lives, to all appearance with the same energy and good spirit they had previously maintained; but, oh! this most assuredly is no proof of want of feeling—rather the reverse; it is seldom their activity is required solely on their own account; there is most frequently direful necessity for them to exercise it on behalf of others, and their casting aside all feelings that would prompt to an indulgence of their anguish, and induce them to sit down and bemoan their lot, is the strongest proof they can possibly give of possessing a tender and feeling heart; and many such are found to beat under the humblest habiliments, and the meanest clad of England's children.

After Mary Ellis had regained her composure, and arranged with her brother concerning the last sad duties which remained to be paid to their departed parent, she stole into an adjoining room, and enclosing the note (of which she had made no mention to her brother) in an envelope, she sealed and addressed it to Frederick Maitland, steadfastly resolving to receive no gift from him.

In the meantime Mr. Ellis wrote to his friends at Sackville, acquainting them with his loss, and likewise of his intention to return to the country immediately after he had seen the remains of his revered parent consigned to their last resting-place.

It was a pretty spot they had chosen in one of the cemeteries in the environs of London—a spot where, of a summer's eve, it would be sweet to sit and think of the departed, to call back to memory the wise counsels and tender advice that had fallen from her lips, while yet a pilgrim here. And, oh! how sweetly preferable to the crowded church-yards, where the long, rank grass grows between the mouldering tomb-stones, that speak so loudly of decay; where, far from having any desire to remain, we are only too glad to depart, and leave the dead to slumber on alone; but, how differently our feelings are acted on, when we are surrounded by all that speaks of life and gladness; when the soft perfume of nature's fairest flowers fills the air with a grateful incense; and we rest on the grave of one we loved, while the soft blossoms growing around remind us of a renewed existence, where not a single leaf decays, but all is brightness and immortality. Oh! then, indeed, we feel that it is good to be there, and we cease to regard the departed as the inhabitant of the narrow tomb, but raise our thoughts and hopes far beyond this sublunary sphere; and, wrapt in pure and holy contemplation, wing our flight even to those realms of bliss, and view the one we mourn, there enshrined in fadeless beauty.

EMILY'S ENCOUNTER IN HER MORNING'S WALK.

[Emily had just time to see and mark the stranger with tolerable accuracy, when her uncle was warmly accosted by Squire Elgood and his son, who, with guns thrown across their shoulders, were starting on a shooting excursion.]

The morning after the funeral, Mr. Ellis and his sister sat over the breakfast-table discoursing with tearful eyes upon the future.

" To-morrow, I shall be obliged to leave you, my dear Mary," said Mr. Ellis, " and it is with an unaccountable presentiment of sorrow that I do so. I wish, indeed, I could have persuaded you to accompany me."

" My dearest brother," returned Mary, " if you knew what charms your proposal offers to me, what a strong desire my heart feels to accept of it, you would attribute my sted-fast refusal to no wish to remain in this dull and gloomy town."

" I would not, my sister, judge harshly of you on any subject, but more particularly on this, as I feel assured that you have no friend or acquaintance here; and, when I am gone, you will indeed be left alone; and it is this that makes me urge my request so per-severingly, that we should for the future have but one home. My income, I know, is small; but neither of us desire aught beyond the necessaries of life, and that, my dear Mary, in your skilful hands, it will surely provide."

" Dear, dear George," she said, rising and throwing her arms round his neck, " I cannot, indeed I cannot accept of your generous proposal. Your income, small as it is, can be barely sufficient for your own wants; were it otherwise, I should not hesitate an instant to comply with your tender request; but, now, I have not only the ability, but the means afforded me of earning an honest livelihood, the doing which will give me far greater happiness than intruding upon your poor pittance. Let us, therefore, part cheer-fully, and, for the present, resign the gratification of living together. If, dear George, you are fortunate enough to meet with promotion, and your income be sufficient to maintain us both, without giving me cause to feel that I am depriving you of necessaries in order to provide for myself, then I shall gladly avail myself of your generosity; unless," she added, smiling, " you may, by that time, be thinking of marriage."

" There is, I think, but little, very little fear of that, Mary," said her brother; " at all events, I have no such thought at present."

" Then," replied Mary, " we may fully hope, at some future period, to spend the remainder of our lives together, for I am resolved myself never to marry."

" You will, probably, alter your determination some day, dear Mary," returned her bro-ther, " as I have no doubt but that it arises chiefly from not having seen the man that you could love."

Poor Mary, with blushing cheeks, hastily changed the subject of conversation; she was conscious of acting with deception towards that affectionate brother; and surely, self-reproach is one of the most painful stings we can carry in our bosom; and, though now resolved to give up an affection that could not be honourably encouraged, yet she felt, with bitter remorse, that it was utterly impossible to repair the error she had unfortu-nately fallen into. And her mother had died heaping blessings on her head, and praising her for the excellence and openness of her character! And, oh! it was torture to her bosom to know, to feel that it was undeserved.

Early the ensuing morning, Mr. Ellis bade an affectionate adieu to his sister, and took his departure for Sackville, anxious once more to be among his parishioners, who so truly loved him, and prized his worth.

Mary had yielded to the wishes of Mrs. Herbert, and consented still to occupy the same apartments she had done during her mother's life.

" But, remember, Mrs. Herbert," she said, when speaking with her on this subject, " I will never consent to see or hear from Frederick or his brother; it is perfectly use-less for me to encourage an affection for one, who, in a worldly point of view, is placed so far above me, that it is idle to suppose for an instant his family would consent to receive me as his wife; and, without their full and free consent, he would never gain mine, were it possible that he sued for it on his bended knees."

" Fear not, my dear Miss Ellis," replied her friend, " that I will ever ask you to see Frederick any more, though I do most firmly believe his affection for you was both honourable and sincere; yet, believe me, when I say that I most bitterly repent of the past, and desire to imitate your example, by determining, that let it cost me what it may, to entirely break off the correspondence that now exists between myself and William. I have already written to him to that effect, and we will for the future endeavour to console and comfort each other. We have both erred; but, oh, I a thousand times more deeply, more irretrievably than you. What is past cannot possibly be altered; but for the future we will act differently."

"You have," said Mary, warmly, "lightened my bosom of half its care by this avowal. I feel that I can now depend upon you as a sincere friend, and most truly I want one."

---

## CHAPTER XV.

IT was a clear frosty morning at Sackville, for the rich smiling autumn had now given place to stern old winter, and the sun appeared in the heavens like a large ball of fire; the ice-bound earth re-echoed the tread of the pedestrian, who stamped his feet on the ground as he walked, and whose breath came curling forth into the clear cold air, acting on the atmosphere like steam. It was a morning on which no one would ever even dream of looking cross; but, under the bracing influence of the weather, all wore a smiling countenance, and warmly complimented each other on the beauty of the day.

Yet there were tears in the soft hazel eyes of Emily Stanhope, as she arranged her dress for walking, for her uncle had just received news of the death of Mrs. Ellis; and, according to her promise, she was preparing to meet Mordaunt, and acquaint him with what had happened since they last met.

As she descended to the hall, her uncle kindly inquired whither she was going.

"The morning is so very fine," replied Emily, "that I thought of taking a short walk before dinner."

"That is just my own intention," returned her uncle; "so, if perfectly agreeable, I will accompany you."

This was the first time Emily would rather have declined her uncle's offer, but not, on any consideration, would she have allowed him to know it; therefore, apparently with much pleasure, she availed herself of his company; and, arm-in-arm, they pursued their way, Emily chatting agreeably to her aged relative as they went.

Emily had no choice as to which road they should take, and Mr. Stanhope almost mechanically turned toward the high street. They had not proceeded many paces down it, when Emily perceived a young man, an entire stranger, who stood leaning carelessly against a projecting wall that turned round by the road that led towards Mrs. Harley's residence. There was nothing whatever in the dress or appearance of the stranger to call forth particular observation; and Emily would probably have passed him with scarcely any notice had he been anywhere but just on the spot of ground he occupied; but she could not help regarding it as somewhat strange that he should be so close to the place where she had appointed to meet Mr. Mordaunt, and consequently looked at him more closely than she would otherwise have done. He was rather above the middle stature, slight made, but muscular in frame; he looked full thirty years of age, but it was probable he had not numbered so many summers; his cheeks were sunken and hollow; wrinkles, apparently caused by deep and harassing care, sat upon his otherwise youthful brow; his blue eyes were lighted up with a glassy brightness, and a burning, hectic flush sat on either cheek, making the rest of his face still whiter by the contrast. His dress was perfectly neat, and betokened extreme cleanliness, yet he was altogether meanly clad.

Emily had just time to see and mark this, with tolerable accuracy, when her uncle was warmly accosted by Squire Elgood and his son, who, with guns thrown across their shoulders, were starting on a shooting excursion.

"And how are you, my dear sir?" replied Mr. Stanley to the kind greetings of the squire.

"Quite hearty," returned the other; "lovely weather, ain't it? Hope we shall meet with capital sport; just going to call for Mr. Harley; he promised to join us, and this is really a brilliant morning."

"So brilliant that it is a pity for us to detain you," said Emily; "though I cannot but think it is rather cruel sport."

"Not a bit of it," returned the squire. "You know, Miss Stanhope, that birds, as well as beasts, were ordained to be food for man."

"Most certainly," replied Emily. "And when man kills them purely because he desires them for food, it cannot possibly be cruel; but it is very different when man destroys solely for the pleasure of the—sport, I believe is the word; though what sport there can be in witnessing the dying agonies of the most beautiful creatures, which, equally with ourselves, are of God's creation I cannot conceive."

Young Elgood had dropped his gun in rather an unsportsmanlike manner, and the colour in his cheek had greatly deepened while Emily thus condemned his favourite sport; and, had it not been for the presence of his father, he would most assuredly have declared his intention of abandoning shooting at once and for ever; as it was, he felt in a particularly awkward and uncomfortable position, and would, for the nonce, very gladly have been anywhere but in the presence of the object he so devoutly worshipped.

"We cannot expect you, my dear Miss Stanhope," returned the squire, by way of retort, "to speak in favour of what our good curate Mr. Ellis so strongly condemns; he has taught you to dislike shooting, and we well know he ever finds you an apt pupil."

It was now Emily's turn to blush and look confused, but she replied with spirit,—

"It is perfectly strange, then, according to your argument, that John still practises the sport, for I believe he is at least equally as apt a scholar as myself."

"Well done, girl," replied her uncle. "Come, John," he continued, smiling, "you ought positively to state how it is that, in defiance of Mr. Ellis's known dislike to shooting, you still continue to enjoy the diversion."

John, in reply, muttered something about having been for years accustomed to practise it, he found it rather difficult to abandon it all at once, especially as his father was constantly urging him to join in the sport; and was about adding something to the effect that he intended for the future to shun it altogether; but he was interrupted by Mr. Stanhope, who, in reply to the last part of his speech, exclaimed,—

"What you have said, my dear John, is perfectly correct. It is difficult, very difficult to eradicate early impressions and feelings, and, consequently, I cannot feel surprised that, in spite of our good curate's well-known aversion to shooting, when pursued as a sport, that you should still continue to find amusement and pleasure in it; but my Emily here, being of the gentler sex, and, moreover, having been early taught to regard it as cruel, naturally feels an aversion to it. But, come, gentlemen," he added, "I fear we have already detained you; so, wishing you every enjoyment that the bracing air and exercise can possibly afford, we will bid you good morning, and pursue our walk."

And a pleasant and cheerful walk Emily and her uncle took, peeping in occasionally at the neat cottages of the peasants, inquiring after the comfort and happiness of the inmates, assuring themselves that the sick and aged were well cared for, and wanted nothing that pecuniary aid could furnish; and everywhere were they greeted with kind smiles and contented faces.

The peasant, with his implements of toil thrown across his shoulder, stopped short in his lively whistle, and, raising his straw hat, bade them a cheerful good morning, as he passed them on his way home to dinner.

After they had walked some distance, Emily and Mr. Stanhope returned towards the mansion by the same route they had taken at the commencement of their walk, and arriving at the corner of the road which led to Mrs. Harley's residence, great was Emily's surprise to see the young man she had remarked when they passed the spot an hour or two before. Yes, there he stood in exactly the same position, apparently not having moved a limb—his eye gazing intently upon each person that passed, as though he were looking in vain for some person. Yet he appeared far from wearied with disappointment, but kept his station in the same fixed attitude, as though still hoping to meet the person whom he wished to see, and perfectly unmindful of the curious gaze the villagers cast upon him.

As they passed, Emily made no remark to her uncle, but wondered greatly in her own mind as to whom the stranger could be in search of—for, in search of some one she felt he must be, or why occupy that one particular spot for so long a time, and on such a cold morning, and he so poorly defended against its inclemency?

It seemed of late that she was to have food for her imagination; for here was another stranger, and, to all appearance, another mystery to fathom, and which she inwardly determined to do her best to unravel.

Having been disappointed in her hope of meeting Mr. Mordaunt this day, Emily on the following morning set out for the appointed rendezvous. It was just such a morning as the last, clear and frosty; and, with an elastic step, she pursued her way, musing, as she walked, on the circumstances that induced her to seek this interview with Mr. Mordaunt, and never, for a moment, doubting she should see him at the place he had himself indicated.

Thus engaged in thought, she advanced down the high street, casting, as she passed, a glance towards the apartments occupied by Mr. Mordaunt, at Doctor Harding's residence. There was no one at the window, and Emily, half unconsciously, hastened her steps, thinking he was probably beforehand with her, and being possessed of a somewhat feverish desire to get the meeting over as soon as possible.

Arriving at the spot where we have mentioned the road turned sharp off to the right, she was somewhat startled at observing the same young man in exactly the same position he had taken up on the previous day, and occupying likewise the very same spot. She cast a searching look upon him as she passed, which he returned with a listless glance; and Emily shortly gained the place where she had last seen Mr. Mordaunt; but no sign of him could she now perceive. Thinking he would speedily arrive, she extended her walk a short distance further, but returned to the spot with the same ill success. In vain she waited; an hour drew its slow length along, but brought with it no trace of him she expected to meet. Vexed at being thus disappointed, after his repeated assurance that he would not fail to be on the spot every morning, and thus give her an opportunity of seeing him whenever she might have aught to impart, Emily, at length, turned to walk home, when, to her surprise, she saw the stranger advancing towards her. As they drew near, she observed he scanned her with a curious eye; and when they met, he stopped abruptly, and without one word of apology for the intrusion, said, in a tone of inquiry,—

"You expected to meet some person this morning?"

"I can scarcely conceive what right an entire stranger has to put such a question," replied Emily, with an air of offended dignity.

"Pardon me," replied the other; "I have for so long a period been separated from society, that I have almost forgotten its usages. I have lived, I still live," he continued, in an emphatic tone, and his eye sparkled with a strange and unearthly fire, " for the accomplishment of one great object; that attained, I care not how soon I lay down this weary head; and everything that tends to that one sole object of my life is pursued by me with an avidity, a joy, that never palls or grows weary; on the contrary, it lightens up my whole frame with ardour, it gives me strength to overcome all obstacles, and, at length, I shall succeed—I know, I feel I shall!"

It was in a lonely spot where Emily and the stranger met, and believing herself to be in the company of a maniac, she shrank as far as possible from his side, and hastened her steps towards the high street; but, stretching forth his hand, he placed it upon her arm, as if to detain her, while he said,—

"Stop, young lady, one moment. I solemnly declare, I mean nothing whatever disrespectful towards yourself; I merely wish to ascertain whether it was Mr. Mordaunt whom you expected to meet this morning? Ah!" he exclaimed, seeing that Emily started at his words; "I am right in my conjectures; that man can have no secrets from me—I am certain to fathom them. I know every feeling of his heart, as soon, ay, almost sooner, than he knows them himself. I am his evil genius, constantly dogging his footsteps—recalling, by my presence, the memory of his evil deeds, which rack his guilty conscience with the most dreadful remorse; and, though my image is truly hateful to him, he cannot rid himself of me, or he would have done it long ago—ay, long ago!"

"Release me this moment," said Emily, who possessed great spirit, and, being more than ever convinced that she was in the company of a madman, strongly felt the necessity of exercising it; she likewise remembered to have read somewhere—probably years ago, and which had long since been forgotten, but now, as is frequently the case, at the moment the knowledge might be of service to her, came back vividly to her memory, as though she had read or heard it but yesterday that the appearance of utter fearlessness completely disarmed a maniac of the desire to injure; while, on the other hand, a show of timidity emboldened them to harm. Acting, therefore, upon this, Emily, with an effort, disengaged herself from the stranger, and turning on him a look of extreme anger, said, in a loud, bold tone,—

"When my uncle is acquainted with your conduct towards myself, he will undoubtedly cause you bitterly to repent it."

"If I have offended you, young lady," returned the other, in a mild tone, " I am sure I humbly beg your pardon; my indignation was not roused against you, but him whom you came here this morning purposely to meet."

"And whom do you suppose, then, I came here to meet?" replied Emily.

"I do not suppose, but know, that it was no other than Mr. Mordaunt."

"Have it so, if you please," returned Emily; "but remember, in case you should find yourself wrong in your conjecture, that you did not gain this information from me—it is merely your own surmise."

"And is it possible that I am mistaken? If so, indeed, I may well ask your pardon; but I feared that you received him as a favoured suitor."

"You need not entertain such a thought for an instant," replied Emily, and a blush, she knew not why, crept to her cheek.

"Had it been otherwise," returned the other, "I should have conceived it my duty to acquaint you with circumstances that would have forced you to shun him."

"It being utterly different from what you appear, most unwarrantably, to have conceived, you will, I trust, no longer force your company upon me, but suffer me to proceed unmolested."

"Certainly," returned the stranger; "and I trust, young lady, to your goodness to pardon this intrusion; nothing would have induced me to be guilty of it, but the fear I entertained that you expected a private meeting with Mr. Mordaunt, by seeing you waiting for so long a time on the spot which I believe I am credibly informed has for some weeks been his daily resort, at the very hour, too, you were there."

"There is no occasion to say anything farther on this subject," replied Emily; and, with a dignified air, she passed the stranger; and, with a steady, and by no means rapid pace, resumed her walk.

She met with no other interruption, and, with a fluttering and thankful heart, once more regained her uncle's residence, and, entering her boudoir, she threw herself on the couch, and gave loose to her imagination. The strange adventure which had befallen her was of course the subject of her thoughts; and yet, the more she thought upon it, the more involved in mystery did it appear. She could not for an instant doubt the insanity of the strange young man, who had so rudely accosted her; but still it was clearly evident that he was acquainted with Mr. Mordaunt, and was waiting about in the expectation of seeing him; and yet, if he wished an interview, why did he not seek it at his residence? This was a question which, of course, with all her ingenuity, Emily could not solve. She could only conjecture that Mr. Mordaunt was as anxious to avoid the stranger, as the other was to obtain an interview with him; and this, most probably prevented Mr. Mordaunt meeting her that morning; as, otherwise, he would undoubtedly have kept the appointment.

As she pondered upon all that had occurred during the conversation of the morning, Emily remembered now how very rational the young man had occasionally expressed himself; still there was nothing in this irreconcilable to his supposed insanity, for how often were persons mad on one subject only, being in all other respects perfectly sane; and thus it appeared to be with the stranger.

He had evidently imbibed some strong prejudice against Mr. Mordaunt; in his conversation, had even stigmatised him as being guilty of crime. And, oh! might there not be something of truth gleaming through the blight of intellect that had fallen upon him. She shuddered at the thought, but still could not cast it entirely from her bosom.

There was much in her ideas in favour of such a supposition, for if he was in truth a maniac, and annoyed Mr. Mordaunt, he would be justified in causing him to be placed under proper control.

However, be that as it might, she herself determined to avoid the spot where she had encountered the stranger, and trust to accident for affording her an opportunity of speaking to Mr. Mordaunt.

Having arrived at this resolution, Emily likewise determined to make no mention to her uncle and aunt of the adventure of the morning, which, though some would deem absolutely alarming, yet was far from displeasing to Emily Stanhope, who had for years sighed in vain for adventure.

The day glided slowly away; and, in the evening, found Emily seated at the casement of her boudoir, gazing intently upon the moon, which shed a soft and silvery light on all around; the trees were leafless, and consequently offered no interruption to the view;

and the frost, which lay thick upon the grass, glistened like diamonds in the pale moon-beams.

Emily was engaged, we have said, in watching the moon, as she apparently skimmed her way through the heavens; now gliding gently under a thick black cloud, and thus causing a temporary oblivion of the beautiful landscape; and anon emerging suddenly forth, and bathing all things in a flood of liquid light; and then darting under a cloud of fleecy whiteness, through which its beams were still visible, but shone with a more subdued and gentle light, and which,—

> " Like the veil by beauty worn,
>    Hides but to heighten, shades but to adorn.''

Thus employed, Emily was unconscious of the dark figure of a man, who stole cautiously along the side of the house, carefully keeping in the shade, and, taking advantage of the darkness, afforded by the moon being concealed by a cloud, came close under her window, and remained for a few minutes perfectly motionless, saving that he cast a hurried and anxious glance around him.

Suddenly the moon shone forth with renewed splendour, rivalling even the noon-tide beauty of the sun; and Emily, with astonishment, perceived the figure standing immediately beneath her casement, and half gave utterance to a cry of surprise; but the person, whoever it was, raised his hat and motioned her to be silent, likewise that she should open her window.

She instantly obeyed, and, leaning forward, discovered the person to be no other than Mr. Mordaunt. He immediately threw something into the room, and once more raising his hat, turned away, and was speedily out of sight; but no sooner had he disappeared than another figure issued from a corner of the building, and darted quickly, but noiselessly, in the same direction.

Emily clasped her hands, and the life blood seemed to curdle in her veins, as she recognized, in this second person, the maniac she had encountered in the morning.

---

## CHAPTER XVI.

THE weather was in every respect propitious for travelling, as Mr. Ellis, with a mixture of joy and sorrow, entered the vehicle that was to convey him back to the country.

He was unquestionably rejoiced at the prospect of returning to the friends he had left, and whom he was assured would most gladly welcome him once more amongst them. Yes, one and all, he felt convinced, would vie with each other in the warmth of their greeting; and yet, though truly beloved by all, he was conscious that his heart singled out one or two objects in a far more tender light than any others; and of these (although, perhaps, he was not himself thoroughly aware of it) Emily Stanhope held precedence.

He knew well enough that it would afford him infinite pleasure again to behold her; but then he deemed he regarded her in the tender light of a sister; and it is, indeed, an easy matter to deceive ourselves on the subject of love.

Unless we very carefully analyze and sift our feelings (which, indeed, it behoves us to do), we may well mistake the regard we nourish in our bosom for some amiable and deserving object, to be only that of a brotherly or sisterly affection (as the case may be), till some untoward event opens our eyes to the real state of our feelings; perchance, at the very moment the cherished love is forced to be crushed for ever.

Regard for ourselves, then, imperatively demands that we should be cautious how we deceive ourselves on so important a matter, and rather smother the passion in the bud, than wilfully blind our eyes to the consequences, till it is too late. Many have nourished in their bosoms the passion that was doomed to destroy them, when a little self-denial and sacrifice of feeling, practised when the wily god first took possession of their hearts, might have spared them the sorrowful harvest of tears and anguish they were afterwards forced to reap.

We are now addressing ourselves more peculiarly to our own sex, although speaking of Mr. Ellis has given rise to the remarks, as it is woman that most frequently suffers from an unrequited or misplaced attachment. For, if a man meets with a disappointment in love, which is not very often the case, it rarely affects him beyond the passing hour. Men, indeed, as Byron says,—" have many resources; we, but one—to love again;" and, probably, meet with renewed bitterness.

Thus far, Mr. Ellis rejoiced at the thought of returning to his flock; and, could he have persuaded his sister to accompany him, he would have hailed his departure with unmixed delight.   And, though he respected the motive which induced her to decline his offer, and appreciated the excellence and dignity of her character, which induced her to prefer gaining a livelihood by her own exertions, to becoming—as she deemed it—a burden upon his paltry income, yet it was with a sad and heavy heart that he thus left her, entirely unprotected, and exposed to the temptations and trials of life, wholly unsupported by the presence of even one tender relative who might have aided her by counsel and encouragement.   And, as he thought upon this, Mr. Ellis was, for the first time, inclined to murmur at the poor pittance he received in reward for his services; for, had it been anything like equivalent to their value, Mary had acknowledged that she would readily have consented to his kind proposition.

And oh! how earnestly Mr. Ellis wished he could have seen his sister united to one worthy of her, and possessed of the means of keeping her in comfort.   Not riches did this excellent brother covet, even for his dear sister; but it grieved him bitterly to know that she was obliged to toil early and late to earn her daily bread.   How gladly would he have borne himself a double amount of privation and care, if by that means he could have provided for his cherished sister!   Even now, he inwardly resolved to abate certain little comforts he had heretofore indulged in (most persons would call them necessaries), that he might be enabled to transmit a trifle more to his sister.   Still, the utmost he could do in this way was so inadequate, that it grieved and vexed him to feel that he could do no more.

Mr. Ellis, of course, returned, as he had pledged himself, to his aged friend, Mr. Stanhope, by coach; and, as it would be but a few miles out of the direct route, he resolved to call at the village where he had left his unfortunate fellow-traveller, in order to inquire after his welfare.

He doubted not that ere this he had been removed to his own residence; still he was anxious to learn what prospect the surgeon who had first attended him entertained of his speedy recovery.

He remembered with pain the mission he had performed for the invalid, and found in his supposed wife one whom he had known when she was fair as lovely; but now, alas, sunk in vice, from which he had in vain sought to extricate her.

On many accounts the curate's musings were of an extremely painful character, as he approached the village where he had but a short time previously parted with his less fortunate companion; on reaching which, he descended from the coach, and bent his steps towards the honest farmer's, who had so hospitably received the wounded stranger.

Arriving at the farm, he was instantly recognised, and before he had time to make any inquiries, " the gude wife," guessing the cause of his visit, exclaimed in a voluble tone,—

" How d'ye do, sir? pray walk in; you have called to see your friend, who, I am sorry to say, is still desperate bad; so much so, that we persuaded him to allow us to send for his wife—not that we were unwilling, or grudged the little we could do for him; but no one can attend upon an invalid, or nurse him so carefully as his own kith and kin; and so, you see, sir, we gained his consent, and sent off for his wife; and sadly she takes on, poor thing, though I think, upon the whole, he has a trifle improved since her arrival."

Thus ran on the good woman, without once pausing, or giving Mr. Ellis an opportunity of reply, till she was fairly out of breath; when, taking advantage of the temporary cessation, he answered, in a tone of suspense—

" What! am I to understand that you sent to London for Mrs. ——."

" Yes, we sent, as I before said, for Mrs. Tierney, but ——"

" Stop a moment, my good woman; was it a lady of the name of Tierney you fetched to attend upon the gentleman whom I caused to be brought here?" interrupted the curate, somewhat perplexed.

" Yes, certainly.  Mrs. Tierney, his wife."

" And she arrived here, from London?"

" La, no, sir," replied the other, interrupting with surprise, in her turn, " she came from the country, where Mr. Tierney left her, when he started on his unfortunate journey to ——"

" That will do, my good woman," returned the curate, more and more perplexed, yet

THE WHITE SLAVES OF ENGLAND.

[On each side of a long table, on which were scattered the necessary articles used in their work, were seated a number of young girls, whose pale and, in many cases, carewern countenances, told but too plainly the life of toil and privation they underwent.]

not willing for his loquacious companion to perceive it. " I understand you; will you now have the goodness to inform Mr. Tierney of my being here, and say, that if perfectly agreeable, I shall be glad to be admitted to an interview."

" I will gladly do your bidding at once; and never fear but he will be delighted to see you, and his wife too, poor soul; for she has expressed herself so gratefully toward you, for the kindness you manifested to her husband, when he met with such a sad accident, that I am sure she will be pleased to see, and thank you personally. Indeed, she has frequently said as much."

"Very well; then, I will remain here, while you announce me in the sick chamber," said Mr. Ellis, seating himself in one of the wooden chairs, while the good-hearted, but talkative hostess proceeded to do his bidding.

She speedily returned with a message from Mr. Tierney to the effect that he would be most happy to see Mr. Ellis at once; and a few moments sufficed to introduce the curate to the room of the sick man. He was greatly astonished at the alteration a few weeks had made in his fellow traveller, who had sustained more serious injury than was at first imagined, and whose cheeks were now pale and sunken, and his whole countenance betokened his having endured much bodily suffering. The chamber was small, and somewhat confined; but how carefully, and even tastefully, was everything arranged! Nothing was wanting that could tend to cheer or solace the invalid, who was doomed for many weary days and nights to toss backwards and forwards in languishing and pain.

Seated by the side of the bed, was an elegant and exceedingly lady-like female, who, rising on Mr. Ellis's entrance, in a sweet, soft voice bade him welcome.

" We are, indeed, my dear sir, indebted to you in an amount that we can never hope to pay; but I have earnestly desired to see you, that I might at least have the gratification of expressing to you my deep sense of your kindness, in so tenderly and effectually extending a brotherly care to an entire stranger; at a time, too, when almost every feeling would have naturally prompted you to hasten your own journey, regardless of the pain or misfortune of others."

There was something so graceful and unaffected in this address of the lady, that Mr. Ellis was instantly prepossessed in her favour; but still more so as he noted her pallid and anxious countenance, which gave abundant evidence of watching and want of rest.

She was remarkably tall, and what would undoubtedly be styled an exceedingly fine woman. Her face likewise wore a very pleasing expression, and amiability sat upon every feature, notwithstanding they were somewhat wanting in regularity—indeed, it more than atoned for it.

And when the curate turned from that lady to speak to him who called her wife, and recalled the memory of his visit to the fair, but frail beauty who had evidently weaned his affections from her who possessed the right to claim them, and, to judge from the gentle, tender tones of her voice, and the soft repose of her countenance, was well worthy of them, he cast an almost reproachful glance on the invalid, who, appearing to understand it, endeavoured to withdraw the other's attention from the apparent subject of his thoughts, by speaking of the injuries he had received.

"Although I purposely called at this village to inquire after your health, yet I did not at all expect to see you; on the contrary, I fully believed ere this you would have been removed to your own residence," replied the curate, in answer to an observation of the wounded man.

" When we parted," he returned, " I myself likewise entertained a hope that the injuries I had received were but trifling; but, unfortunately, I am still unable to rise from this bed, and, in truth, know not when I shall. Confound all railways!" he added after a moment's pause, and with more energy than he had before spoken. " I was prosecuting a journey that I had every reason to desire speedily to accomplish; but this confounded accident has totally upset all my plans, and laid me up here at a time when, of all others, I ought to be most actively engaged."

"You must endeavour patiently to submit to the will of Providence," replied the curate, mildly. And as he spoke, the lady cast upon him a look of grateful pleasure, as though she fully felt and coincided in the wisdom of his remark.

" It is devilish hard to submit patiently to pain of body and anxiety of mind."

" And yet," replied his wife, in a kind and conciliating voice, " you might, my dear Henry, have much more to bear of mental suffering; were I and our dear children, for instance, dependent on your exertions, it would almost be excusable for you to repine at the sad misfortune which has been the means of confining you for so long a time to your couch." And then, turning towards Mr. Ellis, and perceiving, apparently for the first time, his mourning habiliments, she said, " And you, sir, though having, fortunately, escaped the accident which has proved so serious to my husband, yet have suffered from domestic calamity. I trust that the time you so kindly devoted to him, did not prevent you being in time to see your parent."

" By no means," returned the curate; " I am happy to say that I was with my mother some days previous to her demise ; but had it been otherwise, I could never have regretted lending my aid towards mitigating the sufferings of another."

" Such feelings," returned the lady, " do honour to your nature ; would, indeed, more were possessed of them."

" I am willing to believe," said Mr. Ellis, " that few, if any, under similar circumstances, would have acted differently."

After a short time spent in general conversation, Mr. Tierney, addressing his wife, expressed a wish that she would retire for a short time, and seek repose.

" I know," he continued, " that you must greatly need refreshment ; indeed, I have been selfishly inconsiderate in allowing you to attend so closely and constantly in my sick room."

" I do not, my dear Henry, feel at all fatigued," she replied, " and cannot bear the thoughts of leaving you, even for a short time."

" Mr. Ellis," urged her husband, " is almost as tender a nurse as yourself ; therefore, you may safely leave me under his care, and I am certain he will be obliging enough to relieve you for a short time."

The curate returned, that it would afford him great pleasure so to do, and the lady at length yielded to their united persuasion.

No sooner had the door closed behind Mrs. Tierney, than the invalid, turning an anxious look upon Mr. Ellis, inquired if he had fulfilled his request.

" I have," replied the curate, with a serious air ; " and confess that I was deeply grieved, in discovering in her, whom you led me to suppose was your wife ———"

" Stop," interrupted the other ; " I know all you would say ; you would, I am certain, upbraid me."

" I could scarcely do otherwise ; especially after having seen and conversed with her who should possess, and undoubtedly appears deserving of, your entire affection."

" I acknowledge it ; and when I experience her trusting love and kindness, my conscience whispers how sadly and bitterly I have requited her."

" Knowing and feeling assured of that," replied Mr. Ellis, firmly, " you should at once and for ever cast from your mind the ill-fated passion, which is alike discreditable to yourself and your amiable lady."

" Alas!" returned the other, " you know not what you counsel, or the difficulty of casting off the bonds which enchain me. I cannot do it—alas! I cannot do it. Love—all powerful love, which has oftentimes enslaved conquerors, and made monarchs bend before its ruthless sway, has taken entire possession of my heart, to the exclusion of all other thoughts and feelings ; 'tis that alone makes me so bitterly deplore being confined to this dull chamber, as it separates me from the being I so fondly love. You have seen her, and must, I am certain, acknowledge her worthy of my regard. She is, indeed," he added warmly, " the fairest and loveliest of her sex."

" I cannot," returned Mr. Ellis, " regard any woman as worthy, or look upon her as lovely, if she lacks the brightest and fairest ornament of her sex—virtue, which is so graceful and elegant an adornment, that it sheds a lustre on even the plainest, and makes her a thousand times more desirable and lovely than all the meretricious beauty of her who is wanting in this sweet charm."

The curate spoke warmly, nay, almost severely ; and, when he ceased, there was a pause of a few moments, which was at length broken by the invalid, who replied,—

" I cannot seek to justify my own conduct ; but let me do ———"

" Name her not," interrupted Mr. Ellis ; " I knew her when she was virtuous, and then, indeed, regarded her as lovely."

" If you were at all acquainted with the circumstances which induced her to listen to my solicitations, you will believe that she is not naturally inclined to evil, and likewise allow that there is much to be urged in extenuation of her conduct."

" I allow it all," replied the curate ; " but it induces me to lay the guilt more strongly at your door than I should otherwise have done; there is, indeed, no palliating circumstance on your side. United to one you acknowledge amiable and deserving, that should have been a shield against which all temptations would have harmlessly rebounded. I speak plainly," added Mr. Ellis, "though far from wishing to give offence."

"I know I have acted wrong," replied the other; "but love breaks down all barriers, rises triumphant over all obstacles, and leaves the breast of which it has taken possession no choice in its actions; it compels him recklessly to pursue the object of his passion, even at the expense of honour and integrity."

"I cannot by any means agree with you," replied Mr. Ellis; "true, sincere love should refine and purify our feelings, and confirm us yet more firmly in the path of virtue."

"With you such might be the case," returned the other; "but we are very differently constituted; though, had I been fortunate enough to have met with the object of my love before I became a husband, I should have yielded my entire soul to her, and deemed myself truly blessed in my capability of doing it; but, alas! it was otherwise ordered."

"Stop a moment," interrupted the curate, "and boast not of what you would have been; rather consider what you are. When you married Mrs. Tierney, you doubtless deemed yourself in love, and would in all probability have discarded the thought of inconstancy with anger from your heart. Am I not right in my conjecture?"

After a short pause, the invalid, who seemed affected by the other's earnestness, replied,—

"You have guessed rightly. My Amelia is truly amiable and deserving; and when I became her husband, I was what is termed in love; that is to say, I judged most highly of her worth, and deemed she would make a truly excellent wife. I knew she was not what is considered handsome; but, then, she was possessed of so many mental qualifications, that I deemed they would make ample amends for the absence of personal charms."

"And were you deceived?" said the curate, hastily.

"No; I have not that to urge in excuse for my sin. She has been all, and more than my fondest expectation pictured her; and well indeed hath she performed the duties of wife and mother."

"And yet," replied Mr. Ellis, in a tone of reproach, "you could not resist the fascinations of one whose beauty is perhaps her only charm."

"But, oh! what a sweet and precious charm it is! I have, I must acknowledge, ever been a worshipper of beauty's star. Yet never did her bright influence touch my soul into its depths so far; for never before did I meet with one so divinely beautiful."

The invalid spoke these words with so much warmth and animation, that he was obliged to stop from exhaustion; and the good curate spoke not in return, being unwilling to censure, and feeling assured that if he gave utterance to aught it would only be to condemn.

After an interval of a few minutes the invalid again spoke,—

"I know," he said, glancing at the serious expression Mr. Ellis wore upon his countenance, "that you judge very harshly of me; and happiest, I am willing to believe, are those who can rein in their passions."

"All can, if they choose," replied the curate; "only some are unwilling to bear with the restraint that such a custom imposes."

"I was about to observe," returned the other, heeding not the interruption, "that though I am certain you think very harshly of my conduct, still I hope that will not prevent me laying myself under further obligation to you by performing a service that, under present circumstances, I cannot so well delegate to another."

"You may rest assured of my willingness to perform any service for you that I can with a clear conscience," said Mr. Ellis, who guessed what manner of service was required of him.

"I know not how long it may be before I am able to visit London—probably, some months—as when I am well enough to leave here, I shall, for a time, be obliged to return with Amelia to the country. Much as my desire is to be in London, I cannot insist upon going there at once and alone, without exciting her suspicions, which I should be sorry to do, on her account as well as my own."

" You have children, too, whom you will be naturally desirous to see, after so painful an absence, and an accident that might have parted you from them for ever."

" You say right. I have a noble boy, and a dear, gentle little girl, the image of her mother, and I shall indeed be pleased to look upon them again."

" Alas!" thought Mr. Ellis, " he possesses such dear and tender ties as these, which should absorb his every thought; and yet, not content with such blessings, he neglects them for one who has no right to claim even a single thought."

He had left them, too, and his loving wife, to prosecute a journey to London, on an express visit to another; and had, alas, encountered the fearful accident which now kept him a prisoner; and it was impossible to say how much longer he might not be confined to his couch. And she whom he had solemnly vowed to love and cherish, to the exclusion of all others, was in constant and unwearying attendance upon him, fondly believing his heart beat responsive to her own. The curate was roused from these thoughts by the voice of the sick man, who addressed him as follows,—

" The service I am desirous of your performing, is merely to write to her upon whom you called in London, and acquaint her with the nature of my indisposition, which will, I fear, some time longer detain me from her; but assure her that she is constantly in my thoughts, and that I shall joyfully seize the earliest opportunity that offers to visit London. You will not," he added, looking earnestly at the curate, " refuse me this slight favour, after having manifested so strong an interest in my welfare."

" I but now assured you of my willingness to perform any service that I could for you with a clear conscience. This, I am sorry to say, is one of the few things I would refuse to do for you; still, it is with great reluctance I feel myself imperatively compelled to decline interfering in this matter."

" You, then, absolutely refuse to comply with my request," returned the other, somewhat petulantly.

" I cannot," replied the curate, with a mild but serious air, " lend myself, in any way, to the encouragement or countenance of vice. I am grieved to be obliged to refuse the performance of aught that is solicited as a favour; still, my conscience will not allow me."

" Say no more," interrupted the other; " there is no occasion for any apology. I asked a favour of you that, had our situations been reversed, I would willingly have conferred; but, as your conscience will not allow you to do it, there need be no more said; only, I am sorry to have put you to the pain of being compelled to refuse the performance of a service which could have occasioned but slight inconvenience."

These words were spoken with a satirical air, which greatly pained the sensitive mind of the curate, and he considered whether it were possible he could conscientiously perform the required service. But no; the more he thought of it, the more he was confirmed in his original opinion. He had no choice but to persist in the refusal, much as it grieved him to do so.

Mr. Tierney evidently felt mortified and disappointed at the other's objection to perform the favour he had desired of him, and fully calculated upon his granting; yet, feeling that he was already much indebted to the curate, he endeavoured to conceal it from his notice.

But Mr. Ellis was too quicksighted not to perceive how deeply he had mortified the invalid by his refusal.

Consequently, under these circumstances, neither were much inclined for conversation, and an hour was passed in silence, which was at length broken by the return of Mrs. Tierney, whose presence was felt as a relief to both.

The day was too far advanced to allow Mr. Ellis to think of proceeding on his journey that evening; he therefore willingly accepted of a bed at the farm-house, having previously desired Mr. Stanhope, by letter, not to expect him till the following day.

---

## CHAPTER XVII.

WILLIAM and Frederick Maitland were seated on either side of a blazing fire, in the splendidly furnished apartment that served at once for their dining and drawing-room. The handsome features of Frederick wore a saddened expression, and he seemed plunged in deep thought, which was interrupted by the entrance of a private in their regiment who officiated as waiting-man to the brothers, and now placed a letter before the younger, who gazed upon it with a perplexed expression of countenance, turning it over and over for some moments in silence, but without any motion towards breaking the seal.

"Why the devil, Fred, don't you open the letter? You need not, I am sure, mind me. You know I never interfere in any amour you may see fit to indulge in, and your fair correspondent may have something to impart that is necessary for you to know at once; so, Fred, do not stand upon any ceremony, I beg, but peruse your billet doux immediately," said his brother, who had been contemplating him in silence.

"And how know you that this is a billet doux?" replied Frederick, and a smile played round the corners of his handsome mouth.

"That pretty little seal, and the small but elegant handwriting, vouch for the accuracy of my supposition."

"Then you are for once mistaken," replied his brother; "this little billet," holding it up by one corner, "is not a billet doux—at least, not in the sense you take it; neither do I know who or what sort of a person my fair correspondent may prove to be."

"Really, Fred, this savours very strongly of romance. You actually possess a fair incognita, who honours you with her correspondence."

"That is exactly the case; but what do you say to this?" replied the younger brother, hastily tearing open the envelope, and drawing forth a five pound note.

"The devil!" exclaimed the elder brother, with a look of astonishment; and then added, with a knowing look, "come, Fred, you won't make me believe that you have no idea where that note came from."

"On my honour," returned the other, "I can with truth affirm, I have not the slightest suspicion as to whom I am indebted for this, and sundry other notes of the same value."

"Well, Fred, then, I think the old adage holds true, 'That it is better to be born lucky than rich.' I was most decidedly born rich; but the devil a bit of luck has ever befallen me, while on you are showered its choicest gifts. I am not given to boasting, Fred—not at all; still I cannot refrain from just hinting that you have been uncommonly lucky in possessing a brother who not only has the means, but likewise the will, to promote your comfort and happiness—this is luck number one; then, again, when we agreed to try our fortune against each other, as to who should have the entire right of winning a certain pretty girl, you were the favoured party—luck number two; and now, here is a lovely woman—I say lovely, as a matter of course, (because all women are undoubtedly lovely—who ever heard of a woman being otherwise?)—I was saying then, Fred, here is a lovely woman, not only honouring you with her correspondence, but actually making that correspondence more desirable, by supplying you with the most needful of all blessings—luck, undoubtedly, number three. Ah! Fred, my boy, you are, indeed, a lucky dog; while I am a poor devil that no one thinks it worth while to notice. Every pleasure I enjoy, I am forced to purchase beforehand, and often terribly dear."

"You should deem yourself lucky," returned Frederick, while a sarcastic smile curled the corners of his mouth, "in having the means to purchase them."

"True, most true, Fred; still, in every other respect, you are a thousand times more lucky than myself; but, what says your fair incognita, unless you hold her correspondence sacred?"

"As she is entirely unknown to either of us, I see no reason for concealing from your knowledge the few lines I have just received from her. Listen, therefore, while I read them:—

"It is with feelings of sincere pleasure that I again address you. Your worth, as I before intimated, has strongly interested me in your favour. Persevere, I entreat of you, in the cultivation of those virtues, which have hitherto so highly exalted your character, and rendered you a pattern to your sex. Though many miles intervene between us, yet I contrive occasionally to hear of your welfare; and doing so always affords me the liveliest satisfaction. Hesitate not, I entreat of you, to apply towards promoting your personal comfort, the small token of sincere respect that accompanies my letters. I am rich, and in the possession of almost every earthly blessing; while you, at least of equal birth and expectations as myself, are straitened in pecuniary circumstances, and forced to receive aid from a brother, which, however willing he may be to extend it, must be exceedingly painful to such a mind as yours to receive, especially when you are thoroughly aware that his income is by no means beyond his own necessities.

"But from me you need not blush to accept a sum so small; use it, therefore, freely, resting assured that you will continue to hear from me at regular intervals.

"Some day we may, perchance, become known personally to each other. In that case, I can say with truth, that my earnest desire will be to win your friendship and esteem. Till then, regard me in the light of a sister, and sometimes think of me as such. Adieu for the present, and believe me ever, your sincere                      "FRIEND."

"Bravo," cried William Maitland (as his brother concluded the epistle), throwing himself back in his chair; "I congratulate you, Fred, upon my soul I do; you may now, indeed, consider yourself upon the high road to fortune. I quite envy you. I am sorry to entertain so bad a feeling in my breast; still, it is the plain, unvarnished fact, Fred, that I envy you. It is something out of the common, matter-of-fact proceedings of every-day life, to have a charming creature (she is charming, I am sure she is, Fred; it is breathed in every word of her letter)—to have such a delightful creature actually falling in love with you, and writing such tender, yet withal sensible epistles, and delicately hinting at a sister's affection. Ah! this comes of being handsome, Fred, which I ought to have enumerated as luck number four."

Frederick was not altogether free from vanity; and, as his brother spoke, he cast a glance at the opposite mirror, and seemed in no way displeased with the reflection it presented to his gaze; indeed, for a moment, the sadness cleared from his sunny brow, but the next, it gathered again, even more palpably than before, and he sighed as he answered to his brother's remark,—

"You may, William, consider me an object of envy; but not in that light do I regard myself. On the contrary, I am wretched, and not all the effusions of my unknown correspondent can ever produce the effect of rendering me otherwise."

"Then," returned the other, "you are the most unthankful dog I ever had to do with. It is absolutely tempting Providence to be so unmindful of its favours; but, tell me, Fred, what new whim has taken possession of your mind?"

"Whims have nothing whatever to do with my wretchedness; the sole cause of which is that I love, and was, I believe, loved in return, and I have to thank you for alienating it from me."

As he gave utterance to the last part of this sentence, the eyes of Frederick flashed angrily; but his brother answered without any show of excitement whatever, though with manifest surprise,—

"I, Fred, alienated the affection from you! I must confess, I am somewhat surprised at such an accusation, after having done all in my power to forward it."

"You may not have done so directly, but still the fact remains the same. I repeat, I have only you to thank for the utter indifference Mary Ellis has assumed towards me!"

"I should feel exceedingly obliged, Fred, by your being a little more explicit, as I am perfectly at a loss to comprehend you."

"It suits you to be so, just now; but I forget not the last conversation we had on the subject."

"If, in truth, you remember it, Fred, you must of necessity likewise remember that I urged nothing whatever against your entertaining a regard for Miss Ellis. I only stated my intention of preventing your doing what I fancied (perhaps erroneously) you seemed strongly inclined to do, make a fool of yourself by marrying a ——"

"I remember," interrupted the younger brother, "instead of what you call playing the fool, you strenuously recommended me to play the villain; you see that my memory serves me as well as yours."

"I have very frequently occasion, Fred, I am sorry to say, to advise you to be more particular in your choice of words; and, as to recommending you to pursue any line of conduct, I am quite certain I did nothing of the sort; for, as I never take advice, I make it a point never to give it; and, as to the young lady in question, I thought your affair with her was going on quite swimmingly, and am convinced it is your fault, not her's, if it is otherwise."

"Say yours, and then you will be nearer the truth," muttered Frederick.

"Really, Fred," returned his brother, "I cannot allow this—making every allowance for your disappointment, if, indeed, you have sustained one. It is wrong to implicate me in an affair with which, I can truly say, I have had nothing to do—having—so strictly honourably I have acted—even avoided speaking to Miss Ellis, when opportunity offered, fearing your jealous disposition might construe such a civility into an endeavour to win her affections.    Therefore, Fred, whatever change may have taken place in the young lady, attribute nothing to me."

"To what, then, am I to attribute the altered conduct of my dear Mary—she who used to be so gentle, tender, and kind, and confessed feeling a reciprocal affection for me?"

"Had you indeed, Fred, advanced so far?" replied his brother, with apparent interest.

"Yes; and blessed, indeed, I felt myself; the only drawback to my happiness being, that I lacked the means of enabling me to marry one whom I sincerely loved, and felt convinced was, in every respect, worthy of my tenderest regard.    Still I resolved to conceal this from her knowledge, and trust to time, or some favourable circumstance, removing the only obstacle that stood between myself and happiness."

"Well, Fred?" exclaimed the elder brother.

"Well," returned the younger, impatiently, "Mary is lost to me for ever ; my dream of happiness is past, and there is nothing left for me but wretchedness."

"Nothing left you but wretchedness!    You certainly do adopt a most strange and unaccountable way of expressing yourself.    It truly is vexatious, I grant, Fred, to lose such a charming girl as Mary, just at the moment, too, when you were on the eve of winning her ; but to say there is nothing left you but wretchedness, is talking, in my humble opinion, uncommonly like a madman."

"Don't bother me about what it is like," replied Frederick, relapsing into a sullenness that seemed a part of his nature.

"Well, but, Fred," resumed his brother, "do, there's a good fellow, just explain what it is all about.    How came you to lose the girl?"

There was something candid about the elder brother's speech, that induced Frederick at once to believe that he had spoken truth when he said that he had nothing whatever to do with the change that had taken place in Mary Ellis.    He, therefore, replied, with a show of returning good humour,—

"Have I indeed, William, done you injustice in supposing that, by representing to Mary the impossibility of my marrying without your consent, which you would never give as regarded her ——"

"Stop, stop," interrupted the elder.    "I beg at once to deny it *in toto*.    I have had no communication in any shape, either with Mary Ellis, or her friend Mrs. Herbert, since we last conversed together on this subject.    Knowing, from what I then said, that you would not think of wedding her—which, indeed, was but a silly, boyish notion—I was content, and troubled myself no farther concerning her."

"Then," replied Frederick, "I am perfectly at a loss to account for the strange and painful change that has taken place in Mary."

"I would forget her then, altogether,". said William; "in your situation, your fair and considerate incognita should engross every thought."

"Had my heart and affections been disengaged, it might have been so ; but with the lovely image of Mary constantly in remembrance, it is impossible to feel much interested in one I have never seen."

"Oh, fie, Fred, fie!    Consider, your incognita is a woman of birth and fortune, evidently desperately in love with your own sweet self; hints, too, at making herself known to you, at, I dare say, no very distant time ; and then, how deep her mortification will be, to find your heart engaged by one in every respect inferior to her."

"Inferior to her in fortune she may be; but in loveliness of person and mind, sweet Mary Ellis need yield the palm to none."

"Mary Ellis I have frequently, and very justly, acknowledged to be a most charming girl," replied his brother; "but a woman of rank and refinement, who has so far honoured you with her regard, and given you such substantial tokens of it, will expect, as a matter of course, that you will make the slight sacrifice of renouncing the poor work-woman in her favour."

"I know not, and care not, what she may expect ; but I do know that if Mary is induced to receive me once more into her favour, I will not renounce her for even the proudest and loveliest of England's peeresses."

"I can only say then, Fred, that I am very sorry your incognita should have thrown away her affections upon one who has proved himself so utterly unworthy of them ; I wish she had more wisely have chosen me for the object of her regard.    Oh, Fred, how differently I should have acted ; perhaps even now it may not be too late to induce her

CÆSAR ATTEMPTING TO ACHIEVE A DIFFICULT TASK.

[Cæsar at length succeeded in inducing the horses to quit the stables; but, at the first sniff of the keen frosty air, in spite of his remonstrances, they backed into their old comfortable quarters, with greater celerity than they had been induced to leave them.]

to shift her affections from one brother to the other ; she knows me, for she delicately hints at my income being no more than sufficient for my own wants ; which you are aware, Fred, is true enough, only my fraternal affection induces me to make it subservient likewise to yours.''

"I know well enough that I subsist upon your charity ; therefore, you need not trouble yourself to remind me of the fact. If anything could induce me to marry this correspondent, who does, indeed, as you say, appear to nourish a regard for me, it would be the thought that I should no longer be a pensioner on your bounty.''

Frederick had given utterance to these sentiments. There was a pause of a few minutes, which the elder brother at length broke, by saying, with an air of interest for the concerns of the younger,—

"Tell me, Fred, exactly, how you and Mary Ellis are at present circumstanced. I desire to know, if possible, what has given rise to a difference between you.''

"To what does that desire tend?'' said Frederick, as though disinclined to make a confidant of his brother.

"To, if possible, forward your suit with her ; first premising that I shall not consent to your marrying the girl, unless, through some fortunate occurrence, she should become possessed of property. In that case——''

"In that case,'' interrupted Frederick, "I shall of course be at liberty to follow my own inclination.''

"Exactly, Fred ; and now that we so far understand each other, tell me how you and her stand.''

"There is but little to tell,'' replied Frederick. "You are aware that Mrs. Ellis, the mother of Mary, has lately died ?''

"Yes ; but that should be the means of promoting, not retarding, your suit.''

"I have never seen Mary since, or received so much as a line or even a message from her, and all my letters are returned unopened. I have endeavoured in vain to meet her in her walks—she sedulously avoids me ; and it is all to no purpose that I have striven to obtain an interview ; so that at length I have given up the pursuit in despair.''

"Given all up in despair ! Why, Fred, I gave you credit for more courage ; a soldier, and allow yourself to be overcome by a mere ruse of the enemy ! Why, you ought positively to blush at the thought of being so easily conquered. Come, my boy, summon up your courage, and, by Jove, I venture to predict that you will come off victorious. Remember that all stratagems are justifiable in war, and—love,'' he added, after a moment's pause.

"Well, but what am I to do?'' said Frederick, in truth half ashamed at being thought to give way too soon.

"What are you to do ! rather ask what you should not do. Have recourse to stratagem, my boy. You know but little of the sex if you do not see in what quarter the wind blows.''

"I do not understand you,'' replied Frederick.

"Mary Ellis,'' resumed his brother, "has no doubt guessed the truth—that your friends would not consent to your marrying her, however desirous you might be of doing so yourself ; consequently, determined that you shall not gain her on easier terms, she has come to the resolution that you shall not have her at all.''

"I think,'' returned Frederick, "there is some truth in what you say ; and I remember that Mrs. Herbert told me that her only brother, a curate, I believe he is, came to London and stayed some weeks. Now, she may have confided to him her intimacy with me, and perhaps he advised her for the future to discourage it.''

"Nothing more likely ; but, with your handsome face and exterior, it would be absolutely a blot upon our family escutcheon to allow yourself to be outwitted by a sanctimonious parson. The red coats before the black, Fred, for ever ; ask any woman, from the queen down to the lowest of her subjects, and see if they are not, one and all, on our side. Mark me, Fred, though I am by no means possessed of an unpleasing exterior, yet all my conquests—and I may say without vanity they have not been few,—I attribute, without exception, to the irresistibility of my uniform, more than to the fascinations of my person or manners.''

"Well, then, how is it you advise me to act, as regards Mary ?''

"I never give advice, Fred, for reasons that I have already stated to you ; but I have no objection to say what I should do were I in your situation.''

THE HEIRESS OF SACKVILLE.

"That's it," replied Frederick. "Go on."

"I should, of course, profess to be animated by honourable feelings, which, aided by good looks and ardent love, with such a girl as Mary, must ensure success."

"But I know not how to see her, or else ——" and he hesitated.

"Wait for her, my boy. You know for certain that she goes to, and returns from, Madame Florenzi's once every day."

"Yes; but I have striven in vain to meet her. I think she must take a different road every day, on purpose to avoid me."

"Then take your stand, early in the evening, outside the milliner's door, and wait for her coming out."

"Ah, by Jove! that is an excellent thought, and I will most certainly profit by it," said Frederick, assuming a brighter aspect than he had worn during the conversation.

"Remember, there is not, by no manner of means, any appeal to be made to me, in the hope of inducing me to consent to your marriage; as, I warn you, it will be utterly useless."

"I shall not forget," replied his brother, relapsing for a moment into his sullen humour; and then, after a minute's thought, he added, with warmth, "Lovely, incomparable Mary! I cannot exist without you; and though Heaven knows how gladly I would wed you, were it possible, yet, if that cannot be, I have no chance but to win you without it. My heart and soul will ever be yours—only yours. For though

> "'Many lovers look to thee,
> There is but one—one Mary in the world for me!'"

The conversation was here interrupted by the entrance of the waiting-man, who proceeded to let down the thick folds of damask before the windows, and then, bringing in wax candles, spread fruit and wine on the table, stirred up the fire till it shed a bright and ruddy glow round the apartment, and seemed to bid defiance to winter's cold.

Anon the elder brother poured out two tumblers of sparkling champagne, and invited the younger to drink to the success of his enterprise; who, nothing loth, did honour to the toast by draining his glass to the dregs.

And now let us, for one instant, take a peep into a long, low workroom. A scanty fire is burning at the farther end, a narrow table occupies almost the entire length of the room, on which, at regular distances, candles are burning, and upwards of sixty young girls are seated on forms ranged round the table, plying the ever busy needle. No laugh or joke enlivens their labour; all talk is forbidden, but such as relates to the work upon which they are engaged. In the centre of this group is Mary Ellis; her taper fingers seem almost mechanically to perform their office, and the raven hair and mourning dress afford a painful contrast to the chilling whiteness of her cheek. She wears, too, a sorrowful expression on her pallid countenance, as though grief were busy at her young heart, though all unconscious of the schemes of the two brothers, who were at this precise moment engaged in planning how they could best lure her to destruction. Alas! alas! that such things should be; and yet they are of daily, we had almost said hourly occurrence.

Well may we exclaim, as we glance at the splendid apartment of the brothers, and then at the confined work-room, "Look on this picture, and on that."

Alas! Frederick, by nature generous, noble, and good, under the tuition and evil example of such a brother, we tremble for thee. Even now he has led thee to regard the ruin of an unprotected and innocent girl as a matter of necessity; but Mary, we are convinced, will never be lightly won; yet she loves, and this almost makes us tremble for her.

As regards William, the reader, we are certain, will not for an instant attribute his voluntarily offering to assist his brother, to arise from regard towards him. He was influenced merely by a desire to wean his affections from Mary Ellis, whom he had never dreamed of influencing his brother beyond a passing liking; but finding that he unfortunately regarded her too warmly to allow him to indulge in the hope that he would speedily forget her, he judged from his own experience in such matters, that the best and surest cure for love, was possession of the desired object.

Frederick he well knew to be remarkably handsome, and the letter he had read from his fair, but unknown correspondent, delighted him beyond measure. He could easily conceive a woman of rank and fortune entertaining an ardent passion for his young and prepossessing brother; and that such was the case, he considered beyond a doubt; as also, that she would ere long make herself known to him. And thus he hoped to rid himself of the expense he now incurred in maintaining him, and which the reader is already aware was done grudgingly. The silly and boyish love he nourished for Mary Ellis being the only impediment likely to arise in opposition to this desirable state of things, he judged it wise and prudent to lend his aid (should such be requisite) in inducing Mary to listen to his brother's addresses. Once won, he deemed that she would be lightly regarded, and his brother's affections be free and ready to bestow on his incognita. Moreover, he should by this means be enabled to obtain a greater influence over him than he now possessed.

---

## CHAPTER XVIII.

THE snow was falling thick and fast, the trees were glistening with icicles, that hung suspended from their leafless boughs. A cold, piercing east wind blew in sudden and unexpected squalls, driving in all directions, and forcing the traveller to draw his cloak more tightly about his form, and pull his hat further over his face.

Yet on this inclement evening (it was past five o'clock), strange to say, lights were to be seen moving to and fro in Mr. Stanhope's stables, and poor old black Cæsar was engaged in the novel task of harnessing the two sleek, lazy, well-fed horses, who seemed determined to offer every resistance in their power against the process. And Cæsar was fain to have recourse to patting, coaxing, and scolding by turns, till by dint of argument and persuasion, applied separately and together as the urgency of the case required, he at length succeeded in inducing them to quit the stable; but at the first sniff of the keen, frosty air, in spite of the remonstrances of Cæsar, they backed into their old and comfortable quarters with a far greater celerity than they had been induced to leave them, and positively declined going out that evening; in vain poor Cæsar tugged at their heads, till, notwithstanding the extremity of the cold, the perspiration fairly ran down his face with the violence of his efforts. At length, convinced that all was useless, he stood up between the two obstinate brutes, and wringing his hands in despair, exclaimed,—

" Lor a massy !—lor a massy !"

" What's the matter, Cæsar?" said a quiet gentlemanly voice, which he instantly recognised as that of his kind and considerate master.

Cæsar could only reply by pointing to the two animals, who, the sole cause of his misery, were making themselves as comfortable as the case admitted, and looking in the best humour possible, were quietly engaged in pulling hay from the rack; and poor Cæsar could only repeat,—

" Lor a massy !—lor a massy !"

" Well, but what is the matter?" again repeated Mr. Stanhope, in his usual placid voice.

" Oh, de brutes, sar; dey won't come out, sar. Lor a massy, what shall we do ?"

" They won't come out?" inquired Mr. Stanhope, somewhat startled at this unlooked-for announcement; "this is bad news, indeed Cæsar. But have they had plenty to eat —are you quite certain they are not hungry ?" gazing intently on the horses, who seemed desirous that he should give them the benefit of the doubt he appeared to entertain, touching the sufficiency of their food, by munching vigorously at the hay.

" Oh, lor a massy, no, sar, dey can't be de least bit hungry; dey been eating corn all de afternoon; it's cos it so berry cold, sar, nothing in de world else," returned the negro, who, here it may be as well to remark, was one of those faithful creatures who cling to the fortune of their master, be it good or bad. Cæsar had been brought to England, when quite a boy, by a relative of Mr. Stanhope, who, then quite a young man himself, had, on the death of that relative, which took place soon after his arrival in England, from motives of kindness, received the boy into the family, where he had ever since resided, nor ever changed, or wished to change his place. He had commenced his service as an errand boy, but had risen, by degrees, till he at length was promoted to coachman, an office he had now held for years, and which of late had been quite a nominal service, as it was, indeed, but upon very rare occasions that the carriage and horses of Mr. Stanhope were put in requisition.

" It certainly is very cold, Cæsar," replied Mr. Stanhope to the last remark of the faithful old black, " very cold; and, upon any less occasion than the present, I would not desire either the horses or you to go out; but ——"

" Oh, lor a massy, sar, I be so glad to go; neber you fear for old Cæsar. If," he continued, " we could only get 'em out, sar, I'd make 'em go de journey and back in no time."

" But you must be very careful, Cæsar, not to urge them beyond a moderate pace, a very moderate pace."

" Oh, no, sar, neber fear to trust old Cæsar, if we could only get 'em out, dats all, sar."

" If that is all, Cæsar," replied Mr. Stanhope, with his usual urbanity, " of course they must be got out."

" But dey won't come out, sar."

" Oh, but they must," returned his master firmly, yet politely.

The servant shook his woolly head (which age had turned from jet black to a silvery grey), and his face assumed an expression that seemed to say, he very much doubted the possibility of inducing the animals to quit their stable again that evening.

" I think," resumed Mr. Stanhope, in a musing tone, " it would not be amiss to give them a little more corn. You must remember, Cæsar, that they have got a long and, considering the state of the roads, an arduous journey before them, and, consequently, they ought to have a good feed before starting."

Cæsar had ever been accustomed to implicit obedience, and he proceeded quietly to do his master's bidding.

" And now," said Mr. Stanhope, " while the horses are eating, you had better go indoors and get a glass of hot brandy-and-water, and mind, Cæsar, and have it hot and strong."

The negro respectfully touched his hat, and then glancing reproachfully towards the horses, repeated once more,—

" Oh, sar, if we could but get 'em out !"

" Don't make yourself at all uneasy about that, Cæsar," replied his master; " we'll manage to get them out, never fear; but go and see to your brandy-and-water, and then, Cæsar, be sure and wrap yourself up warm. I am afraid you will have a very cold ride."

" Oh, sar, neber tink ob de journey, neber tink ob de brandy-and-water, and notink at all, if we could but only ——"

" That will do, Cæsar," interrupted his master, smiling; " when you come back, we will see what can be done."

The black, at these words, made his exit, but quickly returned, his small black eyes rolling and sparkling from the strength of his potation, and accompanied by the powdered footman, who almost rivalled him in his length of servitude, and with whom the reader is already acquainted.

By this time the horses had completed their repast, and even Mr. Stanhope was convinced that they could no longer excuse themselves from performing the required service, on the score of being hungry.

" Now, Cæsar," said Mr. Stanhope, " are you quite ready ?"

" Yes, sar, me all ready, and John, he be ready too."

" And you are both well wrapped up," replied Mr. Stanhope, glancing approvingly at the thick, warm coats which completely enveloped them.

" Yes, sir," returned John, " we are quite ready to start."

" That's well," replied their master; " and now, Cæsar, gently lead Pompey forward."

This, as the black anticipated, was much easier said than done, inasmuch as the animal in question declined moving an inch.

" Oh, lor a massey, sar ! dey won't come out. What can we do ?"

" Gently, Cæsar," replied Mr. Stanhope. " If Pompey won't do as he is bid, Hector will, I know—won't you, Hector ? (patting him.) Come now, there's a good fellow. It is, I know, a very inclement night, but—he'll go, Cæsar, I knew he would."

This last exclamation was caused by the animal, to the surprise of Cæsar, actually walking of his own accord in the direction of the stable door; and, with a little persuasion and entreaty, to his intense joy, he beheld him once more in the open air.

Having got one horse fairly outside, the other was easily induced to join him; and then Cæsar, having first prudently closed the door behind them, and thus put it entirely out of their power to return, gave vent to his joy in a loud burst of laughter, which put his face into the most grotesque contortions.

" Oh, lor a massy ! dey be got out, and dey can't go back agen till ole Cæsar choose to let 'em; dey can't play him any more tricks.   Oh, no, dey can't cheat ole Cæsar any more, not at all."

And at the thought of his own cunning, in having so quickly closed the door, he indulged in a low, chuckling laugh, displaying his white teeth, which, contrasting with the ebony of his face, had the appearance of the fairest ivory.

After some time and labour had been expended, the horses were harnessed to the heavy, lumbering old family coach, which had belonged to Mr. Stanhope's father; Cæsar had mounted to the box, and the powdered footman was duly installed into the little dickey; and, after much backing, and not a small amount of plunging and rearing of the horses, they were at length fairly started on their journey.

Mr. Stanhope returned to the house, in the hall of which a tremendous fire was burning; the logs of wood, piled half way up the broad, open chimney-place, were crackling and sparkling right merrily, and illuminating the suits of old armour with which the hall was decorated.   And, for such a peaceful, quiet country gentleman, it was strange how well he was stored with implements of warfare.   Pikes, long swords, petronels, and the like, almost innumerable, were ranged in due order against the sides of the hall, relieved, as we have observed, here and there, with suits of curious old armour; shirts of mail, breastplates for man and horse, and huge banners, tattered and nearly colourless with age, were suspended above the armour; and which showed, that though Mr. Stanhope was a remarkably peaceful man himself, he yet gloried in the exploits of his ancestors, about whom he never wearied of relating anecdotes, concerning that very identical armour, which had been worn by his forefathers on memorable occasions, touching the truth of which, he would refer you to history.   And great was his boast that the wearer of one particular suit of armour, to which he never failed to draw attention, had refused the honour of knighthood.   And the portrait of this brave soldier, who had fought in more battles than Mr. Stanhope could enumerate, was placed over the armour, in which he had done his best to discomfit the enemies of his king and country; and a very strange-looking portrait it was, of a man somewhere about middle age, clad in armour from top to toe, "and wore his vizor up," displaying a remarkably long visage, with bushy moustaches, and frowning most darkly on all around, as though he were contemplating with knit brows the enemies of his country.

But Mr. Stanhope paused not, as we have done, to view this and sundry other curiosities in that kind, that held a venerated place in his hall, and likewise in his heart; for that, it would appear, was divided into sundry small compartments, in each of which one of the many cherished objects of his memory held a place; according, of course, to the degree of veneration in which he esteemed them, so they occupied a smaller or larger division.

The good old gentleman, at present, seemed busy with other thoughts; and though he cast, as he never failed to do, an approving glance around him as he entered the hall, he yet did not linger there an instant, but proceeded immediately up the broad oak staircase —so broad, indeed, that even the large, lumbering old coach might have been driven, without the slightest inconvenience on the score of room, up the staircase that Mr. Stanhope now ascended; reaching the top of which, he turned slightly to the left, and entered the drawing-room, over the door of which, on the outside, was fixed a tremendous stag's horn, with wide spreading antlers, which had been shot and placed there as a trophy, by Mr. Stanhope's grandfather, and had never been touched by hands profane.   No; there it had remained for upwards of a century, and looking grimly down upon all who made ingress or egress to and from the apartment; while the hand that placed it there had long forgot its cunning, and, with all who then lived and moved, had crumbled silently to dust.

Mr. Stanhope, as we have said, entered the drawing-room, a large and cumbrously carved oak room, with furniture and appointments to correspond; and now, as in days of yore, a goodly company were assembled, and the old walls re-echoed, as they had done some thousands of times before, to the laugh and jest of the young and fair; and Emily, the centre of the group, and whose dark eyes glanced approvingly on all around, upon her uncle's entrance, ran to lead him to his accustomed seat.

And Emily had certainly taken unusual pains with her toilette this evening.   How exactly the tight satin dress accommodated itself to her well-proportioned bust; not a plait or wrinkle was perceptible, and yet it was made wholly without ornament of any kind, as though she more than suspected her figure required nothing to set off its natural grace.   And then her hair—when did it ever look so glossy, or hang in such long bewitching ringlets, drooping well nigh to the slender waist? And her soft hazel eyes seemed to swim in liquid brightness, and reflected in their dancing rays the brilliant lights that illuminated the apartment; while a captivating archness played round her mouth as she joined in the animating conversation that took place among the visitors.

There was the dear old lady, stiff and erect, in the warm corner, remote from any stray draught that might have presumed to intrude itself into that well-warmed and thickly carpeted room, and which corner was distinguished from all others by the appellation of "My aunt's seat." Yes; there sat the good old lady, in the same chair she had daily occupied for upwards of forty years, smiling complacently on all, but more especially on her niece.

The commonest witticism of the day, uttered by Emily, was received by the uncle and aunt with unbounded applause, and repeated to their acquaintance as specimens of her brilliant and ready wit, and now they both looked upon her with pleased delight.

"And how uncommonly well Emily looks this evening," said her truly affectionate uncle, as he took his seat opposite his aged partner.

"And in what very excellent spirits," returned the old lady.

"I am not surprised at that," replied Mr. Stanhope. "We are all, I hope, in excellent spirits," glancing round the room, which contained, as the principal guests, Squire Elgood, his lady, and daughters, and likewise his hopeful son, John; the widow Harley, accompanied by her gallant nephew, and sundry others of minor importance. Mrs. Harley replied to the speech of Mr. Stanhope,—

"Undoubtedly, my dear sir; we are all, as you say, in excellent spirits; the mere fact of being so pleasantly assembled beneath your roof, would, I am sure (at least I speak as regards my own feelings), itself be sufficient to banish all ennui; but now we are likewise met to welcome home (I think I may be allowed to use the word) our truly inestimable curate."

This, then, was the great occasion which induced Mr. Stanhope to draw from their respective stables, the much prized, though cumbrous old coach, and the fat lazy horses, and send them journeying forth with old black Cæsar and the powdered footman. And this, then, was the reason of gathering into his mansion such a goodly company. And, oh! when you crossed the hall, what a delicious perfume issued from the kitchen—what a tempting smell of venison; and if you could but have taken a peep below, just to see the vast preparations—why Mr. Stanhope must surely be intending to feast the whole village. And all this to welcome the arrival back to his parishioners, after an absence of a few weeks only, Mr. Ellis.

And then, could it be possible that Emily had taken such unusual pains with her toilet, and lingering far beyond her allotted time at the mirror, stepping backwards and forwards, and glancing first over her right shoulder, and then her left, to see that all was perfectly *comme il fait*, and smoothing down her glossy ringlets, again and again, till necessity obliged her to tear herself from the magic spot—could it be possible that all this was on the same grand account that had given rise to the festivities of the evening? This point we must leave the reader to settle as he thinks best, not doubting but he will do it as accurately as ourselves.

The entire party appeared, as the widow had ventured to assert, in the best possible spirits. Frank was gayer even than usual; and, though Mrs. Harley watched, with a somewhat jealous eye, the assiduous attentions he bestowed upon her sweet friend, as she was wont to call Emily, yet this did not, by any means, damp the exuberance of her spirits. No; she aimed this evening at making an impression on the heart of the curate; and, therefore, was not altogether displeased that Emily bestowed so many approving smiles on her nephew, for she shrewdly suspected that she rivalled her in the eyes of Mr. Ellis; and if Emily had paid unusual attention to her toilet, the widow was by no means behindhand with her. Her dress was composed of delicate satin and lace, and made in the newest and most approved style. Her head was, moreover, adorned with a very fascinating little cap, so far removed from the forehead as not to interfere with the redundancy of clustering curls that were arranged on either side of her face. The squire's lady and daughters likewise did full honour to the occasion, by wearing their best dresses, and with them their best looks.

Poor John did not feel quite so happy or in such good spirits as usual. He contemplated Frank, who possessed an envied seat by the side of Emily, who gaily chatted with him, with angry looks; and, if the truth must be told, he was jealous, absolutely jealous of him. As Emily raised her head, and merrily shook back her chesnut curls to laugh more freely at some remark of her companion, the grave and saddened expression of John's countenance for the first time caught her attention, and, astonished to see him apparently dull, when they were hourly expecting the return of his friend, she instantly crossed the room to inquire of him the cause.

"John, I have actually come to scold you," said Emily, gaily, as she seated herself by the side of the young man.

"Although sorry to have incurred your displeasure, yet I would much rather be scolded, than entirely overlooked," replied the youth, with a quickness which was astonishing for him.

"Why, John, you surely are not jealous?" returned Emily, and the old walls re-echoed her clear ringing laugh; but seeing that John coloured, and seemed confused, she checked her mirth, and said kindly, "Well, perhaps, John, I have neglected you this evening; but it has been, I assure you, far from intentional; so, think no more about it. I value your friendship truly, John, believing you to be friendly disposed towards me; and, as I am by no means overburdened with friends, I cannot afford to lose any; besides, John, Mr. Ellis entertains a high regard for you, and that alone ——" and here Emily became confused, and stopped abruptly.

The widow observed the heightened colour of the youth when Emily addressed him, and the confused manner in which she suddenly stopped, and then her cheeks appeared to have caught the reflection of John's. Mrs. Harley, we have said, observed this; but it was impossible at the distance she was from them, to hear a single word that passed. But she whispered Louisa Elgood, who happened to be seated next her, "That she fully believed that Emily would, at no very distant day, become Mrs. Elgood."

"I should be less surprised if you were," answered Louisa, carelessly, and without the slightest idea that such an event would, by any remote possibility, ever take place; merely meaning to express her firm conviction that Emily would never become the wife of her brother.

"La, my dear, how you talk!" replied the widow, affecting to blush; "as if I should ever be induced again to enter into the bonds of matrimony! I assure you, my dear, I have no such intention. A heart that has been wrung with the bitter anguish that mine has" (and here she raised her handkerchief to her eyes) "can never, believe me, love a second time; and, unless I loved, I would never marry."

"Pray do not heed that silly remark of mine," replied the good-natured Louisa, fully believing she had wounded the feelings of Mrs. Harley by recalling her lamented husband to her memory.

"Do not apologise, my dear," returned the widow; "you cannot be supposed to understand how acutely I feel any allusion to the subject of marriage, for you never knew my ever-to-be-lamented husband; had you ever been acquainted with him, I am certain you would have acknowledged him to be the most delightful creature in the world, and so distractedly fond of me, that I did not dare so much as to look at any one else."

"That must have been rather unpleasant, I should conceive," replied Louisa.

"Not at all, my dear, for he was so kind and indulgent, that I absolutely adored him; and that is one very great objection I feel against marrying again. I cannot think, my dear, that I should ever find his equal, and then it would be so mortifying, after having been possessed of so loving and tender a husband, to have one, perhaps, quite the reverse."

"It would, indeed, be a sad misfortune; and as you are very comfortable and happy as you are, I commend your resolution to keep so," replied the considerate Louisa.

"And yet men do plague and worry me so, that I am sometimes tempted to accept one merely to free myself from the importunities of the others. I should not like it to be generally known, but Frank is constantly pestering me on this very subject. And though I am invariably in the habit of assuring him that I will not listen to his suit, yet I cannot get rid of him; he actually quite lives with me, and it makes me so uncomfortable you cannot think, because mischief-making people may purposely misconstrue his motives."

"I should not make myself at all uneasy about that, as Mr. Harley being your nephew, it is but natural that he should like to visit so near a relative," said Louisa, who was entirely deceived by the plausible manners of the widow.

"Why, yes, my dear Frank is, as you observe, the nephew of my lamented husband, but the difference in our respective ages is so trifling; and, moreover, his having con-

THE CURATE'S RECEPTION ON HIS RETURN TO SACKVILLE.

[Mr. Ellis ascended with Mr. Stanhope to the room in which the guests were assembled, and kind welcomes were showered upon him by all.]

fessed a decided preference (I will not call it love) for me, does away with the slight relationship that now exists between us," replied the widow, by no means pleased at being reminded of what she was most desirous to forget.

---

## CHAPTER XIX.

Mr. Ellis passed by no means a pleasant evening with his new friends, Mr. and Mrs. Tierney. The lady, it is true, was all kindness, and endeavoured to make the time pass agreeably in the room of the invalid; but, as the reader is aware, there existed a restraint between the gentlemen which made their company irksome to each other. And though the good curate was conscious of having acted according to the dictates of his conscience, and with strict integrity, yet it was the first time it had ever been his painful duty to refuse the performance of a favour, and he felt more grieved and hurt by his own non-compliance with the other's request, than the occasion perhaps warranted.

After endeavouring to persuade the lady to retire for the night, and leave the invalid under his care, which she politely but firmly declined, Mr. Ellis took possession of the small but clean and comfortable room that had been prepared for his reception, and passed a night of undisturbed repose.

On arising in the morning, he found, to his surprise, the entire village covered several inches deep in snow, which was still falling thick and fast. This was rather vexatious, as the curate, depending upon the fineness of the weather, had taken a place for himself in a coach that went within half-a-dozen miles of Sackville, which last part of the journey he had determined to perform on foot.

As the snow gave no signs of abating, the curate, anxious to be again at home, refused the kind solicitations of Mr. and Mrs. Tierney to remain there another day, resolving to prosecute his journey at all hazards. The probability was great that he should be able, on quitting the stage, to procure a chaise or other vehicle; at all events, if that were impossible, he should have considerably lessened the distance between himself and Sackville, and would be content, if it were unavoidable, to remain in the town for one night, and in the morning he doubted not he should be easily enabled to accomplish that short distance.

Thus resolved, the curate bade a cordial farewell to his friends, receiving from the lady a pressing invitation to pay them a visit at their country seat, which Mr. Tierney seconded, though, the curate could perceive, more out of politeness than any desire to continue the acquaintance.

Mr. Ellis had much desired to speak with him again on the painful subject that had caused the slight difference between them; but the constant presence of his lady forbade any approach to it. And the curate could only hope that he might become sensible of the sin and wickedness of indulging in a connection which, if persisted in, must, Mr. Ellis was confident, result at last in wretchedness and sorrow. Nor did he judge erroneously; but we anticipate.

The heavy state of the roads, and the constant falling of the snow, which continued without intermission throughout the day, delayed very much the progress of the journey, so that it was late in the evening when Mr. Ellis, half benumbed with cold, arrived at his destination. It was a very wretched, dirty-looking public-house at which the stage stopped, and Mr. Ellis inquired of the guard if there were not a better one in the town. He was answered, as he anticipated, in the negative; so, hoping to find the accommodation better than the exterior promised, he walked into the little parlour, debating in his own mind whether it would be better to seek for a bed or a chaise. Reason spoke in favour of the former, but inclination strongly sided with the latter; so much did both urge regarding the respective propositions, that they were pretty equally balanced.

Coming out of the light, reflected on all sides by the snow, Mr. Ellis did not at first perceive that the parlour already had an occupant, who rose on his entrance, and respectfully touched his hat, but with an air as though he were well acquainted with him.

On becoming aware of this, Mr. Ellis was astonished that he should be known, never having visited that particular town before; but on observing the other more closely, his surprise changed into pleasure.

"What, John, is that you?" he said, addressing the powdered footman.

"Yes, sir," replied the man; "glad to see you back again. We have been waiting here some time."

" This is indeed kind of Mr. Stanhope," returned the curate, joyfully ; " he has sent a chaise for me, knowing the difficulty I should experience in procuring one here."

" Not a chaise, sir," replied the man ; " me and Cæsar are here with the ——"

" Surely not the carriage, John ?" said Mr. Ellis, with unfeigned surprise.

" Yes, sir, we've got the carriage, and master is most anxious to see you as soon as possible ; he desired me to present his compliments, and acquaint you that he has a few friends waiting to welcome you once more among us."

Strong as had ever been (since their first acquaintance) the friendship that existed between himself and Mr. Stanhope, yet the curate was unprepared for this convincing proof of the old gentleman's respect and regard for him, and it affected him deeply. He resolved, therefore, to cast aside a slight depression of spirits that recent events had caused to hang over him, and to greet his aged friend without a shadow on his brow.

Having thus determined, he declared his willingness to start for Sackville at once, and was accordingly escorted to the carriage by the obsequious footman.

Poor old Cæsar had resolutely maintained his place on the box, having (notwithstanding the severity of the cold) refused to vacate his seat for an instant, and now presented a rather grotesque appearance, covered entirely with snow, which enveloped him like a garment, and which had a very strange effect, contrasting so strongly with his inky countenance, as to startle any one not cognisant of his presence ; but Mr. Ellis, though prepared for the sight of the faithful creature, yet could not forbear smiling as he kindly inquired after his welfare.

" Ole Cæsar quite well, sar, and bery glad to see you back again.   And massa, oh ! he be so bery glad, and him kind lady, and Missie Emily, all be so bery glad see you.   And massa ask all de grand folk to come see you, and dey be all waiting now."

" Well, then, Cæsar, we will not keep them waiting any longer than we can possibly help," replied Mr. Ellis, throwing himself back on the soft cushions with which the carriage was amply provided.

The old spelling books (now, we are sorry to say, almost obsolete) tell us, " that the horse knows his own stable ;" but Mr. Stanhope's horses went out so very seldom, that they seemed to have but a very vague and indefinite idea as to the road in which their old and comfortable quarters lay.

This was shown by their persisting for some time in endeavouring to trot off in the very opposite direction, and when induced to take the proper route, they manifested occasionally a strong inclination to depart from it.   Indeed, it required all Cæsar's energy and care to keep them in the right road, though doubtless they were equally as anxious as himself to return to their stables.

Mr. Ellis's reflections during the ride were all of the most pleasing character ; he anticipated with joy the meeting between himself and his tried friends, and felt with sorrow how deeply he had wronged them, when, on quitting Sackville for London, the thought had occurred to him, that were he leaving it never to return, not one would grieve for his loss ; and it was indeed with almost unmixed feelings of pleasure that he contemplated the kind reception he was assured awaited him.

However humble the opinion we entertain of ourselves, none of us are displeased at being thought highly of by others ; there is something so gratifying to our self love in a tribute of respect offered in token of affection, and appreciation of our merits, that such is ever received with the liveliest satisfaction, and treasured in our memory as one of the green spots on which we can rest with joy, when dispirited and cast down by the trials and difficulties that will occasionally beset us.   But when we have been induced by untoward circumstances to regard ourselves as uncared for and neglected by our fellows, and have, perchance, under the baneful influence of such feelings, been sunk in despondency and gloom, ready to give up all in despair, oh ! at such a moment, who has not felt the sweet reviving joy of some slight token of tender love, or sincere respect, acting like balm to our wounded spirits, refreshing, and awaking into renewed life the best and purest feelings of our nature, which were almost dead within us.   Like the bright flowers, which have been scorched and parched by a long continued drought, till they were ready to perish for want of moisture, after the benign influence of a genial shower, have raised their drooping heads, and shed once more (as if in gratitude for that sweet blessing) their fragrant incense on the balmy air.

Those who have known and felt what we have above described (and few, if any, we think, have not at some period of their lives been raised by a light token of love from despondency and sorrow, to joy and gladness)—we repeat, those who have done so, will readily understand the feelings of Mr. Ellis, who, conscious of having unkindly misjudged his friends, determined on all the atonement in his power; to Emily, especially, he felt he owed compensation for the cold, nay, almost unfeeling manner in which he had parted from her, and for which he had done penance, by being very unhappy ever since.

The reader must not imagine that in the midst of the pleasant contemplations of the good curate, his sister, and her forlorn and unprotected state, were forgotten by him; such was far from the case; he deeply regretted not having been able to persuade her to share his humble fortune, and thought with sorrow on the utter loneliness she must experience now that he, her only relative, was far removed from her. This was the dark cloud that shadowed his otherwise bright dream for the future; but now that he was returning to friends who were so anxious to receive him, he deemed it but justice to appear before them without a trace of sorrow or anxiety on his countenance.

The roads being very heavy from the snow, which still kept falling, the ride, otherwise but a short one, was prolonged much beyond the time Mr. Stanhope had fully anticipated the return, and the old gentleman became rather impatient at the delay, fearing (and not unreasonably) that some mischance might have befallen them; and Emily at length began to participate in her uncle's fears, when, oh, what a welcome sound of wheels, or rather a heavy lumbering noise, was heard!

"There they are, all safe and sound," exclaimed the old gentleman, with intense delight, as he gazed from the window which overlooked the entrance to the mansion.

This exclamation drew Emily to his side, and Mr. Ellis having just descended from the vehicle, glanced up to the window, and felt not a little flattered by the bright smile which thus bade him welcome back.

Mr. Stanhope hastened to the hall, in order to be the first to receive him, and cordially Mr. Ellis grasped the hand of the kind old gentleman.

"And this is indeed kind of you, sir."

"And, my dear Mr. Ellis, I am right glad to see you back again," was the greeting exchanged on either side.

Mr. Ellis's outer coat was soon laid aside, and, having partaken of some slight refreshment which was spread against his arrival in the dining-room, he ascended with Mr. Stanhope to the room in which the guests were assembled, and kind welcomes were showered upon him by all.

"We are, indeed, pleased to see you with us once more," said Mrs. Stanhope, warmly; "your absence has seemed rather that of months than weeks."

"It has, indeed," said Mr. Stanhope, "for we seemed quite lost without you; did we not, Emily?"

The eyes of the curate followed the direction of the speaker, as he put this query to his beloved niece; and doubly gratified he felt as she replied, with evident sincerity,—

"We have, indeed, sadly missed Mr. Ellis, uncle, for he used so kindly to dedicate so great a part of his time to the company of yourself and my aunt, and never failed to enliven and amuse you, that though I have done my best to supply his place, yet no wonder that you have been dull, and counted the time long in his absence; but," continued Emily in a grave tone, "I am afraid I am arrogating to myself more praise than I deserve; for your old friend John," she added, turning to Mr. Ellis, with whom she exchanged a bright and happy smile, "has frequently spent an evening with us, and admirably succeeded in whiling away its tedium."

"Well done, John," said Mr. Ellis, encouragingly, to the young man; "you have served me most essentially by contributing to the amusement of those I have such reason to love and respect."

The youth blushed as he confessed that the company of Mr. Stanhope was so pleasant and delightful to him, that he feared his visits to the mansion were far more agreeable to himself, than he had been able to render them to others. The squire and his lady bore ample testimony to the regard John entertained for their respected friend.

After some common-place observations from other of the guests, Mr. Stanhope remarked, that during the absence of Mr. Ellis, there had been two new comers to the village.

"Two!" replied the curate, with surprise; "and whom may they be, sir?"

" That is a difficult point to decide," returned the old gentleman ; " one, I understand' bears the name of Mordaunt."

" Oh, I remember," said Mr. Ellis; " he arrived here the evening before I left Sackville, and I had a short interview with him, as he wrote earnestly desiring me to grant him one."

" He seems a very rude sort of man," said John; " he spoke to me one evening as I was returning from here, and asked me about the accident that occurred on the railway, and I took a strong dislike to him at once."

" Oh! John," interposed Emily, quickly, " I think you have strangely mistaken him; he is, I am sure, a perfect gentleman, and possesses a kind and excellent heart."

" Are you, then, acquainted with him, Miss Stanhope ?" said the curate, with surprise, and he fixed his mild grey eyes upon her health-beaming countenance.

Emily was conscious of having spoken too warmly, and not wishing to betray the interview that had taken place between herself and Mr. Mordaunt, she became thoroughly confused and knew not what to say.

Her uncle answered for her.

" Oh, no, my dear sir; Emily has never even spoken to him ; but she judges from his outward appearance, which, I must confess, I think, upon the whole, prepossessing."

At these words Emily's confusion increased tenfold, and she was under the necessity of dropping her handkerchief, in order to afford her a pretext for stooping to recover it, hoping, by that means, to conceal the colour which had mounted even to her temples.

The curate, with astonishment, observed all this; yet willing to give her time to recover her self-possession, he pretended not to have seen her confusion, and, in hopes of changing the conversation, inquired of Mr. Stanhope whom the second new comer was.

" Why," replied the old gentleman, smiling, " he is a still greater mystery even than Mr. Mordaunt; and yet he seems in some way or other connected with him."

" Connected with him !" replied Mr. Ellis, rather hastily.

" We think so," returned Mr. Stanhope; " inasmuch as he made inquiry concerning Mr. Mordaunt immediately on his arrival at this village ; and though we cannot learn that they have ever spoken to each other, yet the stranger appears constantly on the watch for Mr. Mordaunt, who now never leaves his residence till after nightfall."

" 'Tis strange," rejoined the curate, in a musing tone; " because, if he wishes an interview, why not call at his lodgings and demand one ?"

" That," returned Mr. Stanhope, smiling, " forms part of the mystery which hangs over the two."

" Miss Stanhope," said the curate, glancing rather slily at Emily, " used to be famous at solving mysteries. Cannot she interpret this ?"

" Oh, no," said Emily, colouring; " this is far beyond my comprehension; neither do I feel interested enough to endeavour to do so. If you wish to fathom this mystery, I must refer you to Mrs. Harley, who is better able to explain this mystery than I am."

" Emily, dear, what are you thinking of ? I positively declare you are jealous, because Mr. Mordaunt one morning addressed a few words to me; but, as they were concerning—"

" Oh, never mind what it was about," exclaimed Emily, interrupting the widow. " A truce to this foolish nonsense about a mystery, which, if we knew the rights of it, is, I dare say, n mystery at all." Then, turning to the curate, she added, " We have been conversing all this evening of ourselves, and not one present has had the politeness to inquire after your sister. I hope you left her perfectly well."

Mr. F is, as a matter of course, hastened to reply with seeming interest; and divining her wis' to avoid the subject on which they had been conversing, he made no further allusion t Mr. Mordaunt or the stranger during the evening. But the curate, we have alread remarked, was quick-sighted; therefore it was no difficult matter for him to perceive that Emily's professed indifference was merely assumed to conceal perhaps a stronger interest in Mr. Mordaunt than she desired to be known she entertained for him. And yet, this thought was fraught with so many saddening reflections, that he would gladly have cast it from his mind.

The curate was so thoroughly acquainted with Emily's disposition and character, that he knew she was the very girl of all others to desire to penetrate a mystery, one, too, that interested older and wiser individuals; and he shrewdly guessed that if she chose to have done so, Emily could have made plain much that seemed strange.

The manner, too, in which she had interrupted the widow, convinced him that Mr.

Stanhope was sadly deceived, when he said his niece had never spoken to Mr. Mordaunt. And here he thought he could have finished the sentence for Mrs. Harley, as accurately as if Emily had permitted her to do it herself, and concluded (the reader must judge whether erroneously or otherwise) that the widow, who possessed more influence over Emily than he liked, had induced her to act with deception towards her tender uncle and aunt, and he determined to speak to Emily on the subject, the first opportunity that offered; and, in the meantime, to call upon Mr. Mordaunt the following morning, and seek an explanation of him in such a manner, as to prevent any harm occurring to Emily from her acquaintance with him, for that an acquaintance did exist between them, he was confident.

Thus resolutely determined the curate, and not a single selfish thought or feeling found place in his heart.

Had Emily been in truth his sister, he could not have acted with less consideration for self. He had never asked himself the question, "Did he love Emily?" Such a thought had never occurred to him; regarding her as the wealthy heiress, and himself as the humble curate, their destinies were so entirely apart, that the idea of love had not once presented itself to his mind; but, supposing such to have been the case, it would have been smothered at once.

The kindness and affection of his esteemed friend, Mr. Stanhope, would have been ill repaid, by seeking to win the heart of his niece, for whom it was natural he would desire a more brilliant alliance than that of a poor curate.

Neither was Emily Stanhope perfection in his eyes; he saw much in her that required improvement, and did his best to eradicate her failings, as he would have done for a dear and treasured sister. And fondly and proudly he exulted over every good quality that was perceptible in her character.

The evening passed pleasantly and cheerfully away, and not till a late, or, perhaps, we should say, early hour, did the party break up.

---

## CHAPTER XX.

MARY ELLIS stedfastly determined to persist in the line of conduct she had marked out for herself, and sedulously avoided everything that was likely to recall her lover to her memory; she wisely desired to forget him, and though the affection she had reluctantly confessed for him was still fondly treasured in her heart, she yet did her utmost to smother the ill-fated passion.

Mary was not of a mind constituted to please the young and gay of her own sex; so that while all her fellow labourers respected and admired her gentle disposition, and quiet, even temper, she was regarded more as an object of pity than love.

Uncomplaining sorrow was so unmistakeably stamped upon her pallid brow, that her beauty and superior education to the others did not excite the envy they would probably have otherwise done.

Mrs. Herbert was the only female with whom she was acquainted, that seemed to understand and appreciate the excellence of her character, and she even sometimes misjudged her.

There was, too, about Mary Ellis so much natural dignity and innate refinement, that rather forbade than encouraged approach. So that among so many of her own age and sex, she stood alone; not one could enter into her feelings, or sympathise with her sorrows, which were entirely confined to her own bosom.

Mrs. Herbert even thought her cold, and somewhat proud, and concluded she could never have loved Fred so well as he deserved. Young, handsome, and apparently rich, she yet cast him aside almost contemptuously, not even acquainting him with her motive for discontinuing the acquaintance she had previously encouraged.

Mrs. Herbert thus reasoned, although she yet kept faithful the promise she had given to Mary; and though the young officer entreated her to convey a letter into her hands, she firmly and stedfastly refused, as likewise to inform him at what time he should be most likely to meet her abroad.

The snow lay thick upon the ground, and it was still falling fast, as Mary Ellis, toil-worn and weary, emerged from the side door of the fashionable milliner's, and dropping her crape veil, drew her mantelet closely around her form, and proceeded with a quick step towards her own humble abode.

She had scarcely proceeded a yard, when a young man, who had been for some time standing under a colonnade on the opposite side of the street, suddenly cast away the fragment of a cigar he was smoking, and exclaiming, "By Jove! that's her!" darted lightly after her, and before she became aware that she was followed, laid his hand upon her shoulder. Mary started, and at the moment uttered an exclamation of half surprise and half fright; but the next, disengaging herself from his grasp, without even casting a look upon the intruder, pursued her walk.

Perhaps she was not altogether unaccustomed to such treatment; as, for the honour of the opposite sex, we are sorry to be forced to say, an unprotected female can rarely walk through the fashionable part of town of an evening without being made the subject of remark, and, to herself, painful observation.

Mary, we have said, resumed her walk, without the slightest remark or expostulation as to the rude treatment she had received, as she fully believed, from an entire stranger; doubtless, hoping by this means to free herself from the intruder.

But he was not so easy got rid of; one step, and he was again at her side, and the exclamation of "Mary, love, you surely will not refuse to speak one word to me?" in the soft, musical tones of him she loved so well, caused her to stop abruptly, and turn with surprise towards the speaker.

Mary had never before seen Frederick in plain clothes, and for the moment scarcely recognised him; but his voice was unmistakeable—those deep, touching tones, that ever found their way to her heart, could come from none other than him she loved, yet strove so earnestly to forget.

"Oh, Frederick, do not, I entreat of you, force your company upon me. I have stedfastly resolved to avoid you by every means in my power; then do not——"

"Stop, Mary," replied her lover; "I have long sought in vain to converse with you for a few minutes, that I might learn from your own lips what I have done to offend you and cause you to entertain an aversion for my very presence. Now, I have at length succeeded in meeting with you, and we part not, Mary, until I am acquainted with the cause of your dislike."

"How can I answer you?" replied Mary. "Alas! it is, indeed, unfortunate that we should thus have met."

"Answer me, Mary, truly, and as your heart dictates. I repeat, we part not till you have done so. I know there is something more than woman's caprice in your sudden and unexplained renouncement of my love."

"Caprice!" returned Mary, and there was a bitterness in the tone of voice utterly at variance with its usual gentleness. "Caprice! and thus it is that men judge of women."

"No, Mary, I do not so judge of you; I repeat, that I am certain you are not actuated by caprice, but by some deep, though hidden emotion."

"If, indeed, you believe that," returned Mary, earnestly, "be content, and leave me at once and for ever."

"Oh, Mary, how cold, how unfeeling you can behave towards me. I should once have deemed it impossible for you to have done so; but no entreaties or persuasions will induce me to quit your side, till you have informed me in what manner I have been so unfortunate as to offend you."

"Will you be satisfied with my assurance that you have never, either by word or action, given me cause to regard you with less affection than I once professed for you?"

"Then why, Mary, so utterly discard me—is it that you love another?"

"Love another! oh, Frederick, there is not, I believe, a creature in existence more lone or desolate than I. Your love was the one bright spot on my otherwise dark destiny; and Heaven alone knows how fondly I clung to it, or the utter loneliness of heart I have felt since I determined to renounce you."

"Then why do it, Mary?" returned her lover, eagerly catching at the last part of her speech; "but it is cold standing here, and surely you will not refuse me the pleasure of walking with you?" And, as he spoke, he drew her hand through his arm.

Poor Mary's heart was full—too full for utterance; she loved, and the touching eloquence of the young man's voice, as he pleaded for a renewal of their acquaintance, and told how wretched he had been since they last met, how every thought was devoted to her, how fondly and truly he loved her, sunk deep into her heart. Yes, she loved, and sought in vain to remain stedfast to her resolution of renouncing him for ever.

They walked together through the bustling streets of London, alone amidst the crowd, their whole souls wrapped in each other. What heeded they the thick falling snow, or the piercing winter's cold?—their hearts beat in unison, and warm affection glowed within their breasts, making an elysium of bliss to dwell therein. Oh! love, the sweetest boon of existence, what would this world be if thou wert not?—a solitary desert, without a flower to bloom therein, without a sun to shed his reviving brightness, and make our hearts beat with delight, while we bless his glorious rays.

Mary and Frederick, both so young and beautiful, and both loving for the first time, no second-hand passion was given or received by either, as they wandered side by side, thinking or caring for nought beyond themselves. Oh! should they not have been blessed, sweetly blessed in each other. Alas! that a shadow of grief should have clouded the brightness of their bosoms; but love is seldom, if ever, all sweetness, and sad thoughts mingled with the joy of Mary and Frederick.

Frederick felt that he was acting with duplicity towards the gentle being who now leant so lovingly on his arm, and gazed with such tender devotion on his open brow, on which there lurked no semblance of deceit; which indeed was so new to him, that it rankled remorsefully in his breast.

And Mary, poor Mary, trembled for the future; she doubted not her lover's faith—on that she placed full and firm reliance; but would his friends ever receive her as his bride?

Frederick assured her that he had succeeded in gaining his brother's full and free consent, and hoped, through him, to induce his mother likewise to yield her consent to their union.

"And then," concluded the young man, pressing the hand that rested on his arm with fervour to his lips, "oh! my dearest Mary, what bliss will be mine!"

And as he spoke, he bent down, and drawing aside the envious veil, gazed with rapture on her blushing cheek.

Thus conversing, they reached the humble abode of poor Mary. Mrs. Herbert, on opening the door, was surprised to see her accompanied by a gentleman.

"I accidentally met Frederick this evening," said Mary, in explanation, "and he insisted upon walking home with me."

"Well, I absolutely declare that I did not know you, Fred," replied Mrs. Herbert; "but—you will walk in?"

This was spoken hesitatingly, and with a look at Mary, as if to ascertain whether the invitation met with her approval.

"I dare say you are cold, Frederick," said Mary; "and, as you have come so far, you had better walk in and warm yourself."

The young man needed no further invitation, and in a few minutes the trio were seated round the fire.

Mrs. Herbert was soon made acquainted with the renewed intimacy which now existed between Mary and Frederick, which met with her most cordial approbation.

"I assure you, Fred," she said, gaily, "I have ever warmly espoused your cause; indeed, I pleaded so strongly in your favour, that Mary at length forbade me to mention your name."

"Let the past be forgotten for ever," replied the young man. "I confess I was wretched, and feared that I had unintentionally offended Mary; but she assures me to the contrary, and has promised to bless me with this dear hand" (carrying it once more to his lips), "as soon as circumstances will permit. My brother, upon whom, I am sorry to say, I am at present dependent, consents to our union."

"Does William, indeed, consent to your marrying Mary?" interrupted Mrs. Herbert, with surprise.

"Yes; and," replied the young man, "has likewise promised to be present at the ceremony which unites us."

"Oh, that is, indeed, joyful news," returned Mrs. Herbert; "all will end happily at last."

"I trust so, indeed," said Mary, and her large dark eyes appeared to dilate beyond even their ordinary size, as she fixed them earnestly on her lover. "Oh, Frederick, may we never, either of us, have cause to repent this meeting! I feel," she added, and

THE MOONLIGHT MEETING.

[The strange young man stepped from the shade in which he had previously stood, and, in the full broad light of the moon, presented himself before Mr. Mordaunt.]

she spoke as one inspired, "that this night has determined my destiny; be it dark, or otherwise, the future is a blank that remains to be filled up; but I feel I have no longer power to stem the current of events; this meeting, though unsought for, on my part, has resolved the course in which they are doomed to flow. It is in vain to struggle against it. As I said before, I feel that this meeting has irrevocably determined my future career. I love you, Frederick," she added, and the tears came thronging to her eyes, melting her soul to softness, and giving a touching pathos to her voice, always sweet and gentle in its tones; "I love you, and have the fullest confidence in your love for me—which indeed, I never doubted; it was my own humble circumstances that induced me to renounce your affection, fearing that your relatives would never receive me as———"

"My wife," exclaimed the young man, clasping her fondly to his bosom, and raining down kisses on her blushing cheek. Mary started, and endeavoured to free herself from her lover's ardent embrace, but he strained her more closely to him. "One kiss, dear Mary, from those sweet lips, to ratify the promise you have this night given me, to be mine—mine own. Oh, Mary, how long and tedious the time will seem, till I can call you such in truth."

"That cannot, dear Frederick, be yet," said Mary; "Mrs. Herbert———"

"Is gone, love; we are alone," replied the young man.

With an instinctive delicacy, Mary shrank from the circling arms of her lover, and felt vexed with Mrs. Herbert for having left the room. Yet, not willing that he should think she mistrusted him, she gave him the required pledge of love from her lips, which was received with transport; and then, seated side by side, their hands clasped together, how eloquently the young man discoursed of the future, how rapidly the time fled by unheeded; even Mary forgot to lament the departure of Mrs. Herbert; or, indeed, to wish for her return. Love is, indeed, a very sad chronicle of time, counting full oft hours for minutes. And this evening was, indeed, fraught with joy to the lovers; but all things must sooner or later have an end; and, on Mrs. Herbert's return, to their astonishment, they learnt that it was past twelve o'clock.

"I must leave you, Mary, love," said Frederick, rising to depart; "but not, I hope, for long; you will allow me to meet and accompany you home every evening, till we meet to part no more."

Consent was readily given, and the farewell kiss pressed upon the unresisting lips of Mary, who, after her lover was gone, turned to Mrs. Herbert, and, with tearful eyes, exclaimed,—

"Dearly so as I love Fred, and fully as I believe it is returned, yet I feel more sad tonight than I have done for a long time, and almost repent having renewed my acquaintance with him."

"Oh, say not so," returned her friend. "I confess I almost envy you; to be so tenderly beloved by such a handsome fellow as Fred, would completely turn the head of any other girl but you. If I, for instance, was circumstanced as you are, I should be quite beside myself with joy. Everything is propitious, and favours your marriage with Fred; even his brother has consented, and which, I must confess, has surprised me not a little."

"Well," replied Mary, catching some of the enthusiasm that filled the breast of Mrs. Herbert, "I certainly do feel sad; but it may be that my heart is too full of happiness, which has come upon me so suddenly, that I cannot as yet realise it; all that has passed this evening, appears like a dream, from which I dread to awaken."

"It is no dream, Mary; all is sober, earnest, substantial facts; and, before many weeks have passed, I fully anticipate to wish you joy, as Mrs. Frederick Maitland; and you will be happy, Mary—yes, all the happier for the sad and sorrowful days that have passed and gone, and I am sure you well deserve to be so."

The following evening the lovers again met, and the next; and, in short, each night, as Mary left work, she found her young lover waiting for her, till at length the sadness that had hovered over her spirits, had entirely vanished, and she yielded herself to the delight of his society.

## CHAPTER XXI.

AFTER Mr. Mordaunt had seen Emily at the window, he pursued his walk for a short distance towards the open country, which was illuminated by the soft light of the moon, which, we have observed, shone with unusual splendour, lighting up each nook and valley with its rays. And all lovers of nature are aware, that the county of Devon is beautifully diver- sified in its scenery. Having gained a slight eminence, Mr. Mordaunt stopped in his walk, and turning round abruptly, surveyed, with an eye of admiration, the fair landscape that was spread before him ; and then turning his eye up towards the deep blue sky, gazed upon the

"Stars of night,
Sad and intent, as if he sought
Some mournful secret in their light."

As he was thus engaged, he had a half indefinite idea that a shadow glided close by him. He cast an hasty glance around, and seeing no one, with a shudder drew his cloak more closely over his bosom, and prepared to resume his walk, when the strange young man, whom we have already introduced to our readers, stepped from the shade in which he had previously stood, and, in the full broad light of the moon, presented himself before Mr. Mordaunt, who started back as if in horror of his presence, but without giving utter- ance to a syllable.

The other, at first, imitated his silence, and neither spoke for a few seconds. Had any been there to mark the two confronting each other, they would have regarded it as a strange—nay, almost fearful spectacle.

The shrinking attitude of Mr. Mordaunt, as, with louring brows, he gazed upon the stranger with an expression of countenance that might be interpreted either as anger or terror, and, perhaps, partook of both.

While the other stood stiff and erect, his eyes lit up with a wild excitement that seemed to give token of an unsettled reason ; his mouth was closely compressed, and he was apparently endeavouring to calm the turbulence of his heart without giving vent in words.

No other living creature was nigh ; the pale moon alone looked upon the two as they thus confronted each other, and threw their lengthened shadows in strong relief upon the ground, which was bathed in a flood of light.

The spot they occupied was but a short distance removed from the village, and skirted on either hand by tall trees, that seemed to tower to the skies, and which, when clothed in verdure, formed a perfect avenue ; but now, leafless and bare, gave a wildness to the scene, which the hills in the background, rising one above another, till, in the distance, they appeared to melt into the sky, in no way diminished.

On the left of the stranger was a small rivulet, which rippled quietly on with a musical but monotonous sound, reflecting on its polished surface and numberless mimic waves, the clear light of the moon, which gave it the appearance of a bed of liquid silver.

All was in keeping with the still, soft beauty of the scene; and, though a reflective mind might feel a shade of sadness flit spectre-like across his breast, as he gazed above and around him, yet it would be so vague and undefined, that the next instant he would unconsciously grow glad again.

The stranger was the first to break silence ; his voice was subdued and husky, as if with emotion, yet so distinct, that the tones trembled for a moment, and then vibrated in the clear night air.

"Again," he said, "we have met. You see the utter impossibility of avoiding or con- cealing yourself from me. I am safe to track you out."

" To what purpose ?" replied Mordaunt, recovering his composure at the sound of the other's voice ; " your presence, you well know, is hateful to me."

" I do know it," returned the stranger; "and that is one great reason why I thus pursue you ; but there is likewise another."

" Name it," said Mr. Mordaunt, hastily ; " if you want money, state what sum will satisfy you ; then take it, and begone."

" Money!" repeated the other. " You, James Mordaunt, can talk to me about receiving money—you, whose life is in my hands, and whom with one word I could at any moment condemn to prison, and most probably death !"

"Liar!" interrupted Mr. Mordaunt, in a voice of thunder; "I defy you.   None would give heed to the ravings of a madman."

"Not mad, James, though you would fain have made me so;" but the expression of his eye vouched for the truth of Mordaunt's assertion.  "Not mad, or why do you fear me?"

"Fear you!" replied Mr. Mordaunt, and he laughed with bitter sarcasm.

"Yes, fear me," said the other; "for, I repeat, I hold your liberty—nay, even your life at my command."

"I will bear this no longer," said Mr. Mordaunt; "you shall not thus torture me with your presence.  Either quit this village by break of day, or the prison, which you have the audacity——"

"Stop, James, one moment, and weigh well the consequences before you presume to threaten me, who have you so completely in my power, that, as I said before, one word would be amply sufficient to deprive you of your liberty; therefore, you should rather thank me for my forbearance, that as yet I have not given it utterance."

"You hinted," said Mordaunt, without heeding the stranger's last remark, "that you had a reason for thus annoying me, besides the mere gratification of so doing.  Name it at once, and then let us part, and would to God it might be for ever."

"It rests with you, whether or not such shall be the case.  Inform me what has become of Isabel, and I swear to you never more to intrude my presence upon you.  Henceforth our paths shall be as distinct and separate as it is possible for two paths to be.  Here we stand beneath the blue unclouded sky of Heaven;" and as he spoke he raised his hand energetically towards the vast spangled canopy that was spread above them, and tossed back the clustering hair from his fevered brow; "you shall choose which road it best please you to take, and I solemnly swear to journey in an opposite direction.  Never shall a whisper of mine divulge the dreadful secret that is known to none on earth but ourselves."

"Cease—cease," said Mordaunt, and his voice trembled; "there is no such secret existing between us.  You accuse me of committing a deed which was the work of Heaven alone.  Oppressed and trampled on I have been; but never have I been an oppressor.  I am ashamed of my own weakness in listening to you for a moment on this subject."

"Disclose to me the fate of Isabel."

"I know it not, myself," returned Mr. Mordaunt, "neither do I wish to hear her name mentioned—especially by you."

"Once more, James Mordaunt, I warn you that you are in my power; which, though you effect to disbelieve, you yet acknowledge that my presence is hateful to you."

"I hate," returned Mordaunt, angrily, "to have my steps constantly dogged—to be hunted from place to place like a dog."

"Then, remember, I have on one condition sworn—solemnly sworn to pursue you thus no farther—to leave you with no other accuser than your own guilty conscience."

"My conscience," replied Mordaunt, "acquits me of the deed you persist in laying to my charge; and I would gladly spend the remainder of my life in peace and retirement.  I have gained riches by the death of him, whose loss has plunged you into poverty; and, though you have not lawfully the slightest claim to any portion of that wealth, which has descended to me as the rightful heir, yet I have repeatedly offered to make a provision for you, and which, though constantly declined, I am still as willing to perform as ever; nay, mere wealth is so little prized by me, that you have but to state your desire, and it shall be instantly granted.  Alas! alas! riches, once so coveted, became mine at the very instant they were no longer of any value in my eyes."

"James," replied the other, "I little thought I could ever have been a supplicant to you, whom I have every reason to contemn and abhor.  You ever despised me, the illegitimate son of your wealthy uncle, who ever deeply and bitterly regretted not performing an act of justice to my poor mother, till her death, which you are aware occurred in giving me birth, put it beyond his power.  And, oh! frequently has the old man, with tears in his eyes, bemoaned the sad circumstances connected with my birth, which denied me, his only child, the right of becoming, at his decease, the possessor of his vast estate—I, who was his acknowledged son, the constant companion of his old age, the attendant at his couch, ever by his side, thinking and caring for none but him; while you, the rightful heir, remained at a distance, the gayest of the gay, not deeming your relative of any account, compared to your own pleasures; and me you ever treated with scorn and contempt."

" Which you were by no means backward in returning," said Mordaunt; "but to what does all this tend ?"

" Listen, and you will learn. I had, but a short time previous, become acquainted with the daughter of an old and esteemed friend of my father's, who, dying, had bequeathed her to his care, who willingly received the precious trust. Yes, Isabel, though penniless, from the sad reverses of her father, which had indeed hastened his death by preying too severely on his mind, ill constituted to bear up under the heavy pressure of misfortune —yes, Isabel found a warm welcome to my father's house, and an attachment had sprung up between us, when, from some whim, you suddenly announced your intention of visiting my father."

" It was no whim," replied Mordaunt; " I knew Isabel had become an inmate of my uncle's house; and report spoke in such high terms of her extreme loveliness, that I was actuated by an ardent desire to behold her; and, on doing so, found that report, so far from having exaggerated her attractions, had failed in doing them adequate justice, and I instantly became deeply enamoured of her."

" And but too soon succeeded in weaning her affections from me, who had previously possessed them," replied the stranger, in a tone of extreme bitterness; " you persuaded her, James, to elope with you, though she was the promised bride of another, and made her your wife, without possessing the means of maintaining her."

" I naturally considered," replied Mordaunt, " that my uncle would make some provision for the future possessor of his vast estate."

" And because he refused to do so, knowing that you had acted with extreme baseness and duplicity towards his only son, you scrupled not to hasten his end, that you might sooner enjoy his inheritance."

" It is a lie ! and such a one as could never for a moment be conceived by any other than a madman."

" It is truth ; and your own conscience acknowledges the justice of my accusation."

" Cease !" replied Mordaunt. " I will bear this no longer. Nothing but the horror of having my name brought before the public, coupled with guilt and infamy, induced me to bear so long and so mildly with your threats and reproaches."

" You declare yourself innocent, James," said the stranger; " but will, think you, your own unsupported declaration be received as evidence of your innocence by those who may sit in judgment over you ?"

Mordaunt trembled for an instant as the thought flashed across his mind with the rapidity of lightning, that it was difficult, and, in some cases, impossible to prove yourself guiltless of an accusation laid against you, which may, nevertheless, be wholly unfounded ; yet he strove to speak with calmness as he replied,—

" Rather let me ask, whether you conceive it probable that any will give credence to your unsupported evidence against me ?"

" The evidence of your guilt, that I shall be able to produce, will be corroborated in every particular, not by one, but several individuals," returned the other ; and Mordaunt trembled yet more as he encountered the wild, wandering expression of his eye. He scarcely knew what, under the circumstances, would be the best course for him to pursue ; but the suspicious death of his uncle, his own previous poverty, and the especial advantage that accrued to him from it, and him only—for his uncle had died intestate—filled his mind with horror, as he thought that it was certainly possible he might be pronounced guilty of his murder. This determined him, at all hazards, to endeavour to prevent his cousin branding him with a crime he might find it so difficult to prove himself innocent of; he, therefore, replied, firmly,—

" I know myself perfectly innocent, both in thought, word, and deed of the guilt you lay to my charge. You have said truly that we have never, at any one time of our lives, entertained feelings of friendship or good will towards each other ; the very fact that we have ever been rivals, and I the most favoured one, had naturally given you a dislike to me; on the other hand, I well knew that my uncle, and sole relative, entertained an aversion to me, because I stood in the position that he would gladly have seen you placed in, and which you would have occupied, had he been legally united to your mother; consequently, he had none to blame but himself. Yet, this did not prevent him entertaining, as I have just said, a feeling bordering on hatred towards myself, who, conscious of the injustice of my relative, in thus visiting his own sins on my luckless head, regarded you as the sole cause, and treated you, accordingly, with unkindness and contempt. And, when I became the successful lover of Isabel ——"

"Whom," interrupted the other, " you won by baseness and duplicity; indeed, Heaven only knows what arts you used to ensnare her love, and wean her affections from me, to whom, in the presence and under the sanction of my father, she had pledged her faith; and oh! Isabel was all purity and loveliness, and never would she have broken her faith, had ——"

"Isabel all purity and loveliness!" interrupted Mordaunt, with a scornful laugh; "she was nought but deceit and avarice; it was, indeed, an easy matter to induce her to break her faith. Had you been the heir, instead of me, it would have been different—far different; oh, yes—she would then, undoubtedly, have remained true to her plighted word, which was only broken for a more wealthy lover. And I, fool-like, was the dupe—I fondly believed she was true to me in poverty, when ——"

"Liar!" shouted the other, springing towards him with an air of frenzy; "dare to breathe another word against her spotless name, and ——"

"Peace!" interrupted Mordaunt, stepping back as the other advanced; "when I was told that, in my absence from home, she received the visits of one who could be more lavish of gifts than myself, I, poor, weak fool, disbelieved it all;" and again his scornful laugh rang out in the clear, frosty air.

At these words, the anger of the other was instantly, and, as it were, by magic, abated; he shuddered for a moment, and then, in a thick and husky voice, demanded,—

"Tell me instantly the fate of that unhappy girl; divulge but that one circumstance to me, and, as I before said, all else shall be forgiven—forgotten."

"I have told you," returned Mordaunt, " that I know it not myself—would to God that I had never known or seen her. She has caused me all the wretchedness and misery it has been my unhappy fate to know; but for her, you would never have accused me of a crime so fearful that my soul sickens at the very contemplation of it, and yet, sooth to say, there might be found persons who would not hesitate to believe me guilty of it, and urge the presence of a motive as almost proof of crime."

"The motive," returned the other, whose mind seemed to wander strangely. "Ah! the motive—a powerful one, no doubt; tell it me—tell it me; I have promised forgiveness."

"You have nothing to forgive," said Mordaunt; "but time grows on, and it is useless for us to waste more of it here;" saying which, he turned to walk on.

The stranger was instantly at his side.

"You refuse, then, to give me any satisfactory account of Isabel, once so fondly loved that even now I would sacrifice all that is left me on earth—revenge for the death of a parent,—could I learn aught concerning her."

"I tell you I know nothing about her," returned Mordaunt, angrily. " And as to the death of your parent, it was the work of Heaven alone; I defy your malice to the uttermost to prove it otherwise. From this night I cast off the bonds of fear with which you have hitherto held me in bondage. No longer will I be the slave of the childish phantasies with which you have gloried to enchain me; I will no more be the dupe of a cunning madman, who, in revenge for a fancied wrong, has ruled me with a rod of iron. You talk to me of a prison; beware how you pursue me farther, or you may find yourself for life destined to fret away your existence in a gloomy cell; aye, a gloomy cell!" And once more his laugh resounded in scornful mockery.

"Be it so," returned the other. "You have threatened me, James Mordaunt—you have told me that I am mad; yet you dare not even attempt to accuse me of guilt, or of an injury to another; whereas I have proofs against you—proofs so strong that they cannot be combatted."

"I believe it not," said Mordaunt. " You cannot adduce a single proof."

"You called on my unhappy parent to ask of him a provision for the wants of yourself and her who, in defiance of every principle of honour, you had made your wife. He refused to accede to your request, hard words passed between you, and then you suddenly left. A short time afterwards my father was found lying insensible on the floor, and blood flowing from a wound in his head, of which wound he shortly died. He had left no will; all his property descended to you. About the same time, you became jealous of Isabel, and, in a sudden and mysterious manner, she disappeared, none but yourself knows how, or where. You refuse to give any account of her, and I can only conclude it is because you dare not. She, unfortunate girl, has probably likewise fallen a victim to your insatiate revenge."

"As regards Isabel," replied Mordaunt, "you have no right to make any inquiry. She is nothing—never can be anything to you; and my uncle's death was the subject of inquiry at the time of its occurrence, and the wound in his head was satisfactorily proved to have resulted from a fall, caused by being seized with an epileptic fit."

"Knowing that he was subject to such fits, a verdict to that effect was recorded; but, feeling assured in my own mind that his death was caused by your hand alone, I have ever since been indefatigable in procuring evidence that might tend to fix the guilt on you; and I have succeeded, better even than I anticipated; therefore, James, it is useless to attempt to escape by charging me with insanity, there being corroborative evidence against you that will bear out my statement, and witnesses that will vouch to the truth of it. There is but one way for you to escape; it rests with you whether henceforth you live free and undisturbed as far as I am concerned, or be cast into prison, and ultimately die an ignominious death. I have told you on what conditions I condescend to make terms with you, and all you have to do is to refuse or accept them."

The young man spoke these words with a cool but determined tone, that convinced Mordaunt he had no choice between two evils but to prefer the lesser; and as he dwelt for a moment on his uncle's death, a palpable shudder ran through his frame, his breath came thick and short; an accumulation of horrors seemed to impend over his devoted head.

"Oh, death!" he muttered, between his closed teeth, "thou wouldst indeed be welcomed as a boon; but to die on a scaffold, oh, no, no. And yet, I know not what to do." And then, after a moment's hesitation, he spoke aloud,—

"I cannot talk to you of Isabel to-night; I have told you with truth that I know not what has become of her, but I will try to ascertain," he added, in a firmer tone. "To do this, you must give me time, and remember, if I am able to disclose it to you, our compact is sealed. We meet no more on earth. I shall probably go abroad, whither you must solemnly swear not to follow, or in any way persecute me for the future. You will give me your assurance, your oath, to this effect."

"I will," returned the other; "but, James, remember, on your part, that it will be utterly useless for you, in the meantime, to attempt to deceive me. I shall remain in this village, and narrowly watch your movements. I give you a month. Shall I, at the close of that period, call at your apartments, and learn your determination?"

"Oh! no, no," said Mordaunt, hastily; "we never again meet under any roof but this," and he pointed to the starry firmament above them; "here we are alone; no prying eye can mark the workings of my heart, no ear can catch, and perchance give heed to the falsehoods which you unhesitatingly give utterance to; let, therefore, this spot be our trysting place."

"As you please," returned the other, "all places are alike to me. This day month, at the same hour, I will meet you here."

"To ascertain what you are so desirous to know, I may be obliged in the interim to visit London—in that case?"

"In that case," replied the stranger, "I will myself accompany you. Depend I shall watch you with a suspicious eye, and shall not for an instant lose sight of you till the month expires."

"I have no choice but to submit," said Mordaunt, "however much my inclination rebels against it; but I trust you will rest satisfied with the knowledge, that I cannot well leave here unknown to you, and not molest me farther."

"While you remain here without attempting to deceive, or elude me, you have my assurance that I shall offer you no molestation; and now, for one month we part."

"And when we meet again," said Mordaunt, "I trust it will be for the last time."

The other re-echoed the wish, and then Mordaunt returned in the direction of the doctor's, the stranger following at a short distance.

———

## CHAPTER XXII.

IN a particularly spacious and elegant apartment in St. James's, where everything that wealth could procure, or luxury desire, to gratify the taste for modern relish and refinement, was scattered with no niggard hand around, the officers belonging to the regiment of the — Hussars were assembled. They were all in uniform, and their showy dresses and the bright gilding on their sword hilts were reflected in the large mirrors that graced the sides of the apartment; and "glasses sparkled on the board, and wine ran ruby bright."

At the time that we desire to introduce the reader to this assemblage of England's soldiers, their hilarity seemed at its height; their united voices were joined in the chorus of the famous melody—

> " Landlord, fill the flowing bowl,
> Until it does run over;
> For to-night we'll merry be,
> To-morrow we'll be sober."

And at every pause in the song, which was received with deafening shouts of merriment, the decanter was passed round, glasses were refilled, and drained off in bumpers.

After some time thus spent, during a temporary suspension of the festivities, one of the officers remarked, that it was confidently reported their regiment would receive orders to remove into Devonshire early in the ensuing month. Of course all were ready with remarks on the contemplated change—some approving, others disapproving of any alteration.

" It will be decidedly dull, I fancy," replied one, who the reader will recognise as William Maitland, in answer to an observation of another, who had spoken in favour of the change. " It might be all very well in fine weather; but to go into the country just in the midst of the London season, which promises this year to be unusually gay, will be, I must protest, vexatious in the extreme. What say you, Henderson ?"

The young man thus appealed to, was a lieutenant in the regiment, and, though possessing but a very small share of personal or mental attractions, yet by no means entertained an insignificant opinion of himself. He was a complete fop in every sense of the word, affected a lisp, and aimed at being thought quite a lady-killer; and yet, with many drawbacks, he was liked much by his brother officers, for, though frequently their butt, and a never-failing source of merriment among them, he was so thoroughly good-tempered, that he never resented it in the least, and was, in the main, likewise good-natured, and willing to confer an obligation when any required it of him. In answer to William Maitland's question, he replied, first adjusting his hair with great precision, and glancing approvingly in the mirror that faced him—

" Well, Maitland, I pos-i-tive-ly can-not say; but I shall be sor-ry to leave Lon-don just at pre-sent, for I met a ve-ry nice gal at the ball last night, pos-i-tive-ly quite a di-vi-ni-ty, and she seem-ed much plea-sed with my atten-tions, and, if I have time to follow them up, I think I shall make a con-quest."

" Bravo, Henderson," exclaimed a young man from the other end of the table; " what, met with another divinity? Why, I verily believe you do nothing but make conquests."

" Well, Pri-ore, I cer-tain-ly must con-fess that I have had a few con-quests worth boast-ing of."

" Ah! I think you may say that," returned the young man, who was an ensign, and his name, by-the-bye, Prior; " what a charming little girl I met with you the other day, in the park; who was she, Henderson ?"

" No joking about her, Pri-ore, if you please; that, as you say, charming gal, was my sis-tore; con-se-quent-ly, I can-not al-low ——"

" Stuff !" interrupted the other, elbowing his neighbour, to make him alive to the jest; " what, that black-eyed girl, who was leaning so tenderly on your arm?"

" 'Pon honhur, it was my sis-tore."

" Pshaw !" replied Prior, winking at the others. " I could lay my life I saw the same pair of sparkling eyes glancing from under a hood, while the owner of them crept softly

## FRED REVEALS HIS SECRET CORRESPONDENCE TO THE MESS,

[Fred, who, perhaps, was a little flattered and pleased at possessing such an unknown correspondent, proceeded to read the mystical epistle he had that morning received.]

out of your apartments, very early one morning, where, no doubt, you had secreted her over night."

"Ha! ha!" laughed the officers; and "Bravo! well done, Henderson!" resounded from all parts of the room.

"Ah, no; 'pon hon-our, I de-clare this is pos-i-tive-ly scan-dal. You must re-aw-lly have mis-ta-ken some other apart-ments for mine," urged the young man, but with an air that induced them all to believe that the whole glory of the achievement was due to him-self alone; but the reader will, of course, attribute it entirely to the creation of the ensign's fruitful imagination.

"I say, Fred," said William Maitland, from the top of the table, addressing his brother, who was seated near the bottom, "the letters from your incognita all bear the Devon postmark; perhaps we shall light upon her during our proposed stay there. She talks about making herself known to you at some future time, and surely no time would be more suitable than when we are in her immediate neighbourhood."

"Ah," said Frederick, laughing, " and it is strange that my unknown correspondent appears better informed of our military movements than most of us are ourselves. I re-eeived a letter from her this morning, in which she speaks of the probability of my visiting Devon, and the desire she feels to become personally known to me."

"She must pos-i-tive-le be a witch," lisped Henderson.

"More probably a guardian angel, in the guise of a lovely woman, who, knowing the miseries that poor devils of younger brothers, like you and I, Fred, are exposed to, for the want of that most necessary of all commodities, money, kindly provides you with the needful," said Prior, who occupied a seat near his companion in rank.

"But, Fred, let us hear what your fair incognita says. I confess I am greatly inter-ested in her; so read the letter to us, there's a good fellow," said his brother.

"Oh, do!" was re-echoed from one and another.

"Yes, do," said Henderson; "it is a per-fect no-vel-te, and re-aw-le quite a ro-man-tic sort of thing; so do o-blige us by read-ing the let-tar."

Fred, who, perhaps, was a little flattered, and pleased at possessing an unknown cor-respondent, who professed a warm regard for him, and likewise supplied him, with what the young ensign, Prior, had by no means inaptly termed the most necessary of all com-modities,—therefore, nothing loth, proceeded to read the mystical epistle he had that morning received; but, from whom it came, he was utterly unable even to conceive.

"Once more (began the letter) I address myself to the pleasing task of writing to you, though a prospect has been opened to me of a speedy termination of this corres-pondence; and (could I flatter myself it was as agreeable and pleasant to you to receive my letters as I have found it to write them) I should be sorry for it to cease under any other than existing circumstances; but the hope of becoming personally known to you, and, perhaps, being fortunate enough to win your regard and esteem, brings with it such pleasant dreams as sometimes I fear are too bright to be realised.

" I have been conversing this morning with a near friend of yours, and for whom I entertain the highest respect; and he informs me that it is more than probable I shall shortly see you in Devon, when I hope to cultivate your acquaintance.

" Should unforeseen circumstances keep you longer in London, you will hear from me as usual. And now, my friend, adieu, though not, I trust, *pour jamais*."

The foregoing letter, as may be supposed, was received with universal admiration by the gay officers, all of whom were profuse in their congratulations of the favoured youth.

"The devil!" exclaimed William (whom the reader is aware was not very particular in his choice of words) "if I can quite understand who this same dear friend of yours is, Fred, who seems perfectly to understand what movements are likely to take place in the regiment; indeed, he appears cognisant of it before we are ourselves. He must be in-timately acquainted with ——"

"Ah!" interrupted Fred, "that is the only part of the letter that puzzles me; all else is plain and straightforward."

"And I de-clare, po-si-tive-le," said Henderson, "that you ought to be de-light-ed with your good for-tune, to have a love-le wo-man so de-spe-rate-le in love with you, so ——"

"Ah!" interrupted Fred again; " that is the very point. Prove to me that she is a lovely woman, and doubt not that you will find me instantly at her service."

"Hear him," said William, in a tone of disgust; "coldly canvassing the merits of one who ardently adores him. The knowledge of that alone should induce him to award her a place in his affections. I appeal to all of you now present, as to whether you would act in so strange a manner, were you similarly circumstanced?"

All were ready and eager to reply in the negative.

"For my part," lisped Henderson, "I should po-si-tive-le think it my duty to be en-raptur-ed with her, even were it pos-si-ble that one who can ex-press her-self so beau-ti-ful-le, should prove not to be quite so love-le as I an-ti-ci-pat-ed. She is evi-dent-le rich, and that alone ——"

"Ought to make her beloved, of course," said Frederick, laughing. "She is, as you observe, evidently rich, and that, I strongly suspect, is the greatest charm of which she can boast. Were she the lovely being all of you would make her, she would doubtless have lovers in plenty, and need not have recourse to this strange expedient, in order to procure a husband."

"Granted," said William, "for the sake of the argument, that she is neither very young nor very pretty (although I would willingly take the odds against such being the case); yet, granting that, you ought still to feel yourself bound to marry her, on account of the substantial favours she has conferred upon you. For, after all, what is marriage?" he continued, seeing Frederick appeared to dislike the idea of being obliged, as it were, to enter into the bonds with one for whom he could not entertain a sincere affection—"what is marriage? Nothing in the world but standing before a parson, and pronouncing a certain form of words, which, in this case, will entitle you to the unconditional control of some thousands, of which you greatly stand in need, and with which you may enjoy yourself to your heart's content; and if your lady is not to your mind possessed of beauty sufficient to reach the standard of perfection you sigh after, you can, of course, solace yourself with any that are; and that you can find plenty, I do not for a moment doubt."

"Pshaw!" replied Frederick, vexed at his brother's speech. "If I married a woman, I should consider myself equally as much bound to her, were she ugly, as if possessed of the fairest charms."

"Should you, indeed, Fred," said William, contemptuously; "then all I can say, is, that you are a very strange, unaccountable young man, and utterly different from all others."

"For the honour of my sex, I hope not," replied Frederick, spiritedly; "though there are many, I know, base enough to regard the marriage vow as binding only to her who is by nature weaker, and, unless guarded by the love of her husband, more exposed to temptations than ourselves."

"Well done; bravo!" resounded from all sides.

"'Pon my honour, Fred, you ought to have been bred a parson. A black coat would well become such sanctimonious notions as you appear to entertain; but they are positively a disgrace to a gallant son of Mars, and entitle you to be expelled the army, lest you inculcate in the breast of others those old-fashioned and, I had hoped, thoroughly exploded ideas. You must excuse him, gentlemen," he added, turning to the others, "on the ground that he has been brought up in the country, and educated at his mother's knee."

"That has nothing to do with it," replied Frederick, more and more annoyed, as his companions gaily laughed at his brother's remarks; yet, anxious to hide his chagrin, he continued—"If, on becoming acquainted with my fair correspondent, I find her such a one as I can love—if she consent, I will gladly marry her; but marry a woman that I could not love, I never will, were I a thousand times poorer than in truth I am, and she laden with riches. You all appear to think," he added, resuming his wonted gaiety, "that my incognita must necessarily be possessed of personal attractions; while, on the contrary, I firmly believe she is some plain-looking, and not over young maiden, who has long been sighing in vain for a husband, and, thinking a poor devil like me would be glad to catch at that slippery, but desirable thing, money, has spread her nets accordingly."

"It may be so," said Prior, "and yet ——"

"And yet you cannot think as I do."

"Why," said the other, laughing, "the truth is, that you are such a downright handsome fellow, that I can easily conceive a young and pretty heiress being desperately in love with your own sweet self—and as to that letter being written by some disappointed old maid, I'll wager my life against it.   It emanates, I am certain, from a romantic girl; the very style and wording of the epistle vouches for the truth of my surmise.   And I am blessed (if a young and wealthy lady wrote such a billet doux to me) if I could think her otherwise than charming, or be loth to bend my knee in devout homage to her good sense, which she most surely possesses in abundance."

"Ah!" said Frederick, laughing, " you are a professed admirer of the sex, and ever ready to offer homage at their shrine."

"No," replied the young man.   "I leave all that to Henderson—he, you may say, with truth, is devoted to the fair sex."

"Pos-i-tive-le," said Henderson, in a deprecating tone, "you should not say so.  'Pon honour, you should not.   I may have gain-ed a few fa-vours; but I do not like to bo-ast.   There are se-crets which ought ne-ver to be di-vul-ged on any account."

"We all know," said Frederick, "that you are a favourite with the ladies; and, therefore, I think, if my mysterious correspondent makes herself known to us, during our sojourn in Devon, that you must be prohibited from an introduction to her; as, sup-posing I think it worth while to follow up the impression I appear to have made on her heart, I should be absolutely jealous of you—I should indeed."

"I declare, pos-i-tive-le, this is un-fair, and appeal to you all, whe-ther I have not a right to claim an in-tro-ducti-on to the lady equal-ly as the rest?"

"No, no, Henderson," said Prior; "such a known lady-killer as you would cut out poor Fred directly; he would not have so much as half a chance."

"Now, pos-i-tive-le, you are jo-king; but I know Mr. Mait-land will not act so un-kind-le.   I have a great de-sire to see the la-dy, and, real-le, hon-our wou-ld pre-vent me."

"Don't trust him, Fred," said one and another.   " He is never content unless making conquests.   You should see what a pile of love-letters he has got treasured up."

"Now, real-le," replied Henderson, "I would sell them all for a penny.   Per-haps you would like to buy them, Pri-are?"

"Not I," said the young man—"thank you all the same, Henderson; but I don't care to have love-letters second-hand.   They are all very gratifying to your feelings, I dare say; but with me, the only effect they could produce, would be vexation at not being so highly favoured as yourself."

"Come," said an officer, from the head of the table, "this discussion has broken the festivities of the evening.   Fill your glasses, gentlemen, and perhaps Mr. Frederick Mait-land will oblige us with a song."

"Ah," said Prior, "give us, Fred, that song of your own composing."

The young man excused himself on the ground of its being unsuited to the occasion; but his objection was overruled, for all expressed their earnest desire to hear that particu-lar song, in preference to any other.

Having, therefore, begged them to excuse its many faults, he commenced singing, in a beautifully clear and melodious voice, the following stanzas :—

> "Oh, say not in a foreign land
>     That I may happy be;
> This heart with joy can ne'er expand,
>     When far away from thee.

> "I love each sweet and humble flower
>     That blossoms round thy home;
> No other bloom will have the power
>     To cheer me when I roam.

> "With gayer scenes around me,
>     More bright than words can tell,
> I'll sigh for those that bound me
>     In love's enchanted spell.

> "Though softly blue Italia's skies,
>     There's nought beneath their sphere
> Can match their hue like those dear eyes
>     Which make my heaven here.

> " Then think not other beauties e'er
>    This heart can charm from thee;
> Where'er I roam I'll think thee near,
>    My friend and guide to be."

On its conclusion, Frederick was overwhelmed with expressions in favour of his song, though William loudly declared against the sentiment, which, in his opinion, was anything but what a soldier should entertain.

And now the bottle was rapidly passed round the table; song succeeded song, and shouts of approval re-echoed from the hearers.

In the midst of this festive scene, Frederick's thoughts wandered to the humble abode of Mary Ellis, and earnestly did he wish it were possible he could slip from the gay assembly, and spend an hour with her, whose company was far sweeter to him than the most brilliant circles where she was not. And the evening, so rich in mirth and joy to all others, to him was tedious, and irksome in the extreme.

The early hours of morning had been tolled forth from St. Paul's, and repeated by all the neighbouring churches and timepieces, when the brothers sallied forth to their own apartments, not far distant from those of their entertainer.

" I say, Fred, my boy," said the elder brother; " how goes your affair with Mary ?"

" Almost better than I expected," replied the younger; " and yet I have not advanced a single inch towards——"

" What you most desire," returned the other. " Well, Fred, I have a bit of advice to give to you. Harkye, my boy; you must succeed with Mary before we go to Devon."

" Yes," replied Fred, faintly; " I think it would be best."

" You are, surely, not cooling in your ardour, Fred—eh?" said his brother, turning towards him a look of surprise.

" No, no," replied Frederick. " I love Mary as ardently, nay, more ardently than ever, only I am afraid I shall never win her without——"

" Ah, Fred," interrupted his brother, " I must say to you, as I once said before on this very subject, a 'soldier and afraid;' but by nature you most certainly never were intended for a soldier, Fred. I still stick to that."

" It is no use bothering any more about it, then; the truth is, that I love Mary, and would do anything to win her; but she is not the sort of girl to be easily persuaded into what she considers wrong; some might even term her cold."

" Fancy all that, Fred," returned his brother. " I have laid siege to many a heart, that was, to all appearance, far colder than her's, and have ever found them surrender at discretion."

" Yes," said Frederick, " I believe you have done all that; but you must remember I have not, and I am frequently visited with severe compunctions on account of my duplicity to Mary."

" Ah," said his brother, " that, indeed, is a sad bore; and, as a friend, I advise you to get rid of so troublesome a companion."

" It is all very well to give advice," said Frederick; " but it is not always so easy to take it."

" True, Fred, most true; and, as a general rule, I am not prone to give it; but one word more on this subject. If you go to Devon, Fred, without having won Mary, my life for it, you never will win her."

" I wish I loved her less," replied Frederick; " I should then feel less remorse at the thought of making her unhappy."

" There is no occasion to make her unhappy," returned her brother; " at any rate, not till you are tired of her."

" Which will be never," said Frederick, fervently.

" Then, Fred, listen to me one instant. We'll suppose, that before we shift our quarters, Mary becomes your's—good. You leave her, of course, with protestations of eternal love, and so forth. You go to Devon, become acquainted with your incognita, find her rich, and by no means disagreeable, either in person or manners. Feeling assured she sincerely loves you, you marry her, and find yourself in possession of plenty of cash. Good again. Your affection for Mary has undergone no change by your marriage. You go to London, see her, and tell her so; remove her from an employment wearying and harassing to her frame, place her in a situation of competence and ease; visit her often. In short, she is your wife in love and truth—the other only so in name—best of all.  If you can call this making her unhappy," he added, triumphantly, "rather forsake her at once; though I think any one in possession of common sense would rather call it making her happy and comfortable for life, especially as she loves you; but if you ——"

"Enough, enough," replied Frederick, fired with animation; "I hesitate no longer in making myself blest.  I feel that I shall likewise be conferring happiness on my beloved Mary; and yet, how strange that I shall be obliged to use stratagem in order to induce her to consent to our mutual happiness."

"'Tis strange, Fred; but such is the way of the world," returned his brother.  "Yet, now that you have resolved, the sooner you commence operations the better."

"You say right," returned the youth; and then (as lovers are wont), apostrophising the object of his warm affection,—

"Mary, dear, gentle Mary, if I use deception towards you, it is only that I may be enabled to place you in a situation of comfort, and ease you of the irksome toil which you now daily and uncomplainingly pursue."

And here it is worthy of remark, that the young man actually persuaded himself that, as regarded Mary Ellis, he was acting with a praiseworthy motive; as he considered that if he married her without his brother's consent he would be totally without the means of bettering her condition; on the contrary, if, by marrying another, he could become the possessor of wealth, he should thus be able to provide handsomely for her.  And so far, he deemed he was prompted by kind and affectionate feelings for Mary, in following the advice of his designing brother.

Alas! in this subtle reasoning, Frederick forgot that virtue is above all price; and, however bright and gaudy the trappings of vice, it is nevertheless hateful and abhorrent in the eyes of all who are not wholly lost to a sense of sin. And, to a virtuous heart, such as possessed by Mary, the humblest lot, with a consciousness of innocence and purity, is far preferable to the wealth of the Indies, if purchased at the expense of that glorious attribute, virtue.

---

## CHAPTER XXIII.

A FORTNIGHT has elapsed since the evening of Mr. Ellis's arrival at Sackville; the weather is still intensely cold, and the ice-bound earth yet wears its snowy covering; hoar frost glistens on the long, shadowy branches of the leafless trees, which, standing out in bold relief, seem to rise almost spectre-like out of the surrounding snow, which completely envelopes all things else.

It is evening; and the dark blue firmament is thickly studded with brilliant and glittering stars, which fancy might well imagine to be the eyes of angels looking down (from the blest abode above) on to this lower world, where grief and sin so much abound.

The reader, doubtless, remembers the spot where Mr. Mordaunt and his cousin met, and here we again desire to conduct him.  A female figure, wrapped in an almost Siberian costume, well calculated to defend the wearer from the piercing cold, was pacing up and down the avenue, as if in expectation of meeting some person.  Ever and anon she cast an anxious glance around her, as if impatient of delay.  And, as she did so, a pair of sparkling eyes, and a profusion of glossy ringlets, were perceptible through the thick folds of her black veil, which defended her face from the inclemency of the weather.  At length the sound of other footsteps was heard, and, at the same instant, a soft, musical voice exclaimed,—

"Is that you, Mr. Mordaunt?"

"It is I," returned that individual, who now joined her.  "And I am afraid, Miss Stanhope, that I must plead guilty to the rudeness of having kept you waiting."

"It is of no consequence," replied Emily; "I have been here but a few minutes."

"And it is, indeed, kind of you to come at all.  I scarcely hoped to have the pleasure of seeing you.  It was bold, indeed, of me to request this favour; but I am about to leave Sackville."

"Yes," replied Emily; "I inferred as much from the note you gave to my maid, and that induced me to grant the interview; but, oh! Mr. Mordaunt," she added, turning anxiously to him, "I have also received a letter from one who styles himself your cousin, in which he accuses you of being guilty of the most dreadful crimes, the bare thought of which causes me to shudder."

"Alas! Miss Stanhope, can you believe me capable of having committed such deeds? I had hoped that you, at least, would have done me the justice of discrediting such vile falsehoods."

"And you were not wrong," said Emily, frankly; "I did, I do, discredit them."

"Miss Stanhope," replied Mordaunt, "I have had misery and sorrow enough to make me contemn the whole human race. I have met with oppression and cruelty where I most looked for sympathy—for advice. I loved with a tenderness and devotion that men seldom experience, but I nursed in my bosom the snake that was doomed to destroy me. She, too, whom I loved was, in appearance, possessed of every amiable attribute; and, to gaze upon her sweet, ingenuous face, none could believe her capable of deceit. It is not, therefore, surprising that I should (from the moment that I discovered her baseness) have entertained a mean opinion of the sex; but, since I have had the honour of becoming acquainted with you, I have been convinced that I judged most erroneously in taking one as a pattern of the whole. There are some possessed of true, generous, and noble hearts; and you, my dear Miss Stanhope, are one of them, and, for your sake, I am willing to believe there are also many others."

"You will, indeed, oblige me," replied Emily, "by endeavouring to think better of my sex."

"Great as the pleasure is that I feel in your company," returned Mordaunt, "I will not, Miss Stanhope, detain you on such a night as this. My cousin has accused me of the murder of my uncle, of whose death I call God and his attesting angels to witness my hands are free; yet, to escape the persecution of my relative, I intend to leave England for ever; but, though most anxious to be away, I could not quit Sackville without bidding you a long, a last farewell."

"It is a difficult word to utter with calmness, and I am sorry to be forced to pronounce it now," said Emily; "but, wherever you go, Mr. Mordaunt, rest assured that my best wishes follow you; indeed, my thoughts will often wander back to the meetings which have taken place between us."

"If aught could cheer or enliven my breast," replied Mordaunt, "it would be the words you have just uttered, and which I am sure emanate from your heart; but my destiny is sad and solitary. Forgive me, Miss Stanhope, but I cannot part from you without telling you that your numberless good qualities (far more than your attractive person) have made an impression on my heart that will never be effaced. Had we met under different cirumstances, I might have presumed to endeavour to win your regard; as it is, the mention of such a word is almost an insult to you."

This was the first time words of love had ever been breathed to Emily, and it is therefore by no means surprising that they fell pleasantly on her ear, and that her heart gave a faint response to the expressed regard of Mordaunt, which she considered the more flattering, from his having previously been prejudiced against the sex.

She strove for a moment in vain to make some reply, but she found a difficulty of utterance she had never before experienced. Mordaunt mistook her apparent emotion for anger, and said, in a deprecating tone,—

"You will forgive me, Miss Stanhope, for having spoken to you one word connected with my own feelings; I meant not, I assure you."

"There is no occasion for any apology," replied Emily, with that frankness which formed a very pleasing trait in her character; "a woman is never indifferent to an avowal of affection, honourable alike to herself and to him who makes it."

"May I infer," replied Mordaunt, while a shade of joy illuminated his pallid brow, "that you are not offended with me for having dared to nourish in my bosom a regard not, as I said before, for your personal, but your mental attractions."

"Far from being offended, I feel honoured by such a preference," returned Emily, placing her hand in the open palm of Mordaunt.

"We meet no more on earth, Miss Stanhope," he replied, as he carried her hand respectfully to his lips. "If I am fortunate enough to escape my persecutor, this time to-morrow I shall be floating on the broad seas, hastening from England, and all that is dear to me on earth; but the remembrance of this hour will never be effaced from my memory. My days may be few or many, it is utterly impossible for me to determine; but this I know, that, while life remains, you will be fondly treasured in my breast, and never will I cease to weary Heaven with prayers on your behalf. I trust, my dear Miss Stanhope, that your path through life may be bright and pleasant. Indeed, I feel assured that it cannot be otherwise. Virtuous, gentle, amiable, and good, you must, you will be happy."

"And you?" said Emily, in a sorrowful voice.—

" Will strive, in a foreign clime, to banish all thoughts but the blissful one of feeling assured you are interested in my fate, and will sometimes bestow a thought upon me," replied Mordaunt, endeavouring, by speaking in a more cheerful tone, to remove the despondency that was perceptible in Emily.

"I will not," she replied, "seek to turn you from your purpose, or persuade you to remain in England. I am convinced you will be happier when far away. Oh! Heaven grant that you may prove successful in your plan of escape! Every moment," she continued, in a more energetic tone, "is precious for your safety; therefore, I entreat of you, go at once. Do not linger here another instant, or it may prove fatal to your meditated flight."

"I will go at once," replied Mordaunt; "but must first see you nearer the village. I cannot leave you to return this distance alone."

"Oh, think not of me, Mr. Mordaunt," said Emily; "I came here this evening alone, and, in like manner, I can return; consult, I beseech of you, only your own safety."

"Believe me, Miss Stanhope," he returned, "I shall hazard nothing by accompanying you towards the village. Since you have condescended to feel an interest in my behalf, rest assured I consider my liberty too precious to put it lightly in jeopardy; you will not, then, I am convinced, deny me this last gratification of walking a short distance with you."

Emily instantly placed her hand on his arm, and, in that manner, they proceeded towards her uncle's residence.

"I trust," said Emily, "that your cousin entertains no suspicion of your absence."

" I have every reason to hope that I have completely eluded his vigilance, and doubt not that he fully believes I am, even now, at the doctor's. I took advantage of Mrs. Blake's temporary absence, to leave the house unobserved; and, as I had previously desired not to be disturbed on any consideration, my flight will not, I trust, be discovered for several hours, and that will afford me ample time."

"God grant it," said Emily, fervently; "and now let us say farewell."

" Be it as you wish," replied Mordaunt; "we are now close to the village. I will, therefore, bid you an eternal adieu."

"Hush!" said Emily, laying her hand on his arm. "I feel certain I heard steps approaching—there! Do you not hear them now? Alas! all is lost."

"Do not be alarmed," he replied, in a subdued voice, and then, seeing Emily turned deadly pale, and trembled violently, he passed his arm round her waist, in order to give her support.

At this instant the steps became more palpable, and the next moment the curate confronted them.

"Good God! Mr. Ellis," exclaimed Emily, clasping her hands; "what are you doing here?"

"Rather," returned the curate, with evident surprise, "allow me to ask what you are doing here; it is more unusual for you to be abroad at this hour than for me."

"Mr. Ellis," said Mordaunt, " I am happy to have thus met you this evening, in order that I may confide to your care this precious trust. I solicited this interview with Miss Stanhope to bid her farewell. I am about to quit this place; and you will not blame me, for wishing, before my departure, to hear her pronounce a long, a last adieu. We have had meetings before; some days she will impart to you everything concerning them. You will promise me this, Miss Stanhope."

"Yes, yes," she returned; "but do not linger now; pray, pray depart instantly."

"Then, farewell," he replied, pressing her hand tenderly in his own; and then, withdrawing it, he stretched it towards the curate, saying, at the same time, "We have ever been friends, George; you know my unhappy history, and will not, therefore, be surprised at my sudden determination to quit this place; believe me, wherever I may go my best wishes will still be for your welfare."

The curate received his proffered hand, but amazement seemed to have deprived,

MR. ELLIS MEETS WITH A SURPRISE.

The next moment, the curate confronted them. "Good God! Mr. Ellis," exclaimed
Emily, "what are you doing here?"

him of the faculty of speech, and he gazed at Emily and Mordant without uttering a word.

" You will not refuse to say farewell," said Mordaunt, after a moment's pause.

" No, no," replied Mr. Ellis. " Good bye, James ; I trust you may yet be happy."

At these words, Mordaunt, without trusting himself with another glance at Emily, turned quickly round, and was speedily out of sight.

" Will you allow me, Miss Stanhope, to conduct you to your uncle's residence," said the curate, after a short interval, during which they had both remained profoundly silent, gazing in the direction Mordaunt had taken.

Emily started at the sound of his voice, and thought there was an unusual coldness in his tones ; but, then an unwonted oppression weighed down her usually buoyant spirits, and for the first time in her life she seemed to stand in need of sympathy, and would gladly have found it in the curate.

In reply to his question, she merely signified her consent, and accepting of his proffered arm, they pursued their walk for some minutes in silence ; Mr. Ellis was the first to speak,—

" I presume, Miss Stanhope," he began, " that Mr. Mordaunt has acquainted you with the painful secret connected with his history."

" Only in part," replied Emily ; " yet, I confess I feel deeply interested in his welfare."

" I," returned Mr. Ellis, " have known him almost as long as I can remember anything ; we were as boys, school-mates and play-fellows ; and in late life, chums at college ; he was then wholly dependent on a rich uncle, whose estates he now inherits, and who at that time provided amply for him ; though, on account of his having, himself, become the father of an illegitimate son, he treated Mordaunt with a severity bordering on unkindness.

" Soon after we had left college Mordaunt wrote, and informed me of his having become tenderly attached to a young lady, who was at the time an inmate of his uncle's house. It unfortunately happened that Mordaunt's cousin had also conceived a strong attachment for her, which his uncle encouraged, and endeavoured to prevail upon the young lady to receive his addresses. She, however, gave the preference to Mordaunt, and in order to release her from the importunities of his cousin, he persuaded her to elope. She consented, and they came to London. I had just taken orders, and Mordaunt applied to me to perform the ceremony of marriage. It was the first time I officiated on such an occasion, and I felt great pleasure in uniting Mordaunt, whom I knew to be of a generous and noble disposition, to one who seemed in every respect deserving of him.

" Isabel was possessed indeed of the rarest personal charms ; and if her face had formed an index to her mind, she must have been all that is considered amiable and excellent in a woman. Alas ! that it should have been otherwise ; such external loveliness as hers ought to have been joined to beauty and purity of mind."

" It is, indeed, sad," said Emily, who felt greatly interested in the curate's narrative ; " but, pray proceed, for we are drawing very near home."

" Will it be asking too great a favour of you to extend our walk a short distance, as I may not have another opportunity of finishing ?"

" By no means," interrupted Emily ; " it will afford me pleasure to do so."

" I was saying," resumed Mr. Ellis, as they turned aside from the village, " that it gave me great pleasure to unite my friend to the woman of his choice, and they were married with every prospect of happiness.

" Directly the indissoluble knot was tied (and which is just six years ago), we parted, and Mordaunt and myself met not again till he came to this village ; but I repeatedly received letters from him, and which I ever made it a point to answer. And it was with deep regret I learnt, that no sooner had his uncle become aware of his marriage with Isabel, than he signified his intention of withdrawing the provision with which he had hitherto supplied him. This was the more cruel, inasmuch as he had educated Mordaunt for no profession, and he was wholly without the means of providing in a suitable manner for his young wife, who had been accustomed from earliest infancy to luxury and profusion.

" In this unexpected trouble, I can truly say Mordaunt thought not for an instant of himself ; he was so devotedly attached to Isabel, that poverty was felt on her account alone.

After much time and anxiety had been expended, he at length obtained a situation as private secretary to the Honourable Henry Tierney, who was himself quite a young man, but married, and the father of two children. The income that Mordaunt derived from this source, although liberal, and placed by him entirely at the disposal of Isabel, reserving but the veriest pittance for his own wants, yet fell far short of her desires, and she frequently reproached him with having been the means of reducing her to comparative poverty."

"Oh! can it be possible that she could act so cruel and ungenerous a part?" exclaimed Emily, energetically.

"It is but too true," replied the curate; "and yet, Mordaunt so fondly loved her, that he bore it with uncomplaining patience; to me alone did he ever breathe a word concerning her, and then he made every allowance, frequently in his letters reproaching himself for having married her without being assured of a settled income.

"Thus passed the first year of their wedded life, and Isabel became the mother of a girl; soon after which the Honourable Henry Tierney (honourable in title only) chanced to call at the apartments occupied by Mordaunt and Isabel, in order to speak with his secretary concerning some business he wished forwarded immediately, and was immediately struck with the extreme loveliness of his wife, of whose personal attractions he afterwards expressed himself to Mordaunt in the warmest terms, who never dreamed of suspecting that he nourished any base designs towards her, till report began to speak loudly of his frequent visits to Isabel.

"For a while Mordaunt refused the slightest credence to these reports; but at last his suspicions were aroused, and he accused his employer of endeavouring to wean the affections of Isabel from himself. Angry words ensued between them. Mordaunt, naturally of a fiery spirit, could not brook the cool insolence of the other, and the dispute ended in his being dismissed his employer's service. Mordaunt in vain strove to obtain a similar situation elsewhere; the only employment he could procure was occasional copying for lawyers, and though, when he could obtain it, he worked hard, the pay was so bad that he found himself unable to provide for his loved wife and child.

"At length even that precarious employment failed him—starvation stared them in the face. Isabel's reproaches grew daily more intolerable; he parted with almost every article of value to procure her and her child necessaries, thinking and caring nothing for his own wants. Mordaunt, as a last resource, determined on making an appeal to his uncle, to whose estates he must necessarily, at his death, succeed; he therefore sought, and, with some difficulty, obtained an interview with him.

"For her sake alone he bowed his natural pride, and even entreated of his uncle to make him, at least, a trifling allowance. He was answered by angry reproaches and contemptuous expressions.

"In vain he beseeched him, for the sake of Isabel, to do something towards snatching herself and her child from starvation.

"'Let her starve,' returned his uncle; 'she deserves it. And now leave my house this instant, and never let me see your face again.'

"Irritated almost to madness by the cruel and unfeeling conduct of his uncle, Mordaunt, in his turn, answered in anger, and upbraided him with his cruelty. His uncle, still more incensed, bade him, at his peril, remain another instant in his presence, and they parted with anger and upbraidings on either side.

"Almost heartbroken at the want of success he had met with, Mordaunt bent his steps towards his home; having arrived at a short distance from which, he was astonished to perceive his late employer, Mr. Tierney, coming out; and, on his arrival, he questioned Isabel, when she admitted that he had been to see her. He communicated to her the result of his interview with his uncle, and then gently remonstrated with her on encouraging the visits of Mr. Tierney in his absence. She answered him with reproaches on having reduced her to a state of absolute poverty, and inquired, with flashing eyes, if he expected her to stay with him and starve?

"He has since informed me, that he had no power to reply; his spirit seemed entirely crushed.

"The following morning he received news of his uncle's death. He was subject to epileptic fits, and the excitement of the meeting which took place between him and his nephew, had brought on one of the attacks, when, in falling, he struck his head against a corner of the marble mantelpiece, inflicting thereby a deep and frightful wound, which caused his death in a few hours.

"Thus was Mordaunt most unexpectedly placed in circumstances of affluence by the death of a relative who, the evening before, had denied him the smallest donation."

"It would seem an especial act of Providence," replied Emily, who had been a silent and attentive listener.

"It would, indeed," returned Mr. Ellis. "On hearing of his uncle's death, Mordaunt determined to say nothing concerning it to Isabel, till he was actually in possession of the estates. And fondly he pictured to himself the joy of restoring her to wealth, and, he hoped, happiness. He therefore made an excuse for leaving home for a few hours, and hastened to his deceased uncle's steward, to beg the advance of a few pounds for his present necessities. It was, of course, instantly granted, and, on his return home, he stopped to purchase a few trifles he thought would be pleasing to Isabel, laden with which he entered once more his own residence; but, alas! her for whom he suffered so much and so long, was gone, never to return; it was clearly evident, from her own and the child's wardrobe having been carefully removed, that her flight was premeditated."

"Alas!" exclaimed Emily, "poor unhappy Mordaunt, how great his anguish must have been!"

"You say truly; it was, indeed, great," replied the curate; "and you will not, I am sure, feel surprised that the cruelty and oppression of his uncle, and the dishonourable conduct of Mr. Tierney, should have prejudiced him against his own sex."

"Oh! no, indeed," said Emily; "and Isabel, alas! her conduct was enough to prejudice him against ours."

"No, no," interrupted the curate; "he should have felt, as I have often strove to convince him, that she was an exception to the general rule; for women are seldom otherwise than amiable and good."

Emily felt the delicacy of the compliment, and thanked him with a smile. "But," she said, "has not Mr. Mordaunt heard anything of his wife or child since?"

"Nothing; of course he believes her to be living with Mr. Tierney; but he has never ascertained such to be the fact."

"It is a very painful story," replied Emily; "for Mr. Tierney, I think you said, was himself married?"

"Yes," returned the curate; "and accident made me acquainted with his lady, and a more amiable female, or more devoted wife, it would be impossible to find."

"Alas!" exclaimed Emily, "how many are made miserable through the wickedness of one."

"Such is only too often the case," returned the curate; "but my narrative will, at all events, have the effect of causing you to think better of my friend than, perhaps, you have hitherto done."

"I needed it not on that account," replied Emily; "my heart has ever done him justice; but how dreadful it is for him to be accused of having caused the death of his uncle."

"Dreadful, indeed," said the curate; "for he is innocent alike in thought and deed, I am confident, Miss Stanhope; but we are now close home. I hope you are not fatigued."

"So far from it," said Emily, "that I am sorry our walk is well nigh ended; it is one of the pleasantest I ever remember to have taken."

"May I ask, as a favour," resumed the curate, after a short pause, "that what I have confided to you this evening, may for the present be strictly confined to your own breast."

Emily readily gave the required promise, and, having arrived at their destination, they together entered her uncle's residence.

---

## CHAPTER XXIV.

AGREEABLE to the advice he had received from his brother, Frederick the following evening met Mary at the door of the fashionable milliner's. As they walked home together, Mary remarked that her young lover was uncommonly silent, and appeared to lack his usual gay spirits. On inquiring the cause, he informed her that the regiment to which he belonged was shortly about to remove from London, and that dread of separation from her made him thoughtful and unhappy. Mary, herself, though possessed of more fortitude, could not refrain from dropping a tear at the intelligence.

"Yet," she replied, endeavouring to speak calm, "we must, dear Frederick, submit to what is inevitable. I shall, indeed, sadly miss you when you are gone, but will strive to console myself with the hope that you will not entirely forget me."

"Forget you, Mary! Never—never!" returned her lover, vehemently. "But, oh! I cannot prevent the thought constantly dwelling with me, that, if we part without being united, I shall never know the bliss of calling you mine. You are, dear Mary, so rich in loveliness, that—that——"

"Say on, dear Frederick," said Mary, seeing that he paused "You would not, surely, question my love or constancy!"

"I feel, Mary, that I am wronging you by the thought; and, yet, as I said before, you are so lovely, both in person and mind, that I fear (I cannot help it) a more worthy rival may succeed in depriving me of that love which is the brightness and joy of my existence."

Frederick paused for an answer, but Mary made none. Her lover felt that she leaned more heavily on his arm; but her eyes were bent on the ground, and the thick folds of her veil completely hid her face from his anxious gaze.

"Mary," he resumed, after waiting in vain for her reply, "you are not offended with me; tell me, at least, you are not offended with me!"

"Not offended," replied Mary (and her voice trembled); "but, I confess, I feel much hurt that you should, for one moment, encourage a doubt of my faith. Oh! Frederick, how little can you value a love which admits of a doubt of its constancy. How differently do I feel for, and judge of you, who, among gay officers, will mix with bright assemblies, and there meet with others possessing fairer charms than me. Yet, Frederick, I should," she continued, with more animation, "consider myself undervaluing your love, if I encouraged the slightest doubt of your constancy. No! go, Frederick, and believe that, even though your affections should be swayed by others, I will, at least, ever think you true."

How severe the pang that, at these words, shot across the breast of Frederick! Could he longer meditate the betrayal of a heart so trusting, so tender, and so true? No!

"Strange power of innocence, to turn
To its own hue whate'er comes near,
And make e'en vagrant passion burn
With purer warmth within its sphere."

Yet, such was now the case. Had Mary been less trusting, her love less pure and holy, Frederick would have felt no compunction; but now, as he spoke again, his voice had the low, earnest tone of one who speaks with his whole heart, in sincerity and truth.

"Forgive me, Mary, love, that I, in a moment of unhappiness, spoke doubtingly of your love and faith for me. I can no longer entertain the slightest doubt regarding it. Yet, oh! my dearest Mary, do not, I pray you, refuse to give me a right to watch over your happiness—to claim your love exclusive of all others."

"You have it, you have it," interrupted Mary, hastily.

"I know it," replied Frederick; "and yet I dare to ask for more. I entreat of you, Mary, to become my wife before I leave London; the ceremony shall be as private as you please, none but ourselves shall know that we are so nearly and tenderly related."

"Do not press me upon this point," returned Mary, earnestly; "we have both relatives, who ought to be consulted before we take such an important step."

"I cannot comply with your request, Mary; I must, I will press you on this one subject; on all others, dearest, I will be ruled entirely by your wishes. You will not, I am sure, then, refuse me this favour—we shall shortly be parted, it is impossible for us to say for how long; and if we delay being united now, we know not what may occur in the interim, to prevent us ever——"

"Nothing can ever occur, dear Frederick, but the failing of our love," interrupted Mary; "and that we will not speak of."

"Life is ever uncertain," returned her lover; "we know not that we may live to meet again."

"In that case," said Mary, "it would be of little importance whether we were married or otherwise; but we must not dwell upon such gloomy forebodings; rather let us part cheerfully, encouraging the hope of a speedy re-union. Then, if you succeed in gaining the consent of your parent, and I my brother's, you will find, Frederick, that I shall be proud and happy to become your wife. Surely this," she added, striving to smile, " will satisfy you."

" Do not deem me unreasonable, Mary, if I candidly confess it does not. To part with you, under any circumstances, will have the effect of rendering me very unhappy ; but much misery and anguish will be spared me, by the knowledge that you are irrevocably mine. You will consent, then, love—will you not ? If you still refuse, I shall fear that you do not love me as I could wish."

Alas ! how is it that when men seek to carry a point with one between whom and themselves vows of love have passed, when all other arguments fail, they have recourse to the simple expression, " Then you do not love me." Surely, because they well know the implied doubt carries with it a severe pang to the breast of a woman conscious that the reproach is undeserved.

Those simple words have oft prevailed, when the most persuasive eloquence has been expended in vain, when all other arguments have failed. And the woman who has yielded not an inch to the tender pleadings of her lover, has found all her wise resolves melting away before the words, " Then you do not love me." Thus it was with poor Mary ; she endeavoured in vain to continue steadfast in her resolution to deny Frederick's urgent request ; but when he had put it thus, she wavered, and at length yielded a reluctant consent. And yet it is surely ungenerous thus to wring from a woman a favour her conscience whispers she is doing wrong to grant ; but Frederick thought not of this, (alas, when do men think of aught but obtaining their own wishes) ; he was only filled with his own magnanimity in being actually about to abandon the brilliant destiny which he deemed almost within his reach, for his incognita was evidently rich and desperately in love with him, and had likewise avowed her intention of shortly making herself known to him, and endeavouring to win his regard. Her disappointment, he considered, would naturally be severe on discovering that he had plighted his troth to another ; and he could scarcely forbear a sigh as these thoughts passed through his mind ; but when he gazed on the lovely face of his Mary, and looked into the deep wonders of her large black eyes, he felt she was worthy of the sacrifice, and repented not of his resolution to make her his bride.

This, of course, he felt he must conceal from his brother ; while he lived, he should never be able to acknowledge his wife, the chosen of his heart. No ; Mary must be content to bear that holy name only in secret ; but she knew it not, or never would she have consented to the union.

Mrs. Herbert, the only friend to whom poor Mary could look for advice and support, naturally of a weak mind, and particularly short-sighted in all things, looked forward to the wedding with the most joyful anticipations for the future.

As everything connected with that event was to be conducted with the utmost secresy, and though about to become a bride, Mary would possess a husband only by name, she deemed it perfectly unnecessary to make the preparations that are usual on such occasions.

The Sunday following the conversation we have recorded between Frederick and Mary, was the day appointed for the ceremony ; and a more inauspicious one could scarcely have dawned upon this earth.

The frost which had continued in unabated severity for several weeks, suddenly broke up, accompanied with heavy rain.

Mary had promised to meet her lover at an obscure church towards the east end of London, and having procured a hack cab, accompanied by Mrs. Herbert, she was driven to the spot. Here they found Frederick already waiting their arrival ; he had laid aside his regimentals and was dressed in a plain suit of clothes. Mary looked anything but a bride, being attired in her ordinary habiliments, which the reader is aware was deep mourning ; and a thick crape veil concealed her face, on which no soft warm blush mantled : her cheeks were white, and pure as Parian marble, and contrasted painfully with her raven hair and mourning dress ; but though the folds of her veil concealed this, yet it could not wholly conceal the deep glances of her large lustrous black eyes.

" The day was louring, stilly, black," when Mary and Frederick stood side by side at the altar ; there were but few persons in the church, but those few regarded them with a perplexed and surprised air. It was strange to see a bride wearing the ensignia of sorrow, and some hesitated not to affirm that it was adopted as a disguise, and all agreed in regarding it as a luckless omen.

Seldom hath so handsome a pair, both so eminently rich in youth and beauty, been united in the bonds of matrimony, than the two who now pronounced those irrevocable vows. Frederick heeded nothing, saw nothing, but her, who, with all his faults, he yet fondly loved, and injured her not by giving her (as is too often the case) a heart that has deceived or wrung with anguish another. No; she was the first and only possessor of his affections, and he gave utterance to his part of the service in a firm, manly voice.

Mary, on the contrary, was not free from her sex's weakness, and the inauspiciousness of the morning, which appeared to frown on their nuptials, affected her spirits with a sadness not of late very foreign to them; it was therefore in a weak and trembling tone that she repeated the responses.

The ceremony concluded, as had been previously arranged, Mary and her friend returned alone, to prevent awakening any obtrusive curiosity; but Frederick shortly after joined them.

"Mary, love," he exclaimed, as he remarked her more than usually pallid cheek, "you must not look sad on a day so bright and joyous as this one. Come, love, bless me with one of your own sweet smiles."

Mary strove to comply, and a smile did illuminate her features for a passing instant, and she replied,—

"You must not think, dear Frederick, that I am otherwise than happy, because I cannot be so gay as you would wish to see me. I confess that this unexpectedly gloomy morning has rather affected my spirits."

"It is, indeed, vexatious," returned Frederick; "but do not, my love, let that render you uncomfortable; remember, I am now your husband."

"I do," answered Mary, and the long-absent bloom stole momentarily back to her features; "but I also remember that we have not reached the goal of happiness. We must submit to be separated for an indefinite time, and, though I should deeply have mourned the absence of my lover, I must still more deplore the departure of my husband."

"Ah," returned Frederick, impetuously, "it is indeed sad to be parted from each other. Confound the regiment! I wish to God, Mary, I could find some means of remaining behind."

"Stop, stop, Frederick," said Mary, in a mild but deprecating tone. "I have given you proof that my heart is yours, only yours, in consenting to this hurried and secret union; but I am still Mary Ellis. I cannot conceive myself as having a right to your name till such time as you have gained the consent of your parent to acknowledge me as your wife; till then, our paths are separate. You must continue your wonted avocation —I mine; therefore, it is imperatively necessary that you should go with your regiment. Rest assured that I have the fullest confidence in your love; and when happier days arrive the marriage service shall be performed anew. We shall, then, in truth, be one; till then ——"

"I am content," replied Frederick. "You are now, dearest Mary, irrevocably mine; no power on earth can render you otherwise than my own loved wife. I shall go, satisfied and happy with the assurance that nothing can now separate you from me. And yet, it is sad to be obliged to keep our marriage so secret, that even my brother must for the present remain perfectly ignorant of it."

"And mine likewise," returned Mary; "and I need not say that I could much have wished it otherwise, for I am sure he would be much hurt to know that any but himself performed the solemn ceremony that has this day united us; but regrets are now perfectly unavailing."

"They are, indeed, Mary; therefore, I trust you will not indulge in them; we must hope for happier days."

"That is unquestionably the wisest plan," replied Mary; "and I will endeavour to pursue it. You will write to me often, Fred, while you are away; your letters, I can say with truth, will be my only consolation in your absence, which I earnestly hope may not be for many months. I shall count the days, I had almost said, the hours, dear Fred, till your return."

"And shall not I, Mary, be wretched and unhappy at knowing I possess so fair and lovely a bride as yourself, and yet be doomed to a long and mournful separation? I wish, Mary, you could contrive to go into Devonshire likewise; my brother need know nothing of it, and then I could spend my evenings with you as I do now; and we shall still be happy in each other's company. I am sure, Mary, you can so manage it if you will."

"Frederick," said Mary, earnestly, "I must insist upon it that you do not urge me on this subject; remember upon what conditions I consented to this union. It was only upon the full and plain understanding, that we should each still pursue our separate paths; in short, that we should be married only as a form, to prevent any unforeseen circumstances (which might possibly arise) dividing us for ever. And now, dear Fred," continued Mary, "having said thus much, let us not again speak on this subject, equally painful to me as yourself."

The day continued throughout wet and gloomy, which confined the party entirely to the house: they had planned a short excursion from the metropolis; but the unfavourable state of the weather obliged them, of course, to abandon it. Mary felt depressed in spirits, which the circumstances connected with her marriage were anything but calculated to banish; and she felt that this day, a day generally looked forward to by young persons of her own sex as one of unmitigated joy and gladness (though most all have proved the fallacy of such an opinion when they have had an occasion to put it to the test), was to her one of the saddest of her life. Frederick, too, appeared to lack his usual gaiety; they were seated side by side in perfect silence, apparently watching the rain as it pattered against the windows, and ran slowly down the panes; but their thoughts were busily engaged on the future, each hoping for happiness in store, and each half dreading lest they should grasp the shadow, and lose the substance. Thus the day wore on. Mrs. Herbert left the youthful pair, who had so recently plighted their faith, alone, the greater part of the time, thinking her presence might be a restraint to their mutual converse; but, as we have seen, they were little inclined for conversation.

The night set in rough and tempestuous, the wind howled round the corners of the streets, and whistled loudly in the chimneys.

"It is a very unpleasant night to be abroad in," said Mary, as her lover rose to depart; "I am sorry you are obliged to return this evening, Fred."

"I am not absolutely obliged," returned the young man, hesitatingly, ; "and if it will not inconvenience you to afford me accommodation, I am willing to remain here till the morning."

"No, no," replied Mary; and the rich blood forced its way even to her very temples; "by all means, go to night."

Frederick stooped to kiss her blushing cheek, as he prepared to do her bidding; for he had no longer power to urge his request. And, yet, he felt it a painful task to tear himself away from his fair young bride; and the parting kiss was oft given to be again renewed. But, at last, with a promise of meeting her again on the morrow, he tore himself from her side.

---

## CHAPTER XXV.

Our readers, we hope, have not forgotten the elegant mansion, to the fair inmate o which Mr. Ellis paid a visit on his first arrival in London, as we desire once more to introduce him to the interior of that abode.

It is the Sabbath evening, the day on which Mary had plighted her faith to Frederick. On a couch is stretched a suffering and, apparently, dying child; kneeling by the side of which, her hands clasped, and her eyes upraised, in tearless agony, is the young and lovely mother—her who, to save that child from poverty and distress, had sacrificed her all of earth, and, it was too much to be feared, her all of Heaven. That child had been cherished at her heart's core as the one little being that made life sweet and precious; for whose sake she had smiled upon one, and feigned an affection (the most arduous thing in the world) for him she did not—could not feel.

To secure that idolized object of her love a shelter from the rude blasts of adversity—a safe haven, where not even the winds of heaven should visit her too roughly—she had bowed her pride, and submitted to be judged cold, calculating, and avaricious. All, all this, and more, she had borne, not only unrepiningly, but had wreathed her face in gladness—had met the embraces of her betrayer with apparent eagerness and joy—had seemed, not merely content, but delighted with her lot—had drank, day by day, nay, hour by hour, from the bitter cup of self-reproach—had smiled when her heart felt breaking—had carefully, oh! how carefully, cultivated those graces of person which she possessed in so eminent a degree—that beauty, which was doomed to be her bane; had even courted the hand

THE DEATH OF THE LOST ONE'S CHILD.

[And then the mother raised her beautiful eyes to Heaven, now swimming with tears, while her hands were clasped before her, and she still retained her kneeling attitude.]

of the spoiler—had——but we forbear; we have said she sacrificed her all for that one fair child, hitherto healthy and strong, but now suddenly brought low.

What words can depict the agony of that mother, who had thus garnered up and centered every thought in that young child, as she now hung in silence over its dying couch; one little hand, already cold and clammy with the icy grasp of death, she held within her own, striving, in vain, to impart warmth by so doing.

The soft blue orbs that had never before met hers without an expressive gush of childish tenderness and love, now, alas, were fixed in death. No more, oh, never more would they beam with joy and gladness, or return a mother's tender glance; no more would the hoping words of childhood, so precious to a doating mother's heart, again resound with pleasure in her ears. No; the summons had gone forth from which there is no escape—the mandate which all must obey; and again death was about to pluck one of the fairest and purest flowrets that ever bid fair to bloom upon this earth.

How little thought that mother, as she watched the light, elastic step, and saw her bound across the floor where late she trod,—"her beautiful, her own,"—that blighting was so nigh; that even then the canker was at the heart; that the tongue that prattled so sweetly would soon be mute in death; that the hand would no more return her pressure, or the eye her look of love.

Silence had reigned in the apartment for some time, when the mother spoke.

"Oh, tell me, doctor," she said, in a low but touching voice, addressing the physician, who was likewise bending over the sufferer; "oh, tell me, do you not think she may yet recover? Oh, surely, surely, there is a possibility. Children frequently suffer so much, and yet ultimately recover: may it not be so with her?"

The doctor shook his head.

"It would be useless to deceive you, madam; there is no hope."

He spoke these words calmly, but the mother pressed her hands upon her bosom as though to stifle the bitter emotions of her breast, and bent her head till the rich folds of her luxuriant hair, which hung like a curtain around her, swept the very floor.

And oh, she was so lovely, and her beauty of that soft and touching kind which irresistibly appeals to the feelings, and never fails to awaken a deep interest in the beholder.

The physician had watched with her over the dying child for hours; he seemed chained to that spot, without the power or will to leave it. He gazed upon her extreme beauty and the utter abandonment of her sorrow with a feeling almost of sacredness; he would gladly have offered consolation, but he dared not; he felt that words would be a mockery to her grief.

Had it been in his power to have restored that child to health, oh! what a blessed and holy task he would have deemed it; but, no; she was past all human aid; the bud that had given promise of blooming so sweetly here was destined to unfold its beauties alone in the garden of Paradise. It could not blossom here, the climate was too cold. And yet death lingered o'er the couch, as if in pity; though not in anger, not in wrath, he had surely come that day.

A flickering light appeared to play over the pallid (but not wasted) features of the child, irradiating its countenance with an unearthly brightness; and then encircled the small, but beautifully formed head, on which it rested, like a crown of glory. A sweet smile parted the coral lips, the eyes dilated with apparently joyful surprise, as if some surpassing vision met their delighted and astonished gaze; and then the flickering light played again over the pallid features, illuminating them with increased brightness, and then it once more rested as a crown of glory on the head. The face, for an instant, shone as though it reflected back the rays of the sun; and then the crown increased still more in beauty, and the child made an effort to extend its arms, and its lips moved; the mother bent to listen, and caught the words, "I come." And then there was a long stillness, the crown gradually faded, the features settled down into the repose of death; all was changed, save the smile that remained indelibly there.

And then the mother once more bent down to listen, but her darling was gone—gone to a purer and better world; but she could not feel assured that such was the case. Again her voice broke the stillness of the chamber, and, with a beseeching look at the doctor, she exclaimed,—

"Is she not better?—see how still, and in what sweet repose she rests!"

"Sweet, indeed," replied the doctor. "Compose yourself, dear madam; your child is at rest for ever."

Once more she bent over her loved one's couch, and held her cheek lightly over the mouth of the babe; but no soft breath fanned her fevered brow. The doctor had spoken truth; the child was at rest for ever. She knew it now; all doubts had vanished from her mind.

> " The flower she had cherished
> So fondly, was dead ;"

And with it—

> " Her last hope had vanished,
> Her last dream had fled."

And now her agony burst forth in smothered sobs and groans. And then she raised her beautiful eyes to heaven, now swimming with tears, while her hands were crossed upon her breast, and she still retained her kneeling attitude.

"My God!" she cried "thou art just; thou hast meted it unto me even as I deserved." The doctor gazed on her lovely face and form with renewed interest.

"Surely," he thought, "this fair creature, who seems to move in an atmosphere of dove-like innocence—surely she can have done nothing to deserve so severe a chastisement as this."

There is not, there cannot be, anything so touching as beauty sunk in sorrow and utter despondency. The tears came thick and fast to the eyes of the physician as he contemplated the bereaved and disconsolate mother; and yet, he felt any attempt even at consolation would be an utter profanity.

He whisperingly inquired of the servant, who stood near him, if her master was expected shortly to return.

She replied that she scarcely knew; he had not been home for a long time, and her mistress had made no mention of him; but that he rarely stayed away so long, and, therefore, she concluded he might be speedily expected.

"It will be a dreadful shock for him to find his child dead," said the doctor, who had withdrawn the girl to the farther end of the room.

"He will, of course, be surprised," replied the girl; "but he never seemed over fond of the poor child, though a sweeter or more affectionate baby was never born. And my mistress perfectly idolized her; I think, indeed, that her death will break her mother's heart."

"We must hope better," returned the doctor. "I much wish that your master were here, as he might be able to soothe the bitterness of her anguish, which she must feel a great deal more from having to bear it alone."

"Poor soul, it is indeed a heavy trial for her," replied the girl, who appeared attached to her mistress; "but, somehow, I don't think she cares much for master."

"Not care for her husband!" replied the doctor, in a tone of surprise, who had felt assured in his own mind, that whoever owned so lovely a being for his wife, could not do otherwise than adore her; "and, surely," he argued, "she would love him in return."

"Why," returned the girl, "I don't know that I ought to say so, for she always appears glad to see him, let him come when he will; but, to my mind, that alone is not altogether a proof of love."

"Indeed," said the doctor; "I should have regarded it as a strong presumptive proof; what other would you require?"

"As I said before, she is always pleased to see master, when he does come; but then she never seems sorry when he goes, or unhappy in his absence, even though he may remain away, as he has done lately, for many weeks together."

"You are a very accurate observer," replied the doctor; "but what can be done for your mistress? Do you think you could induce her to retire? she must greatly need rest."

"I will see what I can do," said the girl, as they both moved towards the spot, where her mistress still knelt.

Her upturned face and streaming eyes were raised towards Heaven, as if she said,—

> " Nor roof, nor cloud between
> Her own pure orbit and the skies;
> And though her lips no motion made,
> And that fix'd look was all her speech,
> They saw that her rapt spirit prayed
> Deeper within, than words could reach."

And the two gazed on her in silence, but attempted not to interrupt her. At length she turned, and gazing upon the face of her dead child, she pressed a fervent kiss upon its lips, and then exclaimed, " My sweet innocent, for you alone I consented to live a life of sin and sorrow; for never have I known happiness since I forsook the path of virtue. Oh! is there, can there be any return for one so vile as I am? We are parted, my child, I fear (alas! how terrible is the thought) for ever."

" Oh! speak not thus mournfully," said the doctor, with an air at once of respect and admiration. " Your child is but gone before you, to a better and a brighter state of existence. You will most assuredly meet again in Heaven. Oh! think of that, dear madam, and endeavour to compose yourself."

" Alas, doctor!" she exclaimed, rising from her kneeling posture, and casting a bewildered glance around. " You know not to whom you speak of another world. Alas! I have bartered all my hopes of Heaven. Oh, God! I am rightly punished. And yet, oh, yet! it was not for myself, or any consideration of my own sufferings, but for her who " no longer needs my love or care," pointing to the couch, on which lay the dead child; for her, for her alone, who was wasting day by day for want of the common necessaries of life."

The doctor glanced round the elegantly furnished room, and then upon the stamp of nobility that was impressed on that young mother's brow; and the thought occurred to him, " Surely her mind is wandering—she can never have known the want of anything that money can procure." And he said, aloud,—

" Dear madam, I entreat of you to yield to my persuasion, and retire to rest."

" Alas! alas! there is no rest for me," she exclaimed, clasping her small white hands; " no rest, no rest. Oh! the tumult of anguish that rages here," she continued, pressing her hands convulsively on her bosom, " is beyond the power of any to assuage."

Oh! it was a sad and fearful sight to see that fair young creature, in appearance the very type of all that is lovely and loveable in a woman. Her hands were clasped, her eyes upturned, dropping their tears like moonlight rain.

Alas! she should, she might have been blessed in the love of an adoring husband. And though the loss of a beloved child is at all times a bitter grief to a mother's heart, yet she would have known where to look for comfort amidst the storm of sorrow, which now, wholly unsupported, threatened to overwhelm her with its devastating influence.

" Pray, pray be persuaded, my dear madam, at least, to strive and obtain rest," said the doctor, kindly; " your own health may otherwise ——"

" My own health," she hastily interrupted, " is of no value; there is none for whom I need wish to live; that child was my all on earth; for her I wished to live, for her I was content to suffer contumely and reproach; but with her all is gone. All, all at one fatal stroke."

" Consider your husband," gently urged the doctor.

She started as he pronounced the name—a name which should be far dearer and more treasured than even that of mother.

" My husband!" she repeated; " alas! he no longer owns the name; with my own hand, I recklessly rent those bonds asunder. I heeded not his love for his only child, but severed him from ties at once of husband and father. Oh, God! I thought not, cared not for his sufferings, though I now feel how great they must have been. Oh! how acutely he must have suffered, when he found us both gone—fled with another; and that other—alas! alas! my very brain seems on fire!"

Here the doctor again interposed, and at length succeeded in inducing her to seek repose.

She retired to her couch, with an aching, mourning heart. What an awful amount of misery was compressed into that long, long night! What bitter thoughts came thronging back, to render her sufferings still more acute! Days of happiness and sunshine, when tender relatives smiled upon her, and gave her back joy for joy—love for love; when, full of hope and bliss, she fondly looked forward to years of increased happiness. Then the ever busy, wandering mind presented the image of her injured husband, painted his anguished brow and pallid cheek: and then she wrung her hands in increased agony, and sobbingly exclaimed,—

" Oh, James, James! thou'rt fully, amply avenged. Thy misery, however great, cannot possibly equal mine; for no plague-spot is in thy bosom—thou hast never walked hand in hand with guilt as I have done. All are, doubtless, ready to administer consolation and balm to thy wounds; but mine, mine none can heal. All must shun me with detestation and abhorrence. And I deserve it—oh, God, I deserve it! my punishment is well merited. But from this hour, I dedicate myself to a life of virtue. Guilt shall no longer enchain my soul. I care not now what becomes of me; none can deem more harshly of me than I deserve. All is now over for me on earth, save a few short years to hide my shame and sorrow deep in the recesses of my own breast; but these baubles have not, never had, charms for me. I will forsake them all, and seek some lonely, humble spot, where I can spend the remainder of my life in remorse for the past; and, oh, if it is possible, by deep and bitter repentance, obtain pardon of my Maker."

Thus passed that sad night which succeeded the death of the child. Towards morning she gained a little sleep, and awoke more composed.

The dear baby had been laid to rest in its last narrow cradle. A sweet and holy smile just parted the coral lips, and on its downy cheek death had left no stamp to tell of his presence; no sign to show the soul had fled; the beaming eyes were folded for ever beneath their snowy lids, their light extinguished almost as soon as it began to shine. Yet none but a mother could wish it back to this world of sin and grief. Sweet bird of Paradise! what sorrow, what bitter tears, what misery and pain hast thou not escaped, by being thus early transplanted to a more genial clime!

The unhappy mother flung herself on her knees by the side of the little coffin, which held all that was now left her of her treasured babe. No tear bedewed her cheek, but the convulsive throbbings of her bosom and the silent agony of her clear blue eye gave painful evidence of the sorrow of her heart. There she knelt, her eyes rivetted on the child, her fair hands clasped together, and her long auburn tresses hanging in dishevelled folds over her slight but beautifully formed figure. The blue veins in her alabaster forehead throbbed perceptibly, and her whole appearance was that of a subdued but deep-seated misery, fearful to witness in one so young and fair. She moved not, she spoke not; the hours passed unheeded on, and there she still knelt, almost as motionless as the slumbering infant upon whom she gazed.

Thus, day by day, she spent many hours, till a week had drawn its slow length along, and the lid of the coffin was closed for ever upon her darling; and she uttered no sigh, shed no tear; printing a long, long kiss upon its lips, she looked a last farewell upon the infant's sunny brow.

She had spoken but little to any of her attendants, still less signified her intention of quitting the house; and, much to their surprise, the day following the funeral, she carefully selected from her wardrobe a few of the plainest of her dresses, and proceeded quietly, assisted by her maid, to pack them in a trunk; this done, she collected a few other trifles, scrupulously leaving out everything that was not strictly her own. The girl noticed this, but offered no remark, though she wondered much whither her mistress intended going, and several times was on the point of indirectly asking the question; but there was something about her that forbade any approach; an unusual sternness sat upon her brow, and her flushed cheek gave token of feverish mental excitement; perhaps, the more intense, from being so outwardly subdued.

"That will do," were her first words; "there is nothing more I desire to remove; you may close the trunk."

The girl hesitated a moment, and then said, reaching her hand towards it,—

"Your jewel-case, madam, you have doubtless forgotten. Shall I not place it in the box?"

She answered hastily, "No;" but then added, in a hurried voice, "Stay; let me see it."

The girl instantly presented it to her mistress, who opened it, and selected therefrom a gold wedding ring, which she placed upon her finger, and then, withdrawing from her small white hands the heavy glittering jewels, which seemed to weigh them down, hurriedly returned them to the case, at the same time desiring the girl to return it to its usual place, who in silence obeyed.

She then proceeded to attire herself in a plain travelling dress, and casting a hasty glance round the room, as though she were about to bid it farewell for ever, turned to the young girl who stood by her side, and, in a thick and smothered voice, though she seemed endeavouring to speak with calmness, said,—

"Jane, I know I can depend upon your honesty; you have served me well and faithfully, therefore I have no hesitation in informing you that I am about to quit this place for ever.  I entrust everything to your care till such time as you can deliver them to their rightful owner."

The girl burst into tears as she exclaimed,—

"Pray allow me to accompany you—do not, madam, deny me the honour of still serving you."

"Cheer up, girl," she returned, affected by her emotion ; "I no longer need your services, or I would gladly avail myself of them.  It is necessary for you to remain here, in order to take charge of the house."

"But, alas! what am I say to my master when he arrives, and finds you gone ?"

"When he arrives, and finds you gone !"  The words seemed to touch a chord in her heart, which vibrated to the sound, and she sunk into a chair, and covered her face with her hands.

At that instant a loud and hurried knock was heard at the street-door, and which, before the porter had time to open it, was repeated, as though some person was desirous of obtaining instant admittance, and was impatient at the slightest delay.  In less time than it takes us to narrate it, footsteps were heard ascending the stairs ; the door of the apartment was thrown open, and Mr. Tierney, whom we last left stretched on a bed of sickness, pale and haggard, as it seemed, with mental, as well as bodily suffering, entered the room.

"Thank God !" he exclaimed, as he did ; "I am in time, you are not gone yet.  Oh, God! what have I not endured!  But, but——" He stopped, for the unhappy lady had sunk, like yielding snow, slowly and almost imperceptibly to the ground.

———

## CHAPTER XXVI.

WHEN Mordaunt left Emily with Mr. Ellis, he hastened to the railway terminus, and lost no time in engaging a special train to convey him to London, urging for the greatest amount of speed.  Money he declared to be no object—they might charge whatever they thought fit ; his only anxiety was to be in London as early as possible.

"You may depend upon the greatest amount of speed that is consistent with safety," replied the obsequious station master to whom Mr. Mordaunt addressed himself.

"That is, of course, all that I require," he replied; "when will you be ready to start ?"

"Directly, sir, directly ; the engine is now being got out ; we shall be in readiness for you to start almost instantly."

"Well, see that I do so ; I cannot brook delay; would to God we were on the line," said Mordaunt, with an impatience that convinced his hearer he must be some one of importance.  He, therefore, bustled about, ordering one, scolding another, swearing at a third, till he had completely succeeded in throwing them all into an utter state of confusion and bewilderment, retarding, as a matter of course, their progress, and, greatly to the vexation of Mordaunt, consuming the time that was so important, so paramount to all other things as regarded his safety.  Still he felt it would be utterly useless to remonstrate ; so folding his arms across his breast, he surveyed them with a sarcastic smile, and waited till all was in readiness, though ever and anon sending a searching glance around, half dreading to meet the gaze of him he so wished to shun ; but the red glaring lights from the furnace fires reflected only the begrimed and blackened faces of the men, who appeared as if they were meant by nature to live in that mixed element of smoke and fire.

And presently the stoker who was to accompany the engine destined to convey him to London, began to clamber over and upon it ; and then the steam was let off in loud and impatient puffs, as though the engine, itself a thing of life, cavilled at the delay, and was anxious to perform the journey.  And now the engineer and guard, in their shiny-fronted caps, climbed into their respective places, and smiled an adieu to others of the same calling, leaning over to call out some parting admonition, or cut some joke at their acquaintances, which took immensely with the bystanders.

But all this was done so leisurely, that Mordaunt, who had taken his place in the carriage, could scarce refrain from giving utterance to a remonstrance.  Indeed, he was on the point of doing so, and only prevented by feeling the carriage in motion.  Yes; at last they were off, and Mordaunt sank back on his seat, and ejaculated half aloud, "Thank God!" as he felt assured that so far his plan of escape had proved successful.

They had been gradually gaining speed from the moment of starting; and now they appeared to be flying along the line with the rapidity of lightning.

On, on, on, through tunnels (which they entered with a long, shrill whistle, resounding far and wide, like the wild scream of an affrighted animal), over bridges, which they seemed well nigh to accomplish at one leap. On, on, on, through fields, parks, meadows; now running along what had once been the bed of a river, now flying along the top of a high embankment. On, on, on; no cessation: the mouth of a tunnel was for one instant only perceptible; the next, a scream, a bound, a plunge, and they had dashed through it, and were again beneath the canopy of Heaven.

Surely this was speed enough for any one. But no; it did not keep pace with the desires of Mr. Mordaunt, who felt that he was flying from an undeserved prison—perhaps, even, an unmerited and disgraceful death. Oh, when he thought of this, the blood boiled in his veins; he clenched his hands, and the perspiration stood in large drops on his forehead. His heart swelled to bursting; and, in the bitterness of his soul, he exclaimed,—

"Oh, God! dost thou live, and yet permit this relentless man thus to oppress and trample on his fellows? but I shall now escape. If there is justice in Heaven (for on earth I know there is none), God will, for this once, aid me. I shall succeed, and gain a quiet resting-place for the remainder of my life." And then his thoughts recurred to Emily, and his better angel quelled the storm of passion in his heart, and he reproached himself for having, in a moment of despondency, impugned the wisdom of the Almighty.

How much is in the power of woman! what an ascendancy she possesses over the mind of man! Oft, even unknown to herself, doth she pour the balm of consolation into his wounded breast, and wave a magic wand before his troubled spirit, and bid its rough waves subside in peace.

Oh, woman! high and holy are your duties; see to it that you perform them well. You, and you alone, can bend man's rude and stubborn will, and make him gentle, mild, and kind; strengthen his wise resolves, wean him from sin, and make him wise and better by your tender caresses, and your soft, winning words. Man needs and seeks for sympathy at your hands. Oh, never let him seek it then in vain. He has to encounter the storms and buffets of the world, and meets therein much to depress and weaken his spirits, that woman can never know. Then let not light, frivolous pursuits, or vain coquetry, beguile you from the performance of duties which are incumbent on your sex— duties high and ennobling in themselves, and which will not, cannot fail, to shed an halo of light and loveliness around you.

Men are occasionally to be met with, who, judging all from what they have seen of one, think lightly of a woman's character; indeed, hesitate not to pourtray her as cold, calculating, and selfish. Thus it was with Mordaunt; but when he became acquainted with Emily, and experienced her readiness to offer consolation, not by words only, but an unaffected sympathy for his, as yet, unknown sorrows; her eagerness to aid and assist the distressed; and a something which is undefinable in a woman's character—a mixture of tenderness and innocence, which at once cheers and sustains man's fainting spirit; —no sooner, we say, had Mordaunt experienced all this, than he confessed the error into which he had unwittingly fallen, and acknowledged woman's mission to be that of a ministering angel; and so will all who know her aright. Alas! that we should be forced to say, "Woman, it is your own fault, if man think ill of you; a patient and untiring performance of your duties will most assuredly win golden opinions from all men." Then, be careful, very careful, that you give him no cause to think harshly of you.

Directly Mordaunt's thoughts flew to Emily, his mind instantly regained its tone; he felt more kindly disposed towards all others; and, though feeling, with a sense of bitterness, that he had ever been oppressed in no light degree, yet, with a calmer heart, he was enabled to look back upon the past, and forward into the dark future.

"There is," he exclaimed, while a tear trembled in his eye, "at least, one being in the world who feels an interest—a concern for my welfare. Man may brand my name with crime; I may be doomed to descend to the grave with infamy on my head; but she will do me justice, will believe it is undeserved; nay, shed a tear for my fate, which will embalm for ever my memory. She is, indeed, my better angel! her smile has charmed away the dark spot from my brow. My heart melted within me while I listened to her sweet converse, in which tenderness and hope were so richly blended; that love, which I deemed was for ever dead within me, revived at her bidding; and still she knew it not.

Oh! Isabel! I once little thought you could ever possess a rival in my affections. I loved you truly, fondly, with a tender, unwavering affection. Nothing but your own guilt could ever have estranged this heart from you. And yet, I now feel it was a love, based on no solid foundation,—your beauty attracted my eye, and I made you mine without seeking to ascertain aught concerning your disposition. But now I love for beauty and loveliness of mind; it was that I learnt to admire, ere I thought her even interesting in person. And Isabel, thy name is unworthy to be spoken in the same breath as hers who now holds undisputed possession of my heart; and yet she owns not one half thy personal charms; but then her mind and disposition are all excellence and purity."

Thus soliloquised Mordaunt as he was whirled along the line; he heeded no passing object—it was all the same to him whether they passed through towns or villages, or were again in the open country, save as it marked his onward progress to the metropolis. To gain that was now his great end and aim; that attained, he thought he could easily accomplish his escape. London was a vast place to live in, containing many nooks and corners, in which he might successfully conceal himself till he could embark in a vessel that would waft him to a foreign clime.

On, on, still on they went at one unvarying speed, rapidly nearing London—passing other engines and carriages that were drawn off to the sidings to allow them free passage —past stations, where numbers of faces, reflected by the red lights, appeared to glare upon them for an instant, and then were gone.

On, on, still on, till London was reached without the slightest interruption or slackening of their speed. They had performed wonders, even Mordaunt was willing to allow, as he stepped from the carriage on to the platform, and saw by the station clock that the journey had been accomplished in less time than he had expected; and accordingly their reward was liberal. Having ample means, and caring little for it, Mordaunt was ever profusely liberal: we mention this, not that we consider any praise due to him for his liberality, for he was exceedingly lavish of what he set no store by. Had he regarded money with due value, his gifts would have been more, far more to be lauded. It is very easy to bestow upon others what is regarded at a very low estimate by ourselves; but it requires some self-denial to give that which is held of slight value in our own eyes; and the praise for so doing is, of course, commensurate with the amount of self-denial it imposes.

When Mordaunt found himself in London, his greatest desire was to escape observation; so, drawing his hat over his eyes, and wrapping his cloak loosely over his form, that he might conceal himself from the knowledge of any former acquaintance he might chance to meet, he turned down the first obscure street he came to. It was indeed a long and gloomy one, and Mordaunt scarcely knew whether or not it had any thoroughfare; and not wishing to return into the open road, and perceiving a turning to his right, he bent his steps in that direction.

He still pursued the course he thought would most probably lead him to the waterside; and yet, after walking quietly for more than an hour, he seemed farther off than when he first started. Stopping, therefore, to consider which way he had better turn, he observed the street, in which he stood, more narrowly, and for the first time perceived to his surprise that it was within a few minutes' walk of the abode of Mary Ellis. With the recollection of her, came also the conviction, that there he could procure a safe and pleasant asylum for the night, in which he would be subject to no remark; and if his cousin discovered his flight, and followed him to London, before he was enabled to embark in a vessel bound for a foreign clime, he would be far more likely to escape his observation in the humble house of poor Mary than at any public place of entertainment; thither, therefore, he resolved to bend his steps, and a few minutes more found him knocking at the door.

It was opened by Mrs. Herbert, of whom he inquired for Miss Ellis. There was a little hesitation in her manner; and, after she had received his name, and returned to announce his coming, Mordaunt thought he heard, from the parlour, a hurried consultation, and then an unwonted bustle; but, immediately afterwards, Mary made her appearance, and in her usual, quiet, gentle tone bade him welcome, apologizing for having kept him waiting.

Mordaunt followed her into the little parlour, which was vacant, and then made known the object of his visit, addressing her as follows,—

" I have come here this evening, Mary, a supplicant for your kindness. I am about to leave England for ever—stop, Mary," he continued, seeing she was about to interrupt him,

THE RAILWAY STATION AT SACKVILLE.

[Mordaunt folded his arms across his breast, and waited till all was in readiness. The red glaring lights from the furnace fires reflected only the begrimed and blackened faces of the men, who appeared as if they were meant by nature to live in that mixed element of smoke and fire.]

" listen to what I have to say before you make any inquiries concerning your brother. I will only now say, I left him perfectly well and happy ; at least, I consigned him to the care of one in whose company I think he could scarce be otherwise than happy."

At these words a sound, resembling a smothered groan, appeared to issue from some part of the room.  Mordaunt started.

" Mary," he exclaimed, " are we alone ?" as he sent a searching glance round the apartment.

" Yes, yes, perfectly alone," she returned.

" And yet, I could swear I heard ——"

" There are other persons in the house," she interrupted, hurriedly ; " and it is by no means unusual for sounds of voices to appear close to us, when they are in reality some distance off."

" But you are quite certain we stand no chance of being overheard?" said Mordaunt, hesitatingly ; " for I am about, Mary, to impart to you what might ruin all my prospects, if heard by any designing or meddling person."

" Rest assured," replied Mary, " that there is no such person within hearing ; indeed, we are perfectly alone  And if I can aid you in any manner, I scarcely need say that it will afford me pleasure to do so."

" You can, Mary, assist me very materially, and I will not wrong you by doubting your willingness."

" That is right," said Mary.  " You may command my services to any extent, only tell me in what manner you require them."

" You are well acquainted," replied Mordaunt, " with my most unhappy history, and therefore I need only inform you that my ——"

" Wife," said Mary, seeing he hesitated.

" No, no," returned Mordaunt, " I thought not of her, neither have I any desire to do so ; other thoughts have effaced her totally from my remembrance.  Hush !" he added ; " surely, Mary, there must be some person who overhears our conversation.  I could be certain that but this moment I heard a deep sigh, seemingly close to me."

" You are not accustomed," said Mary, eagerly, " to the sounds of this house.  I told you before that there are others who share it with me ; but none, I am convinced, in any other part of it can hear conversation that takes place in this."

" You would not, I am sure, deceive me," replied Mordaunt ; " and it may be—indeed, it must be, that I am nervous to-night, and my weakened imagination ——"

" Undoubtedly that is it," interrupted Mary ; " so make yourself perfectly easy ; and now inform me of the object of your visit.  You look careworn and harassed.  I trust no new misfortune has befallen you."

" No new misfortune, Mary ; but I was about to tell you that my cousin persists in accusing me of the murder of my uncle—has even threatened me with a prison, and probably a shameful death."

" Oh, do not," said Mary, earnestly, " give the slightest heed to his ravings.  He cannot possibly possess the power to harm you."

" I know not that, Mary," returned Mordaunt ; " innocence does not always triumph over guilt ; and he tells me that he has found persons who will unhesitatingly perjure themselves, by swearing they saw me inflict the blow that deprived my uncle of life."

" Oh, God !" exclaimed Mary, " is it possible that men so vile can exist ?"

" Only too possible," said Mordaunt ; " but, to the point : I have so far contrived to elude the vigilance of my accuser, and it is my intention to secure accommodation in a vessel that will leave England the earliest.  I care not whither I go, so that I escape from my merciless and unrelenting persecutor.  Now it is possible, Mary, that he has already discovered my flight, and may be even seeking me at this moment ; here, at least, I am in comparative safety, for it is next to impossible that he will track me hither.  Yet, Mary, believe me, I will not inconvenience you longer than is absolutely necessary.  I desire a shelter for the night, and, to-morrow, I hope to be fortunate enough to procure a passage in some vessel leaving London."

" I am only sorry, Mr. Mordaunt," replied Mary, kindly and frankly, " that I can only offer you very indifferent accommodation ; such as it is, I trust you will believe that I am but too proud to be able to afford it."

" Thank you, Mary," he replied, kindly pressing her hand ; " I was certain that with you I could make bold to prefer this favour ; but, it is now late, and I will not consent to remain here unless you promise to retire to rest; you have need, dear Mary, of repose, for your days are not spent in idleness. For myself, I require nothing beyond a shelter. I need no refreshment, and shall pass the night very comfortably in this apartment."

"Oh, dear, no," replied Mary, somewhat hastily; "not here. I can contrive ample accommodation for us both, without subjecting you to the inconvenience of sitting up; you have been travelling, and must require rest equally as much as myself."

"As you please, Mary; I will be guided entirely by your wishes, with the exception that I cannot obtain rest by depriving you of it."

Mary assured him that she did not desire it; and, after they had partaken together of a slight repast, Mary conducted him to a sleeping apartment; the furniture of which, though exceedingly plain, yet was arranged so neatly, nay, even tastily, by the delicate hand of Mary, and the appointments of the bed were, moreover, of such snowy whiteness, that they would have tempted a far more fastidious man than Mordaunt to seek what is so essential to life, repose.

"You must promise me," said Mary, as she wished him good night, "not to rise in the morning till I call you; I shall sleep in the room below, and, therefore ——"

"I will not make my appearance before you summon me," said Mordaunt, seeing she hesitated. "I shall probably rise early, but will wait till I receive your call before I leave my room; and, dear Mary, good night;" and, drawing her towards him, he pressed a kiss upon her cheek.

The kiss was strictly a fraternal one; Mordaunt had not a thought, or feeling towards Mary that partook not of a tender brother's affection and interest in her welfare; and yet, if Frederick had witnessed the token of love he had given, he might not have been altogether pleased, or satisfied with Mary for receiving it so readily.

Very few persons are willing to admit of the possibility of a tender regard existing between two young people of opposite sex, that is confined entirely to a brotherly and sisterly attachment for each other. It is customary even to sneer at what is termed a platonic affection; and ridicule and sarcasm have done much towards suppressing feelings of regard, that might otherwise very innocently have been encouraged. And that such regard can, nay, has existed, we have not the slightest hesitation in pronouncing to be beyond the possibility of a doubt to any unprejudiced mind.

And why, in the name of common sense, such regard should be suppressed, we are utterly at a loss to conceive, otherwise than a few narrow-minded persons having willed it so, till it has become customary to ridicule the belief in such affection; and such ridicule is a powerful weapon, and often proves victorious, when all others have failed.

Mordaunt slept soundly throughout the night, and awoke not till Mary gently tapped at his door, and pronounced all in readiness below; when he made a hasty toilet, and speedily joined her in the little parlour.

They conversed freely over the breakfast-table; and Mordaunt gratified his hearer by making her brother the subject of his discourse. To hear of his welfare was, indeed, a source of joy to poor Mary; and to converse with one who had so lately seen him, gave her exquisite pleasure.

After the meal was ended, Mordaunt announced his intention of going to the docks to inquire what vessels were about to start, determining, if possible, to engage for a passage in one; and received from Mary advice as to the course he should take, in order to avoid, as much as possible, the more public streets.

The route Mary advised him to pursue, would consume a greater amount of time than going the direct road; but time was of far less importance to Mordaunt than concealment. He, therefore, unhesitatingly followed the line of road Mary had pointed out.

Arriving at the docks, he immediately proceeded to make inquiries concerning the different vessels, and learnt, to his sorrow, that none would sail before three days; but, as one seemed likely to suit him, he entered into an agreement with the captain for a passage, resolving to make every arrangement, now that he was there, and then remain in entire concealment till the hour of embarkation.

Having settled all that was necessary, Mordaunt turned to leave the vessel, when the captain, who had accompanied him to the deck, and was receiving his parting adieu, was accosted by a youth, who, respectfully touching his cap, inquired if he was in want of a cabin-boy.

"No, my lad," replied the captain, bluntly; "we have no vacancy whatever; we have our full complement of men."

The youth hesitated a moment, and then said, modestly,—

"I have an urgent desire to go to America, but possess not the means of paying for a passage; if my services could in ——"

"No, no, my lad," interrupted the captain, who anticipated what he was about to say; "we never do that sort of thing: when we are in want of men or boys, we seek for suitable persons, and pay them for their services. I guess, my lad, you have not been much used to the sea, or you would be less modest in your demand, and find no difficulty in getting a berth."

The boy made no answer to the remark of the captain; but, turning to Mordaunt, thus preferred his request.

"If you have no attendant, sir, I might, perhaps, be useful to you. And, oh! if you will have the kindness to take me, you will, indeed, be performing an act of kindness to a poor, friendless orphan."

"Who told you I had no attendant, boy?" replied Mordaunt, almost fiercely.

"I stood behind you while you were conversing with the captain, and heard you engage a passage for yourself only," replied the youth.

"It is true," replied Mordaunt, "I have no attendant, neither do I wish for any. Good day, captain;" saying which, he was once more on the point of quitting the vessel, when he encountered the disappointed face of the lad, and the thought occurred to him, 'This boy may, as well as myself, have urgent reasons for desiring to leave England; and yet he lacks the means of enabling him to do it;' and, as the thought crossed his mind, he stopped abruptly, and looking earnestly at the youth, he inquired his reason for wishing so particularly to go to America.

"I have not a single friend in England," replied the boy; "and the only relative I possess in the world, I have good reason for hoping to find in America. That, sir, is my reason for wishing to go to that spot, in preference to any other."

"Listen to me one moment, my boy," said Mordaunt, earnestly.

The lad respectfully touched his cap and looked timidly, but hopefully at him.

He was apparently about sixteen, short, and of slender make; his complexion was dark, but bore the appearance of having become so by exposure to the sun, and was naturally of a lighter hue, for his eyes were of the most beautiful blue it is possible to imagine, and his hair of a dark shade of brown, and combed simply to one side of the head.

The features of the boy were regular and good; but in his eyes lay a deep and unfathomable charm—so soft and languishing, that his whole soul seemed to dwell therein; and they seemed at once destined to allure and to destroy. And there was a stamp of nobility on his brow that convinced Mordaunt he had not always been what he now seemed—a poor friendless youth, anxious in any capacity to procure a free voyage from his native land. No; he appeared to have been delicately nurtured, and had doubtless, at one time, been a petted and spoiled boy; kind friends had ministered to his every want, and dwelt with rapture on his growing charms.

"Poor youth!" thought Mordaunt, as he gazed upon him; "thine doth, indeed, seem a hard destiny;" and he felt assured that on him there hung a tale, probably, most probably a tale of woe; and, as he was himself suffering and oppressed, he felt a fellow sympathy for the boy, and drawing him on one side, he informed him of his readiness to pay the captain for his voyage.

"But," he added, "you must understand, my boy, that I do not require your services. We shall be fellow voyagers, mind; nothing more."

"Oh, thank you, kind sir," exclaimed the boy; "you are, indeed, performing an act of generosity, which I can never hope to repay."

"I do not require it," returned Mordaunt. "If you are a good lad, and seem inclined to make your way in another country, I will endeavour to put you in the way of doing so. I need no thanks," continued Mordaunt, seeing the boy was about to express his gratitude. "You had better now return home; you know the day and hour the ship is appointed to sail; see that you are here in readiness."

"Never fear, sir, but I shall be in readiness; would that the vessel were about to start this instant."

"I have judged right," thought Mordaunt; "the boy has certainly a reason for wishing to leave England without delay. I trust he has not been doing anything likely to bring him into trouble;" and then he said aloud,—

"Well, my boy, you had better be moving; I will settle with the captain about you."

Once more expressing his gratitude, the boy bade Mordaunt " good day," and stepping on to the wharf, disappeared among the bystanders.  Mordaunt lost no time in
agreeing with the captain to take the boy, and that done, he hastened home to Mary
Ellis, and informed her what had passed, save that he suppressed all mention of the
youth he had accidentally encountered.  Mary was pleased to hear that he had succeeded
in the object of his visit to the docks, and yet sorry that they must soon part for ever.

" We shall never meet again," said Mary, mournfully, as, on the morning of the day
the ship was destined to sail, they partook of breakfast together.

" Never," repeated Mordaunt; " but, dear Mary, I have ever felt a brother's regard
for you, and I shall still continue to nourish it in my bosom; I shall know, when I am
far away, that I have a dear and ténder sister in England."

" And," said Mary, " you must not forget that you have likewise a wife."

" Hush, Mary, not a word on that subject, if you love me," said Mordaunt, and his
brow assumed a sternness, and his eye an unusual fire.

" I meant not to pain you," replied Mary; " but I wished to ascertain (if it were possible), if Isabel could repent and sue to you for pardon, you would forgive, and again
receive her."

" Never, never," replied Mordaunt, vehemently.  " Oh, Mary, Mary, how can you
speak to me thus ?"

" Forgive me," she returned gently.  " I can only say again I meant not to pain you."

" You do not pain me," returned Mordaunt; " nothing concerning her has power to
wound my feelings now; but the thoughts of my dishonour, wrought by one I so fondly
loved, drives my soul to madness, and fires my blood with angry passions.  But, enough;
Isabel is a libel upon her sex, and one day she will herself be forced to acknowledge it.  I
care not then, how bitter her remorse may be.  I am getting accustomed to the strange
sounds," he added, in an altered voice, " that seem to come out of the very walls of
this house, Mary; or I should declare, at this moment, I heard the sound as of some one
weeping."

Mary smiled faintly, and then endeavoured to pursue the subject, by saying,—

" Isabel is to be pitied, Mordaunt, as well as blamed; it was poverty alone that drove her
to sin."

" Has it driven you, then, Mary," returned Mordaunt, warmly; " have not you been
precipitated from wealth and station to poverty and trouble ?  Have not you, I should
say, been obliged to labour for your daily bread; you, Mary, that were delicately nurtured, and have a soul formed for the enjoyment of refined pursuits and pleasures.  And
yet, Mary, you forego them all, and are content to suffer on uncomplainingly, though your
form grows thin, and your cheek has lost its bloom; but, as I gaze upon you, and feel the
sad cause that has thus altered you, I regard you as a thousand times more lovely than in
your days of affluence, whom your beauty was the theme of all with whom you came in
contact."

" Oh, Mary," he continued, as he pressed her small white hand within his own; " I
have learnt to admire purity and loveliness of mind, far, far more than the outward
charms, which, like the rose, may wither and fade in a day."

" But," urged Mary, " we should be willing to pardon those who are bound to us by
such tender ties as her we are speaking of bears to yourself."

" Enough, Mary," said Mordaunt, hastily; " let us not waste the few precious moments
that are now left us, by discoursing of one whom I no longer regard as having any claim
upon my love or care.  Speak of yourself, dear Mary, and I shall be forced to listen.  I
feel more sorrow at parting with you than ever I expected."

After this, Mary felt that she could urge no more concerning his unhappy wife; she
had done her best to interest him in her behalf; had pleaded her cause more warmly
than many would have done.  Women are too apt to judge harshly of their own sex;
and though this frequently proceeds from thoughtlessness, yet it is not the less unkind
and illiberal, and quite at variance with the gentleness and amiability which should ever
be the most distinguishing characteristic of a woman."

" Farewell, dear Mary," said Mordaunt, as he forced upon her a parting gift; " I wish
you all the happiness you deserve, I cannot say more; give me one parting kiss, and now
I must be gone."

" Heaven bless and prosper you," replied Mary, who was affected even to tears.

In another minute Mordaunt was in the street, and quickly bending his step in the direction of the docks, which in due time he reached, and found the boy who had promised to accompany him waiting his arrival, and, as he approached, touched his cap.

"You are here, I see, my boy," said Mordaunt, in token of recognition ; "and now let us embark at once." The other readily complied, and they were both in the act of stepping on board the vessel, when Mordaunt felt a hand laid upon his shoulder. A dreadful sense of oppression seemed to weigh down his spirit, and cause for an instant a sense of suffocation ; but the next moment he turned fiercely round, and beheld close behind him the face of his cousin, who was accompanied by a police officer.

Mordaunt's brain grew dizzy, his whole frame shook, he reeled like a drunken man, the blood forsook his cheeks, and then rushed back to his very temples in one deep crimson tide, while his eye shot with fiery glances, and he exclaimed, in a deep, stern voice,—

"What is it you want with me?"

"You must accompany me," said the officer. "I have a warrant for your apprehension ; you are arrested on the charge ——"

"Hush !" said Mordaunt, who had completely recovered his self-composure. "I am perfectly innocent of the crime laid to my charge ; but that, of course, is nothing to you ; you are only performing your duty. Call a coach, and I am ready to go with you."

"We have one already in attendance," returned the other ; "I anticipated your desire."

"It is well," replied Mordaunt ; "let us go without delay. The sooner the charge trumped up against me is investigated, the better."

The officer was all alacrity, and, without casting a glance towards his hated relative, Mordaunt stepped into the carriage, and was driven rapidly off.

————

## CHAPTER XXVII.

"MARY," said Frederick, "I am now about to leave you, and the last few days have made me wretched in the extreme."

"Do not let us part in anger, Frederick," replied Mary, gently ; "I have borne your reproaches unrepiningly, and ——"

"You are so cold, Mary," interrupted her lover, "that I sometimes even doubt your love for me."

"Oh, Frederick, doubt it no longer," said Mary, tears overflowing her eyes ; "am I not your wife—what more would you have?"

"Mary, dear Mary," said Frederick, clasping her in his arms, and kissing off her tears, which upbraided him far more than words could have done, for Mary was not a girl given to weeping ; she could not, as some do, sit down and cry over every little trouble that crossed her path ; but now grief and anxiety had taken undivided possession of her heart, and the tide of sorrow flowed in torrents from her eyes.

"Forgive me, Mary," said Frederick, as with tender caresses he sought to stem the current of her grief ; "I meant not to pain you thus."

"You are so impetuous, Frederick," replied Mary, sadly ; "so ready, nay, almost eager, to doubt my love for you—to construe every little circumstance into almost absolute proof that you are no longer so dear to me as you ought now to be."

"Nay, Mary," returned Frederick, "you tell me that you love me, and I know, of course, that you are my wife ; but what does that avail, if I am excluded from your company—forbid, for three days, to come near the house ; and why? because, forsooth, you were engaged with another, whose society you manifestly preferred."

"Oh, Frederick," returned Mary, "what have I—what can I have done, to merit such unkind, such cruel suspicions from you?"

"Ask your own heart, Mary," said Frederick, coldly.

"It acquits me," she replied, "of all that you urge against me. I have done nothing I need blush to own. He, whom I candidly told you was staying here for a few days, had a reason, a fearful reason, for desiring to remain in that strict seclusion, or I would gladly have introduced you to him ; and I am certain that, had he been, in truth, my brother, you would willingly have acknowledged he could not have felt a more truly fraternal affection for me."

"I like not such affections between persons who are not in any way related," said

Frederick, somewhat sullenly; "but, if you can permit others to remain with you for several days and nights together, I am your husband, and may, at least, claim the same favour."

"Hush, Frederick," said Mary, indignantly; "and do not behave in a manner calculated to wean my affections entirely from you."

"To what end have I made you my wife," returned Frederick, "if I am to remain so entirely estranged from you, to allow you to receive the visits of others, and ——"

"You will drive me mad, Frederick," she replied. "What is it you mean by speaking of others? I am utterly at a loss to understand you."

"Then know, Mary," replied the young man, spiritedly, while the blood suffused his cheek to a deeper glow even than usually mantled there, "I have watched this house more narrowly than you imagine, and have proved, by my own eyesight, that you received another visitor, whom you deemed it unnecessary to mention. This Mr. Mordaunt, with his brotherly affections, likewise covered the visits of one who, perhaps, had other views. By God, when I saw him come out, if I had only had a pistol in my possession, I should, for a dead certainty, have levelled it at his cursed head; though I don't know that I ought to blame him, as, under the circumstances, I should, most likely, have acted as he has done."

These words by no means raised her lover in Mary's estimation, and she most certainly began to bitterly repent the hasty step she had taken in becoming his wife; but she likewise felt that now regrets were perfectly useless, and deemed it best to endeavour to conciliate her young and thoughtless husband, who, to confess the truth, we must say, in our own estimation, was utterly unworthy such a noble, high-minded girl as Mary Ellis. But, to proceed; we were saying that she deemed it best to endeavour, for the present, to appease his anger, which, perhaps, was not altogether surprising, under existing circumstances.

"Frederick," she began, after a pause, during which she strove to calm her own excited feelings, "the suspicions that have unfortunately been engendered in your mind concerning me are utterly and wholly devoid of foundation. More at present I cannot say; and if you love me with the warmth you so frequently declare, you will be satisfied with this assurance."

"You have told me something concerning this Mordaunt, and, as far as he is concerned, I am willing to remain content. But who, Mary, is the other that has visited you? a noble-looking, handsome youth, and one well calculated to win a woman's love and favour."

Mary did not like the manner in which her lover addressed her. It offended the dignity and purity of her mind, and was scarcely respectful enough to her, a young and delicate bride; but she answered, without any show of resentment,—

"There is a secret, Frederick, connected with that—that—youth," she added, after a slight hesitation, "which I am not at liberty to disclose, even to you."

"I doubt not," replied the young man, smiling satirically, "there is a secret concerning him, and one you could well disclose, if it so pleased you; but, however, I will not press you on that point—it is a delicate subject, and I will, therefore, endeavour to content myself with a husband's right in you; and mind, Mary, I expect you to award me the lion's share of your affections."

This was said jokingly; but the words, and much more the tone in which it was spoken, greatly offended Mary, and she replied, angrily,—

"I am grieved, Frederick, that you have lost at once all respect both for yourself and me. In a little while, I hope—a very little while, I shall be at liberty to explain to you this seeming mystery, and you will then not only acknowledge the injustice you are now doing me, but will also be sorry that ——"

"Enough, Mary," interrupted her lover; "let us drop this unpleasing topic. I have been absent from you for three entire days; in two more I am destined to quit London for an indefinite time. I have, therefore, made up my mind to devote those two days that are left me entirely and exclusively to you. Mary, I will not quit your side till I am obliged to join my regiment."

"Is this generous?" inquired Mary, in a deprecatory tone of voice.

"Oh! curse all that," replied the young man; "we may never live to meet again; we will not, therefore, be foolish enough to lose the present golden opportunity of enjoying each other's society. Come, Mary," he added, more kindly, throwing his arms round her waist, and drawing her to his bosom, while he pressed a tender kiss upon her lips, "you will not bid me leave you sooner than I can possibly help ; it will be bad enough to part when we are forced to do so."

"Oh! Fred," said Mary, as, completely subdued by his altered manner, she sobbed upon his shoulder ; "you have injured me by your cruel and unjust suspicions ; and then you have spoken to me in so strange and careless a manner that—that, I scarcely know what to think."

"Forget it, Mary, and forgive me ; you will not, surely, be offended at what a careless, good-for-nothing fellow like me has foolishly given utterance to. Come, Mary," he continued, kindly ; "you must acknowledge that I have had reason to feel a little hurt ; you must remember that I have been forbidden by yourself to come near this house for three entire days, and when I begged you to tell me your motive for desiring to keep me away, you at first declined to do so ; and then, when I pressed you more earnestly, you told me that a friend was staying with you, whom you did not wish to see me, although I am your husband, Mary ; now, is that hardly fair ?"

"Not my acknowledged husband," said Mary, "or I would have been proud to present you. The truth is this—Mr. Mordaunt is an old and sincere friend of my brother's, and there were urgent reasons for him to desire to keep the fact of his being in London unknown, and that alone induced him to ask a shelter beneath this humble roof. I could not refuse it him, or I would gladly have done it for many reasons ; but he is now gone, and it is very improbable we shall ever again meet."

"But the other one who has visited you, Mary ; him whom you have not so much as named ?"

"I promise shortly to explain to you everything regarding him of whom you are foolish enough to be jealous ; for the present, will it satisfy you if I give you my solemn assurance that his affections are exclusively and entirely devoted to another ; so much so, that were it even possible I could have desired to gain from him the slightest notice, I never could have done so—his every thought and wish are centered in another."

"Well," returned Frederick ; "I suppose I must be satisfied. I think you love me, Mary ?"

"Think!" replied Mary. "Alas! you know not the terrible injustice you do me by the implied doubt. Had I not loved you, Frederick, with the purest and most exalted affection, I would never have pronounced at the altar those vows which have made me irrevocably thine."

"Then you will allow me to remain with you ?" replied Frederick, persuavively.

What could poor Mary say, what urge, to the pleadings of him, who was in truth her husband ? Nothing ; she felt, under the circumstances, that she was almost bound to make him amends for having kept him so long from her company ; and, smiling through her tears, she consented to his request.

Directly she granted the required favour, Frederick was again the tender, respectful lover he had ever been ; and Mary began to think the provocation he had received, on knowing that Mordaunt remained with her, while he was forbid that privilege, had alone aroused his angry feelings, and caused him to treat her in the cold, satirical manner which (she now fully hoped) was foreign to his nature.

The two days fled rapidly by, and they were happy ; yes, those days were "brief, but delightful," and Mary felt bitterly the pang of parting, which was changed, if not to anger, at least, to sincere regret at her husband's duplicity, when he confessed that he had wilfully deceived her, as the regiment was not destined to remove for another fortnight.

"But," added the youth, "do not look so serious, Mary, or I shall think you are anxious to be rid of me."

"You cannot think that," returned Mary.

"No, no, I will not," he replied ; "let us rejoice, love, that we have a whole fortnight to be together. I should be deuced sorry, I must confess, if I were obliged to part with you now."

"But will a fortnight render us more willing to separate?" said Mary, seriously ; "and your brother will wonder what has become of you."

"Let him wonder," replied the youth ; "I have got a fortnight's leave, and care not a fig for anybody."

Mary made no answer ; there was much in her very youthful husband (now that she came to know him more thoroughly), that she grieved to observe, and would gladly,

THE ARREST OF MR. MORDAUNT.

[They were both in the act of stepping on board the vessel, when Mordaunt felt a hand laid upon his shoulder. He turned fiercely round, and beheld his cousin, accompanied by a police officer.

indeed, have seen altered; still she loved him so fondly, and he seemed so truly devoted to her, that it was no very difficult task to blind her eyes to his many, very many imperfections.

The first week passed in unmixed happiness, and the early part of the second; but, towards its close, Mary, with grief, saw that Frederick began evidently to weary of the monotony in which their days were spent.

"He has," thought Mary, "been so accustomed to lively company, and a constant change of gay scenes, that it is but natural that he should feel dull with only me to cheer and amuse him;" but, though she endeavoured to think and feel that it was natural, a tear glistened on her long, fringed lids, and then rolled unheeded down her cheek.

He was her "sole world," "her universe," and she, alas! (how bitter the reflection) was insufficient for his happiness. Now that there was no recall, no power of retracting, Mary saw, but too plainly, that she was not the sort of girl calculated to ensure the happiness, and keep the love of such a lively, reckless youth as Frederick, and she shuddered as she thought of the future.

Frederick should have mated with one who could have acted her part in the gay scenes and bustle of life; not Mary, who was formed by nature for a life of domestic quietness and retirement. In the gay saloons and crowded drawing-rooms, where Frederick was all life and animation, Mary would have been entirely out of place; it was not her element, and Frederick began to think so. It is well said, that "the lover is blind, but the husband has eyes to see with." And often, oh, how often are marriages made in haste, and repented of at leisure! Love alone, be it ever so true and tender, will not, never has secured happiness. How necessary, then, is it to compare taste, feeling, temper, and pursuits; for a similarity in these things has always attended the happiest marriages; and love, that, perhaps, beforehand was not very violent, has afterwards dwelt tenderly in the hearts that were united in their feeling and desires. Love, be it apparently ever so strong, is nevertheless a delicate plant, and requires constant and daily culture, or it will speedily wither, and die. And, surely, unity of pursuits, a similarity of temperament and wishes, are best calculated to encourage the growth of the tender plant, which, indeed, without it, will never become (as it is capable of doing) a vigorous and hardy tree.

Frederick, as we were saying, began to grow weary of the plain, and, as he termed it, "plodding" manner in which Mary's days were spent. He still loved her—at least he deemed he did; but was anxious again to mix with his brother officers in bright assemblies and fashionable parties. A fortnight's seclusion had convinced him that he was by no means suited for domestic life, and he sighed to be once more in the *beau monde*.

"You seem, somehow, terribly low-spirited, Mary," said Frederick, stretching himself and yawning.

"You surely would not wish to see me otherwise, dear Frederick, when you are so soon about to leave me," replied Mary, laying her hand kindly on his shoulder; and, dropping the work, with which she had been busied, upon her knee, she gazed tenderly and lovingly upon his handsome, yet boyish face.

"I hardly know, Mary," he replied.

"Not know, Frederick!" repeated Mary, sadly.

"Why, the truth is, Mary," he returned, "I can't see any good in your looking miserable now I am with you; and, 'pon my honour, I think a little change will do me good—I do, indeed. You lead a terribly humdrum life, Mary. Don't you get sadly weary of it?"

"Not while you are with me, Frederick. Oh, never—never could I grow weary, when you are by my side."

"Well, Mary," replied the young man, "you are used to this sort of life, and, therefore, it may not seem so insipid to you; but, curse me, if I like it. It don't at all suit my constitution, and that's the truth, Mary."

"It doubtless makes a difference, your being accustomed to gay society," replied Mary, gently; "and, of course, you must miss it."

"Ah! I do, indeed, Mary; and I am afraid I shall not find it very lively in Devonshire; but yet," he added, after a pause, "I should think, if not quite so gay as London, it will be, at least, tolerably passable. I remember, too, Prior told me there is a public ball in the town, soon after Christmas; and, of course, we shall, all of us, make it a point to attend; and ——"

"I think your prospects, so far as gaiety is concerned, are very promising," said Mary, smiling. "I hope, indeed, Fred, that you will be happy," she continued, timidly; "but do not quite forget me."

"Forget you! that would be impossible, Mary," replied the young man, turning to kiss her cheek; "I, who so dearly love you, and run the risk of getting myself into a host of trouble by marrying unknown to my brother; I, who have done this, Mary, could not very easily forget you, you may be sure."

Mary sighed, but found no words to reply to this truly selfish speech.

The morrow came, and Frederick and Mary were seated together, side by side, for the last time; one of his arms was clasped round her waist, the other was fondly held by poor Mary, who gazed upon his handsome countenance, with a fearful foreboding that such would never be again; and then, as the thought forced itself upon her, that absence might estrange his affections, she hid her face in his bosom, and sobbed aloud.

"Don't cry Mary," said the young man, as he smoothed down her raven hair; "we shall soon meet again—a few weeks, or at most months; and then in all probability I shall be again with you."

"Alas! what may not happen in the interim," replied Mary, as she clung convulsively to him. "Oh! Frederick, you have given me cause to fear that it is possible you may love me less. Death," she added, solemnly, "would be a thousand times more preferable, than the loss of your affections."

"You actually make me quite nervous, Mary," he returned, as he tenderly kissed her cheek. "Do, pray, try and calm yourself, or I shall go away so miserable."

Mary was one of the most unselfish beings in the world; she, therefore, strove earnestly to speak in a more cheerful tone, and subdued, in a measure, the violence of her emotions; but when the long, long parting kiss was given, and Mary was strained for the last time to the bosom of him she loved so well, and she had looked her last adieu for she knew not how long, her fortitude forsook her, and she sank upon a chair, and gave free vent to her agonised feelings in a violent burst of tears. In vain Mrs. Herbert sought to comfort her; for awhile she refused all consolation. Mary, we have said, possessed a firm mind; therefore it was not so much the departure of her husband that she mourned, as the conviction (which the short time they had spent together had fixed on her mind), that his love for her had no foundation on which she could rest secure for future happiness. Oh! sad and bitter thought for a young and tenderly attached wife; but rendered ten times more severe when accompanied with the reflection that she has not used sufficient caution beforehand to prevent so sad a misfortune.

Frederick, though anxious to be again amid the bright circles he had mixed in, previous to the fortnight he had devoted to love and Mary, yet felt dull, and, as he termed it, out of sorts, as he wended his way towards his brother's apartments, in St. James's; but when he arrived there, and having once more donned his regimentals, entered the elegant and commodious drawing-room, where his brother was anxiously waiting his arrival, as the signal for dinner, he felt heartily glad to be once more in his old quarters, which contrasted strongly with the humble abode in which he had so lately resided.

"Ah, Fred! is that you, my boy?" said his brother, as he entered. "Well, I must say I am precious glad to see you. John" (this, of course, to the waiting-man), "bring dinner up this instant; I'm cursed hungry. Why, Fred, you have kept me waiting I know not how long. I was just on the point of dining without you."

Fred made some apology as he took his accustomed seat at the table; and now the man appeared, and placed tempting and savoury viands before the brothers, to which Frederick, it must be confessed, did ample justice.

"Well, Fred," began William, when his appetite was a little appeased; "I am anxious to hear all the news. How did you get on?—made it all right with Mary, eh?"

"Yes," replied Frederick, laying down his knife and fork; "I have made it all right at last."

"Well done, my boy; I give you joy of your conquest; but you, surely, have not been staying with her the whole time of your absence?"

"I have," said Frederick, "'pon honour; but I don't mind telling you that I got a little tired at last, and am not sorry to be back again."

"I say, Fred," returned his brother, laughing, "you are not growing weary of Mary already? You, that used to boast of constancy, and sneer so profoundly at such devil-may-care fellows as I?"

"No," said Fred; "I am not weary of her, for I still love her very dearly; but it is uncommonly dull work to sit by her side, and talk love all the day long. Once now and then it is all very well ; but curse me if I should like to be obliged to do it always."

"Ah, Fred, that speech strongly savours of weariness ; and I am afraid you are no better or more constant in your devotions than myself; and I always found that my love just lasted long enough for one object for me to gain her. After that, I ever found my ardour wonderfully abate."

"Well, it may be a little as you may say," replied Frederick ; "but yet I am by no means tired of Mary. I wish, though, she was a little more spirited ; she is, to be sure, very mild and gentle, but then she lacks energy."

"That sort," replied his brother, "are always deemed sly."

"Are they?" said Frederick, quickly.

"You will find it out some day," said his brother, nodding his head knowingly.

"Well, I am sure I should not have thought so," replied Frederick.

"Very likely not, Fred," returned his brother ; "but you are quite a greenhorn at present; but I think you are improving, Fred ; 'pon my soul I do !"

"No letters for me, I suppose," said Frederick, after a pause.

"None, Fred ; your incognita, expecting shortly to see you, I suppose, scarcely thought it worth while to write ; we shall see her soon, Fred, depend upon it. Think of that."

Frederick did think of it. He partook strongly of his brother's character, and anything he was in pursuit of, was to him far more valuable than what he had obtained.

It was, indeed, a sad misfortune for the young man, that, to such a man as his brother, had been delegated the task of introducing him to life, and giving a stamp to his then unformed character. Under good guidance and tender precept, Frederick had been a totally different person.

When his brother first brought him to London, his mind was so pliable, that it was capable of receiving any impression he chose to make upon it, be it good or bad. He did bend it to his will ; and he alone would have to answer for the consequences.

The day following the conversation we have just recorded, the entire regiment, the brothers of course included, arrived at the town in Devonshire we have mentioned as being near to Sackville.

---

## CHAPTER XXVIII.

When Mr. Tierney saw the unfortunate Isabel sink in a fainting fit to the ground, his first impulse was to run to her assistance ; and endeavour to raise her ; but his own weakness, consequent upon the severe injury he had sustained by the railway accident, rendered him totally powerless, and, when her maid had succeeded, by the aid of the usual restoratives, in restoring the unhappy lady to her senses, he could only hang in anguish over her, bedewing her hands and face with his tears.

It is painful, most painful, to see a man weep. Tears to a woman are perfectly natural —they are, as the immortal poet sings,—

> " The weapon of her weakness she can wield,
> To save, subdue : at once, her spear and shield."

When her full heart, o'ercharged with grief, unless it found some outward vent, would break, the tear-drop glistening in the eye, and stealing in silence o'er the cheek, eases the full heart of half its burden, and the sufferer blesses the sweet relief afforded by the flowing tears.

But with men it is far different. They seldom weep ; but when they do, their feelings are, indeed, acute. For, to quote again from the same poet,—

> " Tears, to women, are relief—
> To men, a torture."

And when Isabel witnessed the tears, and observed the pallid countenance of Tierney, her heart reproached her for the part she had acted towards him, and, for one moment, her resolution wavered in its purpose to leave him ; but then, she thought again, "He has a wife—I am told a tender, loving wife ;" and she determined to act up to her original resolve—that of quitting his house and protection at once, and for ever.

Therefore, arising from the couch on which she was reclining, she bade her maid withdraw for a few minutes; and then, turning towards the young man. who was seated by her side, in a tone in which grief and composure strove for the mastery, said,—

"I am glad you have come, Henry; it affords me an opportunity of bidding you adieu."

"Bidding me farewell!" interrupted Mr. Tierney. "Oh! no, Isabel; that must not—shall not be. You will not leave me—me, who so fondly, truly love you—who snatched you and your dear child from poverty, and ——"

"Stop, Henry," said the lady, angrily; "not one word on that subject, unless you wish me to regard you with detestation. Who was it that, in order to gain the wife to his purpose, deprived the husband of the means of gaining a poor but honest livelihood? Oh! shame, shame!" she continued, the burning colour suffusing even her neck with crimson, "that a man should be found so base, so utterly destitute of honour."

"Oh, Isabel! You know how fondly—how madly I loved you. It was that alone that drove me to desperation—that compelled me to gain you at any sacrifice; and you loved me too, Isabel. Oh, yes; my affection was reciprocated by yourself."

"Never!" she returned, drawing up to her full height. "I never could or did love a man whose base conduct I must ever despise. It was a matter of barter only on my part; my lost child"— and at these words her soul melted once more to softness, and her voice trembled—"was dying for the want of the common necessaries of life. I knew not how to procure them by honest and virtuous means; these hands," she continued, stretching out her small and delicate palms, "have never been accustomed to labour—would to God they had—oh! would to God they had!"

"Isabel, my best beloved!" exclaimed the other, tenderly, and imprisoning her hands within both his own, "you have sacrificed much for me, and not even your own avowal will induce me to believe that you were not actuated by a better, a dearer, and more holy motive than the one you have assigned."

He paused, but her head was sunk upon her bosom, and she spoke not.

"You accuse me," he continued "of acting basely, in order to win you to my arms. Oh! Isabel, doth not the end sanctify the means? Heaven knows, I desired your happiness more than my own. You confessed a mutual affection, and to you, at least, I acted openly—honourably, so far as our relative positions would allow. We were both wedded—both parents, when we first met.

"I loved you, and, God knows, had it been possible, I would gladly, ay, gladly have made you my wife. As it was, I felt it impossible not to endeavour to gain your love. I did so, and succeeded; at least, you acknowledged feeling a regard for me, and my earnest desire was then to make you all my own. But I used no artifice to allure you; I had recourse to no stratagem—no mean deception. I told you plainly my desires; I offered you and your child a home, free from all care and anxiety; I assured you, when you whispered your fears that I might weary of you, that you would live in my heart for ever. I secured to you an income that my death even could not deprive you of; and you willingly committed yourself to my love and care. Have I, tell me, Isabel, ever breathed a word to you that savoured of unkindness or ——"

"Stop, stop," she interrupted; "for mercy's sake, stop. I confess that you have spoken truth in all that you have said; and I," she continued, in a bitter tone, "I am most to blame. But it was for my child alone, whom God in his just retribution has taken from me—I say it was for that dear child I consented to sacrifice all else that was precious to my heart. And now that sweet innocent no longer requires it, I am determined to abandon this life of guilt. It is useless to persuade me, Henry, my resolution is fixed."

"If you no longer love me, Isabel," he replied, "I entreat you, for the remembrance of those days when I was dear to you—when you received me with joy—oh, for the sake of the love you once felt for me—the fond, deep passion that now dwells in my breast for you, I entreat of you not to leave me."

"Henry," she replied, seriously, "it is painful to confess my own sins, yet I must with truth declare, I never loved you."

"Oh, God! you never loved me! It cannot be true. You ever seemed so pleased to see me—ran with tender kisses to greet my arrival—looked sad when I spoke of departing. Oh, God! if this was not proof of love, what proof could I hope to find!"

"Alas! it is with shame and anguish I confess I was but acting a part; in sober truth,

> "'You went unmourned, returned unsought,
> And oft, when present, absent from my thought.'"

"Oh, Isabel. Alas! alas! that deceit—such cruel, heartless deceit, should dwell in so fair, so sweet a form; but even now I would beg of you to stay with me, for I loved—what do I say?—I still love you. It may seem madness to speak of it at such a moment as this, but even when stretched on a bed of sickness, from which it was at one time feared I might never again arise, you alone filled my thoughts—your image was ever present to my mind, and made me curse, bitterly curse the sad and unlooked-for accident that kept me from your arms. And now I have torn myself from one who sought in vain by tears, persuasions, and entreaties to keep me by her side—one who has a right to claim my love, and is likewise worthy of it all, and had it, Isabel, before the unlucky hour when first we met; but no, I cannot call it unlucky."

"Unhappy, most unhappy has it been for both of us," replied Isabel. "I have lost state, station, mankind's, my own esteem, and all is now o'er for me on this earth, save a few short years to hide my shame and sorrow deep in my heart's core."

"Recall those words, dearest Isabel, I entreat of you; if not for your own, at least for my sake, recall them, and think better of your sudden determination to quit me, which I can only attribute to the anguish of mind you have endured, caused by the death of your beloved child."

"So far," replied Isabel, "you say truly; for the sake of my child I accepted of your offered protection, and had she lived, I should still have remained with you; but alas! she no longer requires the sacrifice I was only too eager to make, and now I am steadfastly resolved to return to the path of virtue, from which I voluntarily strayed. No inducements on your part, no persuasions will have power to move me from my purpose, I have sacrificed my all to you; you might have saved me from the poverty and sorrow by which I was surrounded at a less price than you demanded and received from me; but let that pass."

"Stay, Isabel," he returned; "I have said, and said truly, that my love for you was so pure and tender, that I would gladly have consummated your happiness at the expense even of my own. Had you intimated by one word that my offer was distasteful to you, and could only be accepted as the means of bettering the condition of yourself and child, I never would have required the high price you intimate as having paid for the beneficial change. I was thankful for possessing the power to assist you; but, Isabel, that word was never breathed by you."

"It was not," she returned. "With shame and sorrow, I confess you have spoken truth. I am convinced, Henry,—more and more convinced, that I am most to blame. Let us part, now and for ever. You have every incentive to induce you to pronounce calmly the word farewell."

"I cannot do it—alas! I cannot do it. I could part with every other tie that binds me to existence; but with you, oh! Isabel—you are so entwined round my heart, that to part with you, would be to rend my very heart strings asunder."

"It must nevertheless be done," said Isabel firmly. "You will soon forget one who has no claim upon your love or remembrance. You have near and dear ties to bind you to existence. You are a husband, and a father; blest in these relations, you will speedily regain your lost happiness, and learn to be thankful that we are for ever disunited."

"But you, Isabel," returned the young man; "if we part, what is to become of you?"

"Heed me not," she replied bitterly; "earth can scarce contain a more wretched, degraded being than myself."

"Oh! say not so," he returned, "while I love you fondly, tenderly, in spite even of all that you have told me concerning the deceit you so long practised towards me. If my presence is hateful to you," he continued sadly, "I will no longer force my company upon you; but do not forsake the protection of this house. It is yours, Isabel, and I am your visitor, and, being an unwelcome guest, will this instant depart."

"No, no," said Isabel. "You have proved yourself possessed of more honourable and generous feeling than I gave you credit for. Oh! never let a thought of one so fallen as me cause you even a moment's uneasiness. Forget if possible the events of the last few years, and you may yet be happy—for myself, I desire to seek some retired spot, where I may spend the remainder of my life in penitence and prayer, trusting, that in the end, I may yet obtain forgiveness of my sins."

"You must, at least, accept from me, the sad cause of your present sorrow and self-reproach, the means of enabling you to command the necessaries and comforts of life."

"My own hands will suffice to procure me these. I shall no longer eat the bread of idleness; I have none to work for but myself, and but little will satisfy my few wants."

"Think well before you attempt to put in practice this wild scheme," said Mr. Tierney earnestly.

"I have thought well," she returned; "neither is it, as you term, a wild scheme."

"Without money, and without friends, unaccustomed to the lightest toil, consider, Isabel, what will become of you!"

"To relieve you of all anxiety on my behalf, I will impart to you thus much of my future plans. Notwithstanding the guilt which encompasses me, there is yet one left, who, though virtuous and excellent in no light degree, will not hesitate to offer me an asylum beneath her roof. Fortune has frowned upon her, and, from independence and wealth, has hurled her well nigh to poverty; but, by honest industry, she has succeeded in gaining a livelihood, and will, I am convinced, put me in the way of doing the like. The knowledge of this will, I hope, remove all your fears concerning my future life. And now there remains nothing but to pronounce the word farewell."

"You absolutely refuse, then, to accept ——"

"Henry," interrupted the lady, "I am resolved, for the future, to depend entirely on my own exertions. Could I, consistent with my present feelings, receive aught from any one, rest assured, I would take from you in preference to all others. I part, at least, with kinder feelings towards you than I anticipated——But," she added, firmly, "we have conversed long enough; it would be utterly useless to protract this interview. What is inevitable is better met at once, with calmness and fortitude; better for both our sakes."

And lightly touching the bell-handle, her maid instantly obeyed the summons, to whom she gave orders concerning the removal of her wardrobe, which, the reader is aware, was packed in readiness for her departure. And then, averting her face, as if fearful of trusting herself with another glance at him she was about so suddenly to forsake, said, in a voice whose tones betrayed the emotions of her heart, stretching towards him, at the same time, her small white hand,—

"Farewell, Henry; believe me, that you are, in this sad hour, more dear—far more respected—than when I first consented to abide with you beneath this roof. I can say no more. Seek not to detain me," she added, striving to speak firmly, though the tears, large and bright, gathered in her soft blue eyes.

He carried the hand she presented to him with fervour to his lips. He loved her; and he deserved that love; merited a kinder reward than the desertion she now meditated. But he had no power to detain her against her own desire. And it was as well for him that a little self-pride came to his aid, and prevented him urging another word to induce her to remain.

For the time, too, he appeared to have lost the faculty of speech. He strove to breathe a prayer for her happiness, but the words died away in murmurs ere they reached his lips. He felt the moisture in his eye, and, in his turn, averted his face, to hide the rising emotion. At the same moment, he dropped her hand—the next, he brushed away the tears, and turned towards the spot where Isabel had stood; but it was now vacant. She had gone, and he was left alone—alone, to indulge in the anguish and sorrow that filled his heart. He cast himself on the couch where she he loved had so late reclined, and for awhile gave free vent to his feelings.

The words of Mr. Ellis, which, at the time they were uttered, sounded prophetic in his ears, now recurred with painful reality to his mind. He had told him, as the reader doubtless remembers, that the end of the guilty connection he then indulged in would inevitably be wretchedness and misery.

"And for this," he exclaimed, in very bitterness of spirit; "and for this I grieved and wounded the gentle heart of my trusting, loving wife! For this I set at naught the wise counsels of him who strove, in all charitableness, to convince me of my sin. My dear, kind, amiable Amelia, will you, can you, receive your guilty husband again to your gentle, virtuous breast? Oh, yes; I feel assured of your love and forgiveness; for, when you unfortunately discovered that my affections had become estranged from you, no reproach, or unkind word even, escaped your lips; with love and tenderness alone you sought to win me back to the path from which I had wandered, and you—yes, you alone shall, for the future, possess all my thoughts and affections; I will sue to thee for pardon, and strive to love thee as thou so well deservedst."

Filled with these thoughts, and animated by the hope of gaining forgiveness from her he had so cruelly wronged, Mr. Tierney shook off the agonised feelings that had so lacerated his bosom, and arranged with the domestics concerning the disposal of the house and furniture ; this done, he set off instantly for the country, determined there, in peace and retirement, to spend the remainder of his life, devoting himself entirely to his wife and children.

## CHAPTER XXIX.

WHEN Mr. Ellis and Emily entered the family mansion of Mr. Stanhope, on the evening of Mordaunt's departure from Sackville, an unusual bustle appeared to pervade that generally quiet establishment.

The powdered footman who preceded them up the broad staircase, wore upon his countenance an air of unusual importance, and stedfastly avoided giving utterance to a syllable, but kept his mouth close shut, as though he were fearful, if he opened it, some intelligence that he desired to keep secret would unwittingly pop out.

Emily and Mr. Ellis looked at each other with puzzled surprise, but on entering the drawing-room, their astonishment increased. Mr. Stanhope's countenance was radiant with intense joy ; an open letter was before him, which had, apparently, conveyed to him intelligence of no every-day character. Mrs. Stanhope's face reflected the joy depicted in her aged partner's, but was evidently chastened with a slight degree of anxiety, and, contrary to her invariable habit, she was the first to address Emily on her entrance, and, as the good-hearted old lady spoke, her tones were even more gentle and kind than usual.

" I am glad you have returned, my dear Emily ; your uncle has received news in your absence, that he is very anxious to communicate, as it especially regards yourself. Your uncle's countenance has, I feel assured, prepared you to expect good tidings ; and, though it is regarded as such by him, yet, my Emily, his very doing so may appear unkind towards yourself."

" My dear aunt," said Emily, completely bewildered, " you speak in enigmas which I am utterly unable to unravel ; whatever is received as good news by my uncle, must surely be regarded in the same light by his niece ; our hopes and interests," she continued, tenderly, " have ever been inseparable, and must ever continue so."

" She is, indeed, a comfort to us," said the old lady, addressing her husband, while her eyes swam with tears, " and I doubt not but she will rejoice with you over the contents of that letter."

" Keep me no longer in suspense, uncle, I beg of you," said Emily ; " I am all eagerness to hear what you have to impart."

" First allow me to wish you good evening, Miss Stanhope," said Mr. Ellis, who conceiving the intelligence to be of a family nature, his natural delicacy made him desirous of departing.

" My dear sir," said the old gentleman, adjusting his spectacles, " pray be seated. I am most desirous you, as well as my Emily, should hear the contents of this letter. It is no secret, I assure you ; nor would I desire to keep it so."

At these words, Mr. Ellis quietly seated himself by the side of Emily, and, with fixed attention, they both listened while Mr. Stanhope read as follows :—

"New York.

" MY DEAR SIR,—You will undoubtedly be surprised at receiving a letter from this city, the writer of which, though an entire stranger, yet claims a near affinity to yourself."— At this passage Emily started, and turned rather pale.—" He has papers and documents in his possession which on inspection cannot fail to prove to you the truth of what he now asserts.

" The Lady Eliza Stanhope, the mother of yourself, when she fled from your father's roof, was pregnant with a son, which, in order to prevent being taken from her (as her husband designed doing, knowing it to be his own), she gave him her word was still-born. Such, however, was not the case ; for he lived to manhood, married, and became the father of myself ; shortly after which, both he and my mother died, and I was consigned to the care of my paternal grandmother, the Lady Eliza. I was reared in total ignorance of my real parentage, as regards the relationship I bear to the Stanhope family,

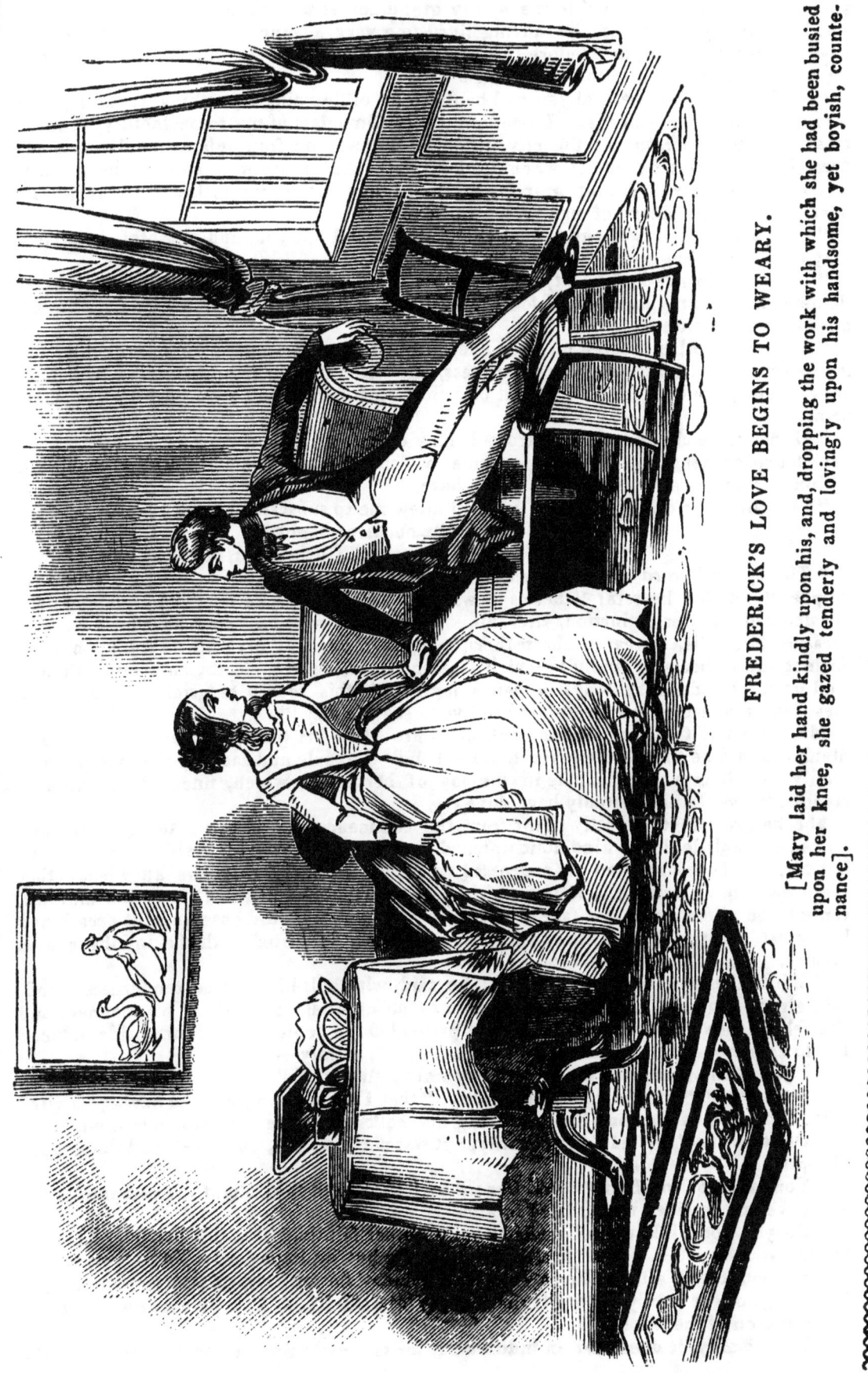

FREDERICK'S LOVE BEGINS TO WEARY.

[Mary laid her hand kindly upon his, and, dropping the work with which she had been busied upon her knee, she gazed tenderly and lovingly upon his handsome, yet boyish, countenance].

and which was only imparted to me by my grandmother a short time before her decease, which but lately took place, she having lived to a very advanced age. By her death, I have become possessed, as I before said, of legal documents every way sufficient to prove my claim, if need be, in a court of justice.

"As I think it but natural you will be desirous of learning something regarding one who claims to be your nephew, I refer you, for testimonials of my respectability, to three most respectable persons of this city, who have known me from infancy, and whose address I have enclosed; one of whom (a lawyer) is one of the most eminent in his profession, and received from my grandmother her dying attestation to the truth of what I have just had the honour of making known to you.

"I am single, and without a relative in the world but you, and any other relative I may discover in England.

"In age, I am five-and-twenty, and have been brought up to the sea, ranking now as lieutenant. It is my intention of following this letter to England immediately, where I hope to find a welcome.

"My grandmother assured me, that she continually received news from Sackville, and learned from that source you were childless, and without an heir to the estates, which, at your decease, would revert to a distant branch of the family, not even bearing the same name.

"Under these circumstances, I trust I may expect to be received with kindness. I have taken a passage in a New York steamer, which will reach England, in all probability, within a fortnight after the arrival of this letter.

"Till, then, my dear sir, I hope you will allow me to subscribe myself,

"Your obedient nephew,

"CHARLES HENRY STANHOPE."

"There," exclaimed the old gentleman, laying down the letter, and glancing triumphantly at his hearers; "there's news—good, delightful news. The Stanhopes are not doomed to utter extinction, after all. You know, my dear sir," he continued, addressing Mr. Ellis, "what a sharp thorn it has ever been in my path to think, that the ancient and respectable family to which I belong, must, at my death, sink into oblivion. And now," he added, rubbing his hands joyfully, "this source of grief is removed. I bless God that I have been permitted to live to see this day!"

Mr. Ellis felt that it was incumbent on him to offer his warm congratulations to Mr. Stanhope, and he therefore essayed to do so; but the pale and saddened countenance of Emily forbade him to participate in the joy of her uncle, which, under other circumstances, he would undoubtedly have done,

She had remained perfectly silent from the commencement of the reading of this unlooked-for epistle. Her kind aunt watched her countenance with evident uneasiness; but Mr. Stanhope had been so engrossed with his own delight, at the knowledge that there was an undoubted heir to his family estates, that he did not, for a few minutes, remark the alteration in the face of his niece; and when he did observe it, it occasioned him great surprise, having expected her to be equally delighted with the intelligence as himself.

"What ails thee, my dear Emily?" he said, with all his wonted tenderness; and, yet, strange to say, Emily fancied there was an unusual coldness in his manner; and she felt a sense of suffocation that almost prevented her replying; but her pride induced her to endeavour to overcome it, and she answered, calmly—

"I am a little tired, dear uncle, with my walk; that is all."

"I am afraid," said the curate, anxiously, "that I must plead guilty to having fatigued Miss Stanhope, by inducing her to prolong her walk beyond her previous intention."

"Oh, dear, no," replied Emily, hastily, "it was not that; but, but ——" and she stopped abruptly.

"You have not, my Emily," said her uncle, "expressed the delight the communication you have just received is calculated to afford."

"Do you not think, uncle," replied Emily, rather faintly, "that this person, who styles himself your nephew, may, after all, prove nothing but an impostor? Your great wealth and unincumbered estates offer a great inducement for any one possessed with a slight knowledge of our family history to claim such close affinity, as at your death will put him in possession of the whole."

"True, Emily, it does offer an inducement for any designing person to pretend to the relationship now claimed; but this person speaks confidently of having documents and papers, which will perfectly establish the legality of his claim; and, moreover, seems so strongly conversant with the history of our family, that I have not the slightest hesitation in believing his statement. What say you, Mr. Ellis?"

"The letter most certainly bears an appearance of truth; yet, it will, undoubtedly, be necessary to investigate, thoroughly investigate his claim, before you receive him as your nephew, and heir to your estates."

"Of course, of course," replied Mr. Stanhope, "I must take steps in the matter immediately; it is my intention of writing to my solicitor in London, and desiring him to proceed instantly with inquiries respecting this person; I shall, of course, transmit him this letter, and appoint him to receive the writer on his arrival, and inspect all documents and other papers he may have in his possession, and shall entirely rely on his judgment in this important matter."

"You cannot possibly do better," rejoined Mr. Ellis; "and if your solicitor pronounces his claim genuine——"

"I shall with pleasure receive him as my nephew," interrupted the old gentleman. "And, after that, I shall seem to have lived long enough; especially, if I find him worthy of bearing our family name. And, to think," said the old gentleman, "that so lately I had a mother living there; it is not many, at my age, could say the same."

"Not many, indeed," said the curate, who stole occasionally an anxious glance at the face of Emily, which wore an expression of increased sadness; and Mr. Ellis desired, earnestly desired, to see again the lovely smile resume its wonted place.

He thoroughly understood Emily's feelings, and was well assured her saddened demeanour was occasioned by no mercenary motive; she grieved not for the loss of the large estates and immense revenue of her uncle.

Her own fortune, which, on coming of age, she would inherit by her father's will, was sufficient to induce her to resign, without a thought of disappointment, the expected wealth of her uncle. And the curate was thoroughly convinced, that not a single sorrow connected with that, cast a shadow over her usually joyous spirit.

But Emily had ever been the petted, indulged child of the aged couple—she lived in their hearts alone; no rival had hitherto claimed even a particle of their regard, which was lavished entirely on her.

"No wonder, then," thought Mr. Ellis, "that she contemplates the arrival of another, possessing, at least, equal claims with herself to their love and kindness, with something of a painful foreboding; such feelings are extremely natural, and, in a measure, do credit to her heart.

And the curate himself was by no means disposed to regard this new claimant to the estates of Sackville, with that favour he considered in charitableness he was bound to do.

And Mrs. Stanhope, with true feminine acuteness, saw deeper into the bosom of her niece than her excellent and kind-hearted partner; and, regarding Emily with tender interest, she said, addressing her husband, but looking at her niece,—

"If, my dear Henry, we are fortunate enough to discover a nephew, it will not cause us to forget that we have, for a long time, experienced the kind attentions and soothing affection of a good and dutiful niece."

"Surely not, my love," replied the warm-hearted old gentleman, with evident surprise; "who, for a moment, even, could suppose it possible?"

"Dear, dear uncle," said Emily, rising, and throwing her arms round his neck; "can you forgive me, if I acknowledge that I did nourish so unkind, and, I feel now, unjust a suspicion in my bosom? But it arose, indeed, dear uncle, from the tenderness of my love for you, which made me dread losing even a particle of your regard."

"My dearest Emily—my own child!" said Mr. Stanhope, as he folded her affectionately to his bosom. "I am, indeed, delighted at the prospect of discovering an heir to these broad lands, and this old mansion, which have never appertained to any but the Stanhopes, who have inherited them in unbroken male descent for many successive generations; and I trust the line may still be thus continued. Your cousin will, of course, marry, and become, I hope, the father of a fresh race. And now I think of it, my Emily, as you have ever been regarded as the rightful heiress of Sackville, if your cousin proves a suitable person, and is not displeasing to you, it would be well for both if you were to marry each other; the estates would then, my child, still be yours."

"There is plenty of time to think of all that," replied Emily, gently ; "at present, I do not feel very desirous to enter into the bonds of matrimony."

Mrs. Stanhope smiled kindly and approvingly on her niece as she gave utterance to these remarks. But a shade of deep sorrow passed over the expressive countenance of Mr. Ellis. He now, for the first time, became fully aware of the real nature of his feelings to Emily : while there was no other person in the village that Mr. Stanhope would be desirous to see wedded to Emily, the curate had fancied that he merely regarded her with the affection of a brother; but now one was shortly expected to arrive at the mansion who would have daily, nay, hourly opportunities afforded, by constant domestic intercourse, of rendering himself agreeable to Emily, who was likely to be impressed in favour of a relative, in every respect so eligible to match with her—a match that would, doubtless, be greatly desired by her uncle and aunt, and which would be the means of fixing her in the mansion as its mistress, upon the death of her uncle, and prevent her foregoing the title she had borne from her earliest infancy, of "the Heiress of Sackville." Poor Mr. Ellis thought of all this as he walked home, and it formed the subject of his reflections for many days after.

He was grieved at the discovery he had made regarding the state of his own feelings. He felt that he loved Emily ; and though some might have termed his regard cold, and deemed it wanting in that passionate warmth which usually attends first love, yet what it lacked in ardour it thoroughly made up for in durability. We say that the discovery of the real nature of his feelings greatly grieved the good curate, and would, he was well convinced, throw a dark shadow over his whole existence. He was naturally of a mild and quiet temperament, and such ever receive lasting impressions. They are by no means easily acted upon ; but when they are, they retain the effect for ever. Thus it was with Mr. Ellis. He knew that his love for Emily would never be effaced from his heart ; and as he could not, under their relative circumstances, dare to hope that he might ever gain her affections, it was necessarily a source of deep regret that he should have regarded her so tenderly ; nevertheless, he wisely resolved to do his utmost to extinguish the passion that existed in his heart.

His visits to the mansion, which had hitherto been his delight, and sweet relaxation from his ministerial toil, now added but renewed bitterness to his gall ; for to hear her speak, and listen to her lively sallies and merry, yet good-natured remarks on persons and things —to answer her kind inquiries after his health, and assure her he ailed nothing, while his heart felt overcharged with anguish ; all this, and more, he desired for the future as much as possible to avoid ; for how could he hope to conquer his love, or subdue even his regard in the presence of the object of his passion !—

> "Severe his task, these visits to forego,
> And feed his heart with voluntary woe."

Yet this he determined to do. He judged that on the arrival at the great house of its rightful heir, as an inmate, his own constant visits might in a great measure be dispensed with, without seeming unkind or neglectful to the worthy old couple, for whom he deservedly entertained a warm affection and sincere respect.

Till then he could not, without exciting suspicions as to his motives, discontinue his visits to the mansion. He therefore went as usual; but with a sorrowing heart and anxious countenance, that Emily strove in vain to account for.

In the meantime, the news of an expected heir to the estates of Sackville flew like wildfire through the village ; and the tenantry, without a single exception, deplored the circumstance that, at the death of their present landlord, would place them under the control of one of whom they knew nothing. He might be as harsh and exacting as the good old gentleman was merciful and considerate. And then, too, the dear young lady, as they called Emily, and whom they had ever regarded as the successor of her uncle, and whom they had likewise known and loved from infancy, it was surely very hard that she should be deprived of the estates for one who was an entire stranger among them; and heartily they wished he had been at the bottom of the Red Sea, before he had turned up to throw them all into sorrow and confusion. So Mr. Stanhope and his lady were about the only persons in Sackville who rejoiced at the prospect of an heir. To be sure, Miss Fraser had been known to express herself to the effect that she was heartily glad that Emily would never inherit the estates; and that now she would be obliged to hold her head a little lower, and not think herself so much better than other people. But then this was well known to arise alone from envy, and therefore may be put down as nought.

A week passed on, and Christmas, with all its festivities, drew nigh ; the old gentleman had much desired his nephew's arrival soon enough to commemorate that time honoured day, but, the vessel being detained at sea, they were obliged to celebrate it without him.

## CHAPTER XXX.

EMILY had promised her friend Mrs. Harley to accompany her and Frank to a ball that was to take place at the adjoining town the week after Christmas, and they now claimed the fulfilment of her promise.

Emily had at this time much food for reflection, and not of the most agreeable kind. Her cousin was daily expected to arrive in London, when his claim to that relationship would, without delay, be thoroughly investigated ; and Emily, in the interim, was nervous and anxious in no light degree, and she felt far from disposed for visiting gay assemblies ; but Mrs. Harley would take no denial.

"Everything, my dear Emily," said that lady, " is arranged ; we have purchased tickets, ordered a carriage to convey and bring us back ; our dresses are in readiness, and—and, in short, Emily, we must go. It will do you good ; you have positively seemed quite ennuied of late ; indeed you have not been yourself since the departure of that Mordaunt, who, I am convinced, was desperately in love with you, and, really, Emily, you ought to have had him. You ought, indeed ; he is exactly the sort of man for a romantic girl like you."

"Probably," returned Emily, " he is the sort of man I might once have been delighted with ; but, as he never made me an offer of marriage, I cannot, of course, be blamed for not accepting of it."

"La! Emily ; what a strange girl you are ; but confess, now ; were you not half in love with him ?"

"Not in love," replied Emily ; " call it not love ; a girlish liking, nothing more, and even that is past ; I seem to have had enough of romance, and desire to turn my thoughts now to the sober realities of life."

"Why, Emily, you could not say more, if you were married, and about to settle down into a quiet country wife ; but I cannot allow you to indulge in such foolish fancies ; gaiety is a woman's natural element, and it is only through a conjunction of adverse circumstances that she ever dislikes it. I see, my dear Emily, that I must take you out as much as possible and show you what life is, or you will be getting the most absurd notions in your head."

"Well," replied Emily ; " I suppose I must go with you for this once, at least."

"Oh, yes ; that of course ; and depend upon it, we shall have plenty of beaux. Frank tells me, that the Hussars are stationed in the town, and the officers have announced their intention of being at the ball. I suppose the creatures thought that would suffice to make all the ladies put on their most becoming looks ; for myself, I dare say, I shall be chained to Frank the entire evening ; indeed, the wretch, has hinted as much already.

It was by no means with very happy anticipations of a pleasant evening, that Emily took her seat in the carriage that was to convey them to the ball-room.

In spite of the assurance of Mrs. Harley, that she should be chained to Frank the entire evening, he seemed determined to allow her to amuse herself as she best liked, while he gave his exclusive attention to Emily, whom he had previously engaged as his partner. Emily had observed several officers in showy regimentals, during the early part of the evening, but had not particularly remarked any one of them, till Mrs. Harley, in an interval of the dance, approached her, leaning on the arm of a very handsome young man, whom she introduced as Ensign Frederick Maitland, of the — hussars.

"This gentleman," said that lady, addressing Emily, "particularly desired an introduction to you ; the master of the ceremonies presented me to his brother, Captain William Maitland, of the same regiment, and with whom, I dare say, you observed me dancing." Emily bowed slightly to these remarks of her volatile companion.

"My great object in desiring an introduction," said the young man, "was the hope of gaining you for a partner in the set of quadrilles which is now forming. If you are not engaged, Miss Stanhope, perhaps you will so far favour me."

Emily replied, that "she was perfectly disengaged, and should be happy to oblige him," and giving him her hand, he led her to the set. Mrs. Harley was engaged to William, and, at the conclusion of the dance, she whispered Emily that they were the envy of the whole room, having secured the two handsomest fellows as their partners.

"Perhaps a change of partners would be agreeable?" said William to his young brother, as they sauntered with the ladies into the refreshment-room.

"By no means," returned Frederick; "I find mine so agreeable, that I am far from being disposed to part with her so soon."

The animating scene, and the exhilarating influence of the dance, had done much towards restoring Emily's lively spirits; and Fred being a handsome young officer, and certainly a pleasant companion, she had exerted her powers of pleasing, and the lively turn of mind she naturally possessed had greatly prepossessed Frederick in her favour; and, in short, they were mutually pleased with each other.

On the other hand, William had found the widow far from uninteresting; and, in her turn, she was delighted with the idea of having made an impression on the heart of the gallant officer, who, she thought, would serve well to play off against her nephew, and perhaps be the means of bringing Frank to his senses.

Fired with this hope she courteously smiled, and bowed her gracious permission, when, at the conclusion of the festivities, the captain begged to be permitted to call at her residence in the morning, to inquire how she felt after the evening's fatigue.

"You have not, as yet, favoured me, my dear madam, with your ——"

"Oh, a card," said the widow, producing a superbly-embossed one, on which was written her name and address in a small but elegant hand.

"I am living in strict rustic retirement," said the widow, as she proffered the card with a graceful curtsey.

"Laurel Cottage," said the captain, reading from the card.

"Yes, that is the name of my little box," returned the widow.

"The name itself prepossesses me in favour of the abode," said the captain gallantly; "and had I not already had the honour of an introduction to its fair inmate, I should most certainly be desirous of seeking one; but, my dear madam, will you allow me to ask if this really elegant penmanship is ——"

"Not to be attributed to me," replied the widow, anticipating his inquiry. "I am indebted for that writing to my young friend, Miss Stanhope, whom I introduced as a partner to your brother."

"The beauty of the writing attracted my attention," said the captain, as, without any show of surprise, he placed the card in his pocket. "I shall most assuredly do myself the honour and pleasure of calling on the morrow to inquire after your welfare. Your friend, I suppose, is frequently with you?"

"Very," said the widow, laying an emphasis on the word; "indeed we are almost inseparable, just for all the world like sisters; neither of us being blest with much tender relations, we seek to supply the place of them to each other."

"She is a good-looking girl, and will be still more so when she is a little more matured," said the captain, with an air of being a first-rate judge of feminine beauty. "No doubt, since she is favoured with your friendship, she is likewise amiable."

"Her greatest fault," said the widow, "is a love of anything romantic, or out of the common path of life, which frequently gives her the appearance of eccentricity."

"She is rich, then," said the other; "or she would not be able to indulge in such fancies."

"She is an orphan," replied Mrs. Harley; "and, when of age, will inherit a handsome competence under her father's will, and till lately she was considered the heiress of Sackville; but unfortunately there is now another whose claims are more legitimate than her own, insomuch as he belongs to the male line."

"Oh! that is indeed, as you say, unfortunate for her; but, as she possesses wealth without the estates, she can better afford to part with them; but," continued the captain, "as I must confess, I feel interested in your friend, will it be deemed obtrusive if I inquire whether her affections are disengaged?"

"Not at all," said the widow smiling, and glancing towards the spot where Emily and Frederick were standing engaged in conversation. "I can only say, that so far as I am aware, her heart was entirely in her own keeping when she entered this room."

"My brother seems to be much pleased with her, and that, my dear madam, was my reason for making the inquiry. He is so very young that I deem myself the guardian of his happiness, and, had the young lady's affections been engaged, I should have deemed it right to acquaint him with that circumstance, for fear her many attractions should otherwise have made an impression on his heart."

" Exceedingly kind of you," said Mrs. Harley ; "it is not every young man who feels so deep an interest in his brother."

The foregoing conversation had greatly increased the esteem of the widow for her new friend ; and when he politely escorted her to the carriage, and pressed her hand at parting, she was absolutely delighted with his gallantry, and on the road home inquired of Emily how she liked her partner.

Emily expressed herself strongly in favour of the young officer's good looks, and also said she had likewise found him pleasant and agreeable in manners.

When the brothers were once more alone in their private apartments, William put exactly the same question to Fred as Mrs. Harley had previously done to Emily.

" I must confess," replied the youth, to this interrogatory, " that she is exactly the sort of girl I admire ; there is some spirit and animation in her. And what an exquisite dancer ! Mary is, I think, better looking ; but, then, she lacks energy."

Alas ! and had Fred began to draw comparisons between his young wife and another already ?

" Ah, Mary is what I call a pretty piece of still life," said his brother, " and one of whom I should uncommonly soon weary. But, Fred, have you forgotten your incognita?"

" Oh, no," replied Fred ; " I have only felt disappointed that she has not as yet discovered herself to me."

" And, yet, you have seen, conversed, and danced with her, for well nigh an entire evening, without yourself making the interesting discovery. La! Fred, what a dull dog you must be."

" Seen, conversed, and danced with her ?" returned Fred. " What on earth do you mean ? You surely do not wish me to infer that Miss Stanhope is ——"

" No other than your fair incognita herself, as I can prove to you. Look here, Fred," drawing from his pocket the card he had received from Mrs. Harley, and holding it towards his brother, " and convince yourself beyond the possibility of a doubt. This, her friend assured me, was the writing of Miss Stanhope ; is it not also of your incognita?"

" Oh! surely," exclaimed Fred, as he snatched it from his brother's hand " it is! it must be so ! There is a decided peculiarity about many of the letters that is perfectly unmistakable. And, yet, my wildest imagination never pictured a creature half so charming as Miss Stanhope ; that, in spite of the evidence of my senses, I feel, as it were, compelled to doubt that in her I behold my unknown correspondent."

" And yet it is nevertheless true ; and being thoroughly convinced of it, I took the liberty of making a few inquiries of the gay widow (who honoured me with so much of her company this evening) concerning her friend, and learnt from her that Miss Stanhope, whose Christian name is Emily, is the very girl, of all others, most likely to have adopted such a romantic way of making her sentiments known to you."

" But how and when can she have seen me before ?"

" All that is nothing to the purpose. She is evidently, from the very tone of her letters, desperately in love with you ; is rich, and willing to bestow herself and fortune upon you, a poor devil who has not a farthing in the world he can rightly call his own. Truly, Fred, I give you joy ; and yet I am positively half disposed to enter the lists with you, and not allow so charming a girl to fall into your arms without even giving you the trouble to woo and win her."

" Oh, no," replied Fred, hastily. " Mind, I permit of no interference. She is mine by right, and, by Jove, I will ——"

" Marry her, of course," said his brother.

At these words a shade of deep sadness passed across the handsome face of Fred. He felt that it was no longer in his power to do so. And bitterly did he curse his own folly for having been so eager to enter into the bonds of matrimony.

The poet sings, with great truth, as well as beauty,—

> " Oh! what a tangled web we weave,
> When first we practise to deceive."

And Frederick had, indeed, got entangled in a web, from which he knew not how to extricate himself without declaring the fact of his marriage to his brother; and that, he was well aware, would be tantamount to plunging himself at once into poverty and disgrace. And then, again, he was assured that Mary would never consent to forego the title he had given her. Now that it was too late to retract, he knew that he had acted with great imprudence, to say nothing more.

He had not even made Mary happy; on the contrary, her letters breathed sadness and anxiety; her health she spoke of as being still more delicate—she could scarcely, indeed, pursue her usual avocation, and was anxious that he should declare their marriage, as she had received an invitation from her brother to visit him at Sackville, which she much wished to accept, thinking it might be the means of restoring her failing health.

All Frederick thought he could do, under these circumstances, he was by no means slow in doing.

He wrote to Mary, informing her of the impossibility of consenting to her wishes at present; and to Emily, with whom he speedily became intimate, he paid marked attentions, which were, he considered, well received; still, he kept from her knowledge the discovery he had made as to her being his unknown, but favourite correspondent, for he demed, that when he confessed that much, he should be obliged to follow it up, with an offer of his hand, which was not his own to give.

His brother certainly cavilled with him on account of his delay, but deeming, that in the end, he was certain of obtaining Emily, he suffered him so far to pursue his own course. and never had Frederick been the subject of so much anxiety, so many doubts and fears that now constantly assailed him.

But still wilfully blinding himself to the consequences, he rushed madly on, determining at one time to wed Emily, if possible, hoping to induce Mary to remain quiet; And then again resolving to declare his determination to his brother, and trust to his ingenuity to extricate him from it. He remembered the visits of Mr. Mordaunt and another to Mary, about whom she refused to give him any explanation. And, as he dwelt upon this, it occurred to him that it might, on an emergency, become the means of enabling him to set his marriage with her aside, and then, of course, he could unite himself to Emily.

And, as he reasoned with himself on the subject, he thought that Emily being so much in love with him, and having showered upon him so many favours, it was his duty to make some sacrifice for her sake; and, from constantly dwelling on the matter, he at last actually persuaded himself that in freeing himself from Mary, in order to unite his fate with Emily, he was making a great self-sacrifice, which could not be otherwise than acceptable to her he wished to make his wife. Alas! what will not selfishness accomplish!

---

## CHAPTER XXXI.

AFTER his patience had been put to a severe trial, Mr. Stanhope at length received a letter from his lawyer, informing him of the arrival of his nephew in London, whose claim to that title he was now investigating; and, as soon as he had arrived at a definite conclusion regarding his claim, he would instantly inform him by letter of the result.

This was some little relief to the old gentleman's suspense; but his patience had to be still more tried before it met with its reward; and it was not till very nearly six weeks after Christmas, that he heard again from the man of law, who took nothing whatever for granted, but sifted the affair well to the bottom, proceeding exactly as if he were endeavouring to prove the young man not to be the person he called himself; and after every paper and document had been well looked into, and scrupulously scanned, seemingly with the desire of proving them not genuine, he (the solicitor) at length, as it were, suffered himself to be convinced that the young man was in sober truth the nephew and undoubted heir of Mr. Henry Stanhope, which he communicated to the worthy old gentleman in writing.

Great, indeed, was his joy at this, to his mind, happy issue; and great indeed were the preparations set on foot to receive and do honour to the future owner of the estate.

The old gentleman bustled about, giving orders and directions here, there, and everywhere, declaring that he felt himself almost young again. And really, to look upon his beaming countenance, and watch his light, elastic step, about which nothing that told of

THE PARTING BETWEEN ISABEL AND TIERNEY.

["Farewell, Henry," she said; "believe me, that you are, in this sad hour, more dear, far more respected than when I first consented to abide with you beneath this roof."]

old age was visible, any one might have been well inclined to believe the truth of his assertion.

"Come, Emily, my child," he exclaimed, on the morning of the expected arrival of his nephew, "you must put on your sweetest smiles to welcome your cousin. By-the-by, it is time for you to see about your toilet; we must be all in readiness to receive and welcome him."

Emily strove to smile at her uncle's remark, but she felt an unusual languor and depression of spirits on this particular day.

Mr. Stanhope had given the whole of the tenantry an entire holiday, in honour of the occasion; and had, likewise, provided every one of them with old English fare, in the shape of a substantial piece of beef, and ingredients necessary for the manufacturing of a plum-pudding; and every chimney in the village was smoking away in right good earnest.

The snow had long since disappeared, and it was a clear, bright, frosty morning, the sun shedding its reviving beams on all around.

And honest John, at the little ale-house, had enough, indeed more than he could do, to dispense Mr. Stanhope's bounty in frothy, creaming pots of real Devonshire ale, on which he so much prided himself.

And the church bells were busy too, sending forth such merry peals, that they, at least, appeared to rejoice and do their best to welcome the heir.

The famous Tally-ho coach passed the door of the mansion, but Mr. Stanhope considered that would not be a sufficiently dignified conveyance to bring his nephew into the village; so he received orders to alight at the neighbouring town, where the carriage would be in waiting to receive and convey him to the home of his forefathers.

A select party were invited by Mr. Stanhope to meet and receive his nephew, consisting of Mr. Ellis, the squire, his lady, son, and daughter, Mrs. Harley and Frank. The fare at the mansion was the same as provided for the villagers.

A large baron of beef was destined to grace the festive board, to be followed by a tremendous plum-pudding.

The horses and carriage had not been put in requisition since the memorable night when they conveyed Mr. Ellis back to Sackville; and the quadrupeds were not, on this occasion, much more willing to quit the stables than when their services were last required; but after the usual amount of coaxing and entreaty, they were at length drawn forth and despatched on their errand.

Great was the speculation among Mr. Stanhope's guests, concerning the sort of person his nephew would probably prove to be. And when, at length, the old coach was seen in the distance, drawing its slow pace along, they all descended to the hall to meet and welcome the expected heir.

Mr. and Mrs. Stanhope, with Emily between them, as the only relatives, stood at the entrance; immediately behind them was Mr. Ellis and the other guests, all placed in due order as to rank.

Emily had pictured to herself, a rough and, perhaps, rather a coarse personage, in her American cousin, and was prepared to find him anything but agreeable or pleasant in manners; and, consequently, was rather surprised when the coach stopped, and a tall and genteel-looking man, without giving the powdered footman time to let down the steps, with one spring, stood at the bottom of the broad stone steps that led to the family mansion: when, observing the tenantry in all their best clothes, and with uncovered heads, giving him silent welcome (for not even Mr. Stanhope could induce them to rend the air with joyful acclamations), with a graceful action he turned round, for an instant, towards them, and slightly raised his hat; a faint cheer was the response of the villagers to this unexpected greeting. And now he ascends the steps; and, as if too anxious to meet his relatives to allow the outside of the fine old mansion to attract even his passing notice, he at once entered the hall, escorted by the footman.

Mr. Stanhope, with his usual courtly grace, stepped forward to meet him, as he exclaimed,

"Welcome, my dear nephew, to the home of your ancestors, and to the estates of which you will be one day the owner."

"May that day be far, very far distant, my dear sir," said the young man, frankly, as he received and warmly pressed the extended hand of his uncle, who politely introduced him to his lady and his niece.

In the stranger's address to Mrs. Stanhope, there was a mingling of respectful warmth and tenderness that found its way to the good old lady's heart.

Emily would merely have curtseyed to the address of her cousin, but he was far from disposed to receive so cold a greeting; and, taking her hand in his own, he carried it, with an air of gallantry, to his lips, as he said,

"I trust, my dear cousin, we shall soon be better acquainted. I feel assured that you must regard me in the light of a rival; indeed, I can scarcely forgive myself for standing in the place you have for so many years been taught to consider as exclusively your own."

"Make yourself perfectly easy, sir," replied Emily, with true feminine dignity, and a little of her father's family pride shone on her beaming countenance. "The only daughter of Sir Beaumont Percy is sufficiently cared for by her father's will, to enable her to resign, without a thought, the estates of her mother's family, on the future owner of which it would grieve her much to be a dependant."

These words were spoken with great spirit, and cordially approved of by all the gentlemen present except Mr. Stanhope, who, without giving his nephew time to digest them, proceeded formally to introduce him to the assembled guests.

And while this ceremony is being performed, we will offer a few remarks upon his personal appearance. He was remarkably tall, measuring full six feet, moderately stout, of rather dark complexion, blue eyes, and brown hair; his features were good, and he was what might be termed a well-looking man, and, to judge from his manners and address, was tolerably educated, and wholly free from any appearance of Yankeeism.

Emily felt rather disappointed on observing this; she entertained a strong prejudice against him, and would rather that his person and appearance had justified and confirmed the dislike with which she had determined to regard him. She had certainly never been in worse spirits, or more indisposed for conversation than on this eventful day; and never before had she apparently been regarded with so little interest by the assembled guests. She was no longer the wealthy heiress whom all were anxious to conciliate and feel flattered at receiving from her the lightest notice; even Mr. Ellis, whom she thought nothing could estrange, seemed on this day, on which of all other she had hoped for his sympathy, purposely to avoid her, and, what was still more, devoted his entire attention to Louisa Elgood, whom, Emily now remembered with a sense of undefinable bitterness, he had often warmly eulogised as possessing stability of character and amiable and agreeable manners.

"Alas!" thought poor Emily, "I am now indeed deserted. I judged better of Mr. Ellis than to suppose my loss of wealth would make me less esteemed by him;" but the next minute she felt that she had done him injustice, and thought again—"It is not riches, or even now I should be more desirable than Louisa, who will never inherit aught beyond her own good qualities; but I am doomed to be unfortunate;" and poor Emily crept unobserved from the drawing-room, and hastening to her own room, gave vent to her feelings in tears.

This was the first time Emily had ever had cause to think herself neglected, and though it was undoubtedly a painful lesson, yet it was likewise an useful one. She had been accustomed to entertain too high an opinion of her own merits; and the attentions that had been so lavishly bestowed upon her, had been received by her as tributes to her superior qualifications; but now she perceived they were nought but offerings at the shrine of her wealth. She now felt humbled, and determined, for the first time, to strive and win affection for her own excellence alone.

With the thought that she was now less cared for, came also the conviction, that had she endeavoured to cultivate the graces and beauty of the mind, she might have still been esteemed and respected, especially by Mr. Ellis; for his friendship she grieved far more than for any other, and the thought of his coldness brought tears to her eyes. At this juncture a tap at the door aroused her, and, in a voice which she strove to be calm, she gave permission for the person to enter.

"Oh, lor, miss, what is the matter," said the maid (for it was her), "on such a joyous day as this for you to be all alone up here shedding torrents of tears?"

"Nothing is the matter, Jane," said Emily, striving to smile; "I do not feel quite well this evening, that is all."

"Lor, miss, that is quite bad enough; and there's your husband that is to be, making all manner of inquiries about you; they want you to play and sing some of your favourite airs."

" My husband that is to be !" said Emily, angrily; " if you speak of my cousin, Jane, I desire you fully to understand that he never will be to me anything more. I cannot possibly think who could have put such a thought in your head."

" Why, miss, all the servants are talking about it, and saying that it is quite a settled thing."

" Then," said Emily, " it is all settled without my consent, which I should suppose was at least necessary before the consummation of the nuptials; and, when it is asked, you may make yourself perfectly satisfied that it will be instantly refused."

" Lor, miss, and he such a fine, handsome-looking gentleman; I should have thought no lady could have refused him."

" He will find there is one that can, if he presumes to make the experiment as regards myself," replied Emily; and, without a word more, she descended to the drawing-room.

When she entered, Louisa Elgood was seated at the pianoforte, and, by her side, Mr. Ellis, who was joining her in singing; there was a seat vacant next to John Elgood, and here Emily quietly placed herself.

When the song was ended, her uncle approached to lead her to the piano, saying,—

" My dear Emily, your cousin is most anxious to hear your performance; oblige him with some of your favourite airs."

Emily complied; and, turning over the leaves of her music book, selected what she thought would most please her uncle.

She was too proud to ask it, but she fully hoped Mr. Ellis would have accompanied her in the song she had chosen, it being one they had frequently sung together, but he had retired with Louisa to a distant part of the room. Emily felt deeply hurt at his neglect, and the evening, as far as she was concerned, passed slowly and sadly away.

Her cousin highly applauded her performance, and expressed an earnest hope that they might hereafter spend their time very happily together. Emily, in order to avoid him as much as possible, bestowed the greater part of her attention upon John, who received it with unbounded delight; indeed it had the effect of inducing the youth to suppose that she regarded him with great favour; and, now that she was no longer the wealthy heiress, he entertained a strong hope of being able to induce her to become his bride.

At a late hour the party broke up, and Emily laid her head upon her pillow with more sadness in her heart than she had ever known before.

She felt so exceedingly hurt at Mr. Ellis's unkind treatment of her, and dwelt so much and so bitterly upon it, that she began to carefully analyse her feelings towards him; and comparing them with what she felt for other gentlemen of her acquaintance, began to fear that she had nourished, unknown even to herself, a tender regard for him.

" How little," she inwardly exclaimed, " should I have cared, or even thought about the matter, had I experienced the like neglect from Frank Harley or John Elgood! Alas! alas! I have loved Mr. Ellis, without being myself aware of it; and, so far from his entertaining a like affection for me, he apparently prefers another. Oh, can it be that he has discovered the state of my feelings, and, as he cannot reciprocate them, has adopted this cold neglect, to convince me of the folly of entertaining such. Alas!" she thought, " I was silly and mad enough, when surrounded by wealth and happiness, to long and sigh for incident, even of a painful nature; my ridiculous and absurd wishes are now realised, and have deservedly brought with them misery and sorrow."

Could Emily by any possibility have ascertained the tender passion the curate felt for her, she would have indeed considered herself blest, as in his love she would have found a sweet and sure reward for every other pain; but she could not, as we have done, penetrate into the inward recesses of his breast, and therefore judged from outward appearances alone.

As days glided on, she perceived with deep regret that Mr. Ellis's visits at the mansion became less and less frequent, while she learned from John that his calls at the squire's were proportionately increased.

Emily, as we have already said, had predetermined to dislike her cousin; but as they became more intimate, she discovered an honest simplicity about him that made it impossible for her to do so. He had received but a very superficial education, and Emily had frequent occasion to smile at his remarks; but so far from manifesting any resentment, he seemed only too glad to see her smile to care anything at all about the cause. He was a pleasant and good-humoured companion for his uncle and aunt, having ever ready at hand a goodly store of anecdote, all of which the old gentleman received in undoubting faith, though to Emily's mind they were most of them at least of very questionable veracity.

Before he had been many weeks an inmate of the mansion, Emily thoroughly understood his temper and disposition, which may be well summed up in five words—simple, good-natured, and easily managed. She therefore, with praiseworthy zeal, strove to interest him in the tenantry, and direct his energies towards improving the estate, and increasing as much as possible the comforts of the villagers.

Mr. Stanhope would listen with pleased satisfaction while Emily conversed with her cousin, and pointed out to him the best mode of managing so large and flourishing an estate as that of which he would one day become the possessor, till at length he became confirmed in the idea that had early possessed him, that these two last remaining scions of his race should link their fate in marriage, and thus become the united possessors of the family estate. Emily's strong mind and energetic spirit, he rightly judged, would counter-balance the natural simplicity and, in some respects, weak mind of his nephew.

"They appear as though they were actually made for each other," said Mr. Stanhope, when speaking on this very subject, to his good lady.

She smiled, and nodded her approbation, and yet in her own mind she felt convinced Emily would never marry her cousin; but the old gentleman, on the other hand, talked, planned, and considered it, till he had fully resolved that it should be. But old gentlemen's plans are not always well matured. Neither was Mr. Stanhope's; for Emily had determined otherwise; and though she found her cousin more pleasant and agreeable than she expected, yet, rather than give her hand to him, she would willingly have seen her name on the old maid's list—a fate that is usually avoided at all hazards by young ladies.

----

## CHAPTER XXXII.

WE think it is now time to return to Mr. Mordaunt, whom we last left in rather a critical situation. When the vehicle in which he was seated arrived at the prison door, and, as he alighted, he cast a glance upward at the heavy walls which seemed to frown upon him, for a moment his composure forsook him, and his very heart appeared to sicken at the prospect of being immured and otherwise regarded as a felon. At the same instant he caught a glimpse of his merciless persecutor, and that sufficed to restore him to his usual firmness. He folded his arms across his breast, and, with an unbending erectness, followed the gaoler to the cell assigned him. The door was closed with a strange, jarring sound, that struck painfully on the ear of the prisoner; and sinking on a seat, he covered his face with his hands, and remained for a long time profoundly silent; and when he did raise his head from his clasped hands, every other feeling gave place to astonishment as he beheld the boy who was to have accompanied him in his expected voyage, seated at his feet, and his deep blue eyes fixed with an earnest, anxious solicitude upon his face.

Mordaunt started, for the moment almost doubting the evidence of his senses; and then exclaimed, in a subdued voice, while he passed his hand across his eyes, as if to clear his vision,—

"My boy, what has brought you here? This is no place for you, and you must quit it instantly."

"Oh! say not so," said the boy, timidly. "When you were arrested, I earnestly craved permission to accompany you, and, not without difficulty, obtained it. Then do not, I entreat of you, compel me to quit this spot till you are yourself enabled to do the like."

"Boy," returned Mordaunt, "you know not the dreadful crime of which I am accused; did you know it, you would shun my very presence!"

"Whatever the crime may be that is laid to your charge, of one thing I am certain,—that is, you are guiltless. You, who were so ready to perform a deed of kindness to a poor friendless youth, cannot possibly have committed an act of crime."

Mordaunt was deeply affected by the sympathy of the boy, and was easily induced to allow him to remain. And, as money can soften even the flinty hearts of gaolers, they offered no objection to the youth sharing the cell with the prisoner.

Two days had Mordaunt been the inmate of a prison, and the third was drawing to a close, when the gaoler suddenly made his appearance, and, throwing wide open the cell-door, told him he was free to go where he pleased.

Mordaunt, astonished no less than delighted, inquired the meaning of this unexpected termination of his imprisonment, when he learnt that two male servants, who had been living with his uncle up to the time of his death, had come voluntarily forward, and made an affadavit, before the magistrate, to having, both of them, seen their master alive and well after the departure of his nephew. And one of them actually swore to being in the room with him, when he was seized with a fit of epilepsy (to which he had been for years subject), and, before he could render him assistance, he fell forward, and, in so doing, struck his right temple against the corner of the marble mantelpiece, inflicting a frightful wound, of which he ultimately died. In addition to these witnesses, there were several others, who bore testimony to the deranged intellect of Mordaunt's cousin, which first manifested itself on the death of his father, to whom he was much attached. They all spoke of him as being perfectly harmless, and, on some points, perfectly sane, his reason apparently wandering chiefly on the subject of his father's death, as he constantly averred, without any foundation in truth, that he was murdered by Mordaunt.

This, together with medical evidence to the same effect, was, of course, quite sufficient to procure Mordaunt's release ; and he now joyfully made his exit from the gaol, accompanied by the youth who had voluntarily shared his fate. A coach was in waiting, and, stepping in, Mordaunt desired the man to drive towards the West-end. And when the vehicle was in motion, he turned to his companion, and inquired if it were still his desire to quit England.

The boy hesitated, and seemed at a loss what reply to make. He looked at Mordaunt timidly, and then said,—

" You, kind sir, are the only friend I possess. If you will allow me to remain with you, all places are to me alike. I ask only to be permitted to serve you in the capacity of a servant."

Mordaunt, in his turn, hesitated, and regarded the boy with a fixed look, and said, as if on purpose to try the effect of the speech on his companion,—

" The result of my incarceration will probably greatly alter my plans for the future. I need not seek to conceal from your knowledge that I am deeply in love with a young lady, whose mental, as well as personal attractions, render her pre-eminently worthy of my warmest regard."

" And she?" said the boy, anxiously.

" Appears by no means averse to my attentions," returned Mordaunt, still keeping his gaze riveted upon the youth, who made no reply to this remark, but hung his head, while an expression of extreme sadness took possession of his features.

" You see," resumed Mordaunt, after a pause, " that I am now free of an accusation that prevented me seeking the lady whom I so tenderly regarded as my wife, and am, consequently, at liberty to declare my sentiments to her. Should they be favourably received, I shall, of course, resign all thought of quitting England, where I may hope to live many years in peace and happiness ; but, as you, my boy, have an only relative in America, I strongly advise you to proceed thither without delay. I will furnish you with ample means to enable you to prosecute the voyage with pleasure as well as comfort."

" Alas!" exclaimed the boy ; " then you will not allow me to remain in your service?"

" You have never been in my service yet," said Mordaunt ; " when you requested permission to accompany me abroad as an attendant, I particularly informed you that I needed none."

" You did—you did !" exclaimed the youth, mournfully ; " and yet ——"

" And yet, what?" replied Mordaunt ; " do not fear to express your wishes ; I feel an interest for you, and am desirous, as far as possible, to serve you. Tell me how I can do so most effectually."

" By allowing me to remain with you," said the boy, energetically. " I ask nothing, nothing whatever, beyond that humble boon."

" You are perverse, boy," returned Mordaunt, " and ask the only favour I cannot grant."

" Oh, pray do not deny me this slight favour. I need not money or money's worth ; only allow me to be your servant ; in that humble capacity I will serve you faithfully—I will, indeed."

" I am a perfect stranger to you," said Mordaunt, seriously. " I cannot conceive

THE HEIRESS OF SACKVILLE. 175

what can have induced you to take so violent a fancy to myself, as to induce you to desire to remain in England merely because I desire to do so."

" Is it nothing that you have treated me with condescension and kindness, such as I have experienced from none beside ? Oh ! is it nothing that you should have taken pity on a poor, friendless, and moneyless orphan ; or is it surprising that I should have conceived an affectionate and tender attachment towards one from whom I have received so many favours, and experienced so much kindness ? I cannot do your bidding if you desire me to depart from you. Gratitude demands some demonstration of my feelings. Let me thus show it."

" I have already told you," replied Mordaunt, " that my entire affections are bestowed upon a worthy object, to whom I propose to unite myself in marriage. How could I introduce you to the object of my regard ? Your appearance is far above that of a menial ; and of your friends and parentage I know nothing. You appear to have been well educated, and possess even feminine refinement ; will you unhesitatingly disclose to me your entire history, keeping nothing back ?"

" Will you take my word for the truth of what I may discover of my former life and friends ?"

" I shall, of course," said Mordaunt, " think it right to make inquiries concerning the truth of your statement, so that I feel assured I am not imposed on."

The boy returned no answer, and shortly after the driver inquired of Mordaunt where he would wish to be set down. He named a fashionable hotel, at which he alighted, followed by his youthful companion.

At the request of Mordaunt, they were shown into a private room. and substantial refreshment was served them ; after they had partaken of which, and the waiter had withdrawn, Mordaunt turned to the youth, and tenderly addressed him as follows :—

" I am now at liberty to hear aught that you think fit to communicate. I should not desire to pry into the secret of your past life, did you not express so earnest a desire to remain in close connection with myself. Before I can return a favourable answer to your reiterated request, it is nothing but right I should learn something concerning your family and previous pursuits ; not that I fear you have been guilty of crime, but ——"

" Alas !" exclaimed the boy, bursting into tears, " you judge me too mercifully. I have been guilty of crimes such as nothing but death can efface. Forgive me for thus intruding upon you. Oh ! pronounce but my forgiveness, and I will quit you, praying that blessings may be heaped upon your head. May you, indeed, be happy, and blest in her who has won your heart ; and may she—oh, she will—prove more amiable and worthy than her who now seeks for pardon at your knees,"—rising, and casting herself on her knees before him. " Mordaunt, the assumed boy is no other than your guilty, faithless wife, Isabel. Spurn me not—cast me not from you, till you have assured me of your forgiveness ; then I will no longer torture you with my presence, but that instant depart."

" Rise, Isabel," said Mordaunt, calmly ; " kneel not to me ; your disguise at first imposed upon me, but, since we have been together, I more than suspected who you were. Tell me the motive that induced you thus to assume a costume wholly unsuited to your person and sex."

There was a stern coldness in her husband that completely awed the unhappy lady. Reproaches and bitter anger she had fully anticipated, and was well prepared to meet ; but his present unmoved yet stern demeanour she never, for an instant, expected, and knew not how to answer him. Without even the power of doing his bidding, she continued kneeling, and, burying her face in her hands, she sobbed aloud.

" This emotion," said Mordaunt, after an interval of silence, " is wholly uncalled for. I have given utterance to nothing that can justify such an exhibition of feeling ; and if you suppose, for an instant, that it will move me in your favour, you are totally mistaken, as, in all probability, it will have a contrary effect ; it will, therefore, be serving yourself better to lay aside all stage attitudes and theatrical effects."

Isabel could only endeavour to suppress her sobs, and drive back her tears to their fount. She essayed to speak, but the bitterness of her emotion choked her utterance.

" When you think fit to inform me of your motive in seeking to force yourself upon me," continued Mordaunt, " I shall be glad, if possible, to meet your wishes ;" and, rising from his seat, he walked towards a window, from which he gazed into the street, apparently utterly indifferent to the emotions of Isabel.

Alas! how severe—how acute were her feelings, at the cold severity of her husband; and the knowledge that her own conduct well merited such treatment, added increased sorrow to the weight of anguish that now pressed so heavily on her heart. Yet she strove to subdue her feelings, at least, in his presence, and, after a short interval, rose from her knees, and, drying the tears that were falling thick and fast, said,—

"My only motive in thus, as you say, forcing myself upon you, was to hear you pronounce my forgiveness. Oh! James, I have long been conscious how deeply I have injured you. Say that you pardon my falsehood, and I shall die content."

"If him you preferred to myself has wearied of your charms, and cast you from him, I can never allow you to remain unprovided for," said Mordaunt, coldly, yet bitterly.

"Alas! such is not the case," replied Isabel; "the poverty and distress to which our child was exposed, alone made me accept his proposal—that child, James, is now no more; and, on her death, I instantly resolved to return to the path from which I had voluntarily strayed. I desire nothing beyond your pardon and forgiveness—that obtained, I shall spend the remainder of my life in peace and serenity."

"If that is, in truth, your desire, you shall be furnished with the means of enabling you to do so," said Mordaunt. "Now, quit me; in your own proper dress, you will find a home and a welcome with Mary Ellis."

"Dear gentle lady," said Isabel, fervently; "I am already indebted to her beyond, far beyond what I can ever hope to repay. Yes, with her, guilty, fallen as I am, I shall ever find a refuge. The sweetest and most innocent of God's creatures are ever, likewise, the most ready to succour the guilty and distressed. Say that you pardon me, James, and, as I said before, I shall go in peace."

"I shall see you again," said Mordaunt; "and if I think you have truly repented, I shall not withhold my forgiveness, if that can avail you aught. I have told you," he continued, "that another has won that love and affection which was once all your own. Yet do I not for a moment contemplate endeavouring to win her regard My heart is too cold and seared for me to offer its acceptance to her, who is worthy of, and should have nothing less than a heart in its first fond gush of confiding tenderness : mine, all cold and dead, would wither and blight her pure virgin affection. When I spoke of wedding her, it was merely done to try you, and it had the effect I intended, of inducing you to throw off your disguise.'

He paused, and Isabel felt relieved at his thus declaring his real intentions; for the thought of his marrying another had shot a severe pang through her heart. Still, she spoke not, and Mordaunt, observing her silence, again resumed.

"I can but feel thankful, for your own sake, that you are resolved to turn to a life of virtue. You have, by your past conduct, planted a thorn in my side—inflicted a wound which made me contemn the entire sex; but, the society of one, virtuous, amiable, and good, has convinced me of the folly, nay, wickedness, of judging so erroneously."

"You speak truth," said Isabel; "and I am truly thankful you are no longer prejudiced against others, because I proved so false and guilty; but you cannot despise me half so much as I despise myself."

"That is nothing to the purpose," said Mordaunt; "you deliberately severed the ties that once bound us together, and we are now entirely and for ever separated. I intend amply to provide for your wants, and hope you may acquire peace, if not happiness; for myself, I shall travel—change of scene may be beneficial to me in a great many respects."

Isabel bowed her head as these sentences fell from the lips of him whom she had once loved, and without heeding them in the slightest degree, turned and left the room.

---

## CHAPTER XXXIII.

JOHN ELGOOD had been of late so flattered and encouraged by the kind attentions of Emily Stanhope, that he resolved to lose no more time, but at once put to her the momentous question that would determine the future course of his life. Fired, therefore, with the full hope of gaining a favourable answer to his important query, he wended his way to the great house, though, it must be confessed, with a fluttering heart, revolving in his mind the best way of procuring a private interview with his lady love.

FREDERICK MAITLAND'S INTRODUCTION TO EMILY PERCY.

["This gentleman," said Mrs. Harley, addressing Emily, "particularly desired an introduction to you. The master of the ceremonies presented me to his brother, Captain Maitland, with whom I dare say you observed me dancing."]

On arriving at the mansion he found that for this once fortune had decidedly favoured him.   Mr. Stanhope and his nephew were from home, the old lady was engaged in her dressing-room, and Emily, with one of her sweetest smiles, bade him welcome, and, after the first salutations were over, invited him to a seat by her side.   John was of course nothing loth, and yet, having seated himself, he was at a loss how to open the conversation, and Emily was the first to speak. She was engaged with her embroidery, and bending over the frame to conceal her rising colour, said, in a low but musical voice,—

" Have you seen Mr. Ellis to-day, John ?"

" I have but this instant parted with him," returned the youth ; " and upon my acquainting him with my intended visit to you, he desired his kind remembrance."

" To me, John ?" said Emily, with an air of surprise.

" He did not particularise you," said the young man; " but ——"

" You mean," said Emily, interrupting, " that he desired to be remembered generally ?" and there was a perceptible sadness in her voice.

" Yes," said John ; and then, after a moment's hesitation, he added, " Are you not well, Miss Stanhope ?"

" Perfectly well, thank you, John," returned Emily, kindly; " but I must confess that my heart is very sad.  I am no longer, John, the wealthy heiress ; and the loss of wealth, though almost valueless in itself, has been accompanied with the loss of friends ; among whom I am sorry to be forced to reckon Mr. Ellis."

" Oh, surely," said the youth, warmly, " you do us injustice ; you do, indeed."

Emily smiled, and laying her hand kindly on the shoulder of John, she said,—

" I never for a moment ranked you, my dear John, among those whom the loss of fortune hath driven from me ; you, at least, have been as kind, as truly affectionate as ever."

" And ever will remain so," replied the youth, warmly.

" I believe you, John," said Emily; " your friendship was for myself, independent of my expected inheritance; and that being the case, it is, and still will be, cherished as valuable and precious."

" Your words, indeed, confer happiness upon me," replied the youth, " and inspire me with confidence to impart to you the secret of my breast."

" What! John," returned Emily, smiling with surprise, " are you in truth possessed of a secret ?"

" Even so," replied the young man, " and one that can be breathed to you alone; it is in your power to render me happy or miserable for life."

" You have succeeded in awakening my curiosity," said Emily, turning her whole attention from her work to give it to her companion; " pray proceed, John, and doubt not my willingness to render you happy; if we are separated from it ourselves, it is nevertheless sweet to make others blest."

" Then you consent to make me so," said John; " that is all I require."

" You must first point out in what manner I can thus serve you," returned Emily, smiling again.

" Dearest Emily—will you permit me to call you by a name so sweet ?—I love you—I love you to desperation;" and he made an effort to throw himself at her feet.

" La, John ! don't be ridiculous," said Emily, making an effort not to laugh; " it is a very excellent joke, but ——"

" Joke !" interrupted the youth; " you do not—you cannot suppose I am joking ; I never was more serious in my life.  Let me sue for the dearest boon I ever craved, as it ought to be sued for, on my bended knees;" and, in spite of her endeavours to prevent him, he flung himself before her.

The poor fellow certainly cut a ridiculous figure, and Emily, ever alive to the absurd, could no longer conceal her risibility, but gave it free vent in a loud, clear laugh, which made the old walls ring again.

In vain Emily strove to subdue her merriment; the disconcerted countenance of John, who gazed on her half in anger and half in surprise, afforded her fresh food for mirth, which was shown in renewed and continued bursts of laughter, till anger took place of every other feeling in the young man's breast.   Few—very few persons can bear to be laughed at ; and John, though a good-natured and well-meaning youth, yet was deeply and bitterly mortified at Emily's treatment of him.   Her refusal of his love, accompanied even with disdain, he would have borne willingly, uncomplainingly ; but to be laughed at— to serve for nothing but her merriment—to appear ridiculous in her eyes, and her not even to think it worth while to conceal it from his knowledge! This—this was too much; he rose from his kneeling attitude amidst her reiterated bursts of laughter, and wore such a rueful expression on his countenance that Emily endeavoured in vain to repress it; and yet, feeling for the young man's evident discomfort, she tried to conciliate him by making an apology for her rudeness.

"My dear John, pray excuse me. Ha! ha! ha! I don't know what I am laughing at. Ha! ha! ha! I don't, indeed. Ha! ha! ha! ha! ha! ha! Don't pay any atten—ti—on to me. Ha! ha! ha !—ha! ha! ha! You are not going, John—Ha! ha! ha!—are you? Ha! ha! ha!" and, throwing herself back in her chair, she was perfectly convulsed with laughter.

"I am happy, at least," said John, when Emily had absolutely exhausted herself, "in being the means of rendering you so merry. If you remember, Miss Stanhope, at the commencement of this interview you complained of feeling sad; but I shall leave you with the assurance that I have driven so unpleasing a companion from your presence; there is some comfort in that."

"Why, John, you are not seriously offended," said Emily, gazing on the youth with unfeigned surprise.

"Not seriously offended, of course," replied John; "I am only too happy to be laughed at by Miss Stanhope."

"Do leave off that nonsense, John," replied Emily, evincing symptoms of renewed laughter.

"Certainly," returned the youth, in a tone of satire; "and that I may avoid the opportunity of offending you in like manner again, I will at once do myself the pleasure of wishing you good morning;" and without waiting her reply he hurried from the room.

"Poor fellow!" thought Emily, as soon as he was gone; "I am sorry I have vexed him, but really he did look so ridiculous, that——" and at the very thought of the rueful appearance of John she laughed afresh.

In the meantime, the discomfitted youth, with a quick pace, walked down the main street of the village, and turned towards the open country in order to tranquillise his ruffled spirits before he again conversed with any one. He was deeply mortified, and he considered justly so, and had inwardly resolved never to speak with Emily again.

So deeply was he engaged with his own thoughts, that he was not aware of the near approach of Mrs. Harley, who was returning from her morning walk, and alone, for Frank had the day before started for London.

"Well met, Mr. Elgood," exclaimed the widow, smiling.

John started at the sound of her voice, and she smiled again.

"Why, I declare, Mr. Elgood, you were absolutely in a profound reverie; if it is not a secret, do pray tell me the subject of your thoughts."

"Oh! nothing very interesting," replied John, "or I should be happy to oblige you. Have—have you seen Miss Stanhope lately?"

"Not very lately," returned the widow; "but your question has given me a clue to the subject of your thoughts, and I am convinced, Mr. Elgood, that you are in love with my fair friend."

"Me in love with her!" said John, with a tone of bitterness. "If I were, Mrs. Harley, I should only get laughed at for my pains."

"Oh! you artful creature!" retorted the widow with a fascinating smile. "You want me to flatter you, but I will not do anything of the sort, so go along with you." Saying which, she endeavoured to pass him, but John with an unwonted gallantry caught her hand, and drawing it through his arm, declared he would enforce a penalty for the impertinence of her last speech, by obliging her to accompany him in his walk.

"Oh! but, upon my word," said the widow laughing, "I am absolutely so weary that I cannot walk a step farther, so it is utterly useless to talk of obliging me; but if you insist on a penalty, I suppose I must submit to be tormented with your company for an hour or two before dinner."

John declared his willingness to accede to her terms, and together they entered her residence. The widow was by no means a bad companion, and so pleasant and agreeable did she render herself to the young man, that time flew unheeded by.

Dinner was served in an elegant and tasteful manner, and after the cloth was drawn the widow managed, with a tact that was natural to her, to draw from John an account of his interview with Emily.

"My dear John," exclaimed Mrs. Harley, and then, as if recollecting herself, "pray excuse me for addressing you thus; really, I am quite forgetting myself."

"I only wish," returned John, "that you would always thus forget yourself; I should then, I think, be greatly the gainer."

"What does the creature mean?" said the widow, affecting a look of surprise. "I have only just got rid of Frank, and obtained an interval of rest from the fatigue of listening to his absurd speeches; and now I declare you are commencing in exactly the same strain. If it is not perfectly unbearable!"

"You must not say so," said John, and, with unusual effrontery, he drew his chair closer to the widow's, and actually passed his arm round her waist.

Now, Mrs. Harley was a very discreet lady; she, therefore, gave no heed to this little piece of gallantry, and John, emboldened by her kindness, strove to snatch a kiss from her rosy lips.

"Upon my word, Mr. Elgood," said the widow, smiling, "you are positively growing too bold; and I must actually chide you—I must, indeed. If Frank was here, or had any idea of your rudeness, I should really tremble for the consequences."

"That would be exceedingly kind of you," said John, "and proves that, in spite of all your scolding, you still entertain a regard for me."

"Why, what will you say next?" said the widow.

"That I am surprised at my own bad taste, in having once been silly enough to prefer Emily Stanhope to yourself," promptly returned the youth; "but you will forgive me when I assure you that it arose solely from not possessing a knowledge of your many attractive qualities."

Mrs. Harley never gave utterance to even the most common-place remark, when conversing with the opposite sex, without having first well weighed in her own mind the effect it was likely to have upon her hearer; consequently, she hesitated for a few minutes before she returned any answer to the last few words that were spoken by John.

She had, ever since her husband's death, sighed for a fresh helpmate, hitherto in vain. Now, she shrewdly suspected, if she chose, she could bring John to the point, and ere long become Mrs. Elgood. This was not exactly the most desirable position; but still she judged it preferable to remaining all her life a widow. Frank, certainly, possessed the greatest share of her affections, and him she had long hoped to secure for her second husband. And then, again, she had of late experienced many gallant attentions from the gay and handsome officer, Captain William Maitland; but neither the captain or Frank seemed much inclined for matrimony, and, consequently, the widow judged it more prudent to secure the bird that was already in her hand, instead of endeavouring to catch the two that were hopping about the bush; so, smiling most sweetly upon the youth, she said,—

"Rest assured, John, I should by no means value your affection less, because it was in the first instance bestowed upon my sweet friend Emily."

"What a delightful, amiable creature Mrs. Harley is!" thought John. "I cannot conceive how I could possibly be such a dolt as to overlook her in the manner I have done;" and then he said aloud,—

"My dear Mrs. Harley, you are good enough to say that you will not value my affection the less, because I was stupid enough to give, at one time, the preference to your friend. May I infer, from that remark, that I am not entirely disagreeable to you?"

"Disagreeable, John!" re-echoed the widow; "you are laughing at me for receiving your attentions so readily; but, really, John, you must spare my blushes—the confession tha—you know, I am sure, what I would say."

"I know that you are an angel," said the enraptured youth, catching her in his arms. "Good God! and is it really possible that you have been honouring me with your regard; and I, dolt, fool, that I must have been, thought little or nothing of any one but Miss Stanhope, who, by kindness and encouragement, brought me to a confession, and then laughed at me for my pains."

"Think no more about it," simpered the widow, endeavouring to extricate herself from his embrace; "I am quite shocked at my own imprudence, in admitting you to such freedom; I am sure I cannot think what Frank will say to all this."

"Never mind what he may say," replied John; "you are not under any engagement to him?"

"Oh, no!" replied the lady, eagerly; "I ever told him, candidly, that I could not feel that affection for him I should desire to entertain for the man whom I called by so endearing and tender a name as husband."

" And do you, can you feel that regard for me?" said John, hastily.

" I have never been given to coquetry," replied the widow, with an air of exceeding frankness, "and will not, therefore, conceal from you that I have, that I do, thus regard you."

" Then I am truly blessed," returned the youth, as he warmly pressed the hand she had given him in his own. The widow smiled upon him in acknowledgment of her own happiness, as she returned the fond pressure.

And the untoward events of the day closed with John, not a little to his own surprise, finding himself the received and favoured suitor of the widow Harley, a state of things which, at the commencement of the day, was the very farthest from his thoughts, and had never before been regarded as belonging to the range of possibility.

This, at first sight, appears strange; but when we remember that John left Emily mortified and displeased at her reception of him, it is by no means surprising that he was easily impressed in favour of one who regarded his merits more tenderly. He knew, with a feeling of anger, that he had appeared ridiculous in the eyes of Emily Stanhope; and he was not at all displeased at the opportunity of convincing himself that the reason of his doing so lay, not in himself, but in the want of proper discernment on the part of Emily. This, he now felt assured, must be the case; for was not (thus he argued) Mrs. Harley equally capable of discerning the difference that existed between absurdity and excellence? nay, she had more opportunities of distinguishing worth, for she had mixed in the gayest and proudest of London assemblies; consequently, her regard must be so much the more valuable than Emily's; and he was perfectly convinced that Miss Stanhope was a young lady totally devoid of all discernment; therefore, he could well afford to pity her non-appreciation of his merits.

This was certainly a very comfortable conclusion to arrive at; and as John gazed upon the really pretty face of the widow, and his arm encircled her slender waist, he would not have exchanged her for Emily, even had the estates of Sackville been thrown into the balance.

John Elgood, the hopeful heir of the family, was impatient of delay, and therefore pressed the widow to name the day when she would again consent to enter into the bonds of matrimony; while she, in her turn, was perfectly willing that her second marriage should be consummated before the return of her nephew.

For Mrs. Harley knew perfectly well that Frank was not altogether unlike the dog in the manger; for, though he was by no means inclined to marry her himself, he nevertheless manifested a strong dislike to any one else doing so.

In the course of a week, under the widow's skilful direction, every arrangement was completed, unknown to any but the two concerned.

The first time Emily met John Elgood, she deemed it right to make an apology for the rude manner in which she had behaved to him.

" I am certainly sorry, John," she said, in conclusion, " to have vexed you; but really you did look so ridiculous, that even the remembrance of it almost compels me to offend in the same way again."

" That is impossible," returned the young man. " I have frequently since laughed at my own foolishness in fancying that I was in love with you."

" I am very glad," replied Emily, smiling, " that it was nothing more than fancy."

" I shall shortly give you convincing proof that I now truly designate it by calling it a fancy."

John accompanied this with an important look; but it was lost upon Emily, who thought nothing more upon the matter, till great surprise and much commotion was abroad in the village, by the strange, though undoubted fact, that John Thornton Elgood had eloped with the fascinating widow, Mrs. Harley.

The indissoluble knot was tied in the adjoining town, and William Maitland had the honour of giving the fair bride away.

From this place John wrote to his father, acquainting him with his marriage, and, like a dutiful son, sued for pardon for this, his first act of disobedience; but also, like a tender husband, stipulated that his lady should be received with respect and kindness, or he could not consent to return to Sackville.

The good-humoured squire blustered a little, and wondered what the devil could induce the boy to make such a fool of himself; and then, in his usual hearty manner, laughed, and supposed it was all for the best. Not so his wife and daughters. Mrs. Elgood, on the first reception of the news, gave symptoms of fainting; but prompt restoratives being administered, she only wrung her hands, and ejaculated, in the most pathetic tones,—

"My brother-in-law, the baronet, whatever will he say to this distressing intelligence?"

Her two eldest daughters wondered how Mrs. Harley had dared to entrap their brother into marrying her without the consent of his friends. Of course, it was all her doing.

"Of course," reiterated Mrs. Elgood; "John would never even have thought of such a thing."

"It is downright scandalous," said Miss Elgood.

"It is, indeed," returned her sister; "and here is Louisa sitting there, and looking for all the world as if she did not care at all about it."

"I am very sorry," said Louisa, "but ——"

"What good will sorrow do?" interrupted her mamma.

"What, indeed?" returned Louisa; "that is exactly what I was about to observe. It is very vexatious, undoubtedly; but our being vexed and sorry at the circumstance will not set the marriage aside, or make John less the husband of Mrs. Harley. Therefore, I conceive it is perfectly useless to render ourselves uncomfortable."

"Bravo, girl," replied the squire; "ever make the best of a bad bargain, has always been my maxim. And here comes Mr. Ellis—ask him if that is not a wise and good plan."

Mr. Ellis, on being made acquainted with the news that had so discomfited the family, although in many respects deploring the unlooked-for marriage of John, yet most cordially approved of the squire's maxim, and gave his vote strongly in favour of giving the young man and his bride a kind and cordial reception back to his family and friends. Mrs. Elgood was the more readily induced to consent to this arrangement, inasmuch as John was her favourite child; and though exceedingly vexed with him for having—to use her own words—"so shockingly thrown himself away," yet, on the whole, she was well pleased at the thought of receiving him back.

"Whatever will Miss Stanhope say?" ejaculated the good lady, who was strongly inclined to believe that Emily entertained a tender regard for her son.

"I was thinking," replied Louisa, "of calling this morning at Mr. Stanhope's, and acquainting Emily with the fact of John's marriage."

"That is well thought of, child," returned her mother; "by all means, go at once."

Louisa immediately left the room to attire herself for her walk, and, on her return, Mr. Ellis rose to take his leave, saying, as he did so, to the young lady,—

"As I am going the same road as yourself, Miss Elgood, perhaps you will allow me the pleasure of walking with you."

Louisa bowed compliance, and arm in arm they proceeded down the High-street, the curate deeply engaged in conversing with his companion about John, and the unfortunate choice he had made of a wife.

"But," said Mr. Ellis, in conclusion, "I hope the marriage may prove happier that we at present anticipate."

"We can scarcely allow you," said Louisa, good-naturedly, "to be a competent judge of the lady's worth, for you were ever rather strongly prejudiced against her."

"There was much in her manners," replied the curate, "that I confess I greatly disliked; and I think, Louisa, you were no great admirer of Mrs. Harley."

"I was not, indeed; and it has often surprised me that she should have obtained so much influence over Emily; their characters and disposition differ so entirely from each other."

"They do, indeed," said the curate. "Miss Stanhope is as amiable and deserving as ——"

"Well, I declare," interrupted Louisa, "here is Emily coming towards us."

Mr. Ellis started as he recognised Emily, who looked pale and sad; but when he kindly inquired after her health, the usual healthy glow returned with a still deeper flush upon her cheek.

"You are quite a stranger, Mr. Ellis," said Emily, with a little show of resentment. "My uncle, speaking of you this morning, declared himself perfectly at a loss to account for the discontinuance of your visits."

"I had the honour of informing your uncle, Miss Stanhope," replied the curate, "that on the arrival of his nephew, I should devote more of my time to others of my parishioners, who felt themselves neglected by the frequency of my calls at his residence, and which left me but little spare time to give them."

"Your excuse is all-sufficient," replied Emily, coldly. "I trust, for the future, that none may have cause for complaint."

"Nevertheless," returned the curate, "it was my intention to call upon your uncle this morning; and Miss Elgood wishing to converse with you, we were coming together."

"In that case," replied Emily, "I will return with you."

The offer was of course accepted, and on the arrival of the trio at the mansion, Emily, having introduced Mr. Ellis to the drawing-room, where her uncle and aunt were seated, withdrew with Louisa Elgood to the privacy of her own boudoir, where, seating themselves opposite each other, the two young girls conversed without restraint.

After Louisa had duly unfolded the strange incident of her brother's marriage, at which Emily could not refrain from smiling rather broadly, though, to her honour be it said, she concealed from his sister the avowal of love John had made to herself, and felt not a little surprised that it should have been (supposing it ever existed) so suddenly transferred to her friend; we say, after all this, Emily, who, though she much liked Louisa, could not refrain from regarding her with an envious feeling, said,—

"Well, Louisa, John has set you an example which I dare say you will be nothing loth to follow."

"Who, me?" said Louisa, in a tone of surprise; "we all of us undoubtedly look forward with the hope of being ultimately settled in life, and so far I may be said to desire some day to follow the example of my brother; but before that day arrives, my dear Emily, I shall hear you pronounce the word of obedience at the altar."

"You are laughing at me," replied Emily; "Mr. Ellis ——"

"I should suppose, will perform the interesting ceremony," interrupted Louisa, gaily.

"I shall not trouble him so far," returned Emily, in a very different mood to her friend's.

"Really," said Louisa, in the same gay strain, "then you are determined ——"

"Not to marry," said Emily; "but all this is nothing to the purpose; what I alluded to, was your marriage with Mr. Ellis."

Louisa changed colour at these words, and then said, hesitatingly,—

"My marriage with Mr. Ellis! Who informed you, Emily, that there was even a remote possibility of such an event?"

"I merely drew an inference," replied Emily. "When a gentleman pays particular and exclusive attentions to a young lady, which are well received, it is usual to conclude that a wedding will, in all probability, be the result."

Louisa changed colour again, as she answered,—

"It is impossible for me to say what motive may actuate Mr. Ellis in the few slight attentions he has paid me; but I can, with truth, declare that he has never breathed a word that I could, were I ever so disposed, construe into more than a friendly interest."

Emily seemed relieved, but not perfectly satisfied; and, in answer to the last remark of her friend, said,—

"But you admit, Louisa, that his attentions are agreeable to you, and, if he made a proposal, would be willing to accept it?"

"You press me very closely," returned Louisa, laughing, "and I suppose I must even confess that you are not altogether wrong in your conjecture. The truth is, I cannot afford to be very particular; gentlemen are not quite so plentiful at Sackville that a portionless girl like me can pick and choose. I must, therefore, be content to like the first person who offers himself, providing, of course, that he is any way eligible."

"Cannot afford to be particular, and must, therefore, be content to take Mr. Ellis!" re-echoed Emily, in astonishment.

"That is a plain statement of the case," replied Louisa; "and not very difficult to comprehend, I should think;" seeing Emily appeared completely bewildered.

"Alas! how truly unfortunate," exclaimed Emily, "you do not love Mr. Ellis, and him so calculated to inspire affection."

"I very much differ from you there," said Louisa; "for I do not conceive Mr. Ellis at all the man to inspire regard; respect he most certainly does, but surely not affection; he is too cold and reserved, easily to win a woman's love."

"But that love which is difficult to obtain, and which is not lavished on any, or every object that chances to please the eye—oh! that love is a thousand times more valuable than any other; it is, indeed, the only regard I should ever care to win. I would not," continued Emily, with increasing animation, " value a love, be it ever so passionate, that was won, without any desire on my part to gain it. It is something to make a conquest of an obdurate heart; and to be the first that ever inspired affection therein, must indeed be productive of the sweetest bliss."

" That is your romantic ideas," replied Louisa, laughing good-naturedly; " but I, and likewise I think the generality of our sex, prefer a man that is open and warm-hearted; such a man for instance as—as——" and here Louisa hesitated for a moment, and then with an heightened colour, added, " as your cousin."

" Surely," exclaimed Emily, eagerly, " you would not draw a comparison between such a man as my cousin, and Mr. Ellis?"

" Why, it is scarcely fair," returned Louisa, " as the balance preponderates so greatly in favour of——"

" The curate," interrupted Emily. " I thought, Louisa, you had better judgment, than to prefer my cousin."

" Indeed," returned Louisa, " then you are in error, for I must even plead guilty to thinking Mr. Charles Stanhope by far the handsomest, and, in every other respect, the most desirable of the two."

" Ah! is it—can it be possible?" cried Emily, her face radiant with joy. " I entirely forgive you for the sad want of taste you display; for, to you, I need not declare that I am so thoroughly alive to the good qualities of Mr. Ellis, that I do not by any means wish others to regard him in the same light."

" And you really prefer Mr. Ellis to——"

" To all the world," interrupted Emily, warmly, and a deep blush mantled to her cheek.

" Wonders will never cease," replied her companion. " I thought—indeed we all thought, Mr. Ellis, I assure you, among the number—that you were engaged to Mr. Charles Stanhope, and, in my heart, I confess I secretly envied you."

" How strange," said Emily, smiling; " for I was envying you for being, as I supposed, beloved by Mr. Ellis; but ' all's well that ends well;' and I trust that this little comedy of errors will end in happiness to all concerned; there is but one obstacle, and——"

" That, of course, is to make the gentlemen do as we wish," interrupted Louisa.

" I have no fear for one," replied Emily. " It will be a matter of no difficulty to induce my cousin to fall in love with you; he has frequently expressed a strong admiration of you already."

" But he loves you," said Louisa.

" Say that he fancies he loves me, for in truth I do not believe it is aught more, though my vanity might make me desirous of thinking so; but I'll undertake to manage him, and in a few weeks expect to find him your acknowledged suitor; and for myself I shall be glad to be well rid of a troublesome lover."

" I need not say, dear Emily," urged Louisa, " be careful to act with delicacy and caution; it would pain me greatly if your cousin entertained a thought——"

" I know what you would say," interrupted Emily, " and in return beg you not to mistrust me. I will be doubly careful as regards yourself."

" And you?" said Louisa, in a tone of inquiry.

" I will endeavour to ascertain the true nature of Mr. Ellis's feelings towards me. I must manage him. Leave everything to me, Louisa. I begin to hope, with, oh! what sweet delight, that he regards me more tenderly than he wishes me to know. Many, many things now recur to me to favour such a supposition. If I can satisfy myself on this point, no false delicacy on my part shall stand in the way of our mutual happiness. I regarded you, Louisa, as a rival; he may have done the same by my cousin. Let us see you two united to each other, and I shall then be able better to understand Mr. Ellis."

" But can you wait patiently for so long a period of time?"

" I could wait patiently, very thankfully, for years, with the hope of being his at last," said Emily, with warmth. " Louisa dear," she continued, after a short pause, " I know I can depend on your secrecy; let this conversation remain unknown to any but our two selves, and, moreover, hint not by a word, even to Mr. Ellis, the deep affection I nourish for him in my bosom, and shall ever do, for I have determined some time since to be the bride of none but him. If it is decreed that I am not to be his, I shall willingly resign myself to the fate of an old maid."

ISABEL'S DEVOTION.

[Sinking on a seat, Mordaunt covered his face with his hands, and remained for a long time profoundly silent.]

"Those words are easily uttered; but it requires a larger amount of moral courage than I can give you credit for, to put such a speech in practice," returned Louisa, smiling.

"Well, we shall see," replied Emily; "but now it is time we joined the gentlemen below;" and, with a beaming countenance, she preceded her friend to the drawing-room.

---

## CHAPTER XXXIV.

Now it so happened, that when Mr. Ellis communicated the intelligence of John's marriage to Mr. Stanhope, the old gentleman had been meditating the whole of the previous morning upon the match he was so anxious to forward between his nephew and niece, and he now communicated to the curate his desires upon the subject.

"There must, there will be another wedding shortly," exclaimed Mr. Stanhope, joyfully; "and you, my dear sir, must officiate. Yes, Emily must be married within the same walls in which her mother and uncle were wed before her, and wherein she was herself baptised. Oh! it seems but the other day that she was carried to the font, and a right merry day it was for the whole village. There was not even a child, my dear sir, but rejoiced, and made merry, on the auspicious occasion; and so they will again. Yes, yes, it must be a joyful wedding, a joyful one indeed." Here the old gentleman paused for want of breath, and Mr. Ellis, conceiving it necessary to say something, though much shocked at the thought of Emily being about to yield herself to another, said—

"Miss Stanhope, then, is shortly to be united to her cousin."

"I hope so; I hope so indeed," returned the old gentleman.

"Then it is not definitely settled," thought Mr. Ellis; "here at least is some relief," and he breathed free.

"I am naturally," resumed the good-hearted old gentleman, "anxious to see my nephew married, and in a fair way of having heirs to the estate, previous to my own death."

"Very natural, of course," reiterated the curate.

"And Emily," returned Mr. Stanhope, "I am likewise anxious to see settled in life, and where could I find another person in every way so suitable as her cousin?"

"Where, indeed?" re-echoed Mr. Ellis.

"The match is so extremely eligible," continued Mr. Stanhope; "the estates will be retained entirely in our own family; and Emily will enjoy them equally as much as if her cousin had never appeared to prove his prior claim."

"Exactly," returned Mr. Ellis, who felt himself obliged to say something, and who was quick-sighted enough to perceive all the horrid eligibility of the match as clearly even as Mr. Stanhope.

"I hope," resumed the old gentleman, "to persuade Emily to give her hand to her cousin very shortly."

"What," said the curate, in a tone of surprise; "does Miss Stanhope offer any objection?"

"As yet nothing decisive has been mentioned to her; but, when I have hinted it, I have observed that she has endeavoured to evade the topic; but that may not, and I think does not, arise from dislike to Charles, who I think, independent of being the heir of Sackville, is a very desirable young man, and one that she could mould to her own wishes, which is more than can be said of most others."

The curate merely assented; and the old gentleman again went on. "I am sure of Charles; he has declared his willingness to comply with my wishes, and wed Emily whenever her consent can be obtained—he cares not how soon."

"Very kind of him," replied the curate, satirically; but the old gentleman observed it not, and answered seriously—

"Yes, I am thankful and proud to say, that my nephew is very kind and dutiful; always anxious to sacrifice his own wishes in deference to mine."

"But surely," interposed Mr. Ellis, "he will make no self-sacrifice in marrying Miss Stanhope; the joy and honour of so great a favour as her hand must bestow upon him unmitigated delight."

"Certainly, certainly," replied Mr. Stanhope. "Emily is an excellent and amiable girl, and Charles is thoroughly alive to her good qualities, and will, I am convinced, make her a kind and excellent husband."

Here the conference was interrupted by the entrance of the two young ladies.

The old gentleman, with all his wonted politeness, rose to lead Louisa to a seat, and as he did so, remarked, smiling kindly—

"So, your brother John has stolen a march upon all you young people; well, it is a good example, and one that I hope you will all follow." Then turning to his niece, "What say you, my Emily?"

"I am not going to disclaim matrimony, like a silly girl, who thinks of nothing else from morning till night," she replied smiling; "at the same time, uncle, I confess I do not feel in any particular hurry to change my condition."

"But I am very desirous, my love, to see you united to your cousin, before my own decease, and ——"

"This is a subject," interrupted Emily, while the colour mounted to her very temple, "only suitable for private discussion; and when you wish to converse with me concerning it in privacy, you will find me perfectly willing to entertain the subject, which, in the interim, I promise seriously to consider."

"That is right, my Emily," replied her uncle; and then addressing Louisa, he said,—

"When may we expect the pleasure of seeing your brother again at Sackville?"

Louisa replied that it was their intention to send him an invitation to return immediately. Mr. Stanhope highly approved of this arrangement, and continued conversing with Louisa, who was perfectly willing to amuse him, and keep his attention from Emily, who, seated by the side of Mr. Ellis, had succeeded in drawing him into converse, with something of the freedom that at one time so particularly marked their intercourse.

"Have you heard very lately from your sister, Mr. Ellis?" said Emily, in a tone of kind inquiry.

"I had a letter this morning," returned the curate, "and am grieved to say that she complains very much of ill-health; indeed, I cannot help entertaining serious fears on her behalf."

"Does she consent to visit Sackville?"

"No; for the present, she declines my invitation, but gives me hope that she may do so when the spring is more advanced."

"I am sorry, indeed, that she defers coming," replied Emily; "the climate of Devon is considered highly salubrious, and she would likewise have the benefit of Doctor Harding's medical treatment, which has already restored many, whose health was greatly disarranged on their arrival here."

"I am exceedingly anxious concerning my sister," said Mr. Ellis; "for she is usually very open regarding her motives for not complying with my wishes, and now she sedulously avoids assigning any reason for her reiterated refusal of my pressing invitation."

"Perhaps," replied Emily, "she may calculate upon enjoying her visit more fully when the season is milder, and more genial for an invalid."

"I trust that is her only motive; but yet, I have been harassed with sad anxieties concerning her."

"Do not distress yourself, I entreat," said Emily, with a show of friendly interest. "Ladies, you know," she added, smiling playfully, "do not always feel themselves bound to assign the motive that may actuate their decision, be it on what subject it may, and general rules will not always apply to particular occasions."

"Is it thus that I may interpret some of your actions?" replied the curate, smiling in his turn, and catching some of her animation.

"Most certainly," said Emily.

"Then ladies are perfect enigmas," returned Mr. Ellis.

"And are not gentlemen sometimes equally as inexplicable?" replied Emily, bending her soft hazel eyes intently on his countenance, as she waited his reply.

He seemed slightly confused, but answered with a show of frankness,—

"I scarcely think so, Miss Stanhope; what (may I take the liberty of inquiring) has induced you to entertain such an opinion?"

"I answer, candidly—yourself! You seem surprised," she continued, seeing he started; "but, allow me to explain. We were once on friendly terms, you came here often, and appeared pleased with my company. I never, to my knowledge, offended you, even in the slightest degree."

"Offended me, Miss Stanhope?" returned the curate. "I was only too proud of the honour you conferred on me by your kindness and consideration."

"Then," said Emily, with an air of triumph, "I have proved my argument; you suddenly discontinued your visits, treating me with a coldness amounting well nigh to indifference—even avoided me as much as possible; and all this, you confess, without my having given you the slightest offence. Truly, some men are utterly inexplicable."

"I acknowledge the correctness of what you have stated; but I was actuated in my conduct by a powerful motive, though such a one as I could not explain to you. Will you forgive me, Miss Stanhope, and receive me again into favour?"

"On one condition," said Emily.

"Oh, no," returned Mr. Ellis; "I ask for an unconditional pardon."

"You throw yourself, then, on my mercy?" said Emily, gaily.

"Entirely," replied the curate; "gentleness and forgiveness are feminine attributes; and, therefore, I do not despair."

"Since you condescend to flatter, I suppose I must exercise the grace you give me credit for; but you must promise not to offend in the same manner again," replied Emily.

"Oh! no, no," returned the curate; "in that case, I should be unworthy of the grace I ask;" and he bent his mild, grey eyes upon Emily with an expression of kindness that sent a rush of exquisite gladness through her heart.

She was prevented from replying, otherwise than by a grateful look, by her uncle, who appealed to her at this moment on some subject he was discussing with his fair companion; and Mr. Ellis shortly after took his leave; and Emily sought her boudoir, to indulge her blissful feelings alone.

"He loves me!" she repeated, again and again, each time with renewed rapture; "we shall yet be blest. How thankful I am to drop the chains that once held me in bondage. I am no longer an heiress, and may wed whom I please;" and the knowledge that she would likewise be enabled to confer happiness on her friend, added to the joy that filled her breast. There was but one drawback to the pleasing anticipations she indulged for the future, and that was, the disappointment her uncle would undoubtedly experience when she refused to become the husband of her cousin. And at one time it is probable Emily would have sacrificed her own happiness in deference to the wishes of her guardian; but she had, of late, wearied of the romantic notions that once were her delight; and she resolved (in spite of all her favourite novels said on the subject of feminine delicacy), boldly to declare her love for the curate, should it be necessary for the consummation of their mutual happiness. In sober truth, Emily began to discover that romance was very interesting in theory; but totally the reverse when reduced to practice; and she, therefore, wisely resolved, on no account, to allow it to stand in the way of her future happiness.

The grounds attached to Mr. Stanhope's residence were extensive, and commanded some of the most beautiful prospects in the lovely and fertile county in which they stood; and the afternoon being fine, Emily accepted the invitation of her cousin to accompany him in a walk round the garden. They had strolled together for some time, conversing on indifferent topics, when the young man, who had evidently been tutored by his uncle, said, as he pressed the small white hand that rested on his own,—

"England is a beautiful country; and I have heard much in praise of its scenery; but I much doubt if it contains a lovelier spot than this."

"It is, indeed, a beautiful prospect that we are now gazing on," replied Emily; "and I confess I love it well. At one time," she added, "I had a great desire to view other scenes, deeming I should find them more lovely, if less dear; but now I have lost all wish to quit this spot. Here I hope to live and die."

"And you will, dear Emily," returned her companion; "there is sufficient happiness for us both in improving our estate, and attending to the comfort of our tenantry."

"Listen to me one moment, Charles," said Emily, seriously; "it is a delicate subject upon which I am about to enter. I have kept silent long—perhaps too long; but my having done so has arisen from the reluctance I felt to dash the hopes my uncle seems so determined to encourage."

"Go on, go on," said the young man, hurriedly, as Emily paused for a few moments.

"To come at once to the point," returned Emily. "In speaking of these grounds and my uncle's estates, you appeared to suppose it probable, at the least, that I should one day enjoy them with you."

"Surely, surely," replied her cousin, "I did, I do fully look forward to such an event."

"Dismiss those hopes, then, at once, and for ever, from your mind. I value your friendship. I love you as a brother; but never, never can I be more to you than a sister— a kind and affectionate sister, who, as such, would gladly see you united to an amiable and deserving woman, one worthy to become the mistress of this old family house, and these broad lands; one with whom you may be truly blest with happiness."

Emily spoke with unusual warmth, and with the image of Louisa full in her mind's eye, and never having dreamed that her cousin was really attached to her beyond what their affinity would warrant, she was completely startled, as well as shocked, now that she turned to look upon his face, to observe the expression of utter despondency that it exhibited. "Is anything the matter, Charles?" she exclaimed, as she lightly pressed his arm to attract his attention.

"Anything the matter! and can you, Emily, coolly ask me such a question, when you have cast me from the highest pinnacle of hope, down into the very depths of despair?"

"Alas! alas!" exclaimed Emily, "I am wretched beyond measure. I never thought that you really loved me; if I had ——"

"Would you," interrupted her cousin, catching at the last part of her speech, "have endeavoured to return my affection? If so, it is not too late; promise that you will strive, I care not how distant the day, to regard me with a more tender feeling than you now entertain, and I will bless you, Emily, and wait patiently; aye, you shall see how patiently."

"Stop, stop," said Emily earnestly; "I would gladly do as you desire, but I cannot, indeed, I cannot."

"Why not?" said her cousin, earnestly; "you have no engagement; you have assured me I am not disagreeable to you; and if your love is not given to another, may I not hope, by kind attentions and          ."

Emily's face was suffused with the deepest crimson, as she replied, firmly,—

"Pardon me, Charles; I did not say my affections were disengaged; had they been, my own heart would have prompted me to comply with what, I am well aware, is the fondest wish of my uncle."

"Then you love another," returned the young man; "and I am, indeed, wretched."

"Say not so," replied Emily; "there are others, more worthy of your regard, and who would willingly accept your proffered love."

"To speak of others at such a moment as this," said her cousin, "is a bitter mockery; and if, as you say, you know what love, the heartfelt passion, really is, you might have spared me this infliction."

"I was wrong," replied Emily, mildly; "but, believe me, I do so love; yet the object of my warm and tenderest regard I must for the present conceal even from you, as he is himself ignorant of the love he has inspired in my breast."

"You love," said the young man, with an air of perplexity, "and the object of that love knows it not. Oh! surely, Emily, you have not given your affections to one beneath you."

The pride of Emily was thoroughly aroused at this question, which sent the burning blood, in a rich glow, to her cheek, and she released herself from the arm of her companion, and drew up to her full height, as she answered,—

"I am sorry, Charles, you think so meanly of me, as to suppose that Emily Percy could bestow her love upon an inferior, either in birth, or education; rest assured that my desire to keep this love a secret for the present, arose from no feeling that I need blush to own such existed; so far from it, when I think of his moral excellence, and his superior mental qualities, I am only fearful that I am unworthy of possessing so great a treasure as his affections; which, if I were convinced were bestowed upon me, I should be proud and delighted to acknowledge before the whole world."

Charles Stanhope was astonished to hear his usually proud high-spirited cousin thus expressing herself, and exclaimed, rather satirically,

"And does this paragon of perfection reside in the neighbourhood of Sackville?"

"Charles," said Emily, kindly, "do not press me on this subject; you will one day, I fully hope, know my secret; till then, allow me to assure you, that the affection which exists in my breast, is no girlish liking, no silly romantic passion, founded on nothing more than a showy exterior; but it is a love that is founded on the best and surest foundation—a deep respect and a high opinion of the mental endowments of him who has inspired it.    It is, perhaps, a love that some might account cold; but it is likewise a love that will outlast a more violent attachment, for it is lasting and endurable as time itself. It is a love that would prompt me to ensure the happiness of its object. at the expense of my own.   I know not," she continued, with warmth, "when this love first took pos-session of my breast, it seems to have grown with my growth, and strengthened with increasing years; but not till others had spoken to me of love, had linked my name with yours, did I become aware of the nature of my regard ; then, the repugnance I felt to a union in every respect so desirable, led me to analyze my feelings, and the result proved to my entire satisfaction that I loved; yes, truly and devotedly."

"Every word you utter," returned her cousin, mournfully, "while it convinces me of the hopelessness of my own love, at the same time plants a thorn in my breast.   Emily," he added, "you may form an idea of my feelings, when I tell you that this large estate, and the numberless advantages I derive from being the heir of Sackville, sink, now you have rejected me, into utter worthlessness.   A dark cloud has passed over the brightest picture of my imagination, and since you care not for me ——"

"Speak not thus mournfully," interrupted Emily ; "I feel equally as sad as yourself. I shall be forced to disobey an uncle whom it has hitherto been my greatest delight to please ; and were my own happiness alone concerned, I should be almost tempted to sa-crifice it; but I believe that of another is at stake, and I dare not."

"Hush, Emily," said her cousin.   "Were you to offer me your hand, I could not, after this conversation, accept it.   Your uncle intends conversing with you this evening regarding our proposed marriage, and doubtless he will be deeply hurt when you acquaint him with what has passed between us."

"And the more," said Emily, sorrowfully, "as I cannot explain to him my reason for refusing you."

"It is unfortunate," returned the young man ; "but as uncle is so much attached to you, he will, I hope, readily accept of your excuse.   You can tell him that it is impos-sible for you to return my affection ; and now let us part.   I must strive to forget how dear, how very dear you are to my heart."

"I shall still," said Emily, " regard you as a sister.   Think of me as such, love me as such, and we may yet be happy."

Charles made no reply, save by a long lingering pressure of the hand ere he resigned it, and then bowing low, he turned into the shrubbery, and Emily, with a sorrowing heart, once more sought the seclusion of her room.

———

## CHAPTER XXXV.

POOR Emily, who had so lately trod on air, in the joyous gaiety of her heart, was now sunk once more into the deepest despondency ; she felt, indeed, perhaps more than the occasion warranted ; but those who are the soonest elated are ever the easiest depressed.

"Alas !" she exclaimed, as she threw herself on the downy cushions of the couch that ornamented the apartment, "I shall be forced to sound a note of discord where all has hitherto been peace ; and the task I thought so easy to accomplish is surrounded with difficulties, so much so, that I almost despair of success."

But then the thought of the bliss that might ultimately crown her efforts determined her to go on in the course she had marked out for herself.   She had certainly never for a moment contemplated any obstacle on the part of her cousin, never having believed that he entertained any very tender regard for her, till the deep sorrow he manifested on receiving her decided refusal of his love convinced her that it was no foolish boyish fancy he had conceived for her, but a true and tender passion, which would require time to be effaced from his memory, before his heart could be open to receive new impressions in favour of another.   Yet, such she trusted would one day be the case.   Yes, she hoped for Louisa as well as herself.

Emily certainly dreaded meeting her cousin at the tea-table, and was half inclined to frame an excuse for her absence.   She felt there would be an awkwardness in their first meeting after the explanation that had taken place between them ; and this determined her to have it over at once.   Therefore, summoning her maid, she proceeded to array herself in an evening dress, and, striving to smile with her usual gaiety, she descended to the drawing-room. Mr. and Mrs. Stanhope, with their nephew, were waiting her arrival, and Emily, according to her invariable custom, presided over the tea equipage. Her uncle was unusually gay, and even her aunt, Emily thought, smiled more frequently than was usual with her; Charles, too, joined in the conversation more cheerfully than she expected, but he carefully avoided looking at her; indeed, Emily had done the same by him, only once venturing to glance at his countenance, which certainly, to her eyes, at least, gave token of extreme dejection, and which was by no means calculated to banish her anxiety. Tea over, Emily resolved, with a sort of desperation, to come at once to an explanation with her uncle, and though her voice trembled, she gave no other token of the emotion that swelled her breast, as she said,—

"Uncle, Charles has informed me that you are desirous of speaking with me in private; will an hour hence be convenient?"

"Perfectly, my dear child; indeed, the present moment will."

"Then let it be now," replied Emily, quickly; "the sooner it is over the better." And she followed her uncle to his study, and, seating herself opposite to him, waited to hear what he had to say.

"I am sure, my dear Emily," began the old gentleman, "you are well aware of my anxiety on your behalf, and that I must first have well weighed in my own mind the benefit likely to accrue to you, before I advised you to take an important step of any kind, more especially so solemn and important a one as marriage."

"Oh! yes, dear uncle," replied Emily, warmly; "I am, as you say, thoroughly convinced of it."

"Well, then, my child, when I strongly express my earnest desire to see you married to your cousin, you will believe it is not alone the eligibility of the match as regards pecuniary consideration, but that I, likewise, consider him a man every way calculated to ensure your happiness."

"Uncle," said Emily, seriously, "you do not think there is even a possibility of happiness in the marriage state without mutual and warm affection?"

"No, my love, I do not," replied Mr. Stanhope.

"Then, uncle, you will not urge me to a marriage with my cousin, when I assure you that I do not so regard him."

"But he loves you, Emily," returned the old gentleman, in sad surprise.

"I believe he does," said Emily; "and most bitterly do I deplore the circumstance."

"My dearest love," replied the old gentleman, in a tone of extreme surprise, "deplore the affection your cousin so warmly bestows upon you? I surely cannot understand you aright."

"It is but too true, uncle," said Emily, sorrowfully. "I do not—I cannot love him; and, therefore, for his sake, deeply deplore that he should have given his affection to me."

"But you do not intend, surely," said the old gentleman, in a tone of extreme sadness; "you do not intend to refuse your cousin's offer?"

"I have no alternative but to do so. Believe me, uncle, it pains me greatly to be obliged to grieve you, and act contrary to your advice; but on this one important subject I can be guided only by my own feelings."

"My dear child," said Mr. Stanhope, "think well before you decide."

"I have thought well, uncle, and considered it deeply in my mind."

"Emily," resumed her uncle, "do not, I beseech of you, allow any romantic notions to stand in the way of your cousin's and, I believe, also your own happiness. From infancy you have been regarded as the heiress of Sackville. You are beloved and respected by the tenantry, who have always indulged the hope of your becoming the owner of these estates, and they naturally look to you, when in trouble or difficulty, for aid and advice. By this marriage, all these hopes are confirmed. You, and your children after you, will inherit the wealth of your mother's family."

"I am fully aware of all you observe," replied Emily; "and though, by remaining steadfast in my refusal of Charles, my means of assisting others, in a pecuniary manner, may be lessened, yet, as I shall still reside on the estate, my advice and attention to their comforts will be as much their's as if I were indeed the owner."

"You know not that, Emily; you may marry, and quit the village for ever."

"In that case," replied Emily, "I hope first to see Charles united to an amiable and worthy woman, one who may more than fill my place to the tenantry."

"Emily, my love," said her uncle, kindly, "for my sake, do not decide upon refusing your cousin at once; take time to consider of it, and you will probably alter your deter-mination."

"Never, uncle; I am not actuated, as you suppose, by any romantic notions, neither has caprice aught to do with my motives. I could not, therefore, refuse him to-day, and accept him to-morrow."

"I did not expect so sudden a change in your ideas, Emily," said her uncle, anxiously; "but I see you are determined not to oblige me."

"My very dear uncle," said Emily, rising, and throwing her arms round his neck, "oh, pray forgive your child this one act of disobedience; could I, consistent with my own feelings, do as you wish, believe me, uncle, I would gladly do it—I would, indeed."

Mr. Stanhope folded her to his bosom; he was greatly hurt at her refusal, but he loved her so tenderly that he could not chide her, even had he supposed it would have induced her to comply with his wishes; and poor Emily was so unhappy at having pained her uncle, that she leant her head on his shoulder and wept aloud.

"My dear Emily, my darling child," said the kind old gentleman, striving to console her, "do not weep; I cannot bear to see your tears—dry them, my love, and forget for ever this conversation; let me see you smile, again, and you shall never more, my Emily, be pressed on this subject. I will forbid your cousin even to mention it in your presence."

"My dear, kind uncle," sobbed Emily, "but, will you, can you forgive me for my seeming unkindness? Some day you shall know all, and then ——"

"And then, my child," replied Mr. Stanhope, "I am convinced I shall approve of your conduct this day. I think, my dear Emily, you are actuated by some good and powerful motive."

"Oh, bless you, uncle, for those words; you but do me justice—you do, indeed."

"I am sure of it, Emily; only let me, my love, caution you on one subject—that is, never, Emily, be induced to take any step in life without consulting your uncle."

Emily's brow flushed to a deep and burning crimson at these words, and she answered, "Oh, uncle, do you suppose it possible I could thus forget myself, or what is due to you?"

"I do not, my child; but this conversation has convinced me that your affections are already bestowed. I will not, my love, injure you, by supposing they are given to one unworthy of you."

"You say truth, dear uncle," replied Emily, hiding her blushing face in her uncle's bosom. "I will not attempt to conceal from you that my love is, has, long been given to another."

"And that other, my love?" said the old gentleman, in a tone of inquiry.

"Dear uncle, will you forgive me for saying that I cannot name him to you?"

"Why not, my child? Surely ——"

"Oh, uncle!" interrupted Emily, "I should be but too proud to own him; to tell you how dear, how very dear he is to my heart; but he knows it not himself, and that is the only reason I desire to conceal his name from you."

"But of course, my love, if Mr. El ——"

"Uncle, you have guessed right; but spare my blushes, and pray do not breathe to any one the secret I have imparted to you, alone. I should die with shame, if I thought it possible you would even hint to him the state of my feelings. Oh, promise—pray, dear uncle, promise not to discover aught to him?"

"Peace, my child: I will be guided entirely by your wishes; your happiness is alone concerned, and it is but right your desires should be studied."

"Thank you, oh, thank you, dear uncle; I am now content."

"But, my child, how can your happiness be insured, if he who is necessary to it, is never to know the regard you entertain for him?"

"Pardon me, uncle, I did not say he should never know it, but that I desired you should not mention the subject to him; you know, uncle," she continued, with some-thing of her native playfulness, "that I was always a wilful girl, and ever coaxed you into letting me have my own way. I will not now, uncle, ask you if you would consent to give your Emily to the man of her heart; but, when I do solicit your approbation, I trust, dear uncle, it will not be withheld."

"It will not, my child; I know of no man, with the exception of your cousin, I would more willingly receive as your husband."

## MRS. ELGOOD'S RECONCILIATION WITH HER NEPHEW.

In less than half an hour, Frank was seated in his usual snug little corner, puffing away at his eternal pipe, happy in himself, and perfectly satisfied with the course events had taken.

No. 25.

"This conversation," said Emily, "has relieved my heart of much anxiety, and, for the rest, time and patience will, I hope, accomplish much."

"I am unhappy on Charles's account," replied Mr. Stanhope; "but I hope it will prove for the best. The saddest reflection, my Emily, is, that I shall now probably, most probably descend to the grave without seeing my name perpetuated in another generation."

"You must not indulge such gloomy anticipations, dearest uncle," said Emily, tenderly kissing his forehead. "I feel assured that you will live to see the family again revive, and the children of your nephew playing around your knee."

Mr. Stanhope smiled, though rather faintly, as he answered,—

"I shall have the painful task, Emily, of breaking this intelligence to your cousin."

"I have spared you that, dear uncle, by acquainting him with the state of my feelings, when we walked together this afternoon."

"Did you indeed, my love? I thought he seemed thoughtful, and less inclined for conversation; but I attributed it to the excess of happiness, and not to grief; but I hope he will endeavour to conquer this unhappy passion."

"I hope, and likewise believe he will," said Emily; "and now, uncle, you must promise me not to be sad yourself, for, if I see you unhappy, I shall indeed be wretched."

Mr. Stanhope gave the required promise, and, to do him justice, we must say that he strove hard to keep it; but, when day by day he witnessed the gloom and despondency of his nephew, not even the attentive kindness and playful gaiety of Emily could dispel the sadness of his breast.

In due time, John and his bride made their appearance again at Sackville; the little box underwent thorough repair, and several new pieces of furniture were ordered direct from Bond-street, to grace the habitation of the new married pair.

Emily was, of course, among the earliest of the visitors who called to wish them joy and pay her respects on the important occasion. There was something in the manner of John, towards her, she thought anything but agreeable; and, as he introduced the widow as Mrs. Elgood, the expression of his face seemed to say, "Though you would not have me, here is one everyway preferable who was but too proud to become my wife." The widow smiled, and affected to blush, as she simpered out,—

"Well, Emily dear, I am almost ashamed to see you, and fully prepared to receive a good scolding for having behaved so deceitfully towards you; but you know what men are, and John was so urgent, that really ——"

"Make no apology," returned Emily, "especially to me; I assure you it is wholly uncalled for."

"I suppose you will be the next, Emily," continued the lady, in her usual bland tone. "By the bye, how came you so rashly to refuse your cousin?—I attribute it entirely to my absence, for, had I been here, I would not have allowed you to act so silly."

"Your presence or your absence could not possibly have aught to do with my refusal to marry Charles."

"Well, but, Emily, do tell me all about it—how came you to decline his offer?"

"For the simple reason," returned Emily, "that I did not, and do not love him."

At this juncture, the two brothers, Captain and Ensign Maitland, were announced.

"Oh, show them in, John," said the lady; and then whispered Emily that she really protested John was jealous of the captain already.

"Then, I am sure," replied Emily, "I would not admit of his visits."

"La, child," said the bride, "what old-fashioned notions you have got into your head. I would encourage them for that very reason, even if they were disagreeable to me, which I assure you they are not, as the captain is such a gay and gallant companion, and, moreover, such a handsome man."

The entrance of the object of her remarks prevented the lady farther eulogising him at present, but she greeted him with a most fascinating smile, and invited him to a seat by her side, which the captain was nothing loth to accept, having first bowed politely to Emily.

The young and handsome ensign, with whom Emily was on friendly terms, gave his entire and exclusive attention to her, and, in light and cheerful converse, the morning passed pleasantly away.

On Emily's return home, she was met by her cousin, who informed her that Louisa Elgood had been there during her absence, and concluded with saying,—

"I am sure she is a very pleasant and amiable young lady, and far more worthy of your regard than that showy, though, to me, disagreeable widow."

"She is not a widow now, you know," replied Emily, laughing; "but, to confess the truth, I am not overfond of her; I am perfectly wearied of being called her sweet friend, and am so flattered by her on any and every occasion that I am quite tired of it; the sweetest things clog our palates, you know, the soonest."

"They do, indeed," said Charles; "and you have been unfortunate enough to lose the company of Miss Elgood."

"I do not think that a very great misfortune. Louisa is ———"

"A most delightful companion, surely," said the young man; "you cannot gainsay that; and then she is evidently so amiable and good-tempered."

"Rather plain in person, do you not think?" replied Emily, in a tone of inquiry.

"What, Louisa Elgood?" said her cousin. "I thought, Emily, you were possessed of better taste, for she is certainly a very pretty, interesting girl."

Emily laughed.

"That will do, Charles. I only wished to gain your true opinion of her. I should, indeed, be possessed of bad taste, if I regarded her otherwise than interesting in person and in mind. I know she is all, and more than you describe her. I hope," she continued, "you spent a pleasant morning."

"Oh, yes, very," returned her cousin; and, for the first time, he began to think that, as his uncle was so very anxious to see him married, he could scarcely do better than unite himself to Louisa, who, he rightly judged, was possessed of every requisite to ensure his happiness; and Emily likewise shrewdly suspected that her wishes, so far as her friend were concerned, were now in a fair way to be realized. As regarded herself, the prospect was not so bright; she felt it at present impossible to ascertain the nature of Mr. Ellis's feelings towards her. Since their renewed intimacy, his visits at the mansion were more frequent; and he even treated her with the greatest respect and consideration; but yet there was a restraint which marked all their intercourse; and, though he frankly communicated to her the intelligence he received from his sister concerning Mr. and Mrs. Mordaunt, and any other event he thought calculated to interest her, yet Emily thought, especially at times, that there was even a marked coldness in his manners towards her, and which checked the warmth of her own feelings, which were constantly rising to the surface. Yet Emily was by no means discouraged; the comparative poverty of the curate, to her mind, offered a sufficient explanation: and she, therefore, resolved to wait patiently, till time should remove this, she hoped, only obstacle, to her happiness.

Though Mrs. John Elgood was not the companion and friend of Emily she had once been, yet she very frequently spent her mornings at her cottage, especially when she had reason to suspect Louisa would call at her uncle's; for she judged there was nothing so likely to bring about her views, as leaving her cousin alone with her friend as much as possible.

We had forgotten to acquaint the reader, that when the widow gave her fair hand to John, she wrote immediately after the nuptial knot was tied, to inform her nephew of the important event: and, no sooner was Frank made acquainted with the intelligence, than he set off in great haste for Sackville, and arrived at the cottage the day after the return of Mr. and Mrs. Elgood.

The bride received him with her usual affability, and bore the reproaches of her nephew with most praiseworthy forbearance.

Frank was absurd enough to consider himself very ill-used in not being consulted on the occasion; and appeared to consider great credit was due to him for not being in a towering passion.

"Harriet!" he exclaimed, in a subdued though angry voice, "what the deuce could you have been thinking of to marry that smock-faced boy? If you had only patience, I always intended to marry you myself; but, instead of even giving me the refusal, in my absence, you go and act in a manner to make me forget the friendship that has for so long a time existed between us."

Mrs. Elgood was extremely mortified at this speech; and bitterly she began to repent not having asked her nephew's advice before she became the wife of John; but she knew that now regrets were useless; and, therefore, hastened to do all in her power towards mollifying the anger of Frank.

"I am sure, my dear nephew," she began, "I was anxious, nay, desirous to ask your advice; but John would not listen to anything of the sort; he so dreaded you might throw some obstacle in the way of our marriage, and was so exceedingly urgent to have the wedding take place in your absence, that he positively overruled all my objections."

"But I tell you," replied Frank vehemently, "I intended to have married you myself."

"You never before said so," returned the lady.

"I thought, of course," said her nephew, "you guessed as much; what else made me so frequent a visitant here?"

"Well, Frank," said Mrs. Elgood, gently "had you told me this some months earlier, I might have profited by it; now it is too late. I am married to another, and——"

"And," said her nephew, angrily, "you can now dispense with my visits; of course they are no longer agreeable, or pleasant to you."

"Stop, stop, Frank," said his aunt; "you are too hasty; I will not, cannot add ingratitude to the list of my offences against you. You are not the less my nephew, because I am again a wife; and I should hate myself, if it were possible I could ever behave to you with coldness or neglect."

"Then," he replied, "you will still allow me to occupy my old seat by your fireside, and smile upon me as kindly as in days gone by?"

"Can you doubt it, Frank?" replied his aunt, with a slight show of resentment; "I thought you knew me better."

"Well, aunty," returned the young man, completely subdued; "I must confess that I think I have judged you rather harshly; you were ever kind and indulgent, so I must trust to your goodness to forgive me."

"I can refuse you nothing, dear Frank; let us forget the past, and for the future I hope we shall be happy."

"I hope we shall," re-echoed the young man; "and, in token of forgiveness, dear aunty, kiss me."

In less than an hour after the commencement of this conversation, Frank was seated in his usual snug little corner, puffing away at his eternal pipe; happy in himself, and perfectly satisfied with the course events had taken.

"I say, aunty," he began, after some minutes spent in full enjoyment of his pipe, and which he now reluctantly removed from his mouth, to give utterance to the aforesaid words.

"Well, Frank?" replied the lady.

"You are now no longer a widow," replied her nephew.

Mrs. Elgood returned, "that since her second marriage, she had certainly ceased to be such;" and then waited patiently for him to speak again; for the pipe engrossed so much of Frank's attention, that whoever attempted to converse with him, had great need to exercise that gift.

"Well, aunt," he began again, after two or three fresh whiffs, "since you are no longer a widow, you are by no means bound to reside, constantly, at a distance from the metropolis."

"Certainly, by no means, my dear Frank," replied the delighted lady, in full anticipation of what her nephew was about to remark.

"Then I should like you to accompany me back to London for a few weeks. I have made a few alterations in the house that I should like to have your opinion of; it is some time since you were there, and the change I should think would be agreeable to you; besides, I have taken a box at the opera for the season; and Grisi is now singing divinely; and—and in short, aunt, you must come."

"It is very kind of you, indeed, Frank; and I should certainly very much like to visit London, once more; the country is certainly very dull in the winter."

"Then it is settled," replied Frank; "your husband, of course, must go with us; and I think it would be as well to invite Miss Stanhope to accompany you."

"What, Emily?" said the lady, not quite so eagerly as before; "if you wish it, Frank, certainly."

"Yes," replied the young man; "I think she will be a pleasant addition to our little circle."

"As you please, Frank," returned his aunt; "I am ever anxious to oblige you."

"Thank you," replied Frank; "and, now I think of it, I may as well inform you that, sa for the future I am determined to live entirely with you, it is nothing but right

I should pay handsomely for the accommodation. So, anticipating the result of my present visit, I have brought with me this little document," drawing a paper from his pocket, and handing it to his companion. Mrs. Elgood received it with evident surprise, but, on opening it, every feeling gave way to one of unmixed delight as she perceived the paper was a legally drawn up deed of gift, conveying to her, for her own especial use and benefit, a munificent yearly provision.

"My dearest Frank," cried the delighted lady, "I am absolutely overwhelmed with gratitude, and yet I know not how to express it."

"Say nothing about it," replied Frank, gallantly. "Am I not already deeply indebted to you, and also looking forward for renewed kindness? Indeed, it is become so habitual to me, that I could not live without it; 'pon my soul, I could not."

"You flatter me, Frank," replied his aunt, smiling sweetly; "but you well know, that I have always entertained a strong preference for yourself, and the only way you can permit me to show my gratitude, will be by constant and unwearying affection."

"That's it, aunt. I begin to think, after all, it is quite as well that you have married John. You will now be able to return to London, and the society you used so much to delight in."

"And we will go soon," said the lady. "I declare, you have made me quite anxious to be again in the gay world; and John, as you say, suits me as well, or better than any other, for I can manage him, and have my own way equally as much as when I was a widow."

Frank assented, and then added, "You must speak to Miss Stanhope about our arrangement."

"Oh! certainly," replied Mrs. Elgood; "and Emily I am sure will be delighted to accompany us." But for this once the lady was wrong, for, on speaking to Emily on the subject, and giving her a most kind and pressing invitation to accompany the bridal party to London, Emily, to her mortification and astonishment, absolutely and decidedly refused it.

"I am sure, my dear Emily," said that lady, "we should all do our best to make you happy."

"I do not doubt it," replied Emily; "but I have no desire to leave my uncle. We have never been parted for a day, and he is now no longer a young man; and should anything happen to him in my absence I should never forgive myself."

"Well, my dear Emily," returned Mrs. Elgood, "you must of course judge for yourself. I know Frank as well as me will be greatly disappointed; still, I would not persuade you against your own inclination. We propose leaving here in a fortnight; if you should alter your mind, I can only say we shall be greatly pleased with your company."

"Thank you," replied Emily, "but I beg leave to decline your invitation entirely. I hope you will enjoy yourself; but for myself, I have not the slightest wish ever to quit this village; I have ever been accustomed to a country life, and a London one I am convinced would ill suit me. You, on the contrary, are formed by nature and education for gay and animating scenes."

Mrs. Elgood entirely coincided with this remark, and in due time acquainted her nephew with Emily's refusal of their invitation. Frank only remarked that it could not be helped, and he dare say they should do very well without her; a remark his aunt was by no means disinclined to agree with, and she bustled about to make everything ready for her departure with a light heart and unwonted gaiety of spirit.

---

## CHAPTER XXXVI.

The two brothers, the younger of whom has formed a somewhat prominent character in this little history, were *tete-a-tete* in the apartments they occupied in the best hotel the town afforded, and conversing about Emily Stanhope.

"I tell you what it is, Fred," said the elder; "you are now in the way of making your fortune, but you seem devilishly disinclined to do it, and for what reason I cannot tell."

"No, I am not," replied Fred; "and if I was sure Miss Stanhope really loved me, I should be only too glad to win her,"

"If you have not had sufficient proof that she loves you, I know not what proof you can expect to have; she has told you that she loves you, and if you can't believe her own words, why, what can you believe?"

"I sometimes doubt," replied Frederick, "whether Miss Stanhope is really no other than my fair incognita; indeed, all my conversations with her induce me to think there must be some mistake."

"The fact is, Fred," replied his brother, "you don't wish to marry Miss Stanhope—a girl that any other would be proud to win; but you are a strange, unaccountable sort of a fellow, and that's the truth; 'pon my soul it is."

At this instant, the servant entered, and placed a letter before Frederick; the handwriting convinced him at once that it came from his young and trusting wife, and tearing open the envelope, he read the following lines:—

"My dearest Frederick,—I cannot doubt the truth of your love for me, though your letters are few and far between; yet I am aware that you have many calls upon your time and attention, which prevent your dedicating a greater portion of it to me. I will not grieve you, by dwelling upon my own sadness and loneliness of heart in your absence; and I love you too dearly to regret having become your wife; and God forbid, dearest Frederick, that you should ever regret it. For your sake, and through your urgent entreaties, I have consented so long to conceal from all but ourselves the dear and holy bond that exists between us—but, concealment much longer will be impossible, for I feel it my duty to inform you that I am likely to become a mother. Dearest Frederick, may the knowledge of this induce you to consent to my earnest desire, to make our marriage known to the few friends we mutually possess. I have ever been a decided enemy to all deceit, and my heart accuses me of ingratitude in practising it now, towards a tender and affectionate brother. I do not wish to alarm you, still I will not attempt to conceal from you that my health fails daily; I am now almost incapable of pursuing my usual avocation, and were it not for the kind and assiduous attention of a dear and affectionate friend, I should stand in need of the necessaries that my situation so imperatively demands. I hope, dear Frederick, to receive an early answer to this; God grant that it may be favourable to my earnest desire, that concealment may be at once abandoned. With best love, believe me, faithfully your's,                        "MARY."

After Frederick had perused this tender epistle, he proceeded without any appearance of emotion to commit it to the flames, watching it in silence till it was destroyed.

"Not from your incognita, aye, Fred?" said his brother, scrutinizing his countenance with an air of perplexed surprise.

"No," returned the young man, "it is from Mary; I am afraid I shall find her troublesome; she tells me," he added, after a moment's hesitation, "that our intimacy is likely to result in the birth of a child."

"Whew! whew! whew!" whistled William; "that is bad news indeed; but, of course, her claim upon you must be met."

"Her claim! what claim?" said Frederick, hastily.

"I mean on account of the child. You must make some arrangement with her, Fred."

"I am sure I don't know what arrangement to make," replied the young man, with an air of vexatious anxiety.

"You must come down with something handsome, and sufficient to relieve you of any further claim, should she be disposed to make it."

"And where am I to get the money to do so?" replied Fred, evidently much annoyed.

"Where are you to get the money?" returned his brother. "Why, Fred, excuse me; but I must confess, you are the veriest ninny in such affairs as the one we are discussing, that I ever had to do with. Here is a splendid girl, with a handsome fortune, ready, nay, eager, to become your wife; and yet you talk as though it were utterly impossible for you to obtain a few hundreds at any cost."

"That is all very well," returned Frederick, testily; "but what am I to do with Mary? She appears fully to expect that I will redeem my promise, and make her my wife."

"My dear Fred," replied his brother, "if you cannot talk a little more sensibly, do pray be silent. It is perfectly ridiculous to go on in the absurd manner you do; and I am heartily sick of listening to such a farrago of nonsense."

"Curse it all!" exclaimed Frederick, angrily; "I wish I had never seen Mary. I have paid dearly for my folly, and it seems I must still continue to do so."

" Excuse me, Fred, but you need do nothing of the sort.   Your path is plain, straight, and, I should have conceived, pleasant."

" I have acted like a cursed tool in making all sorts of promises to Mary ; and now I don't know how to extricate myself.   I wish to God I had only followed your advice a little more closely, and that's the truth."

" Then resolve to do so for the future ; that is far better, my boy, believe me, than sitting down and bemoaning the past."

" Then tell me what I had better do."

" In the first place, you must write to Mary, acquainting her with your deep regret, and so forth, that you cannot fulfil your promise to her, inasmuch as you are on the point of marriage with another ; but, in consideration of her remaining quiet, you will, for the future, provide handsomely for her and the expected child."

" I don't at all think that Mary will accede to those terms," said Frederick, despondingly ; "but," he added, striving to speak more cheerfully, " I will take your advice and try her."

" She will accede to them, safe enough.   Her doing otherwise would be only injuring herself."

" She may not think so," replied Frederick ; " for she is, in some respects, a strange girl, and accustomed to make a great fuss about virtue."

" She won't now, Fred, take my word for it.   It was all very fine when she thought it would answer her purpose ; but now that she knows it will only have a contrary effect, you will find her as meek and humble as you please.   Oh !" he continued, gaily, " I should think I ought to know ; I have had experience enough to enable me to be a very competent judge."

" I do not doubt it," replied his brother ; " still, Mary may be, and I think is, different from most others.   I have, however, determined to follow your advice, and shall write to her at once."

" Then I will leave you.   I was just thinking a stroll might improve and sharpen my appetite for dinner.   Till then, Fred, I shall do myself the honour of wishing you good morning :" and gracefully waving his hand, as a parting salute, he left the room ; and Frederick instantly set about writing to his truly unfortunate wife.   In doing so, he took care artfully to attribute entirely to his brother, upon whom he was wholly dependent, the placing of him in such a position that he was all but compelled to offer his hand to Miss Stanhope, assuring Mary that she alone did, and ever would, possess his unalterable affection ; beseeching her, by her love for him, to consent to this second union, which, he assured her, was only rendered endurable to him by the thought that it would endow him with the means of providing for her comfort, and that of her unborn child ; declaring, that if she made known the fact of his union with her, his brother would utterly cast him off, and by this means he should be utterly deprived of any provision for himself, much less for her and the expected infant.   The letter was a long one, and concluded thus :—

" I throw myself, dear Mary, entirely on your kindness, nothing doubting that you will exercise it this once in my behalf.   I have given you convincing proof of my love in marrying you without the consent of those upon whom I am wholly and solely dependent. It is painful, dear Mary, and humiliating in the extreme, to solicit—earnestly solicit your consent to my uniting myself with another ; but what can I do?   Had I the means of supporting myself and you—who are still dearer to me than self—in even humble circumstances, you may, my dear girl, feel assured I would not desire to do what is so repugnant to my feelings ; but I have not even the slightest possibility afforded me of doing so.   Believe me, Mary, I have opposed my brother's views as long as possible—I have told him my heart and affections are only yours ; but he heeds it not, and I have no longer any choice.

" I loved you too well, Mary, to act unkindly towards you when I had reason to suspect your truth and faith towards me, though I might have sought, under the peculiar circumstance to which I allude, and I think with success, to set our marriage aside. I do not mention this little matter to grieve or vex you, but merely to remind you, in case it should have slipped your memory, that I have a claim on your gratitude and kindness, and which you have now an ample opportunity afforded you to repay.   By doing so, you secure my affection your own for ever, and with but little sacrifice on your part, for, so far from yourself being benefitted by a declaration of our marriage, I warn you,

Mary, that my brother would sift the affair to the bottom, and the little circumstance I have above alluded to would not escape his observation, and he would undoubtedly take legal measures to separate us for ever; myself being under age, and he my guardian, would be sufficient authority for him to do so; but I forbear. Your own good sense will, I am sure, dictate to you the best course to pursue; and, trusting that you will give it immediate attention, believe me, dearest Mary, in heart and affection, ever yours truly                              "FREDERICK MAITLAND."

After Frederick had despatched this cruel and unfeeling epistle, he waited with feverish impatience her reply, half hoping she might accede to his wishes, and half fearing she would unhesitatingly refuse his request. He fully expected an early reply, but in less time than he anticipated a letter from Mary was placed in his hands. Hope strongly preponderated in his bosom as he broke the seal, and drew the important letter from the envelope; but the first line convinced him his hopes were all fallacious—the note conveyed to him her angry and indignant refusal. Poor Mary, usually so mild and gentle, was completely roused by the cruelty and oppression she experienced from him who had vowed to love and cherish her, and who but so lately had sought her hand as the dearest boon of existence—had sworn unalterable and never-dying affection to her whom he was now so anxious to rid himself of, that he would even condescend to bribe her to silence—for the sake of money, make her consent to appear what every feeling of tenderness and delicacy ought to have made him shrink with abhorrence from even naming to his young and gentle wife. Truly, the worm will turn, if cruelly trampled on; and Mary, who by nature possessed the meekness of the dove, felt every feeling merged in anger and resentment when she read her husband's letter; and, without giving herself time to consider its contents, or seek the advice of the few friends she could call her own, immediately wrote an answer, in which she gave free vent to the resentful feelings of her heart, declaring that as she was in truth his wife, nothing on earth should induce her to forego her claim as such, and challenging him to dare to attempt to set their marriage aside.

This letter was unfortunately by no means calculated to induce Frederick to consider the injustice of his desire to marry another; on the contrary, it fermented his ill feelings, and he began really to regard himself as unkindly treated by Mary, and resolved to acquaint his brother of the circumstances in which he was placed, preferring at once to encounter his anger than longer continue the deception he had practised towards him.

Therefore, taking advantage of an opportunity when his brother seemed unusually good-tempered, Frederick in the gentlest manner possible broke to him the intelligence of his marriage with Mary. Prepared as the young man was to witness his brother's extreme displeasure, he had yet never even dreamed of encountering the absolute fury and passion he displayed on the occasion. We will not deface our paper or shock the ears of our readers by telling of the oaths and curses he heaped upon Frederick's luckless head.

The young man bore all in silence for some time, and then mildly deprecating his brother's anger, hinted at the probability of the marriage being set aside; and concluded by expressing his deep sorrow at having so wilfully taken such an imprudent step. His brother listened more calmly.

"Why, the devil, Frederick, what could you have been thinking of? You must have been mad, downright mad; and I should be perfectly justified if I placed you under confinement for life."

Frederick assented to this remark, and then led him back again to the subject of his marriage, on which they conversed for some time; and at length came to the conclusion that if Mary persisted in asserting her claim, they should endeavour to obtain a divorce.

"It will cost a heavy sum, Fred," said his brother; "and you must now lose no time in pressing your suit with Miss Stanhope; it is essentially necessary that you gain her, in order to get the money to pay the requisite expenses; for, curse me, Fred, if a farthing of my property goes to pay for your fool's tricks. I have brought you to London, and kept you like a gentleman for something!"

A week after this conversation, a week of wretchedness and bitter anxiety to poor Mary, she was seated in the little parlour that had witnessed the sad parting of herself and Frederick, and since that ill-fated day that had made her his wife, sorrow and ill health had committed sad ravages on her fair face; beauty was still there, but it was the beauty of

FREDERICK'S PROPOSAL AND DISAPPOINTMENT.

"I pardon, you, sir," said Emily ; "this is, indeed, my handwriting. But what must you have thought of me to suppose, for an instant, that these expressions of affection were intended for yourself ?"

the fading flower, which, lovely even in decay, drops its sweet-scented leaves one by one, and sustains its purity in undiminished brightness to the close.

Mary's face was fairer even than of yore, and a soft unwonted bloom sat upon her cheek ; and yet that soft, still bloom that revelled in such beauty there,

> "Spoke to those who watched its hue
> Of sickness, death, and suffering too."

Mary was not alone : by her side, and whispering words of hope and comfort to cheer her to the end, sat one whom it would be no difficult task to recognise : the luxuriant auburn ringlets that hung over her small but beautifully formed figure, and the angelic purity of her soft blue eyes, now swimming in moisture as she gazed upon the wasted features of Mary, proclaim her at once to be no other than the unhappy and guilty Isabel.

"Alas! dear Mary, how is it," she exclaimed, "that those who so richly deserve happiness in this world rarely, if ever, obtain it. You, so gentle, virtuous, and lovely, should have been blest with happiness above the common lot of mortals."

"Hush," said Mary gently ; "it is not ours to impugn the all-wise providence of a just and merciful God ; and, dearest Isabel, you judge me too kindly, too leniently. I do not deserve happiness ; I acted with unkind deception towards the best and tenderest of parents,—and again, after I had voluntarily resigned all acquaintance with Fred, I suffered myself to be again drawn into the net, from which I had with difficulty succeeded in extricating myself, and so far forgot what was due to my only brother, that I even consented to a private marriage with Fred, though my heart at the time told me I was doing wrong, and——"

At this moment Mrs. Herbert entered with a letter, which she presented to Mary, whose hand trembled violently as she received it ; the writing was unknown to her, and, with a quivering and palpitating heart, she proceeded to make herself acquainted with its contents. After she had perused it she handed it to Isabel, with a tearful eye, saying,—

"Read, dear Isabel, and tell me, if you deem it possible Frederick could ever have loved me." Her friend took it from her hands, and read as follows—

"Madam,—My brother has informed me (upon whose bounty he is entirely dependent) of the imprudent alliance he formed some time since with yourself ; such a marriage, of course, cannot for a moment be entertained by his family, who have designed a match for him with one in his own station in life, and who is fondly attached to him.

"The extreme youth of my brother, and the knowledge we possess of the acquaintance you carried on with a person bearing the name of Mordaunt, immediately after my brother had been (by your specious conduct) drawn into a marriage with you, will, we have reason to feel assured, amply suffice to procure a divorce, which will entirely deprive you of all future claims on my thoughtless and inexperienced brother, who equally deplores the imprudent step he was induced to take.

"I trust this will convince you of the folly of persisting in asserting what you please to call your rights ; the doing so will only expose yourself to the deeper mortification of having your conduct made public ; and, on the other hand, by merely keeping silent, you secure to yourself a handsome provision for life. Under these circumstances, I will not insult your good sense by supposing it possible you will act contrary to our wishes.

"Madam, I have the honour of subscribing myself, your's obediently,
                                     "WILLIAM MAITLAND.

"P.S.—If Frederick's love is any object, he begs me to assure you that he still entertains a tender regard for you ; and, on his again visiting London, will be happy to renew his acquaintance with you on the same terms as formerly."

Isabel had scarcely patience to read it to the end. "Cruel, insulting wretches!" she exclaimed, indignantly ; "heed them not, dearest Mary. God be praised, money is no object to you ; James has amply provided for us both. Courage, dear Mary," she continued, seeing that the tears coursed each other in rapid succession down her pale cheeks, "James will be here to-night, and will, I am sure, advise you for the best."

"He will—he will," returned poor Mary, almost choked with her emotion ; "but I shall not need it long. Patience—patience, Frederick, and death will sever the bond that exists between us, and save you all the trouble of a divorce ; but while I live I am your wife ; nothing—no, nothing on earth shall induce me to forego that title ; not if you lavished on me the whole wealth of the Indies, and my refusal plunged me into the utter depths of wretchedness."

"Do not, dear Mary, excite yourself," said Isabel, seeing that the hectic flush of disease sat in a burning spot on either cheek; "calm yourself, dearest Mary," and she threw her arms lovingly round her, and pillowed her head upon her bosom; "rest there, dear, gentle Mary," and her own eyes swam in moisture.

---

## CHAPTER XXXVII.

ON the same eve as Mary received the unfeeling and insulting letter from William Maitland, with which we made the reader acquainted in the last chapter, Frederick and his brother, as had been previously arranged, were spending the evening at the house of Mrs. John Elgood, who entertained a few friends previous to her departure for London. Mr. Ellis had received an invitation, but he politely excused himself. Emily would willingly have done the same, but as her cousin and the young ladies of the squire's family had engaged to be present, she could not very well decline the invitation.

Two rooms on the ground floor had been decorated, and duly appointed as the ball-room; and among the visitors were a goodly sprinkling of the —th Hussars. Frederick, on this occasion, paid Emily particular and marked attention, but she scarcely observed it, her own notice being pleasingly attracted to the attention her cousin Charles bestowed upon Louisa Elgood.

In the course of the evening, Frederick contrived to lead Emily, who had been his partner in the dance, to a room more free from the pressure of guests that thronged the ball-room. After a few common-place observations, to which Emily replied kindly and cheerfully, Frederick felt encouraged to make an avowal of his love, and pressing her hand with fervour to his lips, "My dear Miss Stanhope," he began, "you must have deemed me cold and backward, in so long delaying making known to you the passion your beauty and accomplishments have inspired in my breast."

Emily started with surprise, but astonishment chained her tongue, and the young officer proceeded.

"Diffidence alone, my dearest Emily, has made me so backward in declaring my affection; for, from the first moment that I beheld you I loved you; but my own unworthiness prevented me telling you so. I dreaded you might ridicule a passion which has nothing but its truth and constancy to recommend it to your notice."

"You entertain too mean an opinion of your own merits," said Emily, kindly; "for I cannot feel otherwise than flattered at the preference you acknowledge."

"A thousand thanks, dearest Emily; you will consent then to be mine, my own. Oh! if a life of constant devotedness and attention to your lightest wish, can prove my grati- for your ——"

"Stop," said Emily, mildly; "listen to me for a few minutes. I should have thought, Mr. Maitland, that you could not possibly have supposed your protestation of love would be otherwise than favourably received by such a girl as me; who, educated and residing constantly in the country, must naturally feel proud of winning the affection of so gay and handsome an officer as yourself."

"You greatly flatter me," said the young man, gazing at the playful expression of Emily's countenance, which he thought appeared more lovely every hour.

"No such thing," replied Emily, gazing in her turn upon the really handsome face of Fred. "It grieves me to be forced to refuse the addresses of one, whom, under other circumstances, I should be pleased and proud to accept."

"Oh, do not," cried Frederick, "crush the hope I have fondly nourished—the sweet blissful hope, that I might gain your love."

"Under other circumstances," replied Emily, "I have said you might have done so, but existing ones render it impossible."

Frederick was puzzled, and could only account for Emily's conduct, by supposing that she had by some means become possessed of the secret of his marriage; he, therefore, hastened to ascertain if such was the case.

"If, dearest Emily," he exclaimed, "you have heard aught to prejudice your mind against me, for mercy sake, tell me at once, that I may be enabled to explain."

"No, no," interrupted Emily; "I have never ever heard a word breathed to your discredit; the circumstance to which I alluded, rests wholly with myself."

"I entreat of you," said Frederick, despondingly, "at least, to name it to me."

"It is simply this," returned Emily, "I love another."

"You love another?" returned the young man. "Alas! there must be some mystery, or you have suddenly transferred your affections from myself."

"Neither," said Emily, in a tone of unfeigned surprise; "there surely can be no mystery in my having long loved one who is pre-eminently worthy of my tenderest regard; and, as to yourself, Mr. Maitland, I can truly say, that not a particle of my regard was ever yours."

"But, but," said the young man, hesitatingly, "you wrote to me from time to time while I was in London, speaking of your affection for me, even anticipating my coming to Devonshire, and ——"

"Never," exclaimed Emily, in a tone of indignant surprise.

"Do not be angry, Miss Stanhope, I beg, I entreat of you. I must have mistaken another's writing for your own; yet, the similitude is so striking, that I think it might deceive even you. Look, judge for yourself, Miss Stanhope," he continued, presenting her with the last letter he had received from his incognita.

Emily took it from his hand, and with a burning cheek carefully perused it; and then, turning to the young officer, said, in a tone of womanly dignity,—

"I pardon you, sir; this is, indeed, my handwriting. But, what must you have thought of me, to suppose, for an instant, that those expressions of affection were intended for yourself?"

"For whom, then, could I suppose they were meant? They came sealed, and addressed to myself."

"You could not, then, perceive," said Emily, "that the address on the envelope is written in a totally different hand. The truth is," she continued, "that this letter, and many others, in a similar strain, were written, and sent by me, to Miss Ellis, at the request of one who knew her intimately. How they happened to fall into your hands you can best imagine."

A light broke upon Frederick at these words.

"Alas," he exclaimed; "I see—I understand it all. You sent them, conveying an enclosure to Mary, and she, unfortunately, supposing they came from me, constantly returned them to my address. It is—it must be so," he continued, gazing intently on the envelope he held in his hand; "for, now I look at this more closely, I perceive the handwriting is her own.

Emily was surprised, for the young ensign had never mentioned his being acquainted with Miss Ellis, but her pride prevented her seeking an explanation; so, merely bowing, she proposed, if agreeable, they should return to the company. Frederick assented, and hoped she would pardon what had seemed bold in his conduct. Emily, interrupting, begged he would dismiss the matter from his thoughts, assuring him that she should adopt that course herself.

When the brothers retired to their own apartments at the hotel, Frederick informed William of the blunder they had unfortunately made regarding Miss Stanhope, who, though excessively vexed, could not, on this point, very well blame Frederick; but he loudly and bitterly cursed his folly in marrying Mary Ellis, assuring him he would not advance a farthing towards extricating him from the dilemma. Frederick retaliated, and a scene of recrimination ensued, and they parted for the night in mutual displeasure. When they met at breakfast the following morning, no allusion was made by either to the occurrence of the night before. William was gay, as usual, and rallied Fred upon his downcast appearance. It was an unusually late breakfast, and as the brothers were seated near the window, William recognised his acquaintance in the street, and had plenty of employment in bowing and kissing his hand to the ladies, and nodding familiarly to the gentlemen. He was interrupted by the entrance of a servant, with a letter on a silver salver.

"For me, John?" said the captain, abandoning the window for a moment.

"No, sir, for your brother; arrived express, and ——"

"Give it me, John," interrupted Frederick, hastily. The next moment he had torn it open, and devoured the contents. As he did so, the colour receded entirely from his cheeks, leaving his face of an ashy paleness; then the blood rushed tumultuously to his very temples, and his eyes flashed with a brilliant and unwonted fire; and turning fiercely to his brother, he exclaimed, as he threw the letter towards him:—

"You have murdered her! Now are you contented?"

"Hush! Fred," said the other; "you are surely beside yourself. What has happened to affect you thus?"

"Read for yourself," exclaimed the young man, in a hoarse, broken voice. "Mary is dying, and you have killed her!"

William stared in astonishment, and then taking the letter, coolly read the contents. They were but a few lines, stating that Mary's health had long been on the decline; but no immediate danger was apprehended till she received the letter from William, which had taken such an effect upon her as to produce an attack of hectic fever, which was succeeded by long and continued fainting fits; that, in short, she was now dying; and though she expressed an earnest desire to see Frederick before her death, it was scarcely possible that she would survive to do so.

"This is certainly rather unpleasant," said William, pouring himself out a fresh cup of chocolate; "but nevertheless it will have the good effect of ridding you of her without more expense or trouble."

"Wretch!" exclaimed his brother, in a violent passion, "this is all your doing. I tell you, you have murdered her!"

"Fred," returned the other, deliberately buttering a round of toast, "I cannot allow you to talk in this manner; it is exceedingly unpleasant. There are persons about who might, possibly, overhear your language, and my character, as a matter of course, would suffer materially in consequence."

"Your character!" returned the other, with a bitter sneer; "did I blacken it as it deserves, you would be universally hated and detested, as ——"

"Fred," interrupted his brother, "I'll thank you to ring the bell."

The young man seized the handle, and gave it a violent jerk, which immediately brought in a servant.

"You will have the goodness, John," said the elder officer, in the same cool tones he had before spoken, "to pack up my brother's wardrobe. He will remove to another hotel in the course of the day."

"Yes, sir," said the man.

"And," added the other, "the sooner he departs, the better."

"Yes, sir; where did you say I was to take the boxes?" replied the servant.

"That information you must seek of him. As far as regards myself, you may take them to the devil, if you please."

"Yes, sir," said the man, and, with a profound bow, he departed.

Frederick rose from his seat, and turning towards the door, which he held open, he exclaimed,—

"From this hour I disown you, as unworthy of the relationship that exists between us. My bitterest curse will ever rest upon you. May you ——"

"My good fellow, don't flurry yourself, I entreat," said his brother, cutting a slice from the ham. "I forgive you—I do, indeed, Fred. You have been guilty of great ingratitude, but forgiveness is a Christian's duty, and I am pleased to be able to exercise it towards you. You may go, Fred."

"I may go," returned the other, "and you forgive me. Yes, I will do your bidding; it is an utter waste of breath to talk to you. You are dead to every sense of feeling and ——"

"May I ask as a favour, Fred, that you will go at once—there is a draught of air from the door which is anything but pleasant?"

The door slammed violently, and Frederick sought the commanding officer, obtained leave of absence for a few days, and, with a heavy, sorrowing heart, took his way to the station to engage an express train to convey him to London.

On this selfsame morning, when Emily entered the breakfast-room, she observed that her aunt and uncle wore a look of importance on their countenances, while her cousin regarded her on her entrance with a half embarrassed air. After the usual salutations had been exchanged, and Emily had seated herself in front of the hissing urn, her uncle said,—

"Emily, my love, your cousin has something which he wishes to show you."

"Indeed!" replied Emily, smiling; "am I to expect a gift, or ——"

"No," replied her cousin, anticipating her remark, and at the same time pushing a little three-cornered note towards her; "I merely wish you to read this, and give me your opinion of its contents."

Emily instantly recognised the handwriting of Louisa, and read with unmingled delight the following lines,—

"Dear Charles,—I can now, without hesitation, confess that you are dear to me. The conversation we held together last evening has relieved me from all embarrassment; and as I promised to convey to you by letter this morning my real sentiments, I hasten to do so by declaring that if your aunt and uncle will consent to receive me as their niece, it will ever constitute my greatest pleasure to administer as far as it is possible to their comfort and happiness. I shall be at Mr. Stanhope's this afternoon, when we can converse on this subject more freely. Till then, dear Charles, adieu; and believe me ever affectionately yours,                                                                    "LOUISA."

"Oh! happy, happy news!" exclaimed Emily, laying down the letter, and extending her hand to her cousin. "You have, indeed, dear Charles, made a good choice. Uncle, aunt," she continued, turning first to one, and then to the other, "both of you, surely, approve of it?"

"Most cordially, my Emily," said her uncle; "and the sooner all things are arranged the better."

Mrs. Stanhope likewise expressed her full concurrence, and congratulations, warm and truthful, were showered upon the young man, till his heart was fully satisfied. In the midst of this conversation, Mr. Ellis was announced, and duly ushered in by the powdered footman. At the first glance of his countenance, Emily felt convinced that he was the bearer of painful intelligence.

"Welcome, my dear sir!" exclaimed Mr. Stanhope, who was not quite so close an observer as his niece. "We shall speedily require your services; we shall have a wedding after all. Charles has just received a letter from Louisa Elgood, accepting him as her future husband."

"I am much pleased to hear it," returned Mr. Ellis; "but I am come to bid you farewell once more before I start again for London."

These words chased away all the bloom from Emily's countenance; and she could only look at the curate for an explanation; her tongue refused to assist her with words.

"You will excuse me, I am sure," Mr. Ellis continued, addressing Mr. Stanhope, "when I inform you that I have just received the distressing intelligence that my dear and only sister is dying," and here his emotion choked his utterance, and he was unable to proceed. Mr. and Mrs. Stanhope expressed their sincere regret, and deeply commiserated his feelings.

"I must again," said the curate, after he had, in a manner, recovered his composure, "have recourse to the rail; and this time, I shall engage an express train."

The old gentleman slightly remonstrated, and reminded the curate of his last perilous journey; but Mr. Ellis was firm, and promising to write instantly on his arrival, proceeded to wish them respectively adieu. Emily followed him from the breakfast-room to the hall; but the curate was so engaged with his own sorrowful feelings, that he did not observe her, till she laid her hand on his shoulder. He turned instantly, and beheld her pallid cheek and tearful eyes with pleased surprise. Sympathy is, indeed, sweet, and he pressed her hand warmly as he exclaimed,—

"This is, indeed, kind of you, Miss Stanhope."

"Oh! Mr. Ellis," she replied, as the tears she could no longer suppress forced their way unheeded down her cheek. "You are going on a mournful errand; but do not allow sorrow for your sister to cause you to neglect yourself; for ——" and here her bloom for an instant returned, and she hesitated.

"For your sake?" he said, while a smile of pleasure lighted up his whole face.

"Yes, for my sake," she replied.

"For your sake, I would do anything."

He still retained her hand; but as he spoke he drew her closer to him, and his disengaged arm found its way round her waist.

"It seems selfish," said Emily, "to speak of myself at such an hour as this; but I shall, indeed, be wretched till I hear of your safe arrival in town."

"And am I really happy enough to be cared for by you?" said the curate, in a tender tone.

"You are—you are, indeed," replied Emily, hiding her blushing face upon his shoulder.

He gently raised her head, and pressing his lips to her's, in one long tender kiss, murmured,—

"Farewell! dear one. God bless and keep you till I return," and tore himself away.

Emily, with a lightened heart, sought her boudoir, to weep over her own unexpected happiness, and pray for blessings on her lover ; while he, with a heart throbbing at the newness and sweetness of his bliss, half reproached himself for giving one thought to happiness while his sister was so near the grave. On arriving at the station, Mr. Ellis encountered the young ensign, Frederick Maitland, who had just ordered an express train to London on the same errand as himself ; and the curate, at his invitation, consented to join him.

During their journey, Frederick acquainted Mr. Ellis with the connection that existed between himself and his sister, avowed his own unkindness towards her in desiring to set the marriage aside ; in short, placed the whole affair in its proper light, without seeking to extenuate his own conduct, and ended by solemnly declaring his own deep regret at what had passed, and his firm intention of acknowledging Mary for his wife, should she fortunately recover from her indisposition. Mr. Ellis, though greatly affected and surprised by the recital, yet felt convinced the young man was far less to blame than his wicked and unfeeling brother. Frederick, consequently, experienced but little difficulty in obtaining the curate's pardon.

On the arrival of the train, they immediately procured a coach, and drove direct to the humble abode of the truly unfortunate Mary. Mrs. Herbert received them with tearful eyes, and a reproach to Frederick that rose to her lips was but half suppressed, as she noticed his altered countenance.

"My sister still lives ?" said Mr. Ellis.

"Yes, she still lives, and that is all I can say."

"Conduct me instantly to her," returned the curate ; "you," he added, turning to Frederick, "had better remain here till I have seen her." He silently assented, and Mr. Ellis, alone, was introduced into the sick room of his dying sister ; everything was hushed, and Mary lay in so calm and sweet a sleep, the curate could scarcely believe she was so near her end. Seated on either side of the bed were Mr. and Mrs. Mordaunt. Isabel was greatly altered since he had last seen her ; but, oh, to his eyes, she was now a thousand times more lovely. A plain mourning dress, without the slightest ornament, was fastened at the throat, and her own beautiful, luxuriant hair hung in rich folds over her shoulders, while her bowed head concealed the anguish that was depicted on her countenance. Mordaunt rose, and, warmly greeting the curate, informed him that the doctor had warned them that, in all probability, Mary would never wake again. "She has slept for hours," he continued, "and it may be a satisfaction to you to know that she has not during her illness wanted either for sympathy or kindness. Isabel, though guilty as regards myself, has yet lovingly supplied her every want, even before she had time to name them."

The curate wrung his hand in mute acknowledgement of his kindness, and then, without speaking, placed himself by the bedside.

After the lapse of an hour Mary awoke, like an infant from its slumber, and, with surpassing sweetness, gazed upon her attendants.

"Mary, love," said Mr. Ellis, approaching, and taking her hand, "I have come to see you."

"What, George!" she exclaimed, in a clear, sweet voice, "my dear, dear brother, God be praised that I have lived to see you once again ; kiss me, dear George, before I go ;" and then turning to Isabel, she said, "Give me, dear Isabel, your hand." The lady complied. "Now, Jane, yours," said Mary. Mordaunt stretched it forth ; she joined it with that of Isabel's, and conveying them to her lips, kissed them with fervent tenderness.

"Dearest James," said Mary, collecting all her strength to give energy to her dying words, "promise, promise to love and protect her—she is repentant. Oh, receive her back to your arms and heart ; promise this," she said, earnestly, "and I shall die happy."

"Forbear, dear Mary," said Isabel, gently ; "crimes, such as mine, admit of no pardon like that you plead for."

"Isabel," said Mordaunt, "I have watched you narrowly when you thought it not, and am convinced you are truly repentant; that being the case, I have no right to refuse to receive you back; my arms are open to welcome your return, and my heart also."

Isabel at these words sunk weeping into the extended arms of her much injured husband.

"Mary," said Mr. Ellis, after a short silence, "there is one below who owns a near relationship to yourself, who is desirous of asking your forgiveness; have you strength to bear an interview with him?"

"Oh! yes," replied Mary, eagerly; "it is, it must be, Frederick; let him not delay a moment."

Mr. Ellis left the room at these words, and speedily returned with the young officer.

"Frederick, dearest Frederick!" said Mary, extending her arms to clasp him to her bosom; "my, my——" her voice failed, her arms relaxed their hold of him, her head sunk upon his bosom, and Frederick became conscious that he was pressing warm kisses on her lifeless cheek; her gentle spirit had taken its flight to a land more pure, more blissful than this.

Thus did the kind, lovely, and loving Mary Ellis, "blossom and bough, lie withered with one blight;" sinless, as far as possible to be so in this world, she fell a victim to the cruelty and oppression of others. She might have been a fond, proud wife, and a tender, happy mother, but her child was doomed, through the sufferings of its parent, to close its little being without birth; but enough, she sleeps well; who would wish her back to this dull earth?

The grief of Frederick Maitland admitted of no consolation, though the good curate was the first to offer it; he nourished no enmity in his bosom against the man, whose unfeeling conduct had deprived his sister of life, and, though his own anguish was acute at the loss of his sole surviving relative, yet the thought of Emily Stanhope tended greatly to mitigate the violence of his sorrow. To be loved by one his own humility pictured as so much superior to himself, and whom he had so long and tenderly regarded, caused his heart to throb with bliss, even in the midst of his sadness, and he sat down to write to Mr. Stanhope, with his mind filled with the (to him) sweet image of Emily.

After Mr. Ellis had seen his sister laid in the quiet grave by the side of her departed mother, he turned his thoughts again to Sackville, resolving now to bid adieu to London, he hoped, for ever. Mordaunt had acquainted him with his intention of quitting England, with Isabel, for the continent, where they should, in all probability, pass the remainder of their lives; and, in return, the curate imparted to him his own hopes regarding Emily Stanhope. We need scarcely say, that Mordaunt warmly approved of his choice, and wishing each other all the happiness that can possibly fall to the lot of mortals, they separated, each to pursue their different journeys. Isabel, with tearful eyes, bade the curate farewell. Indeed, the parting of all three was sad and painful; but a promise of epistolary correspondence cheered their hearts. Isabel and Mordaunt were thankful and happy; their love and trust in each other was fully restored, still their happiness was of the quiet thoughtful kind.

Mr. Ellis had never much liked Mrs. Herbert; therefore, he parted with her without regret; yet he deemed it right to address to her a few words of friendly admonition, and which, we are happy to say, were not lost upon her. Indeed, the illness and death of Mary had tended greatly to alter her character, and she was now in every respect more worthy and amiable than when we first introduced her to the reader. And here it may be as well to remark, that this alteration was by no means evanescent; for the painful yet useful lesson she had learnt in the sad school of sorrow, remained indelibly fixed in her memory during the whole of her subsequent career, which was no longer marked by folly, much less by vice.

Frederick was wretched and melancholy. Immediately after the death of Mary, Mordaunt unfolded to him the seeming mystery of his own rather prolonged visit to her; and from him Frederick likewise learnt with surprise, that the handsome youth of whom he had been so foolishly jealous, was no other than his wife, Isabel, who, for reasons which he exlpained to him, had adopted that disguise.

Frederick was now an outcast, without provision, or the means of maintaining himself, save what he derived from his commission. England, London especially, had become hateful to him, as being the scene of his former happiness. The Indian war was then at its height, and a regiment being about to embark immediately for that clime, Frederick

THE DEATH-BED OF MARY ELLIS.

[Her gentle spirit had taken its flight to a land more pure, more blissful than this. . . . . . . . She sleeps well.   Who would wish her back to this dull earth?]

easily succeeded in effecting an exchange with an officer of his own rank, and bidding adieu to Mr. Ellis and Mrs. Herbert, was shipped off with the regiment for India.

Immediately after witnessing his embarkation, the curate placed himself in the Tally-ho coach, and was shortly after set down at the door of Mr. Stanhope's residence. He had not previously written to name the day on which he might be expected, and his unlooked-for arrival was hailed with gladness by the little circle, now so doubly dear to him. And the soft blushing smiles of Emily, when, grown bold by her kindness, he ventured, the first moment they were alone, to rapturously kiss her cheek, would have been cheaply purchased by double the sorrow and anxiety he had previously endured. Very soon after his return, Mr. Ellis's services were required to unite Charles Stanhope to the amiable and truly excellent Louisa Elgood.

The squire and his lady were, of course, pleased and proud of the match; the two elder daughters certainly wondered what the young man could see in Louisa, to give her the preference, which, they considered of right, belonged to themselves; still, though indignant, they did not suffer their displeasure to prevent them honouring the wedding with their presence, and a right joyous wedding it was; the tenantry were feasted, as tenantry were never feasted before, and wore such joyous, happy faces, that Mr. Stanhope declared it made him feel quite young, only to witness their hilarity.

Mrs. John Elgood, with her husband and Frank, tore themselves from the gaieties of London, in order to be present at the wedding; but the lady was very anxious to be again in London, declaring to Emily that the country was very dull and insipid, and that she was sorry Frank had ever purchased the cottage, as it would be now perfectly useless.

"Will you, then, sell it to me?" said Emily, smiling.

"To you, my dear?" replied the lady, in astonishment.

"Yes, to me," returned Emily; "I am willing to give you the same sum as your nephew paid for it."

Mrs. Elgood expressed her own willingness, and said she would speak to Frank, who, on being applied to, professed his entire concurrence, and the cottage was transferred to Emily, who was likewise permitted to select what articles of furniture she chose, Mrs. Elgood promising to purchase on her own account any she might desire to have from the great mart, London. Emily thanked her, and the same evening expressed a wish to her uncle, to speak to him in private.

"I wish, dear uncle," said Emily, when they were alone, "to know what money I am entitled to by my father's will."

"Certainly, my love," said Mr. Stanhope; "I should have entered upon this subject before, but you always manifested an aversion to it."

"Yes, uncle, I did; but I ask now, because I wish you to advance me a few thousands."

"When of age, my Emily, you are entitled to thirty thousand; how much do you require for present use?"

"It seems a large sum, uncle, but I shall be glad if you will advance me ten thousand."

"It is a large sum, Emily; still——"

"It will be spent to advantage, uncle; but at present, the manner in which I shall dispose of it is a secret."

"Enough, my child; I will give it you in the course of to-morrow."

The following day the money was placed in Emily's hands; part of it was paid to Frank, for the purchase of the cottage, and a still larger portion of it was likewise given to Frank for the purchase of something else; but that, as Emily said, was at present secret.

After the departure of Mr. and Mrs. Elgood and her nephew, great alterations were made at the cottage, the whole of which were superintended by Emily; but this was attributed to the friendship that existed between her and Mrs. Elgood, every one fully believing that Emily acted for her in her absence. New and very tasty furniture was sent from London; and Emily was constantly overlooking and ordering the management of it, till at length everything was complete. All this while, of course, old time has not been standing still, and sweet spring had now began to clothe the fields in verdure, when, one afternoon, unusually bright for the season, Mr. Ellis, his face beaming with gladness, called at Mr. Stanhope's residence, and inquiring for Emily, and learning that she was walking in the shrubbery, he instantly sought her, and scarce had the first salutations passed, before he drew her to his side, and passing his arm round her waist, exclaimed with joy,—

"Dearest—dearest Emily! I can now with honour ask you to become my wife. I am no longer, dear one, the poor curate; the rector has most handsomely presented me with the living, in reward, as he is pleased to say, for my zealous and faithful services as curate. He is himself in possession of many other more valuable livings; and has, he informs me, long determined to part with that of Sackville; but he might have sold it, instead of which, he has generously presented it to me."

Emily manifested no surprise. This, then, was her secret; knowing the rector wished to part with Sackville, she had undoubtedly become the purchaser, under the consideration that the incumbent should appear to present it gratuitously to Mr. Ellis.

"I love you, Emily, with the fondest and most enduring affection," said the curate, "but, for this unlooked-for occurrence, I should scarcely have dared to ask you to honour me with this dear hand," pressing it in his own.

Emily fondly returned the pressure, but her eyes were bent upon the ground.

"Look up and smile, dear Emily," he continued; but Emily was smiling rather too broadly and meaningly to comply with his request just at that moment; but, when she had conquered her feelings, she did look up and smile upon him with all her wonted sweetness.

Mr. and Mrs. Stanhope, with Charles and Louisa, were speedily made acquainted with the pleasing intelligence; and joy reigned supreme in all their hearts.

Directly Mr. Ellis had received the presentation of the living, he had hastened to Emily, that she might be the first to hear the thrice happy news; but it was very soon spread abroad in the village, and joyfully hailed by all; the little bells of the church rung forth a merry peal, and Emily felt herself truly blest. Mr. Ellis claimed, as a reward for his long and enduring affection, that an early day should be appointed for their marriage, and Emily blushingly consented.

"We must all live together," said the old gentleman, smiling kindly on his niece; "the old house is plenty large enough."

"You know, uncle," replied Emily, smiling archly, "that I always contrive to get my own way, so it is useless to thwart me now. I intend having a house of my own; you will be a great uncle by-and-bye," looking at Louisa, "and, if I remained here, I should be sure at length to get turned out among you."

"No, no," returned the old gentleman, "there is no fear of that; and there is no suitable residence, my Emily, in Sackville, that ——"

"Stop, uncle!" she exclaimed, smiling; "if Mr. Ellis will promise to accompany me, I can show him a residence that will in every respect suit our moderate wants."

The curate was, of course, all willingness; and, arm in arm, their faces radiant with happiness, they proceeded down the High-street, turned off towards the open country, and finally stopped in front of the cottage that had once been known as Widow Harley's. Emily knocked at the door, and, on gaining admittance, led the surprised curate through the rooms, which were fitted up with tasteful elegance.

"There is one room you have not yet seen, and which I hope, more particularly than the others, will please you; this way," she said, smiling. The curate followed her to a room that had been the widow's boudoir, but was now arranged as a study; a select library adorned the walls, and the gothic window looked out upon the beautiful scenery of hill and dale.

"Dear Emily," said her enraptured lover, "this is your doing; how much I owe you."

"Here," said Emily, seriously, "I hope to spend many happy hours; you must allow me to sit here while you are studying. These are books," pointing to the walls, "which will not only amuse, but instruct me. I shall have no separate boudoir; this room, love, will serve for us both."

"My Emily, my own dear Emily," he exclaimed, as he clasped her to his bosom; "what have I done to deserve such happiness?"

"Dearest love," she returned, as she fondly clung to him, "you deserve it all; nay, more;" and the fulness of their mutual bliss found vent in tears—sweet, graceful tears. How pure and holy, how bright, how extatic, is virtuous love! Well might the poet sing,—

"Oh! happy they, the happiest of their kind,
    Whom gentle stars unite."

Reader, our tale is told; a few words more, and we are done. We have not sought to excite your imagination by wild and improbable adventure; we have merely related a simple, every-day story, seeking to cull therefrom lessons that may improve the mind. We have met you with pleasure, week by week, and are sorry that we are now forced to bid you adieu.   If any desire to inquire farther respecting our heroine, we are pleased to be able to inform them that both her and Louisa were happy and blessed in their respective partners.   Mr. and Mrs. Stanhope lived long enough to see a whole host of nephews and nieces, and the family pew was filled again, as in days of yore, with bright, rosy, happy faces.   Mrs. John Elgood managed her husband admirably; Frank constantly resided with them, and, of the two, was rather more master than John.   Frederick, as we have said, went to India, fought bravely in several battles, but, before peace was declared, was shot dead whilst heading a small number of determined soldiers.   His brother, continuing to enjoy life after his own fashion, passed among those who slightly knew him, as a most excellent tempered and delightful man.

Mr. Mordaunt never repented having received the erring but repentant Isabel back again to his arms and heart.   They resided entirely abroad, and were blessed with a fine and healthy family, whom they reared in the path of virtue, and, consequently, of happiness.   Mrs. Tierney received her husband on his return to her with open arms—not one reproach or unkind expression escaped her lips; and when he confessed his error, and implored her forgiveness, she clasped him to her heart, and, with tears of gladness, hailed his contrition and promised amendment; and, from that mome ., she forgot the past, nor ever alluded to it by the slightest remark. He never again visited London; his whole care and attention was henceforth devoted to his gentle, loving, and forgiving wife, and the tender offspring of their love.   Need we say they were happy?   Surely not!   Happiness is ever a close attendant upon virtue.   And, in peaceful serenity, their lives were spent; and Mr. Tierney learnt to bless the day that Isabel resolved to return to that path which he had once induced her to forsake.

ELLEN T ————

THE END.

www.ingramcontent.com/pod-product-compliance
Lightning Source LLC
Chambersburg PA
CBHW080839250626
47161CB00009B/3122

* 9 7 8 1 5 3 5 8 0 3 9 9 1 *